One Final Shot

One Final Shot

Aubreé Pynn

www.urbanbooks.net

Urban Books, LLC
300 Farmingdale Road, NY-Route 109
Farmingdale, NY 11735

One Final Shot Copyright © 2024 Aubreé Pynn

ISBN 13: 978-1-64556-640-3

First Mass Market Printing November 2024
First Trade Paperback Printing April 2024
Printed in the United States of America

10 9 8 7 6 5 4 3 2 1

Distributed by Kensington Publishing Corp.
Submit Orders to:
Customer Service
400 Hahn Road
Westminster, MD 21157-4627
Phone: 1-800-733-3000
Fax: 1-800-659-2436

Acknowledgments

God, I thank you because without you, the last two years of life would have taken me out of here.

All the stories you placed on my heart would never see the light of day, and I would be another lost soul. I am so full that you are merciful and allowing me to be your vessel and humble servant.

My family and my team, thank you for loving on me, encouraging me, and steadily pushing me forward. I love you all dearly.

Foreword

This book took me forever. I started over four times. Telling this story of healing and purpose was so very important to me. I wanted to do so correctly and not rob you, my loyal readers, of any detail, any pain, or lesson. I so thank you for trusting me, allowing me to shed the most personal parts of me.

Happy, tearful, healing reading.

Feels

"Charlene" x Anthony Hamilton

"Put On A Smile" x Silk Sonic

"Stuck On You" x Giveon

"Wrong Places" x H.E.R.

"Pick Up Your Feelings" x Jazmine Sullivan

"Hurt Me So Good" x Jazmine Sullivan

"Just Because" x Joyner Lucas

"B.S." x Jhené Aiko ft. H.E.R.

Trigger Warning

Things are happening that may or may not trigger you. Please read with caution.

I did kill someone. You won't miss them. You're welcome.

Prologue

Three Summers Ago

Austin

"Ay, ay, man, listen. Little homie a shooter," Musa boasted from the corner. He stood in his fresh white Nike Air Force high-tops on the edge of the concrete sidewalk covered in old gum and minimal litter spilling over from a nearby trash can. Every word he spoke was full to the rim with pride. A Newport hung from his lips, and another was tucked behind his ear. The sun beamed down on his umber skin as well as on the group of men posted up on the corner with him. In the circle were Keyston, Eman, and the star of the hood, Austin. All conversation and attention had been laser focused on him.

Austin's refusal to leave Fiftieth and McClendon was an outright headache for everyone around him. If he wasn't outside the four walls of the small house he grew up in, he was surrounded by the roughest gangstas in the hood. Each of them proudly sported a cross tattoo on their faces, necks, or hands. In Musa's instance, it was all three. You had to look close to see it. But everyone knew Musa was loyal to the crosses his skin bore. Between him, Keyston, and Eman, they ran Prophet Park.

They controlled the tempo of their part of the hood, the pickup games and the hustles on the street. The work came from Saint, but the money was made due to them serving fiends tirelessly. They all touched the work, the weapons, and the money. All of them except Austin.

Austin was their golden ticket out of the hood, their better way of life, and anything attached to it had to be protected by any means necessary. The draft announcement was set to be released in two days. There were active bets about what team he was going to and who he was taking with him.

Austin's mind was made up. He would be entering the league with his girl, his boys, and his mother. No one else was tagging along for the ride, and no one else would sway his attention. As he stood adjacent to Musa, clad in a white T-shirt and college-branded shorts, he chuckled.

Musa could make anything sound good. His gift of gab made him the hustler he was. He'd talked many women out of their panties, and if all went well, he'd have another on his roster before vacating the ten blocks of Ganton Hills' ghetto.

"I'm nice, I'm nice," Austin jeered, soaking up the compliments from his boys. "I'm about to take the league by storm."

"Hey, Austin." The sound of his name being called pulled his attention slightly from his boys to a cluster of scantily clad women prancing by. Since the announcement that he was going into the league shortly after his sophomore year, the girls around the way had been flocking to him more than usual. No one could break his gaze from Mone't, though.

She was the epicenter of his world. From middle school through high school, it was them. Hand in hand, side by side. She even made it a point to spend her weekends with him on campus. While he had a full ride to Ganton Hills A&M University, otherwise known as GHAMU, she studied data entry at Ganton Hills Community College. They were loyal to their soil. Ganton Hills was the city to bring them together, and it would be the city to make them stronger.

Austin hadn't said it, but he was banking on his draft to the Ganton Hills Monarchs. Despite him being raised and groomed by the Prophets, sports were neutral ground just like church. One thing was for certain—you could worship and cheer in peace.

He threw them a nod and a friendly smile. Nothing too friendly because, without a doubt, someone who knew Mone't was lurking around a corner. His girl was easygoing about a lot. She never asked where his money came from, where he was, or what he was doing, but if word got back to her that he was too friendly, heads were bound to roll.

"What's up, y'all?" he greeted them in return.

"Don't forget about us when you blow up," one shouted from the thick of the cluster.

Briefly his eyes observed her from head to toe. She had scars from bullet wounds, butterfly and leopard-print tattoos, gawdy gold-beaded jewelry, a pair of eyebrows that were drawn on by Sharpies, and a pudgy stomach that lapped over the waist-band of her too-small denim shorts.

"Nah, I could never forget you," he managed to say before Musa and Keyston released a twin chuckle. "Man, y'all hell."

"We ain't do shit," Eman muttered as his eyes scanned the block for potential customers. When his eyes landed on LeAngelique, he frowned. "Watch out. It's the mouth of Fiftieth."

"I know your ass is probably saying something smart, Eman!" LeAngelique shouted as she penetrated their circle. "Austin, who you over here grinning at?"

"Man, get on. Don't you and Mone't got some business or something?" Eman asked, slightly pushing his baby sister's best friend out of their circle.

Wriggling her way back in, she smacked her gum and rolled her eyes. "Uh, no. Ain't shit to do out here but wait until tomorrow night and put my girl up on game about these hoes grinning all stupid-like at her man."

Austin's head bowed slightly as he laughed to himself. "I assure you I'm not grinning at nobody."

"How about you take your nosy ass to the house and get her for this pickup game? And tell her little ass not to be wearing all that fly-girl shit." Eman gnashed his teeth toward LeAngelique.

He couldn't show he was sweet on her. He couldn't even act like he remotely was feeling her. She had dreams and aspirations that were supposed to take her outside of the death corridor of the hood. He would never be the man to hold her back. Their fates were sealed. Eman knew that the only path for him was straight to the penitentiary. But for her, the road she would travel would be so bright it was blinding already.

"Matter of fact, you change, too. Every time y'all come out of the damn house y'all naked as fuck. You and your nappy-headed friend trying to have me catch a charge."

LeAngelique curled her lip and rolled her eyes. "You get on my nerves, Eman LaDon."

Eman completely removed her from the circle and pointed toward her primer-painted Ford Taurus with spinning hubcaps and black dice hanging from the mirror. "Take your ass on, Angie."

She huffed, turned to face Austin, and gave him a death stare. "Keep your eyes and that cheesy-ass smile to yourself."

"Go mind your damn business," Eman grunted before closing the circle fully. With no other option, LeAngelique pranced to her car, hopped in, and zoomed down the block toward the house where his sister and mother laid their heads.

"Yo, she be bugging," Keyston said, breaking the silence. "She need a nigga to shut her ass up."

Eman grunted again, waving him off. "Shorty is my sister's bestie. We're going to get off of that and back on this nigga. You ready for the amount of pussy that's going to be thrown, tossed, handed, slid, and passed your way?"

Austin shrugged his shoulders as he proudly spoke. "Mone't is all I need. I'm going to the league to make a life for us. Give my mama that house she wanted and put Mo through school. Shit is simple."

Musa scoffed in objection. "Yeah, it's simple until it ain't. Them lights gon' get bright, them hoes gon' be hoeing, and the noise gon' be loud. If you can't keep that tool packed away, don't sell her no dreams. Don't interrupt her journey if you're going to fuck up her path."

Keyston blew the smoke into the air from the blunt he'd lit and puffed. "Shit, this shit getting deep as fuck. It's cool and shit, but I got niggas' money to take."

Musa waved his hand in the air. "Nigga, the superstar can't fail a drug test fucking around with you."

"Oh, shit," Keyston grumbled. "My bad, fam."

Mone't

"You're not wearing that to the Saint courts. I just know you aren't," LeAngelique abruptly commented, sifting through the unimpressive amount of clothes in Mone't's closet. "You mean to tell me you're about to be on the arm of the NBA's newest prodigy and this is all you got?"

Angie, as Mone't affectionately called her, kissed her teeth and turned her nose up at the articles of clothing that comprised most of Mone't's wardrobe. There were GHAMU basketball T-shirts with Austin's number and name printed across them, a handful of Austin's jerseys from middle school until now, T-shirts, leggings, some jeans, and a pile of clothes with the tags on them.

Angie squatted and rummaged through the neatly folded piles of new clothes. "Why aren't you wearing any of these?"

Mone't's stammered answer wasn't immediate. Although the two were best friends, she kept the ways of her mother hidden from everyone around her. Any gifts, or anything deemed worth something, was bound to be sold. If tomorrow night unfolded the way she anticipated, she would need to hide his jerseys in the ceiling along with the extravagant treasures Austin had gifted her throughout the years. Despite Austin being the league's newfound golden child, the only thing that would be added to Mone't's reality were spotlights. She'd grown accustomed to the bare minimum, especially with the mother she had the misfortune of being cursed with. Bare minimum was the only way to make it under her roof. Flashiness was a beacon for money, and for green-eyed women like Arayna Swift, flashy would get you hustled out of your check. That was the sole reason Mone't hadn't uttered a word or shown a fraction of excitement surrounding the nearing events.

"Leave those alone," Mone't muttered from the edge of her bed. She'd been quiet, almost too quiet for Angie's liking. "Please."

"Oh, I get it, I get it. You need to be fly for tomorrow night's lights and cameras when they announce Austin Graham as the pick for Ganton Hills."

Mone't winced. If Austin got drafted, she prayed he'd go somewhere far from the Hills and the politics it would take for him to thrive here. Surviving the hood was difficult enough. Surviving the league as a product of this environment would be harder to swim through.

While everyone here would have their hands out for something, all she'd required from him was to thrive. Whether it was with her didn't matter. Mone't wasn't her mother, and she promised herself she would never be the type to ride someone's coattails for a come-up.

She had her own plans, goals, and dreams. They were far more than being Austin Graham's girlfriend. Honestly, it would have been easier if he went on and forgot about her and the raw young love they held for one another. They were all each other knew. If the time came when he knew another, it would crush her.

"Mm, I think I'm going to sit it all out," she muttered to herself more so than Angie.

Angie could hear a pin drop. Her ability to hear everything she wasn't supposed to was exactly why she could regurgitate people's business without missing a beat. Mone't swore it was going to make her a great journalist one day.

Angie popped up, tossing her best friend a minidress with the tags still on it. "Put that on. I'm not playing with you."

Mone't's toasted brown face screwed up in dis-
taste. "I'm not going."

"You are because these thirsty-ass hood rats are
going out of their way to get your man's attention.
I'm not having it. Not now, not ever. Get out of your
head, stand your pretty ass up, and get dressed."

Grudgingly, Mone't obliged her friend. Angie
was the only one who could make her listen the
first time. It was the only advice she heeded outside of Ms. Graham's.

Once they were dressed and on their way to the
courts, Angie slightly turned her gaze to Mone't,
who was staring out the window, watching the
graffiti-painted block flash by.

"Are you nervous that he's going to forget you or
leave you behind? I heard girlfriends get nervous
during draft time."

"I'm not nervous. I'm not concerned. This is
about Austin. It's about him doing what he needs
to do to be who he needs to be. If I'm invited along
for the ride, okay. If not, I'll understand."

Angie frowned somberly at Mone't's comment.
It wasn't a secret that Mone't had sacrificed her
time and years of her life to be a good girlfriend.
She cheered the loudest and got up early to run
or lift weights or whatever he needed. Mone't was
Austin's rib, and to hear that she'd sacrifice her
love so he could fly was beautifully heart-wrenching.

"Wow," Angie blew after moments. "You really love him. That's some biblical, forsaking-all-others shit. It's deep. I want that."

Mone't chose to stay silent. She loved Austin how her father had loved her mother. It was a dangerous type of love. A love that had him locked away for twenty-five to life on charges she should have taken. But Symon Lucas was a man of honor, and his woman would never be taking a charge as long as he was alive to see to it.

Angie parked her Taurus and killed the engine. The pickup game was already underway, and the crowd lined around the basketball court thickened as the minutes passed. Around-the-way girls with their cutoff shorts and cropped tops were feening for attention from the local hustlers and the ballers. Anyone who could keep them laced in the latest, flyest shit was who they were leaving with . . . or attempting to leave with.

While the scantily clad women were on the prowl, the dope boys were coolly trying to get recognized too. The name of the game in the hood was come-up. The game? Rub elbows with the movers and shakers and prove they weren't bitch-made. But there was no purpose in the show. The real ones smelled the disparity in the air. It was thick and fell on them like the mugginess of a summer afternoon after a shower of rain, sticky and uncomfortable.

Hand in hand, Mone't and Angie pushed through the crowd until they were safely tucked behind Keyston happily collecting fives, tens, twenties, and fifties from bets, Musa shouting for Austin to drive the ball down court, and Eman standing imperturbably, his eyes surveying the crowd for any potential threat. The protector in Eman kept his head on a swivel. He'd gotten that from his father—Mone't's father.

"Girl, your man is balling out!" Angie squealed. "I can't wait to see him play this next season."

A rush of euphoria washed over Mone't. Containing her excitement, shouts, and grins was out of the question. Austin's performance was precise and agile all while being aggressive as hell. That, coupled with the charisma and arrogance that popped out when he was in beast mode, was the most majestic thing she'd ever experienced.

Austin had everyone entranced with his ability to control the rock and the tempo of how fast or slow the game moved. His opponents, and even his teammates, were having a difficult time keeping up with him. Through his high school and collegiate careers, he'd pushed everyone around him to the max. Austin wouldn't ever slow down so that his opposition could catch up. Being the best was drilled into his head. In turn, he drilled it into everyone around him. They held on to the lessons shown and spoken by the young man. Especially Mone't.

She watched him while he calculated everyone's moves in his head, ran plays, and solidified which way they were going to move. That set her body ablaze with desire. No matter how she tried to psych herself out, she burned only for Austin, and her entire being was his.

"Yo, that nigga is ballin'!" Keyston jeered, nudging Musa with his elbow.

Musa stood proudly, hands in his pockets. His hand always rested on one of his guns when the crowd was too thick to be controlled. A smile threatened to take over Musa's lips, but he remained as stoic as Eman.

Musa's head nodded before he looked over his shoulder and down at Mone't. She looked different to him. Something else was setting the way for a metamorphosis in her life. That made him smile, reach out for her, and pull her against his side. She might have been Eman's baby sister, but she was his too. Shit, she was a baby sister to all of them. Her being attached to Austin meant just an added layer of protection.

"You see how yo' nigga balls out when he knows you're watching?" Musa asked. Only the two of them could hear him with the rising noise of the crowd.

Mone't's grin was on full display. Her narrow eyes had disappeared behind her high cheekbones.

"You that nigga's heart. I love that shit. I want you to remember how this feels right now. After tomorrow, shit is changing. Lean into the change and flow with the river, a'ight?"

Mone't's almond-shaped and hued orbs drifted up to Musa. "I'm afraid of tomorrow." She finally admitted it out loud.

He shook her slightly and hummed. "Tomorrow has troubles of its own. Stay in this moment. Lock this shit in. This is a legend in the making. King Austin. Mark my words."

Mone't's attention returned to Austin, who'd taken two steps back and hit a fadeaway shot that knocked out the lights in the park. The crowd went crazy. This was a moment the hood would remember forever. Pride filtered through the bodies on and off the court. Austin had rocked the block, and after his announcement tomorrow, he was going to rock the hood.

In the midst of excitement, Austin maneuvered through the crowd to stand in the warmth of Mone't's light. He knew without a doubt that the moment she knew her power, everyone would have to bow at her feet.

Cupping her face, he kissed her sweetly. It was a display of affection that had every girl in the hood grimacing with jealousy at the sight. "How you like it?"

"That shouldn't even be a question," she crooned. "You did your thing."

"I wasn't playing that good before you showed up."

"Let me get a pic of the cute couple!" Angie squealed, interrupting their ogling of one another.

Austin adored Mone't. Regardless of what she chose to tell herself, he loved her as much as his young mind could process. "Your mama home tonight?"

Mone't shook her head no. "She's out of town with some old playa until tomorrow night."

She didn't need him to say what was on his mind. They were on the same wavelength. They always were. They turned to face Angie. Sweaty and valiant, Austin held his lady close and smiled at the camera. Mone't hugged his waist, grinning from ear to ear.

"Y'all cute as hell," Angie cheered.

"Let's get out of here," Eman spoke up.

Mone't turned to her brother and nodded. One by one, they all moved to Eman's voice. That was until someone shouted Austin's name, drawing his attention from leaving with Mone't to them. He stopped, his hand wrapped around Mone't's.

Mone't turned with him to see Gabe leering down at her and then up to Austin. "I see you, superstar."

Her tiny eyes rolled. She hated when anyone referred to him as superstar, money, or big time. They were all signs of snake shit, and she couldn't get behind that. Mone't was still pure and un-tainted, a blessing Austin wouldn't understand yet. Only time would reveal what stood by his side.

Mone't's grip on his large hand squeezed tighter, discomfort pulsating through her being. Austin knew the subtle signs that it was time to get her out of the throngs of people and back into her safe space.

Austin smirked and slightly threw his head toward him. "What's up, G?"

Gabe clasped his hands together and rubbed them over one another. "You need to give me a chance to win my money back."

Austin's annoyed chuckle resounded. "You got to take that up with Keyston."

Gabe released his hands and pressed two fingers into Austin's chest. "I'm not talking to Keyston. I'm talking to you, big money. I can get my money back now, or I can get it back in blood. Either play or say bye-bye to your career, pretty boy."

Austin let go of Mone't's hand. The happiness in the air shifted. Now there were two men glaring at one another. The dispersing crowd started to lin-ger at signs of the tension. Eman, Musa, Keyston, and Angie halted their progress to the street. The only thing on Austin's mind was defending his honor, his pride.

Mone't was pulled from Austin's side and replaced with Eman. "We got a problem, G?"

Gabe thumbed his nose and sniffed a bit before turning his attention from Austin to Eman's overpowering presence. "I was just telling your man here that I want to win my money back. You know, a little one-on-one action."

Eman laughed. "That's cool and all, but Austin ain't over the money. Keyston is. Roll up off my nigga and follow the chain of command. Your bitch ass talks to Keyston. Keyston talks to Musa. Musa finds me, and I tell you it ain't fucking happening."

Gabe closed the space between them, choosing to stand toe-to-toe with Eman. He snarled as he removed the Glock .45 from his waist. "Y'all motherfuckers better get to playing ball before he doesn't walk again."

"Eman, I'll –"

Eman held his hand up. "Take Mo back to your spot and don't leave."

"Man, it's nothing. It's a one-on-one pickup game. I can play whoever he's putting me on in my sleep," Austin said, defending himself.

"Nigga, hear me. Take my sister and get the fuck on," Eman harshly spoke.

Against his ego and pride, Austin took two steps back and regained Mone't's hand. Angie stood near, watching Eman and Gabe, stuck in place as her heart thundered.

"Yeah, listen to daddy, little nigga!" Gabe shouted their way.

"Angie, come on," Mone't spoke up before her eyes floated to Eman removing his piece from the front waistband of his shorts. Gabe held his gun in the air as though he was getting ready to surrender. One shot fired into the air sent the park into pandemonium. A scuffle ensued, growing bigger by the moment.

Gabe and Eman fought. The guns scattered. A member of Gabe's crew grabbed one, aiming it directly at Austin. Mone't's fight or flight response was in full effect. As she shoved him out of the line of fire, her feet trampled over into the mess of men, and she grabbed Eman's gun out of the back of his shorts. Without warning or a bat of an eye, bullets flew, and only one struck.

Mone't couldn't hear anything. The blast from the gun deafened her momentarily. Austin yanked her from the mess and pushed her and Angie toward her car. The ride three blocks over to Austin's house was full of heaving, distant sirens, and loud thoughts that would not be silenced.

Before Angie could stop the car, Mone't jumped out and barreled into Austin's house through the side door. She ignored the shouts of surprise from Austin's mother, who was in the kitchen checking off a list for the festivities the next day.

"What in the world is happening?" she screeched, dropping her list and rushing down the hall behind Mone't. "Mone't Swift."

It was unlike Mone't to disrespect Aneica's home, and any other time, she would have answered if her head weren't stuck in the porcelain bowl. She'd barely eaten over the last week, and up until now, she'd done a good job of hiding it. But the nerves in her stomach, the smell of gunpowder, and the worry of what-if were shedding light on her little secret.

"Oh, my goodness." Her thick Jamaican accent came through. "Mo, are you pregnant?"

It wasn't a question that Aneica needed an answer to. It was Austin, now standing directly behind his mother, who needed the answer.

"You pregnant, Mo?"

Upon hearing his voice, Mone't flushed the minimal contents in the bowl and wiped her face with the tissue nearby. With another eruption soon on the way and her breathing labored, she looked at him, tears streaming down her face, and whimpered, "Yes."

Everyone's hearts sank. Aneica quickly turned to scurry down to her room to get a fresh set of clothes and fresh towels for her from the hall closet. Austin stepped fully into the bathroom and wiped her face with the back of his hand.

"Baby, why didn't you tell me?" he questioned in a soft tone. It only coaxed the tears to flow faster and harder. "Don't do that. I'm right here."

"I promise I wasn't trying to trap you or get a bag. I don't want you to think I'm trying to tether you to me forever."

Austin's face scrunched. "Mo. I ain't leaving you here. Baby or not. That was never an option. It's been me and you, and it'll always be me and you. You didn't make this baby by yourself."

"Mm-hmm, she sure didn't," Aneica responded, returning with towels and clothes. "Austin, help her get cleaned up and come to the living room when you're done." She left them alone.

Austin was hyper-focused on Mone't. He was attentive to all her needs throughout the night until the doorbell rang. Mone't was curled up on the couch, trying to not fidget or have her nerves get the best of her.

"Have you told your mother?" Aneica asked, prompting Mone't to shake her head no.

"She'd use it and me for a check. I can't get behind that. I don't really know what I'm going to do. I need a job and—"

"Let tomorrow's troubles be tomorrow's troubles, Mo. We have tonight and tomorrow to get through. We'll figure it out after."

Austin had spent the last two hours in the kitchen, quietly breaking down the events of the evening while Mone't stared aimlessly at the TV screen. Aneica had taken Mone't under her wing when Austin started bringing her around years ago, having known her mother from around the way and seeing that her brother was on his own path. She knew that, more than guidance, Mone't needed someone to care.

The mug of ginger and peach tea on the coffee table was cold, and there wasn't anything on TV worth staring at. Mone't's ears and attention were tuned toward the door. Her view was obscured by Austin's tall frame, but she could hear Musa's voice clearly.

"You gon' let me in, nigga? The block is hot."

"Yeah," Austin spoke once he cleared his throat.

Musa stepped inside Aneica's home and scanned the area. Instantly, he frowned when his eyes landed on Mo curled on the couch. "Yo, you good?"

Mone't's puffy eyes found Musa's marijuana-glossed orbs. He glared at her intently before coming closer to her. "Don't trip on that shit at the park. We're handling it."

"How are you handling it?" she questioned, sitting up.

Musa took a beat of silence, his eyes bouncing from Austin standing next to the locked door, to Aneica resting at the threshold of the kitchen, then back to Mone't, who was full of worry. "Eman took the wrap for it all."

"You serious?" Austin questioned.

"Wait, what do you mean 'it all'?" Mone't asked.

"Mo, that bullet hit a vein in his leg. He bled out before the medics could show up."

Terror took over Mone't's being. "Oh, my God. Oh, my God! I killed . . ." Mone't was on her feet, pacing in small circles, tears rushing from her eyes. Before she was too far gone with panic, Musa grabbed her shoulders.

"Mo, look at me."

"E can't take that charge for me. He only has one strike left."

"Baby, breathe," Austin chimed in, now standing on the other side of her. "You can't stress out like this. The baby—"

Musa froze, his eyes lighting up. "You pregnant?" It was almost as if a light bulb went off in his head. "That's what it was," he muttered to himself. Then he spoke to Mone't. "E is doing what real niggas do. Tomorrow, everything is changing. Your life out of here starts tomorrow. E ain't gon' let you stay, especially not with Austin's baby inside of you. Now hold your head up. You got things to do, mama."

Mone't's eyes fell to the floor. "How am I supposed to do this knowing what I did? I didn't mean to. I was just . . ."

Austin pulled Mone't to him. Holding her firmly, he coached her to breathe. "You were just protecting me. I'm indebted to you for that. We'll get through this."

"We're handling the streets, but y'all probably need to get into the city tonight."

Aneica had rented out a suite at 4Oaks for the big day. Initially they were supposed to check in on draft day with the mountains of food for the big day. The NBA camera crews were set to meet them there. This latest turn of events changed everything. Austin's life in the hood, life as he knew it, was over, and the lights of tomorrow were brightening and becoming more anxiety inducing by the second.

"Mo, I told Angie to go get all your stuff from your spot. She'll meet us in the city. Ms. Graham—"

Aneica stood erect. "I'll pack up all of this and meet y'all there."

"Keyston will take you. You need a shooter with you."

The silence throughout the small house weighed on Mone't like a ton. The rest of the night was deafeningly silent. Austin moved around the small house gathering his things, while Aneica and Mone't secured the large pans of food into the totes. Per usual, Aneica had gone overboard with the food for the small group of people who would be in attendance tomorrow.

"Stop blaming yourself," Aneica finally spoke up, slicing the silence with her words. "Everything is a part of a plan, a bigger plan than us all. He could have shot Austin, or worse, he could have shot you. You did what had to be done, Mo."

Mone't quickly wiped her face with the back of her hand. "It doesn't feel that way."

Aneica hummed. "It never does. We're women. We do what we need to despite what it feels like. No matter how hard or painful it is, we do it, sometimes with tears in our eyes and sometimes with a smile on our faces. Tomorrow calls for a smile. Despite what you feel like, when those cameras turn on and he accepts his job, you'll smile. Tonight will never be mentioned to anyone again."

"Yes, ma'am."

Aneica nodded and returned to the tasks at hand. Within hours they were packed and fleeing the ten blocks that made them. Mone't couldn't help but feel as though she were in the Twilight Zone. Everything was playing out around her, but she couldn't reach out and grasp any of it. There were so many variables she had to consider.

Her brother was gone and would probably get stuck with a public defender who couldn't remember his name. There was a child growing inside her and depending on her quiet serenity to nurture and care for it. Her mother would show up when it was beneficial for her. And Austin was hours away from showing the world what he was made of, regardless of whether he was a second-round pick.

"Mone't, I'm talking to you," Angie huffed with her hands on her hips.

"Huh? What'd you say?" Mone't questioned, finding herself on the edge of the bed, staring at the wall. "I'm sorry."

Angie's initial reaction was to be annoyed by Mone't's ability to zone out for minutes at a time. Considering the current events and her friend's mental state, she sighed and took a seat by her, clasping Mone't's hand in hers. "I know this is a lot and it's scary. You're not alone. You won't fail, and I won't let go of your hand. Okay?"

Mone't looked over to Angie, her eyes still exposing the painful toll of her mind. "Okay."

"Now, Austin is out there with his agent going over tomorrow's announcement. Aneica is being a helicopter, and I need to know what you're wearing." Angie pointed to the bags full of clothes Mone't hid from her mother. "Let's try them on."

"Let's?"

Angie nodded her head confidently in response to Mone't's question. "Yes, because whatever you aren't wearing, I am. I'm trying to catch me a baller too."

Mone't cut her friend a knowing expression. "Oh, really?"

Angie inhaled deeply, trying not to allow her mind to run marathons when it came to Eman. Despite how annoyingly rude they were to each other, what their hearts knew and what they experienced was the greatest love story yet to be written.

She talked a good game, but moving on from Eman with his scent on her was nearly impossible. Angie was willing and ready to ride out this bid with him. She knew every free moment would be dedicated to the long drives to whatever prison they assigned him to, writing letters, and making sure that when he was finally free, he knew that above all else she would be his.

Angie's words came out just above a whisper. "No. I wish I could. I can't. I won't. So it's me and you and this little baby while I count down seconds, minutes, hours, days, months, and years."

Mone't rested her head on Angie's shoulder. "Me and you until the end."

"To the end."

Austin

Austin was a bag of nerves. Although he stood confidently in his tailored teal-green suit, crisp white shirt, and diamonds dancing around his neck, he felt like he was suffocating. The moment he'd been preparing for was here. His mother was proud, his girlfriend glowed, and he was surrounded by people who truly loved him and wanted him to thrive, with the exception of Eman.

Yet and still, he felt unprepared and undeserving of this optimum opportunity. In a matter of minutes, the cameras would be on and he'd be on his way. He couldn't control any of it. His home was being packed in boxes, his best friend was locked away facing the most time he'd ever faced, and he was here. Austin's dreams were here: NBA superstar, soon-to-be father, and if Mone't would have him, soon-to-be husband. It was all so much at once.

Anxiously running his hands through the curly locs on top of his head, he rushed out of the room and onto the balcony where Musa and Keyston were finishing a blunt. Austin's tawny skin glowed red, and his face was scowled.

"Nah, youngblood, you're supposed to look like you're on top of the world," Keyston stated, waving the smoke out of the air. "What's up?"

"Pressure on your shoulders weigh a ton, don't it, nigga?" Musa asked, eyes focused on the city. "Welcome to manhood."

"I can't breathe."

Musa leaned on the rail of the balcony and looked at the city moving below. "That's because you aren't breathing. You've been holding your breath, waiting to wake from a dream. Guess what? You're up, nigga. This is happening. You'll have millions in your account by tomorrow, your girl is having a baby, and you promised your mama a house. Contracts, endorsements, responsibilities, and obligations are coming at you, and you can't pass out now. Breathe through that shit. Your light skin as red as a bitch because you can't control none of this."

Keyston joined in with commentary of his own. "I mean, you can if you go back to the hood. Then you'll be dead or in jail in, what, two months?"

"And who the fuck wants to see that talent wasted? You wanna see it, Key?" Musa posed.

"Nah, not at all," he responded.

Musa stood up and strolled over to Austin and pressed his pointer finger into his chest. The aroma of marijuana was still pungent on his knit. "Breathe. Poke your chest out, hold your head up, and do what the fuck you got to do for you, for your lady and your mama, and for Eman. Don't fail yourself or them."

"What about y'all?"

Keyston laughed and held his arms out. "You ain't got to worry about us. We're with you every step. Eman ain't having it no other way. Take your moment."

Musa grabbed Austin by the back of the head and pressed his forehead to his. "You got this. It's in you, nigga. Show the world who the fuck you are and what the Hills made."

Releasing him, Musa stepped back and trailed Keyston inside. Austin was left alone to fill his lungs with air. His heart thundered in his chest as he released the air slowly. When nearly all the breath from his body had expelled into the air around him, his phone vibrated in his pocket. Inclined to ignore the device, he snaked it out. The unknown number scrolled over the screen, coaxing him to answer. Hesitatingly hitting the green icon, Austin was met by a monotone voice.

"You have a call from an inmate in the Ganton Hills Correctional Facility. Press one to accept."

With haste, he accepted. A cheer roared through the receiver. Someone passing by would have thought it was a group of men, but it was just Eman. "You better go the fuck off, boy!"

A smile pinned itself to Austin's face. "You know it."

"I know you over there stressing the fuck out. Don't do that. You got it. I'm cheering for you the whole way. Promise me you'll take care of her and my nephew or niece."

"You knew?"

"That's my baby sister. I knew the moment you touched her. I know her. I don't want her worrying about me. Neither of you. I'll be cool. I can't talk long, but hear me, man—everything is everything. Rumble, young nigga. Rumble."

"I'm getting you a lawyer."

"Don't waste your money on me. You taking care of her and doing what you have to will be all I need. Tell Angie's annoying ass to stay out of people's business when y'all get there," Eman commented.

Austin chuckled and ran his hand down his face. "I'll tell her you asked about her, although you could do it yourself."

"Nah, she doesn't need no one like me. See to that shit."

"I will." Emotion started to tighten Austin's chest. "I'm—"

Eman's voice dropped. "Don't do that shit. I didn't call to hear the soft shit. Make me proud."

"Without a doubt."

Without saying goodbye, Eman hung up. Austin took a step closer to the rail and looked at the vastness of the city. The journey here wasn't easy, and the one he was getting ready to embark on wouldn't be either. Regardless of how he felt about his readiness, it was do or die.

"I'm going to do this shit like it's never been done before."

He took the next moments to level himself before entering Mone't's space. She was beautiful, so much so that he had to catch his breath before closing the space between them. She'd been holding tightly on to the bottle of water. Her nerves were just as bad as his. Neither of them slept or said much the night before.

"You good?" he quizzed.

Mone't's eyes drifted to his as her hands released the bottle to straighten his lapel. "I'm okay. You?"

"I'm okay. Nervous."

"It's okay to be nervous and scared. Your dream is coming true though. Focus on that."

He grabbed her hands, squeezing them as he brought them to his lips. "Our dreams. A dream ain't a dream without you."

Mone't smiled faintly. "I seem to be adding a lot to your plate."

He shrugged nonchalantly. "So what? As long as you're on that plate, what does it matter? We're in this together."

"You sure?"

"Don't ask me again if I am. The three of us are going to be fine. A'ight?"

A voice interrupted their moment. "Austin, lights, camera, action in two minutes." Jermel Green, his agent, was excitedly clapping his hands.

The tightening of Mone't's already-anxious demeanor rooted Austin. For as long as Jermel had been around, he and Mone't never saw eye to eye. Jermel thought Mone't was a distraction, and Mone't didn't trust anything about him. His cheap white teeth, slick grin, and overly greased hair were all the signs she needed not to buy into his campaign. Jermel looked like a used-car salesman who made a quick come-up. He was some guy from around the way whom the college had recommended to assist Austin with the transition.

It seemed easier for Austin to ignore their issues and focus on the task at hand. His insatiable appetite was going to get him and his entire family to the top. That was the only median between Jermel and Austin. He was a greedy, greasy man who used his connections to the culture to influence young players to march to the beat of his drum.

Jermel was going to be the liaison who took Austin Graham and turned him into the Greatest of All Time—for a small price, of course. Twenty percent of Austin's money was his for the duration of their contract. The agenda was clear and precise.

If Austin stuck with him, he'd make millions while he was young. If that meant interrupting his time with Mone't, then so be it.

Austin lingered in her gaze. "A'ight?"

"All right. Go. It's your time."

"Our time. Come on."

The lights shined as brightly as everyone's smiles. Keyston and Musa stood in the background, proudly watching Austin sit between Aneica and Mone't. It seemed like the ten minutes of filming waiting for the phone to ring were the longest. He attempted not to glare at it, but it was impossible. When it rang, he couldn't bring himself to pick it up until Jermel snapped him out of his trance.

Austin swiped the icon and put the phone to his ear. "Hello."

"Austin Graham! Gerald Bennington, owner of the Ganton Hills Monarchs. I'd like to personally welcome you to the team! Are you ready to change the game?"

Austin beamed. "I'm ready!"

Chapter One

Now

"Ay, Mo!" Austin shouted her name throughout the 12,000-square-foot mansion. He checked all her usual places only to find her tucked away in a cabana on the far end of the pool. She was in her most natural state: thick, curly hair falling over her face and shoulders with one strap of her dress down so their 6-month-old son could nurse without obstruction. Her legs were crossed, and her eyes were trailing the words in Izzy's princess book.

Austin was a few feet away when Isabella spotted him. Leaping from her mother's side, she ran down the concrete-block path into her father's arms.

"What you doing, stink? Hm? Reading with Mommy?"

"Yep. We got a lot of books today!"

Austin joined Mone't and AJ in the cabana, giving them each a kiss. "You went out today?"

Mone't shook her head no. "Your mother took Izzy to the store. They came back with a ton of books. How was practice?"

"Intense. Tomorrow is game one of the playoffs. Are you coming this year or enjoying it from home?"

Mone't looked down at Austin Jr., who was grunting greedily as he nursed for the umpteenth time today. "I don't know if I can leave him."

"Bring him. I'll get y'all a private skybox. You can do what you have to do. But I need you there. You know I go off when you're there."

"I remember."

Austin chalked up the change in his wife to hormones settling post pregnancy, but deep inside of him, he feared it was something much more. That same fear kept him from asking. The thought of hearing the heaviness of her feelings and what it would take from him for her to feel whole again was stomach lurching. "What do you say?"

"Say yes, Mommy. Please say yes!" Isabella begged, clasping her tiny hands together while giving her mother puppy eyes.

Austin joined in with the plea, knowing that his wife couldn't tell him no. "Please say yes. I need you."

"Daddy needs you," Isabella chimed.

"Are you two double-teaming me? Really?" Mone't replied with a chuckle. "If I say yes, are y'all going to stop?"

Isabella and Austin looked at each other, sharing the same thinking face. Hell, they shared the same face. Austin couldn't deny his children if he wanted to. Isabella was almost 4, with her father's mannerisms and height. Austin was sure she was going to be the next WNBA phenom due to her inheriting his athleticism as well.

"Yes!" they said in unison.

"Okay, I'll go," Mone't yielded. Austin hoped that getting her out of the house would change her mood.

"Izzy!" Aneica shouted from the floor-to-ceiling sliding glass door. She stepped out and proceeded over to the small family. Aneica was the star advocate of their marriage. She actually cried when Austin proposed after a few short months of being in the league. Their wedding wasn't glamorous or announced in the blogs. It was simple, Mone't in a dress that hid most of her growing belly, and Austin in jeans and a button-up. The wedding wasn't the work. The marriage was, which was why Aneica vowed to be there for them as long as they needed her help.

"Yes, ma'am?" Izzy asked from behind one of the curtains of the cabana.

"Help me give your brother a bath," she announced as Mone't pulled her breast from AJ's mouth.

Once she handed him off to Austin, she fixed herself and lay back, allowing herself a moment of peace.

"Thanks, Ma," Austin spoke after covering both of his children with kisses. When they were alone, he closed the curtains and lay by his wife. "All he does is eat."

"All day and all night. He won't take the bottle either," Mone't said.

Austin swept her hair out of her face and adored how beautiful she was. His hand trailed from her chin down her neck to her full breasts. "They're bigger this time."

"Neither of you will stay off of them. Let me guess—that's what you're out here for."

"I wanted to tell you." Each word was trailed with a soft kiss to her exposed skin. "The Herb and Nutrition endorsement is a go."

"Oh, that's good. Congratulations, babe."

"Nah, that was all your hard work setting up the events and making sure everyone who came into town had what they needed while managing a house, two kids, and me. Fifty percent of the shares are in your name."

Mone't turned to Austin with shock on her face. "Are you serious?"

"Hell yeah. I wouldn't be here without you, baby." He kissed her lips tenderly and, in the same motion, pulled her on top of his body. Immediately she tensed up. "Mo, come on. Stop it."

The self-doubt had embedded itself in Mone't's orbs. He was partially guilty for that, guilty of putting his needs above hers and allowing her to accept the minimum treatment. Not just from him, but everyone around her.

"I'm too heavy to be on top of you and . . ." Her words trailed off at the sensation of Austin's thumb gliding over her bud.

He did it again, inducing her flood gates to open, and the arousal from his touch distracted her just enough to fall into his demand. Giving her an orgasm and a momentary release of endorphins was easy. Trying to understand the complexity of the woman he vowed forever to was a task he couldn't wrap his mind around. So he didn't. Austin provided her an escape while he got the release he'd been thinking about for most of the day.

Pushing her dress up over her thighs and hips, Austin removed his erection from his basketball shorts. It was second nature and muscle memory. He didn't have time for foreplay or finding the new spots on her body. He wanted her with haste, and she yielded.

Mone't's walls wrapped around him, pulling him into her as deep as he could go, covering his erection with her silky wetness. Removing the straps of her dress from her shoulders, he palmed her milk-filled breasts and squeezed them. He latched his mouth around them. Austin's obsession with her breasts started when Izzy was a newborn, and now he couldn't get enough of them or her.

The more he desired her, the more it seemed that she pulled away from him. He hoped that his sex could undo whatever had been done over the last year and a half. She held him close, letting her mind drift off and relish the pleasure his sex provided her. Austin drove into her while her hips ground around him until they were spent, clinging to one another, panting, chests heaving against one another.

Austin kissed the center of her chest. "We should do that more often."

"If you were home enough," Mone't replied.

Austin huffed as she removed her body from his. "Here we go. Can we have a moment without that shit? You know what it is, Mo."

"Forget I said anything."

"I just want to enjoy my wife and stay in a moment without a smart comment."

"It's not a smart comment when it's true, Austin. I know you're fighting for that playoff spot and another championship. I know it's hectic. You come home and stay for a few hours and you're out the door again. When's the last time you really asked me how I was doing?"

"This morning, but you shushed me and fed AJ."

"Austin, you slept last night, right? Your clothes are clean. The house is clean. I . . ." She stopped herself. "You're right. I'll do better."

Yanking the curtain open once she fixed herself, she slipped her feet into her designer slides and stormed into the house. Austin's eyes trailed his raging beauty up the concrete path and into the house. "She's just going to leave me like this, dick in my hands and shit."

His shorts were returned to their original position, and his body remained reclined. Austin grumbled to himself, "A man can't even have pussy and peace. Something is always wrong with her, goddamn."

He lay in the cabana silently, letting his mind turn over with ways to get to the root of what was going on with his wife. His mind didn't get too far into the never-ending loop of Mone't before his phone rang out.

Choosing to ignore the festering emotions in his house, he answered the call from Jermel. "Yo, what's up?"

"Tell me you can get downtown in the next hour," Jermel started without so much as a "Hi, how's the family doing?"

"Man, I just got home. My wife is trippin' over something. I got to tend to this."

"You just gave her half a million. What's there to trip over? Listen, her attitude isn't going anywhere. This money might." Jermel dangled the carrot in front of Austin's face. "Trust me, I've had three wives. They come and go, but the money, that's the sweet spot."

Ignoring the latter part of his comment, Austin asked, "Who is it?"

"Ian Sanders from Sanders Tech."

"The *HOOPS* developer?"

"Yeah, and he wants King Austin. So what do you want me to tell him? You can't come because your wife has an attitude, or you're on the way?"

Austin removed his tall body from the cabana and walked toward the house. He could see Mone't moving around the kitchen, fixing Izzy's dinner while his mother did bath time with their little ones upstairs. The scowl on her face said it all. He was damned if he did, damned if he didn't. The decision was made for him.

"I'm on my way."

He hung up, dropped the phone into his pocket, and strolled into the kitchen. "Don't make anything for me. I have an endorsement thing to head to."

"I thought you were free tonight," Mone't chimed back, looking at him over her shoulder. "We promised Izzy movies tonight."

"Tell her I'll do it this weekend."

Mone't turned to face him. "Let me guess. Jermel has an opportunity you can't miss? You can tell your daughter why you're breaking your promise. I'm not being the bad guy another night."

"Why can't you help me out?"

"Because helping you out puts me on the shitty end of the bargain. Perhaps if you stood where I stood, you'd understand."

Not wanting to fight with her, he fell back. "All right, Mo. You win. I'll be back later tonight."

Chapter Two

"King Austin is in his zone tonight! The Monarchs are on the verge of securing that playoff spot," one announcer spoke through the surround sound of the skybox.

Typically, Mone't would be on the floor, almost courtside with the rest of the fans, but AJ had ruled her life since he came by breech birth into the world, kicking and screaming. Not to mention, Isabella loved the snacks that came along with watching her daddy play from the skybox.

Mone't's eyes watched the screen as she swayed from side to side while nursing the newest addition to their family beneath the receiving blanket. Austin dribbled down the court, sweat pouring off his golden skin covered with intricate art in permanent ink. His tapered cut and curly locs had been traded in for a low-cut Caesar.

Even in the last minute of the game, Austin still looked put together. He looked, moved, and embodied every part of a franchise player. These ticking seconds were crucial. After three years in the league, Austin was hungry to bring home another championship for Ganton Hills.

He had affectionally been dubbed the King of the Hills, and he proudly carried the title and city on his back. It showed on the etch of his brow as he drove down the court, passing the ball to Cypress Jones. The play was fast, but Mone't had seen it over a dozen times.

Mone't knew this play. Before juggling two kids and a household, they ran this screen together. Cypress would pass the ball back to him, and Austin would take it to the hoop for a game-buzzing shot. Except they weren't accounting for Ramsey Edwards of the Lavendale Vipers to steal it and drive it down the court. It was a fight to the finish. Lavendale was down by three. A stolen shot and foul would tie the game.

She smirked at the determination on his face. "Don't sweat it, baby. You got this."

"You got this, Daddy! Take it to the hole!" Isabelle cheered from her hoisted position on Musa's shoulders.

Austin was in a race against the clock. The seconds felt infinite as he ran down the court to retrieve the ball that had the game tied. Twenty seconds, and the rock was in Austin's palms. Mone't held their son tightly while he peacefully suckled.

"Come on, come on, come on," she anxiously chanted to herself. "Three-peat, baby, three-peat."

In the blink of an eye, Austin rushed mid-court, and the ball hit the glossy floor twice before he curled it back and released it. It was poetic the way the ball glided off his fingertips at the perfect arch.

The anticipation almost caused her to clamp her eyes shut. She couldn't. She had to see this. She'd missed so many games in person due to tending to their growing family. The swoosh of the net in concurrence with the buzzer could be heard throughout the skybox.

"Yes!" she shouted, startling AJ in the process. "Oh, sorry, bubba." Adjusting herself and her breastfeeding-friendly top, she held him upright and kissed his head through his thick curls. "Sorry, bubba. Mommy got excited. Daddy won."

"He did it again. Playoffs here we come!" Aneica spoke proudly as she removed AJ from Mone't's arms. "Three seasons back-to-back. He owes you a vacation."

Mone't smiled convincingly. It was a trait she'd adapted over the years with Aneica's help. "Let's hope he gets another ring, and then we can think about vacation."

Aneica's expression remained the same. If it were up to her, Mone't would have found a back-bone when it came to her son and demanded his time. Unsure of what it would take for Mone't to finally step into herself, she settled with the answer she was given and gathered the children.

Mone't tried not to internalize Aneica's words, but she knew home life really hadn't really felt like home since giving birth. The off-season schedule was just as hectic as the actual season. If Austin wasn't training, he was shooting commercials, appearing on sitcoms, and making appearances at nightclubs or lounges. Mone't tried to be present at everything until she couldn't. Traveling while maintaining their home life resulted in her on bed rest for the final four months of her pregnancy.

She expected things to get easier after giving birth. AJ's entry into the world wasn't nearly as easy as Isabella's. Mone't couldn't snap back or get her mind together. When she needed Austin, he was away, too busy to talk or be present, all too involved with the business side of his brand.

Six months later, she was finally out of the house at a game, by persuasion of course, and it all felt surreal. This had to be the best he'd played all season. As they traveled down to the media room where the after-game press conference was being held, she fidgeted with her top.

Musa and Keyston were back to work securing Austin and his prized possessions. Angie sat in the media room with her pass, awaiting a juicy story to post on her blog. Aneica and Mone't were the last to enter with the children.

"Stop fidgeting. You look fine." Aneica grabbed Mone't's hand and squeezed it. "You look beautiful. Stop."

Mone't didn't feel fine. She'd gone from slender and petite to thick. New curves. Full hips and breasts placed her outside of her comfort zone. This was her first public appearance, and the last thing she wanted the media to say was that she was fat, homely looking, and an embarrassment to Austin's brand.

Austin was showered and dressed in the latest threads from his clothing line, waiting for her to enter. Isabella captured his attention first. Happily scooping her in his arms, he covered her face with kisses, making her giggle loudly.

"You did it, Daddy!" Isabella shouted, making the journalists and sports analysts "aw" or laugh at her outburst. Her daddy may have been the superstar, but she stole the show.

"You saw that?" Austin matched her energy.

"Mm-hmm, it went swoosh. Mommy was ascared though. But I wasn't," she said in a matter-of-fact tone.

Austin's attention shifted from Isabella to Mone't, who had no idea what to do with her empty arms. He observed her from head to toe, a smirk forming over his lips. Mone't's full lips were painted with clear gloss, her wild hair pulled into a high bun. The loose-fitting draped top fell over her full breasts effortlessly, and her hips in distressed denim made his mind swirl with thoughts of removing the articles of clothing from her body and burying himself deep inside.

"I wasn't scared. Nervous maybe. Good game, baby." She smiled at him and took a step closer, sure to position herself behind Musa so the cameras wouldn't get a good photo of her.

"I knew you were up there chewing on your lip or swaying," Austin teased. "You look good."

A genuine grin formed over her lips for the first time in a while. It was wide enough to make her small eyes disappear. "Thank you."

Austin's gaze became more lust induced by the passing seconds. "Dinner after this is over?"

"Just us?"

"Yeah. Just us."

"Austin, they're ready for you," Jermel interrupted. It was a nasty habit Austin hadn't corrected yet, and for the sake of not causing a scene, Mone't didn't say anything. "Oh, Mone't, nice to see you out supporting King Austin. Didn't think we would see you tonight."

Her narrow eyes squinted at him before turning back to Austin. "Go do your thing."

Austin gave her a quick kiss on top of the head and proceeded with Izzy in tow to the setup at the front of the room. Mone't inhaled sharply and scanned the room. Angie caught her eyes and swooped her finger over her face and mouthed, "Smile, beautiful."

Just like that, Mone't's face lifted in the practiced smile. She stood on the other side of Musa and watched Austin explain how he brought his team this far, crediting his teammates for the success although the reporters in the room made him sound like a basketball god. One reporter even called him the GOAT while praising his ability to save his team in the clutch.

"Your nigga is that nigga," Keyston proudly stated in a low tone. "You got to be proud of that."

Without a doubt she was. However, Mone't knew who Austin really was when the lights turned off. He was just the boy who stole her heart.

"I am proud."

Musa added to Keyston's commentary. "The king ain't shit without the queen. Don't get so caught up in the hype."

Tuning out their back-and-forth, Mone't watched how Austin and Izzy effortlessly kept the post-game conference entertaining. It went on for almost ten minutes before Austin looked in her direction.

"Thank you. I have a beautiful woman to take to dinner. Cypress and Paul can take it from here."

When he stood to leave, all the attention in the room turned to Mone't, who could've disappeared behind Musa's large frame. The questions were being fired off, and shutters of the cameras were almost deafening. Behind Musa's lead, Austin clasped Mone't's hand and trailed them into the hallway.

Aneica stood in the hall holding a sleeping AJ. She watched her son walk out hand in hand with his wife and felt a sense of hopefulness for the two. Being a young couple with two children and a demanding career was taking a toll on them. She could only pray it wouldn't swallow them whole.

"Good game, son," she greeted him once he entered her space.

Austin proudly smiled. "Thanks, Ma. Do you mind keeping an eye on them? I want to take Mone't out to—"

"Austin, Austin!" Jermel shouted down the hall behind him.

Aneica and Mone't shared a twin expression of annoyance in response to Jermel's rude behavior. By now she should've been immune to his ways, but they only seemed to aggravate her more.

"There's some investors here to see—" Jermel started, but Aneica happily cut him off.

"Can't you see we're in the middle of something? Did your mother ever teach you manners?"

Jermel cut a coy look over at Aneica. "Actually, I never knew my mother. I'd love to get into that, but money is calling."

"Mel, can it wait?" Austin asked, hoping to ease some of the tension. "My kids are tired. I want to spend time with my wife."

"The offseason wasn't enough?" Jermel sarcastically asked.

"Nigga," Austin grunted, forcing Musa and Keyston to close in.

"That was a joke. Right, Mo? It was a joke!" Jermel attempted to backpedal to no avail.

"Don't call me that," Mone't replied with a harsh undertone. Looking up at her husband, she pressed her lips together. "Go do what you have to do. I'll wait in the car."

"Five minutes, baby. I promise." Austin bent over to put Izzy down but not before kissing her face. "I'll tuck you in when I get home."

"Okay, Daddy!" Izzy shouted before trekking over to her grandmother.

"All right." Mone't hummed, feeling the sting in her ear when he released her hand.

"Five minutes, baby, and then it's you and me," Austin assured her while taking two steps back from her.

The group watched Austin venture down the long hallways with Jermel. Once they were behind a closed door, Mone't turned on the heels of her feet. "Key, can you make sure they get home safely?"

"You got it," Keyston spoke up.

"I'll let you know when we get home. You two try to enjoy tonight, okay?" Aneica said, touching Mone't's arm.

"Yes, ma'am."

Mone't was left in the empty hall with Musa, who was more than keen to what was happening between them. It was a slow, gradual distancing. If their ship didn't get back on track soon, this ordeal would be too far gone.

"You got to tell him you don't like that man or what's happening between you two," Musa shared, leaning on the wall adjacent to Mone't. "You got to communicate, Mo."

"There's been enough fights over his job and his agent. I'm tapped out."

"You better tap back in. That pull leads to trouble. I'm telling you."

"I hear you, Musa."

"I hope so. Let's wait in the car."

Five minutes turned into ten, ten turned into twenty, and soon an hour had passed when Austin met them in the car. "Baby, great news."

Mone't couldn't pretend to be interested in what he had to say. She was visibly irritated. Musa was standing outside the car in the once-buzzing players' parking lot, smoking. "Yeah? You rented out a restaurant or something? Everywhere we go to is closed now."

Austin groaned, swiping his face with the palm of his hand. "Shit, I'm sorry. We got caught up."

She said nothing.

"Damn, do you want to hear my news at least?" he asked, taken aback by the show of her festering feelings. "They want to headline me on the next *HOOPS* video game."

She was still silent.

"Damn, at least pretend to be happy," he snapped, climbing into the back seat of the Cullinan. "Can you do that for me?"

"I do. All the time, Austin. I've done it for years, and I don't ask you for much in return. Five minutes is what you told me, and you couldn't bother to tell me that it was going to take longer? You have no consideration for me."

"Mo, it was business." Austin's hunger to never return to the ten blocks of the hood had skewed the vision of what was really important. If he didn't have Mone't, he didn't have anything.

"No, it was Jermel finding another way to impede. It's getting old. This is getting old."

Austin's face scrunched, and he drew his head back. "What's getting old, Mo? This?" Austin twirled his finger around the interior of the luxury car he paid cash for. "I busted my ass tonight. I expected my wife to be excited about that. It's the same shit day in and out. You have an attitude about this and that. You have help!"

"Help isn't you!" she shouted back.

"Two part-time nannies and my mama. I'm out here providing. The least you could do is meet me halfway and be grateful for this shit!"

"Whoa," Musa interrupted. "The Hills have eyes and ears. Don't give these people a story. Table this."

Mone't sucked in a deep breath and looked out the window. "No need. Just take my ungrateful ass home."

"You know damn well that's not what I meant." Austin slammed the door of the truck and sank into the leather. His words were echoing in his head, but pride had sat itself between the couple and refused to move.

Austin's frustrated wife sighed heavily and rose her eyes to the stars on the roof. "I feel like I'm—"

Austin's phone rang out, cutting Mone't off midsentence.

"It's Cypress," Austin announced as though it would make a difference to Mone't, who was moments away from having a break of her own.

"Cypress is more important than what we have going on right now?"

"It'll only be a second, damn. Calm your ass down," he grumbled, answering the call. "What's up, Press?"

Musa dropped his head and shook it slightly as he pulled out of the parking garage. He tried his best not to interject himself into their issues. He made a mental note to talk to Austin later without Mone't around or anyone else who would have a rebuttal to the commentary.

The tension in the car was too thick to be cut with a knife. They would need a sledgehammer to break through this. Mone't leaned into her nook of the back seat and scrolled through IG posts. In between the clutter of sports content and mommy videos, there were self-love posts and affirmations. She'd followed all these accounts to give her some sort of reprieve. None of them helped.

Faintly, she could hear Cypress speak to Austin. "You comin' out tonight? Or you playing daddy?"

"I don't play shit, nigga. I am Daddy."

Cypress laughed. "Yeah, I hear you. We're hittin' the lounge. Come through and celebrate this W."

Austin lowly shifted his eyes over to Mone't. "I'll let you know when I get to the crib."

"A'ight, nigga. We got money on you not showing up," Cypress joked, forcing Austin to grunt.

"Every time someone bets against me, you'll lose."

"You might be right," Cypress commented before they ended the call.

"Musa, you can take me home so the king can get to wherever he needs to go," Mone't said more to dig under Austin's skin the way all of this was digging under hers. It was childish and trivial.

Communication wasn't their strong suit, especially with one another.

"Cut it out, Mo." Austin's agitated grumble seemed to do the trick for the duration of the ride.

Mone't entered the house ahead of Austin, bypassing their bedroom to check on AJ and Isabella. Finding both of her children sound asleep, she sighed in relief and trekked aimlessly down the hall.

Austin was climbing the stairs two at a time with two glasses of wine and a bottle. Mone't's eyes trailed the length of his body, observing the rigidness of his frame. "I hope that's not what you're using tonight to get some."

Instead of firing off a smart-ass comment of his own, Austin tightened his jaw while taking a sharp inhale. "No, Mo. We got to talk."

"Don't you have to go out with Press and the team? Don't worry about me." Mone't walked around his frame into their bedroom and kicked her shoes off. Frustration had her pulling her hair out of the holder prior to plopping down at her vanity.

Austin stood in the background and watched his love remove the makeup from her face without so much as looking at her reflection. She seemed so foreign to him. If only he knew how foreign she felt to herself.

Invitation wasn't needed as he took large steps into the bathroom with a glass of wine.

"You know I can't drink."

"Pump and dump."

She huffed. "Austin, just go do what you want to do."

"I'm standing here, ain't I? What's going on with you, Mo?"

She paused the vigorous swiping of her makeup. Her eyes filled the moment his gaze met hers, admitting that she felt weak when she carried him and their family on her back and went against everything she was taught.

Austin coaxed her response. "Baby, tell me. This ain't you. You haven't smiled or laughed since AJ. You won't leave this house. You're moody."

Her eyes fell to her hands, and the truth she couldn't run from was on the tip of her tongue.

"Is it postpartum depression?" Austin asked, concern riddling his voice.

"I think it's more than that now. He's six months. I'm supposed to be over this."

Austin neglected his spot and squatted beside her. "What do you need from me to get through this?"

"I need to feel like I'm the first option. Not the second or the third. I don't want to feel like I only have your attention when you need help swaying a potential deal or when you want some. I feel like we're slipping away from each other."

His sigh was littered with relief. The way they'd been hot and cold, he was sure she was on the brink of wanting out of this life with him. It was demanding. He was away from her more than he was home. His kids were sprouting before his eyes, and he was missing moments all while Mone't was struggling to do it all.

"Baby, I'm sorry."

Mone't quickly wiped the tears from her cheeks. "Me too. Can we try this date night again after the season?"

He nodded. "Yeah. Can I hold you tonight? I won't try no shit."

"Turn your phone off and it's a deal."

"Not you in here doing everything." Angie's voice cut through AJ's cries, Isabella's off-key singing, and the sizzling of bacon on the stove. "Where is Austin?"

Mone't whisked around the kitchen, trying to prepare the bottle she silently prayed AJ would take. While Austin slept, she spent the night pumping and feeding her needy infant. It was taxing. All of it was taxing, and despite her admitting that her mental health was in shambles, she got up to take care of her family.

"It's what I do," Mone't muttered, in pursuit to pick AJ up and feed him.

"Ah, I got it." Angie intercepted her godson and cradled him in her arms. "Why are you screaming like this, huh, *papi?* I bet you've been up all night, nursing. Mommy is running around with no head on her shoulders. Yes, she is. If you're hungry, just say that."

Angie cooed at AJ, distracting him. "You're six months and you weigh eighty-five pounds, chunk-a-munk. All you do is eat, sleep, and cry for Mommy's titty."

Mone't handed over the bottle and spun to flip the turkey bacon. "Thank you."

"Why are you thanking me? This is what we do. You okay?" Angie could take one look at Mone't and know she was hanging on by a thread. "And don't give me no bullshit. I saw your face last night, and the security guard told me about the shouting match in the parking garage. They even took pictures."

That grabbed Mone't's attention. She turned off the stove and removed the pan from the eye. "What are you going to do with it?"

"Nothing. I paid them for it, had them send it, and deleted it from their phone. They'll never see the light of day. But when did you two start fighting, especially in public like that?"

Mone't sighed and pushed her hands through her hair. She watched AJ calmly take his bottle without fussing or fighting her. Not only was her husband playing in her face, but her son was also. "Since I went on bed rest. I think he's so accustomed to me doing everything and being everything to him and the kids, he can't see past that. And I'm tired, Ang. I don't sleep. I'm a twenty-four-hour feeding machine. I have to bend over for him when he wants it. I have to be present. But who's present for me? Who takes care of me?"

Despite Mone't trying to fight back tears, they fell from her eyes like an avalanche. This was the moment she was trying to avoid—the break. Angie's heart swelled for her. It hurt for her. Mone't had sacrificed herself for Austin, proudly standing by him, bearing his children, while being the epicenter of his peace.

"This shit was supposed to be over by now. Postpartum is kicking my ass. I struggle every day just to make it through the day. I can't look at myself. I don't feel like I'm worthy to be desired, but I'm superwoman, right? I have to keep going, right? Because if I stop for just a second, Angie, I'm selfish or a bad mother or a neglectful wife, when in reality I take care of everyone and I'm alone."

Angie reduced the space between them. Balancing AJ in the crook of her arm, she reached out and hugged Mone't.

"Austin could walk out of here today and find another woman who is whole, and what am I left with? Huh? Wasted time and fucking depression that won't get off of me. I want it gone."

"You're not alone. I'm always here, but we don't know what you need if you don't tell us, Mo. You're so worthy of everything you give. You can't get what you don't demand, baby."

"What's going on in here?" Austin's baritone rumbled, making Mone't quickly wipe her face and jump back into the swing of her morning routine.

Austin stood in the middle of the large kitchen and watched the concern riddle Angie's face. Mone't avoided eye contact, feeling silly for even letting herself get to this point.

"Nothing. Sit down. I'm almost done." Mone't's voice was just above a whisper.

"Angie, can you give us a minute?" Austin asked. "Izzy, go with Auntie Angie and get Mama."

Isabella jumped to the command of her father's words. "Okay. Come on, Ang. Mama's doing yoga."

Angie flashed Mone't a look that urged her to talk and then herded the kids out of the kitchen and down the hall.

"That's how you feel, Mo? For real? Like I'm going to leave you?" he asked, brows pinned together. "You know that's never going to happen."

"I don't know that, Austin. I honestly don't. You don't even want to be here with me. The phone rings and you're gone, but I've said this. All I have is my kids. That's it. Nothing else of my own. No business—"

"You have me."

"It's not enough."

Austin's shoulders tightened along with his expression. "Yo, I can't do this today. I have practice, film, and—"

It was his inability to step outside of himself for a moment to hear and feel the gravity of Mone't's words. She was drowning, and she expected him to be the one to save her like she'd done for him countless times before.

"That's it right there. You can't see anything past King Austin. I'm telling you I'm suffering. That I hate this shit. I hate that my mind doesn't stop. I hate myself for feeling like this. I hate that I don't feel good enough for you or our kids, and yet you can't see a damn thing past dollar signs and contracts and what everyone has to say."

"That's fucked up, Mo. I work fucking hard for this family."

She was tired of having to repeat herself. Tired of him not getting it. "This isn't about you! My God!"

"Stop it."

"No! You can't see past your fuckin' self!"

Mone't's outburst prompted Keyston to run into the kitchen to see what the shouting was about. Not being one who was well-versed in handling emotions, he paused. "Uh, y'all having some married shit right now?"

"What is going on in here? We can hear you downstairs!" Aneica shouted, rushing past Keyston.

"It's nothing," Austin dismissed, attempting to get everyone out of his business. It was too late for that.

Scoffing, Mone't wiped her face and slammed the plate she'd been clutching the entire time on the quartz counter. The blue porcelain plate shattered into tiny pieces across the counter. "Fuck you, Austin. Make your own damn breakfast and pack your own shit."

Mone't charged out of the kitchen and up the stairs to their bedroom. Slamming the door shut, she released everything holding her hostage. Crying was just one layer. The work that had to be done under the surface was expansive. She needed a break. She needed a shoulder to lean on before she slipped so far under the water that it overtook her.

As she fought to pull herself together, Angie slipped into the room. Bypassing Mone't and her sobs, she trekked into the bathroom and turned the tub on. As Angie zipped around the room collecting various things, Mone't silently coached herself to pull it together.

"Stand up," Angie ordered.

Through the tears, Mone't questioned, "What?"

"Stand up."

She stood with puzzlement dancing in her eyes.

"Go get in the tub and calm down. I am going to help you. I'll finish breakfast, help Mama, and when Austin goes to practice, you and I are getting out of this house. I'm not going to let you drown in this. Now go. There's oil and bath salt already in there."

"AJ needs—"

"Between me and the rest of the adults in this house, we are more than capable of handling two children. Go."

Heeding the demand, Mone't pulled herself into the bathroom. She removed her tired body from the oversized Monarchs T-shirt and basketball shorts and slipped her body into the water. Drawing her knees into her chest, she hummed to herself, embarrassment now settling on top of the mountain of all the other things she'd felt.

"Unball yourself and breathe, girl," Angie directed as she walked out of the bedroom.

It took Mone't a minute before she could. Once she stretched out and laid her head on the bath pillow, she sighed and covered her face with her wet hands. "You have to get yourself some help."

Chapter Three

"What the hell was that?" Aneica snapped at her son as she cleaned the remnants of Mone't's breakdown.

"Ask her."

"Boy." Her tone was stern and her gaze even more paralyzing. "I asked you. What was that?"

Austin groaned, running his hand down his face. "She's been up and down."

"And you think telling her to suck it up and get over it is how you handle that? You don't know half of what it takes to be a woman, a wife to a man who is larger than life, and a mother, all while trying to find your place in all of that."

"Ma, we talked last night, and it was fine."

Aneica kissed her teeth. "Oh, yeah? What she say last night 'bout this? Hm? What she tell you? That's not a woman who is okay or fine."

"What do I do?"

"For starters, help her out. You have a boy who won't let her have a moment. You don't help. Not a diaper or a shirt has been changed. But you come home demanding her time, not keeping your word. Not making space for her. You wouldn't even be here if it weren't for her. And that's how you treat her?"

"Ma—"

Aneica held her hand up. "I am not done talking. Sit down."

Austin did exactly what he was told. An upset Aneica was nothing to play with. Her accent was thicker than usual, and the look in her eyes was murderous. Mone't didn't have to be of her blood to be hers.

"Three seasons, three playoffs, three championships. Not one complaint. She showed up every time she could. She cheered the loudest. Ride or die without question. Being a husband is far more than throwing some dollars her way. I assure you, she doesn't give a damn about this money. And it is very unfortunate that you can't see that."

"I'm never going back to Fiftieth. I've told all of you that. I'm going to work until I can't."

"At what cost? Huh? If you lose your family, you'll lose everything."

Austin didn't want to hear that. He stood up and waved it off. "Both of you are tripping. I got to get to work. Keyston."

"Huh?" Keyston asked from the living room. He'd been ear hustling and was going to give Musa a play-by-play when he returned.

"Get the Cadillac. I'm out of here in ten minutes."

"A'ight, young'un."

Austin trekked down the hall, knowing everything Mone't and his mother had shouted to be true. He warred with himself constantly. He wanted to be the GOAT, and he wanted to feel what it was like to be with Mone't before worry took over. The demands of his career and his wife didn't fit in the same space. One was going to overtake the other. It was survival of the fittest, a war between his heart and soul and his brand and career.

He whisked through the laundry room, packing his bag for practice and clothes for after. He even went so far as to pack an outfit just in case he went out with the fellas. Mone't needed her space, and he needed to decompress from the weight of responsibilities he didn't know how to take care of. This was supposed to be easy. They were supposed to fall into this dream turned reality, thrive, and grow together, but none of that was happening. A year of them growing apart instead of together was coming to a head.

"This is bullshit," he muttered to himself. "I built her a damn castle, and she's crying because I'm out hustling to pay for the shit. Got me fucked up. For real."

After collecting his practice sneakers from the shoe rack on the other side of the laundry room, he walked out past the kitchen to the garage. His mother had finished the cleaning and moved on to finish making breakfast.

"Come grab your breakfast," she directed.

"Nah, I'm cool," he called as he walked out the door and met Keyston in the SUV. "Take me to get a smoothie."

"Nigga, I ain't Mo. I'll knock your top off talking to me like that," Keyston rebutted. "I'll knock that bass out your damn chest."

Austin groaned, annoyance coursing through his blood. "Where is Musa?"

"Upstate to see Eman. Or you forgot about him on your money chase?"

"Nigga, shut up. No one forgot about Eman. I keep money on his books."

"There you go again. That's that shit Mo in there crying about. Money ain't everything, nigga. It's here today and gone tomorrow. Money ain't you, young'un. When you get Jermel out of your ear and get that shit through your thick skull, you'll see what we're talking about."

"All of a sudden everyone got an issue with this come-up? What the fuck?"

"It ain't the come-up we got issue with. It's you. You arrogant, dismissive, and self-centered. Motherfuckin' King Austin can't do no wrong. Everyone loves him. Shit feels good, don't it? But if your kids don't know you and your wife can't stand you, what kind of king are you really?"

Austin pulled the headphones he wore around his neck over his ears and turned the music to the maximum volume. Keyston chuckled and shrugged his shoulders. "A'ight, nigga. You'll see."

Musa walked through the visitation room with a wide grin on his face. Every month on the same day, he took the four-hour drive upstate to see Eman. Due to his direct connection with Austin, he came with paraphernalia for the block, snacks they couldn't get on commissary, and photos of his family.

"You looking good, man. You spending all your time lifting weights?" Musa asked, greeting Eman with a tight brotherly hug.

"You know I got to pass this time somehow. You don't look too bad yourself, fly nigga," Eman replied prior to releasing him. "How's everything?"

Musa took his seat and playfully shrugged. "You know how it goes. Protecting the fam, keeping the business tight."

"Oh, yeah, sounds like some shit is hitting the fan. I know Austin is balling out. I see the endorsements rolling in, but what's up with Mo? She ain't been taking my calls," Eman said, looking Musa square in the eye.

Musa clenched his jaw. "She's going through it. You know your sister. She holds everything close to her chest, but this shit is different."

"Postpartum ain't off of her yet?"

"No. It's heavier than that. She needs him or you or something."

"Where the fuck is Austin? How doesn't he see this shit?" Eman asked, the frustration of being inside these walls starting to show itself. "How fucking hard is it to see that she needs something?"

"That nigga Jermel," Musa stated. "All Austin sees and hears is money, money, money."

Eman sat back in his seat and grunted to himself. "What are you saying to him about this?"

"I haven't said nothing to him, yet. I'm caught somewhere between letting him learn and staying out of married people's business."

Eman's head swayed. "What else is it?"

Musa smirked. "Angie slid me some letters for you. Pictures of AJ and Izzy and an appeal motion you need to sign."

The stack of envelopes was slid across the table. Eman took his time looking over the pictures of AJ and Izzy. "They're getting big. AJ must be eating all the fuckin' time."

"Man, he's latched on to her every second he gets. He's gonna be a linebacker or something. He's a butterball."

"I can tell." Eman's words broke with laughter, only dying down when he picked up the appeal letter. "Mo did this?"

"You know she doesn't listen."

"Hardheaded as hell. Shit is a headache. Can I think on this?"

Musa shook his head no. "You can't. It took three years to get this letter. Who knows how long it's going to take them to review it after you sign it? I got a feeling."

Eman's eyes popped up from the letter to Musa. "About this?"

"No. About them. Whatever is going to happen, they're going to need you. Angie needs you. She's been holding it down, keeping herself busy with everyone's business, but you set the tempo."

Eman released a slow breath. "It feels like I've been in here for an eternity. The gangs are at peace. My baby sister ain't a baby, and you're here pushing me to go back out and fix some shit that I don't even know—"

"We made them a promise. We all got dreams attached to them. If they win, we win."

"No one wins when the family feuds."

Musa nodded. "Exactly."

Eman stared at the appeal letter a while longer before reaching for the pen Musa slid over. "You can hold it down until I'm home?"

"You're my brother. You know I'll hold it down forever."

"I appreciate you. I mean that shit."

"This is what we do. Keep your head up. It's almost over."

Musa and Eman's conversation switched gears. When Musa came upstate for his visits, he was intentional about filling them with purpose. Eman was supposed to be managing Austin. That was what Musa kept at the front of his mind—the dream of his sports agency, the plan of them reaching back to the hood and pulling niggas out one by one. Although Austin was stuck in his own way, he was intentional about setting money aside for his people. Eman especially.

"That's time," the correctional officer sounded off from the corner of the visitation room.

Musa looked over his shoulder at the time. "Damn."

Eman stood. "Thank you."

"Don't mention it. I'll be seeing you."

"For sure."

They dapped each other, embraced, and departed until later. Musa retrieved his property from the officer and made his way out of the prison. Keyston had called three times over his typical limit. Keyston was only going to call once. Four times was excessive for him. Musa tapped his name on the screen and waited for Keyston to answer before pulling off.

"Damn, nigga, what were y'all up there doing? Braiding each other's hair and sharing gossip?"

"Fuck you. What's going on?" Musa asked, getting straight to the point.

"Besides Austin sending me home and sending all our calls to voicemail? Nothing," Keyston replied coolly.

"How the fuck are you security and he's out without you?"

"Jermel took him to some party to network and shit. Ain't heard from him since."

"I'm about sick of that nigga," Musa grumbled. "Is Mone't cool?"

"Besides Angie taking her out and getting her wine drunk, she's calmer than she was this morning."

"A'ight. That man is grown. He's going to do what the fuck he wants to do. He wants to be the man, let him."

"You sure? It ain't nothing to—"

"Nah, we can't keep saving him, regardless of whether we see the train coming and he's playing on the tracks. He wants to be the man? Let him."

"A'ight, I'm headed out. I got a little shorty to catch a vibe with."

"Don't get your ass robbed messing with these hood rats. I'm not coming to help your ass out of a jam like last time," Musa warned before disconnecting.

There were a million words he could've said to Austin and Mone't. There were things he could've done to get Jermel out of the picture. Regardless of all the things he could have done, this was Austin and Mone't's path to travel. He couldn't stop it from happening, but he could be there to lessen the impact of the blow that was sure to come.

When the time came, Musa would be there. Until then, he was going to take this ride back home and lie in his peace until the morning. Musa's peace was a woman he should've had no dealings with. But the heart wanted what it wanted, and his wanted her. Whether she felt the same or she was using him as a rebound would be determined later.

The second he parked his car from his travels, he looked at her front door and grinned. Shooting her an I'm here text, he climbed out of his car and proceeded to the door.

When his feet hit the welcome mat, she pulled the door open in a satin robe and a lustful grin. "Didn't think I'd see you tonight."

"You know I wasn't going to leave you hanging."

He grabbed her by the waist and backed her into the house, kissing her in tandem with shutting the door behind them. Whatever was happening outside of these four walls would have to wait until the morning.

Chapter Four

Austin didn't drink often, especially during the season. Tonight was an exception to his rule. The marketing mixer Jermel invited him to was more of a party. The rented space was packed from the front entrance to the back. As he towered over the crowd, his mind recalled how Mone't would accompany him to these events regardless of whether Jermel thought it was a good idea.

He felt naked. Mone't had a natural charisma that could sway the crowd in his favor. Until now, all Austin had to do was show up, smile, pose for some photos, and the deal was sealed. She was his greatest asset. Somewhere deep in the crevices of his mind, he knew that. What he knew was clouded by the vision being sold to him. The material things were too blinding to see past.

Women had shown up in throngs. Some were feening for his attention, and others really wanted to talk shop. Jermel filtered them through to him and kept a drink in his hand.

"Austin," Jermel called with a wide grin showing his veneers too big and too white to pass off as real.

"Have you met Pandora Herrera? Sports leisure designer, social media creative, and fan."

Jermel was laying it on thick with this particular introduction. Not playing too much into it, Austin threw the woman a nod without really looking her way. "What's up? You want a pic for the Gram?"

Pandora smirked as her dark eyes ran up and down his body. Austin had his Caucasian father to thank for his dancing bronze eyes. His strong features screamed every bit of Aneica. His thick hair, beautifully golden fawn skin, broad nose, lean body, and height were to be marveled over. His swag, however, was the pure product of Mone't. She knew what he needed to be seen in and how he needed to walk, talk, and make people feel when he spoke to them.

The Caribbean descent vibe that ran through his blood was cultivated and nurtured, and Mone't's product shined like a diamond, all of which was alluring to Pandora. Her placement into his space was not accompanied by pure intent. Truly, Austin had no need for her. She couldn't add value to his expansive empire.

However, having the stamp of King Austin over her would take her career to heights she'd only dreamt about.

"A pic for the Gram?" she repeated in a friendly tone different from the women who were trying to shamelessly throw themselves at him.

He gave her a small glimpse that lasted longer than it needed to. Pandora was dangerously sexy. Her profound curves, thick, cascading curls down her back, and smoky-style makeup intensified her exotic look. Without a doubt, she was a temptress.

"Yeah," he spoke over the music, lowering himself enough for her to hear him. "That's why you over here, right?"

Pandora laughed, flirting. "No, not at all. I don't need you to boost my followers."

"But you need something, so what is it?"

Pandora faced the bar of the section Jermel had propped Austin in. He had no security of his own, no one close to him to advise him against being too friendly or too close. No Mone't to get to the root of the business this woman had with her husband.

As though Pandora had cast a spell over him, Austin trailed her to the bar, requested another drink, and waited for the seductress to answer his lingering question.

"I shouldn't even present this to you. Word on the street is that your wife is the gatekeeper." Pandora looked down at his ringless finger. Neither the absent ring nor the M tattooed on his finger meant anything to her. Pandora looked over her shoulder. "Where is your wife?"

Austin's ego refused to give way to his common sense. "Not here. I am. So what's the pitch? Aren't you supposed to come with some sort of numbers and projections? A team?"

Pandora took a long, slow sip of her drink while looking up at him from under her thick lashes. "I roll solo. No team, no gimmicks or hype. Just me. You should collab with me. I'm a good look. If we look good together, the possibilities are endless."

"I have a clothing line."

Pandora slowly licked her lips, took a step in his space. It was just enough to brush her body against his and swipe the scent of her perfume over his designer knit. "I know, and it's okay, but it's not me. I'm telling you, I think you and I can make magic." Gently rubbing her hand down his arm, she held her other hand out. "Let me give you my number. You take tonight and think about it and tell me tomorrow what the answer is. You know, after you discuss it with wifey of course."

"I don't need her permission to make my own decisions." Stupidly, he pulled his phone from his pocket and handed it over.

Pandora took the device, held it to his face to unlock it, and smirked at the photo on the screen. Mone't smiled brightly with the Mediterranean Sea as her backdrop. She was smaller in the photo, holding a small baby bump. That was the last time they went on a trip, a few months before Izzy was born on this babymoon.

"She's cute." Pandora hummed before navigating her way around his apps and calling herself. "That's my number. I'll be looking forward to your call."

Austin was taken aback by her boldness. His body reacted to her regardless of his heart warring against it all. Licking his lips, he bobbed his head as he took possession of his phone. "I'll sleep on it."

"I hope so. Dream about how good a collab with me will be."

He chuckled. "Sounds like you're selling something else."

"The arousal of your senses is to be expected when you're on the brink of something game-changing." Pandora took a step back. "Nice meeting you, Austin Graham."

She held her freshly manicured hand out for a professional shake after laying her game on him. Without a doubt, she knew she had Austin in her web. Soon, she was going to have everything she wanted. Maybe him and his namesake, too.

Austin took her soft hand. "Same to you, Pandora."

"Have a good night." She withdrew and pranced away, knowing Austin would watch her make her exit.

"Damn," he muttered to himself. His dick was on brick. It would be wrong to dive into the sea of temptation, so his only option was to finish this drink and go home. Maybe a night of good sex would loosen his wife up some. Maybe it would bring them back to center.

Sliding his glass back toward the bar, he tipped the bartender and exited his area, surveying the crowd for Jermel. The crowd was too thick for him to find his agent. With his phone in hand, he pulled up the JoyRide app. Exiting the building without security, he hurriedly ordered a ride home.

"Where's your ride?" Pandora asked.

He turned slightly to see her waiting by the valet stand. Holding his phone up, he said, "Ordering it."

"Cancel it."

He considered it before Mone't's scowl flashed in his mind. "Thanks. I'm cool though."

"You want to ride in a car with someone you don't know? I can take you to where you have to go."

"I appreciate it, but—"

"But you've been drinking, got a couple dozen missed calls. You might need something to soak up that liquor. I'll drive you to Juicy Lucy's and you can get a car from there."

"My wife—"

"I thought you didn't need her permission to make your decisions." Her words left her lips like a challenge as her SUV was pulled around. "More than enough space for you to stretch out."

Impaired judgment carried his legs over to her. A superstar with too much to lose took the one step forward that would change everything. "I'll skip Juicy Lucy's. You can drop me off at my spot a few blocks away."

The spot was a luxury condo he'd bought as an investment property. He was going to rent it out but hadn't made his way around to sharing the idea with Mone't. Neglecting his original idea of going home and connecting with his wife, it was easier to spend the night out and sleep the liquor off.

The explanation would be simple: he went out with Mel, drank too much, and crashed at the condo. Nothing else to it if it stopped there. Austin was in the front seat of Pandora's SUV, not giving a fuck about the photos or spectators.

"You keep a spot in the city? I thought someone like you would have the family life down to a science."

He looked over at Pandora, the alcohol supporting the reaction of his erection pressing against the inseam of his pants. The dress she wore seemed to be riding her thighs with every passing second.

"It's an investment condo in the new GH Capital building."

She screeched, "Are you serious? That place is super elite. I applied for a spot there."

"They have so much red tape."

"Who are you telling? My Realtor couldn't even get me in to view it."

"You want to see it?"

Pandora's face lit up. "I'd love to."

Meaningless conversation filled the time it took to get from the event space through the parking garage of GH Capital. The building housed seventy floors, twenty of which belonged to GH Capital Banking and Trust. Above those were a dozen businesses and then residential spaces. At the top was an exclusive restaurant he'd planned on taking Mone't to.

Austin ushered Pandora through the private entrance toward the elevators after a brief conversation with the security guard. A thick sexual tension filled the elevator as they ascended into the air. Pandora stood inches away from him. So close. So dangerously close.

Before Austin acted on his impulse to take her in the elevator and send her on her way, the bell dinged as the doors opened to the luxury condo. The lights in the space were on motion sensors, and they lit the way as Pandora took off inside.

"This is gorgeous." She gawked over the view, the modern decor, and the tempered glass floors. "I have to get on this level." Stopping at the sofa, she inhaled. "This is why this collaboration is so important, Austin."

"It's definitely something to aspire to."

"Has your wife been here yet?"

"Nah, we can't seem to find the time."

Pandora turned to him. "That's a shame. If I had a man like you, I'd be wherever doing whatever needed to be done."

He scoffed, enjoying the feeding of his ego. "A man like me?"

"Yeah. A provider. It's obvious you love her and your family. You take care of all of them, but I can't help but wonder who takes care of you."

"I get by."

Silence fell as she moved toward him. "I can take care of you." Pandora's hand gripped the erection through his pants.

Whatever blood Austin had left in his brain was gone.

"It's clear you need to be taken care of."

Without warning, Pandora dropped into a squat and freed him. Austin knew to run, to go home, to remove all temptation from his space. His feet were rooted, pleasure coursing through his being as Pandora took him into her mouth without complaint. His eyes were cast down at her making his dick disappear and reappear. She used no hands to work him. One hand was pressed against his thigh, and the other played with her kitty.

"Gahhhdamn," he groaned, yielding to the trouble he found himself in.

Pandora moaned in response. His hands gripped the roots of her hair. She allowed him to fuck her mouth until his seed shot down her throat. Pandora's touch opened a box and brought out on a prowl the beast Austin kept locked away.

"Go to the sofa and bend over."

Austin dipped into the nearby bedroom Keyston used from time to time to flex, and he rummaged through the drawer for a condom. Finding a pack of six, he returned to a naked Pandora sitting on the couch, her legs spread-eagle. She played with herself and fondled her breast. She was free and open about what she wanted. Austin wasn't a master of women. He was a master of his wife's body as far as he knew.

What Pandora possessed was erotic and played into his fantasies.

"You want to swim in this, don't you? Do it. I'll take care of you."

Austin sheathed his length with the rubber. He lowered himself to his knees and pulled her to the edge of the cushions. It took five strokes to push the guilt to the back burner. Pandora allowed Austin to have his way with her until they passed out in a bed.

The rising sunlight hit him like a freight train along with the sensation of Pandora sucking him to life.

"Fuck, what time is it?" he questioned, patting the bedside table for his phone.

"Shh," she hushed. "I'm not finished taking care of you."

"Shorty, I got to go. You got to go. Last night—"

Pandora hoisted herself on top of him and slammed down on his erection, up and down, her juices leaking all over his dick. "It was perfect."

Her moan was so sexy, but he couldn't help but see Mone't bouncing up and down on him. Sense finally returned and was having a war with the sensation she possessed.

"Yo, we . . . Fuck." He told himself he'd already crossed the line. What was one more ride? After he left her, he'd delete the number and forget he ever stepped out on his wife.

He didn't forget. How could he? Even after he washed her evidence off him. He didn't delete the number either. He couldn't. His phone was dead. He sat in the back of a JoyRide he had the front desk set up for him. He would get through practice with enough time to build his story.

"Fuck."

Chapter Five

"Mommy."

Mone't woke up to Isabella standing at her bedside with her phone's screen illuminated in her face. Going out with Angie the day before and getting drunk had proven to be a bad idea. She hadn't even heard Austin come in. Through her wild hair, she squinted. "What is it, baby?"

"Daddy isn't picking up," Izzy answered.

"He's probably in the gym, baby."

Izzy shook her head. "Nope. I looked."

Following a deep sigh, Mone't sat up and noticed Austin's side of the bed was untouched. She took her phone from her daughter and looked through the texts: drunken texts from her to him, a few apologies, a slew of tempting photos, and an offer to suck and fuck him the way he'd always wanted. No response.

"Is Mama up?"

"Yep. She's downstairs."

"Can you help her with your brother until I get down? I'm going to find Daddy, okay?"

"Okay," Izzy dragged out. "He owes me."

Mone't swung her legs off the bed, eyes fixed on Austin's last known location. She walked down the hall to peek into the guest rooms, but there was no sign of her husband. As she trampled down the stairs, she spotted Musa just coming in.

"You good, Mo?" he asked, feeling the anxiousness exude through her pores.

"Have you seen Austin?"

He shook his head. "He should be at practice. They have three-a-days until the first game. Speaking of which, you ready for that? I got the pilot booked for the duration of the first round."

She shook her head. "I'll get ready, though. Did he go with Keyston?"

"He ain't here, so probably. You sure you good?"

She wasn't good. Her gut was twisting and turning. Something wasn't right. They'd fought before, had disagreements, but he had never stayed out without a call or at least passing out in his man cave.

She forced herself to lie. "I'm cool. Thanks."

"Don't mention it."

"How's Eman?" That was the perfect distraction. If she dwelled on where Austin was or what he was doing, she'd experience the very manic episode that sent her through bottles of wine.

Musa smirked. "He signed the appeal. I dropped it off. We're a step closer."

Mone't's heart skipped. She couldn't wait until the day she could hold her brother. "Good. I'm ready to see him."

"I know you are. You sure you okay?"

"Mm-hmm, yeah. Hungover and I need to get myself together."

Musa waited before nodding and breaking himself away from her. Going back up the stairs, Mone't showered, pumped, and dumped before joining Aneica and the children.

As the day went on, she couldn't stop checking her phone. She couldn't stop texting or calling. One thing was for sure—when Austin came home, he'd have a world of explaining to do.

"Damn, you tired?" Cypress asked, sitting next to Austin. "You played like shit all day."

Austin slid his feet into his slides. "I didn't sleep for shit last night. Tomorrow is gonna be a better day."

"I hope so. Three-peat!" Cypress shouted as he hit Austin with a towel. The locker room went into an uproar. Over the noise of his teammates, he heard the ringing of his phone. Dreading answering it after seeing Mone't had been blowing him up all day, he grabbed it and peeked at the screen. Angie called back-to-back, then sent a text.

It was a photo of Austin and Pandora entering the building last night.

Angie: You need to meet me on the vacant parking level. Now!

Shit.

He stood, coolly packed his stuff, and slid out of the locker room. He took the players' elevator to the vacant parking level and spotted Angie leaning against her baby Benz.

"How'd you get that?" Austin asked after reaching her. "Who sent that?"

She answered him with a smack across the head. "Are you fucking stupid?"

The answer was yes. Austin could hardly get through practice due to the guilt weighing on him. "Ow!"

"Oh, shut up. I'm tempted to beat your ass up here. Tell me you didn't do what I think you did."

He didn't say a word.

Angie hit him again. "What the fuck were you thinking?"

"I wasn't. You can't tell her."

Angie yanked her head back. "I can and I'm tempted to, but knowing the state she's in, this will send her over the edge. You're going to tell her."

"You crazy?"

"Yes, certifiable. You know there's twenty photos being shopped around? I'm in a bidding war against Shady Palms for these and one that little bitch took this morning. You need to tell her before I am forced to."

"You're not going to leak this story. How much do you want to buy all of it and get rid of it?"

"Austin!" Angie screeched. "That doesn't take away what you did. Why would you do this to her? Huh? With a ho like Pandora?" She landed a series of hits on him again.

"Yo, cut that shit out."

"I'm preparing you for the ass beating she's going to put on you if you don't get in front of this. I refuse to hurt my friend with this. I am so disappointed with you. I just knew you were one of the good ones despite the issues you two are having. You have kids, Austin."

"I don't need you to remind me! Fuck!"

Angie ran her hands through her hair and then dropped her hands to her hips. "How do you even know that ho?"

"Jermel introduced us last night."

"That motherfucker. Where was Musa and Keyston?"

"They had the night off."

"Goddamn it, Austin. You're a stupid-ass nigga," she said through gritted teeth. "I have until tomorrow to get these photos and destroy them if they don't come out on one of these sorry-ass blogs. Take your ass home and get ahead of this shit show."

"You're not going to let that happen, Angie. I'm your biggest investor."

"Austin, you're my best friend's husband, so I say this with all respect. Fuck you and your money. That doesn't sway me. I have a duty to her above all else. Go fuckin' fix this!"

"Lower your fucking voice, Angie. I'll handle it."

"You'd better. Time is ticking," she warned, pivoting to get in her car. Before she was tempted to run his ass over, she rolled the window down and added, "If you lose her, kiss everything you have goodbye."

The tires screeched as she sped off.

"Fuck," he cursed to himself as he made his way down to the players' level to climb inside a JoyRide and go home.

Upon his entering the house fully, Izzy rushed him. "Daddy! You're home! Where you been?" she fired off. "I've been calling you for all days!"

Austin forced himself to lie. His heart was in his stomach. There was no way he could look Mone't in her eyes and act as though he hadn't ruined their lives.

"Daddy had to work. You want to watch a movie?"

"Yes. Mommy is putting AJ to sleep. Let's watch in the big room."

The big room was the theatre located in the basement of the house. For now, it seemed like a great avoidance mechanism. Austin watched as many movies as he could with Izzy before she was passed out and snuggled into his side. He stared at the movie credits, playing Angie's warning in his head.

Images of the night before flashed in his mind. He needed to forget about it. He needed to step up and be present for his life.

"Get ahead of this."

Austin carried Izzy up the stairs to her room, tucked her in, turned on the night-light, and slipped down the hall. Entering his bedroom, he spotted Mone't in the bathroom, brushing her hair into a ponytail.

"You going out?" he asked.

"Dinner with Angie. You would know that if you checked in. Jermel called me."

Austin's heart skipped a beat. "W . . . what he want?"

"Just making sure you made contact with potential deals from last night. He said you left your watch in his guest bedroom." She dropped her arms to her side and tugged at the hem of her black dress. "You could have told me it was a late business meeting instead of ignoring me all night. And day."

Austin dropped his head in relief. At least someone was looking out for him. He entered the bathroom where she was. Mone't looked good in the form-fitting black dress, natural beat, and red lipstick. He loved when she wore that color.

"You going out like this?" he asked, pulling her into him.

"Austin, stop. I gotta go."

"I'm sorry. Baby, I mean that. Sorry for blowing up and ghostin' you. I'm adjusting to all of this too. But you're right. You need me, and I've been distant."

Mone't's small eyes floated up to his. "You serious?"

"Dead ass. If I lose you, I don't have shit. I have to start acting like it." He kissed her soft, full lips repeatedly.

"I just want to be okay. I want us to be okay. I'm sorry for blowing up. I just—"

He silenced her with a kiss. "Let me make it up to you."

"Austinnn," Mone't whined, "you're going to make me late."

"Angie will be okay. You know she will. I have to apologize to you." He yanked her dress up over her ass. "I owe you time. Good lovin'. My presence. A vacation or two."

He rubbed her center from the front to the back until she was putty. Mone't couldn't ever deny him when he had her this hot.

She moaned softly. "You do owe me a vacation. Without the kids."

"Mm-hmm, for tonight, though," he started, lifting her off of her feet and placing her on the counter, "I'm going to eat this pussy until you pass out."

He ripped her thong off her body and latched on to her bud, running his long tongue from the front to the back. Mone't pushed his head into her center. "Oh, yes, baby."

Her toes curled while Austin did everything to her body to make her cum without penetration. For as long as it took, he did what he needed to do. As badly as she wanted to be wrapped around his length, he refused, claiming to make tonight about her, not him. He achieved his mission. After the fifth orgasm that ripped violently through her body, Mone't dropped to his side and passed out.

As for Austin, he'd bought himself enough time to keep her away from her phone and Angie for the night. His phone chimed, the screen lighting up their dark room. Reaching over to grab it, he opened it.

Pandora was blowing up his line.

Pandora: Let's collab again.

Pandora: No reply? Damn, are you ghostin' me?

Pandora: I want to take care of you again. Let's link.

He peeked over to see if Mone't had woken up. She hadn't even moved.

The final text was from Angie.

Angie: I know what you did. Lucky for you, I handled it.

The weight of being outed fell off his chest.

Deleting all the texts and blocking Pandora's number, he powered down his phone and rolled over to cuddle his sleeping wife. "I love you, Mo."

Chapter Six

There was a glow on her face, and for the first time in a while, Mone't felt like everything was going to be okay. She felt like she was going to be okay. She didn't know what had gotten into Austin, but he'd been present, balancing his time between work and home without finding reasons to leave.

Aneica even saw the change and opted out of attending the next three games so Mone't could travel and have stolen moments with her husband. Angie and Mone't were sitting in the players' family section, watching the back-and-forth of the game. Austin was cold. He was missing points, rebounds, and blocks. His head wasn't in it at all.

"Damn, he's playing like shit tonight," Angie grunted. "You put that snapper on him before the game, didn't you?"

"No, he hasn't wanted it. He's been on this 'I'm going to please you' kick. He's off, though, that's for sure," Mone't commented, wincing at the missed shot.

The arena was loud, a mix of boos and hand-claps filling her ears. Mone't stood tall, cheering for her man. There was a gut feeling nagging her, but she'd been ignoring it due to Austin laying it on thick.

"Come on, baby, get focused. You got it."

Angie didn't cheer. Her eyes were glaring across the aisle at a woman Mone't had never seen before.

"You know her? What's tea?"

"No tea. I'm just trying to figure out what she's staring at." Angie gave Pandora an evil eye before refocusing her attention. "I'll keep it cute since I'm with you. You know how I feel about these groupie hoes staring."

"I appreciate it," Mone't replied as the buzzer ended the third quarter. Angie's comment didn't bother her. Groupies came a dime a dozen. Austin may have been selfish, among other things, but Mone't knew that he wouldn't step out on her.

"He's got to get it together," she mumbled, casting a glance up at the scoreboard. "I'm going to get a drink. You want something?"

Angie shook her head and grasped Mone't's arm, a subtle attempt to keep her within eyeshot until the game was over. "Let Keyston get it. He's about to ball out, and you don't want to miss a minute."

The Monarchs were down by ten. They could come back. That wasn't her concern, though. What was plaguing his mind that he couldn't focus was her worry. Staying put, Mone't sat nervously, watching Austin struggle through the quarter. He made four buckets, which was 70 percent under his average.

Defeated, the team walked off the court toward the locker room. No one wanted to lose at home. Austin avoided eye contact with everyone as he trekked to the locker room.

"Pick your head up, baby," Mone't shouted over the boos. Musa and Keyston stood up, preparing to escort Angie and Mone't to the media room. As they maneuvered their way out of the row of seats, Pandora made her presence clear.

"Mone't Graham." Her voice was cool, calm, and collected as she held her hand out for Mone't to shake.

Mone't refused. She never shook hands at the arena. She'd seen fans and wives not wash their hands, and she refused to take anything home to her babies. "Hi," she politely responded, following Musa's lead to the exit.

"I've been trying to get in contact with your husband."

Angie was beside Mone't, trying to pull her away. "Let's go."

Mone't was frozen. "Excuse me?"

"You know, to collab. I have a line. I made this. I brought an extra one for you. Maybe you can put a bug in his ear about collaborating with me." Pandora spun around, proudly displaying a rhinestone first-grade project bearing Austin's name and number on it. "We can be twins."

"I'm sorry. I have to go. Keep working at it. Maybe another investor will be willing to work with you."

"Pandora Herrera. He'll regret it."

Angie pulled her completely away from the woman who knew more about her husband than she was letting on. Mone't got a good look at her: pretty, surgically enhanced, but the confidence that woman exuded was sickening. She was too friendly and too close to what belonged to Mone't.

Mone't walked into a caravan to the private elevators. "Do you know her?"

Angie pretended not to hear her. Lying to Mone't was on her short list of things she would never do.

"After we leave here, we're going straight to the airport to head to Eastover," Musa announced, assisting Angie in her delay to answer.

Mone't's intuition never steered her wrong. When she didn't like someone, there was always a reason. Whoever that woman was, she needed to stay far away from her and hers.

As she traveled down the hall, Mone't's name was called by the general manager of the team, Lamont Wright. He was a larger-than-life pro baller who'd retired and found himself on the business side of the game. He was tall, like all the other giants who played this sport, and a little heavier than he was in his heyday, but he looked great and was aging gracefully. He had smooth milk chocolate skin, a low salt-and-pepper fade, and a beard to match.

"Damn, he's fine," Angie grunted as he jogged closer to the group.

Musa nudged her. "Cool out."

"What? I was just saying," Angie defended herself.

"Don't," Musa grumbled.

"What's up, y'all?" Lamont greeted them, acknowledging everyone who accompanied Mone't. "Mone't, quick question: are you still doing the concierge service?"

"Depending. Who's asking?" Mone't responded with a squint.

Lamont smiled brightly. That smile could melt any woman's panties off. Mone't only had a desire for Austin. She wasn't fazed at all by his charm. "I am. I have some execs I'm trying to impress, and I've watched how you assisted Austin and was wondering if I could commission your time."

"I'm not cheap, Lamont," Mone't warned.

Lamont threw his hands up. "You're the wife of the highest paid man in the league right now. I'd never lowball you."

"All right then. Email me, and I'll set up a meeting with you when we get back from Eastover."

"Sounds like a plan. Thank you. Enjoy the rest of your night."

Musa squinted as Lamont swaggered off. "Yo, I don't like that nigga or that other one with the teeth."

Keyston chimed, "You don't like no one, nigga."

"For good reason, too. All these motherfuckers around here are snakes. Growing to your size to eat you alive."

"Mm," Angie grunted. "Still don't mean he ain't fine."

Musa smacked his teeth. "Take your ass in there. You too, Mo."

The post-game conference went as expected. Austin took the blame of losing on his shoulders and assured the fans of Ganton Hills that they were bringing home another championship come hell or high water. His demeanor was plagued.

Mone't made a mental note not to ask him until they were alone. She was settled on the back of the jet, lying out on the twin-sized bed parallel to the one Austin's long body occupied. Musa was sitting at the front of the plane with an eye mask on and his noise-canceling headphones. The only reason he boarded the plane was because Austin gruffly told him to move his ass along while sliding him a roll of cash.

"Do you know a Pandora Herrera?" Mone't asked from behind her phone screen. Pandora had followed her on every platform. Either this woman was desperate or there was something else that Mone't was missing.

Austin faked like he didn't hear her. The headphones over his ears were just for show.

"Austin? Austin? Austin," she called, only for him to seem as though he was in his own world. Reaching over to remove an ear pad, she repeated herself. "Do you know a Pandora Herrera?"

Austin's face twisted as if Mone't was on his nerves. "Baby, what? Don't even start that."

"I'm not starting anything. I'm asking you a question. She stopped me as I was leaving. She said something about collaborating with you on a line and you'll regret not working with her. She tried to give me some tacky-ass art project, too."

Austin's ears were burning. "You took it?"

"No, you know how I am with other people's stuff. She just seemed too familiar with you. I didn't like it."

"Could you be overthinking it? You do that from time to time."

"I'm not overthinking. I'm just asking you a question, damn."

"Here we go," he groaned, sitting up.

"Don't do that."

"You don't do that. It's already a terrible-ass night, and you're asking me about some woman who wants to collab. I have my own line. Why would I need her?"

"You collab with people every day, Austin."

He nodded. "That may be true, but not everyone is on my level. Look at her, and then look at me. Look at what we got going on. She probably got shut down by Jermel and tried another way of reaching out."

"All right, Austin, whatever you say," Mone't verbally yielded, but she wasn't going to let this one go. Something was up, and she could only pray it wasn't what her gut was telling her it was.

Austin turned his phone off and rolled over. "Any other questions before I try to sleep?"

Mone't's eyes were back on her phone. "Nope. Not a thing."

Chapter Seven

"Rip the damn thing out of the wall," Austin shouted from underneath the pillow.

Since landing in Eastover, sleep hadn't been an option when his head hit the pillow. If his guilt wasn't keeping him awake, the ringing of the phone was. Mone't had given up on sleep hours ago. Instead, she propped herself up in the corner of the room with her breast pump and worked at filling the little Baggies of liquid gold as if AJ was going to be screaming for her at any moment.

Sleep hadn't come for her. Her mind ran in a continuous loop. "You rip it out the damn wall. It's for you anyway."

Mone't's words were filled with annoyance. She'd fallen into the rabbit hole between pumpings. She'd gone from Pandora's page to her friends' pages and pages of friends of her friends, trying to connect the dots of how a woman like her knew her husband.

As far as she knew, Austin had avoided the groupies and the trouble that came along with them. And up until she was placed on bedrest, he couldn't get enough of her. Only recently, with her mental health and adjustment to her new normal, did she feel like he wasn't pleasing her the way he had.

The ringing stopped for a second. Austin threw his legs off the bed in tandem with yanking the covers off him. He stomped around the bed, cutting his eyes at Mone't the entire time. "What's wrong with your feet, Mo?"

Mone't's eyes lifted to him with a look Austin had never seen before. "I told you it was for you."

Austin couldn't gauge whether she was in one of her moods. Guilt had him trying to deflect her attitude as if it were her. Shifting blame while gaslighting her would make a terrible mix.

"How you know that?"

"I answered it the first time. It was someone claiming to be the front desk saying that a black card of a Mr. Graham didn't go through. I hung up. It hasn't stopped since."

"Ain't shit wrong with my card," he grumbled.

"Yeah, and who knows that we're in this room? Musa booked it under someone else's name. Fix that before I fix that."

Austin's heart beat triple time. Instead of answering the phone, he ripped the cord out of the wall. Mone't sat calmly in the corner and watched Austin zip around the room for his phone, a shirt, and a pair of slides. "I'm going downstairs to handle this shit."

"At three in the morning?" Mone't quizzed, not trusting anything about this or him anymore. "A'ight."

His brows furrowed. "A'ight?"

"That's what I said. A'ight."

Austin mistook Mone't's meekness over the years for weakness. She was still from the hood and was taught by the toughest of them. Eman taught her how to spot bullshit, and whatever Austin had going on was some bullshit. She wasn't going through his phone. She wasn't going to question him until he showed his hand.

Austin reluctantly pulled himself from their suite and headed down the hall. His face grew hotter by the step. Pandora was playing games, constantly calling from different numbers, sending photos of him sleeping, his tattoos, and his dick. She was going to keep going until she got a reaction from him.

Opting out of taking the elevator, he took the stairs only to find Pandora in the stairwell with a smirk on her face.

"You blocked me, Austin."

"Are you out of your fucking mind?" he semi-shouted through gritted teeth, bucking at her. Despite the environment Austin came from and the things he'd seen, he'd never been the type to put his hands on a woman. Aneica raised him better than that and would have a fit if she saw him now. Hell, if she knew the half of it, she'd snatch her grown son up and read him his rights.

After three years of stifling the hood in him, it was showing itself. "My wife is up there, and you're playing these stupid-ass games. I fucked up, it happened, it's over. Stop this shit before you regret it."

Pandora smiled that same spellbinding smile she entranced him with. "It's not over, baby, until I say it's over. Quite frankly, I'm just getting started."

Austin slammed the palm of his hand into the brick wall next to Pandora's face. She didn't flinch at all. If anything, it seemed to turn her on more.

"Come on, Austin, you know what my pussy can do for you. I've experienced how good you feel. You think I'm going to just walk away from it?"

"You better get the fuck on." He bucked again, growing tired with the back-and-forth with her.

"You can start paying up, or I'll shop these babies around." Pandora wasn't playing fair, but nothing was ever fair when it came down to playing with matters of the heart and, in Austin's case, his livelihood.

He had to control Pandora and make her fade away quietly without Mone't getting a whiff of what was going on. Juggling his mistake and his wife's heart was going to kill him if the thorn ready to pierce her heart didn't wither quickly.

"You already did that."

Pandora hummed. "Mm, no. Just the photos of your back and your hidden condo, but not these, baby. These the money shots. You know how many women are going to drool over these dick pics? Then they're going to hate you for all the texts you sent me."

"I didn't send you shit."

Pandora giggled. It fused into a moan as she tried to reach out and grab Austin's bulge. He wasn't having it. He was clear-minded and without a doubt knew that Pandora was a world of trouble if he lost his mind again. "Don't fucking touch me. How the fuck did you even get here?"

"You're not hard to find, baby. Now—"

Austin's actions were swift and rough as he grabbed her by the neck and shoved her into the brick wall. Every action since allowing her in his space was going to be questioned and pulled apart by a jury ready to convict him of the ultimate crime. "Hear me motherfuckin' clear. Get your ass out of here before I have you dragged out this bitch."

Pandora moaned, continuing to provoke him. Once she had him warped in anger, he'd be hers to toy with. "You like it rough. That's why you fucked me. Isn't that right, baby? You wanted to be free and have your way. Have your dick sucked without a bitch gagging. I bet your prudish-ass wife doesn't do any of that."

Following the small voice in his head for once, he released her and took a full step back. Austin was in a race to calm himself before he did something there was no coming back from. "I need you to get your shit and leave."

"I need some money."

"I can't do that."

She scoffed in laughter. "You can and you will. Walk your ass up the stairs and get me some money."

"I'm not doing this shit. You're not going to extort me out my fucking money." He started up the stairs.

"You'll regret that. You could've beaten me and then fucked me, but not paying me . . . yeah. I'm going to make sure I destroy you and everything you built."

Austin blocked out her empty threats. She could post and do whatever she wanted to. It would take one call to shut her up forever, but it wasn't a card he wanted to pull.

Returning to the room to Mone't, Austin pretended everything was okay and lay back in the bed. It was going to be a long day and a half, and Mone't's silence would make it even longer.

Fourth quarter. It was crunch time. Austin's heart thundered in his ears. Sweat poured out of every open pore on his body. His personal troubles didn't exist while he was engrossed in the paint. Austin could control everything here.

The rock forcefully left his hands in a behind-the-back pass to Cypress. Shot. Point. Check. Steal. Shot. Two-point game. Forty-five seconds left on the clock for the Monarchs to win by a point.

The intensity of this dance he was engulfed in erased everything. Where he came from, what he'd done to get to this position, and the fear of losing it all faded. The buzzer sounded, the score changed, and his hard work for another night had advanced him further in his career.

The euphoria of winning made him feel like he could conquer anything. Players, staff, and media personnel flooded the floor. Sienna Lawrence of Ganton Hills Sports Program Network stood five foot five to his six-foot-eight frame.

"Austin, you played a hell of a game tonight, forty points alone. What was going through your mind?"

Heavily breathing, he briefly looked down at Sienna. "I was just focused on securing our spot. The first game was rough. I was determined that this one would be different. We balled out tonight."

"Do you think you can get past Eastover without another loss?"

Confidently, he replied, "Without a doubt, Sienna."

"All right, thank you, Austin. Back to you, Emya."

Austin's victorious jog to the locker room was stifled when he was met by the pained curiosity pinned to Mone't's expression. Musa was standing proudly next to her, clapping in celebration of Austin's victory.

"You're the one, nigga!" Musa affirmed.

That statement used to light him up with pride.

Austin's faded reality crashed down to the glossed pinewood floor of the arena. Pandora, two rows behind his wife, was the reason behind Mone't's expression. He knew it. He knew it in the churn of his gut that Mone't was on to him.

The cheering fans clashed against the anxiety attempting to deafen him. With a slight nod, Austin retreated deeper into the tunnel behind Cypress.

"Why you look like you saw a ghost?" Cypress asked, throwing his arm over Austin's shoulder.

Austin typically didn't share much with his teammates outside of the things he was truly proud about: his accomplishments, his growing family, and his business. What was weighing on him couldn't be told. If he had the magical shot to go back in time and never open Pandora's box, he would sacrifice the championship for it.

Austin shrugged Cypress off him. "I'm cool, nigga. Just tired."

Cypress slapped his palm against Austin's shoulder before leaving him to his own thoughts. "Liven the fuck up for this press conference."

Chapter Eight

"Goddamn, this nigga is playing like he had a point to prove!" Musa shouted excitedly in the thick of the crowd booing. The game was neck and neck.

It was too close to dub a winner and definitely too close to cheer through her nervousness. Mone't sat silently in her assigned seat, watching as Austin made a full turnaround from the last game. She was shocked that he was playing the way he was after a night of no sleep and suspicious behavior.

She wanted to be focused on him, but the mounting anxiety that had held her in a chokehold for a day and a half wouldn't let her be. The heat cascaded over her body as her mess of a mind continuously turned on a loop and what felt like every eye in the stadium peered at her.

An ever-present onset of her hypersensitivity had her in the gripping effects of paranoia. At times, she was unable to place herself. She was unsure if she was coming or going. Balancing her attention between the game and the crowd around them, her eyes landed on Pandora, who was sitting in her section.

Mone't's interest in the game was zapped completely at the sight of Pandora. Questions were squirming through her mind as she observed the thirsty woman clad in her husband's jersey. This time, the custom jersey was one that was limited in quantity. How the hell did she get it, why was she here, and who invited her to keep showing up? Did Austin invite her to be here?

Inclined to trust her man, Mone't was certain her mind was playing games on her. She tried to chalk up the swirl of anxiousness and lack of sleep to her current mental state. She tried to take blame for her paranoia, but little did she know, she was faultless.

Her mind was spinning. Her thoughts grew louder and louder. Mone't was teetering on the brink of another breakdown, another outburst, another embarrassing moment that would take her days, even weeks, to recover from.

The third basketball game of the series wasn't the place nor the time for her to shout and scream about her issues with Austin. Unfortunately, she wouldn't be able to until she was 30,000 feet in the air at cruising altitude.

Perhaps if she told Austin again, at the top of her lungs, that this feeling was absolutely unshakable, he'd listen. It was wishful and almost naive in her thinking to believe that their relationship would change after one night of a sexual exchange.

"Yo, Mo!" Musa jeered. "This nigga showing out. How you sitting down?" Musa reached over and pulled Mone't to her feet. Throwing his arm over her shoulder, he gently rocked her back and forth. "Whatever is on your mind right now, baby girl, let it go until this is over. This is history in the making."

Mone't forced a smile over her face. Unequivocally, Austin was aggressive in his pursuit of another W. Mone't had seen this fire from him playoff season after playoff season. Austin refused to go to game seven. He always said if he couldn't get it by then, he failed.

Although she was proud of who he'd become—second-round pick to the franchise player—the nagging feeling wouldn't allow her to focus fully on him. Not with Pandora glaring a gaping hole in the back of her being.

"Yo, E would be so proud of him," Musa muttered, but Mone't couldn't help but hear it. Musa was up and down with his shouting and coaching from the stands.

"Tighten up, Austin! What is wrong with you!" Musa shouted after Austin, Cypress, and TC fumbled with their passes. Quickly recovering, Austin shot a three-pointer and sprinted down to the other end of the court. "There you go, young'un, there you go. If he's going to play like this for the rest of the series, I'm leaving your ass at home and coming out here with Keyston."

Mone't mindlessly watched Pandora's enthrallment with Austin and his sportsmanship. She cheered, called his name proudly, and then shouted phrases of encouragement as a scuffle broke out among the players.

Austin was fouled, shoved into the goal post to be exact. Shoving his opponent back induced a scuffle full of high emotions and pending technical fouls. Cypress intervened, talking Austin down until he dropped his sweaty body down on the folded padded chair.

"That's all right, Austin, you got this. Keep your head up," Pandora shouted, cutting her eyes at Mone't to add insult to injury.

"Do you know her?" Mone't asked, nudging Musa. "To your left, two rows back with the build-a-body?"

Discreetly, Musa looked over his shoulder and replied, "Nah, probably some groupie looking to get a rise out of you. Ignore that shit."

She couldn't ignore it, and that was the issue. Any other groupie feening for Austin's attention didn't faze her. She knew her position, and she was confident in the way he regarded her. Pandora's presence was a direct violation to everything she'd grounded herself in.

Musa purposely focused his attention on the game. He didn't have all the details, but he could piece it together. He was front row to the fault lines in their relationship. He saw Mone't's constant despair and Austin's fight against the current to keep his family from returning to what they knew before.

For the final quarter of the game, the two women Austin was hoping to control were having a stare down. Mone't missed the final forty-five seconds that sent the arena into a frenzy.

Overwhelmed with emotion, Mone't turned to the floor, spotting her giant husband in the thick of the sea of people. Her chest heaved up and down. Her sweaty palms gripped the glass railing in front of her. Mone't watched closely as Austin's pride swelled his chest.

Basketball seemed to replace her in his life. It was a competition she was fully aware of and didn't fight against. At a point in time, she was willing to share space with all that it took up. Mone't wanted to blame basketball for the pull of this union.

As Austin made his way back to the locker room, he looked up at Musa and Mone't. The happiness on his face dropped upon seeing Mone't's face. The glance was brief, although it seemed like an eternity.

"Is there something I need to know about my husband?" Mone't asked Musa once Austin was out of sight.

Musa looked around to find a clear path to escort Mone't through. "Like what?"

"Like where his attention is? Or what he's doing when he isn't with me?"

"I wish I could tell you, Mo." Musa shook his head. "As far as I know, the nigga be working his ass off."

"Yeah," she muttered. "He's working something."

Musa found a path to usher Mone't from the arena down to the makeshift media room for the visiting team. As though they were at home, they stood off to the side of the room, Mone't's view obstructed by Musa.

The festering of her emotions beneath the surface wouldn't allow her to pay attention to the line of questioning. Her only requirement was to show up and be present for her husband. Be his number one fan, look the part, think for him, hold him down, suck and fuck him on demand, and keep his house a home.

So much was required for what she received in return. Quite frankly, she was tired of the exchange. For every hundred thousand she put out, her return on investment wasn't even a quarter of the cost.

"Austin! Austin! What happened? You've had a hell of a season. Your last game was hard to watch, but tonight you were on fire. What contributed to that?" a reporter shouted out in a hurry to be answered first.

"Every game is about improving and securing our championship spot. There's a team of us, and we're all fighting for a three-peat. One rough start shouldn't define our tenacity moving forward."

"Austin! Hell of a game—forty points, twenty assists, and ten rebounds. You were in your zone. Glad to see the cheating allegations haven't affected your performance. Do you want to comment on that?"

The room erupted with questions. Austin laughed it off, quickly trying to save face and his wife's, as he answered. "I've never cheated in the game of basketball."

"But you did cheat in the game of life, is that correct? With a Pandora Herrera."

Reporters were on their feet now, all shouting questions as every phone in the room was going off with alerts. Noise filled every crevice of the room, though Mone't heard nothing.

Musa left Mone't's side in aid of Jermel, who'd jumped in quickly to remove Austin from his seat and rush him out of the room. It didn't make a difference. Reporters swarmed Mone't, cornering her where she stood.

"Mone't, did you know your husband was having an affair with Pandora Herrera?"

"Did you know about the penthouse he kept her in?"

"Are the rumors true that you two have an open marriage?"

"How do you feel about your husband cheating? Are you going to work this out?"

"Mone't, what about the kids?"

Musa snatched a stunned Mone't out of the swarm of reporters and rushed her to the elevator where Jermel was coaching Austin on what to do next. "Tell them it's a private matter between you, your wife, and Pandora."

Austin looked up to see the look on his wife's face. Anger. The cluster of cameras and shouts followed her into the elevator until the first door closed. "I asked you who she was."

"Baby, it was once," Austin confessed, guilt straining his voice as he took a step toward her. He was trying to smother her growing rage. "I swear, I can fix it. Let me fix it."

"I asked you if you knew her," Mone't repeated, this time the words heavier than the first.

"I swear. I was drinking, I—" The doors glided shut, leaving the four occupants to privacy from the media on the other side.

Mone't's vision was obscured by the hot tears. "You looked me in my face and told me it was nothing. You fucking lied to me."

Austin had put himself in the path of her wrath. Mone't's tiny fist balled up, cocked back, and landed on the side of his face. Hit after hit. Kick after kick. The only person who tried to restrain her was Musa. Mone't's rage couldn't be contained. She fought Austin without protest.

"You're a fucking liar! Had me walking around here like I was just going fucking crazy! Had that bitch in my space! You were fucking her the whole fucking time!"

"Stop, Mo!" Austin bellowed, trying to contain her. It was impossible. Mone't had been so calm and collected that he'd forgotten his wife could tussle and scrap with the best of them. She learned it early from her mother. She was far too beautiful not to know how to protect herself.

"Fuck you, Austin! Fuck you! Fuck you, nigga!"

Musa tussled to control her. "Calm down, Mo. The cameras."

"You think I give a fuck about these fuckin' cameras? The world knew he was cheating on me! Me!"

Mone't's shouts could be heard outside the elevator where more reporters waited. King Austin had fallen, and no one was going to miss it. Mone't didn't give a damn about the cameras or his image anymore. The fight in her was unrelenting as she gnashed and fought him from the elevator car into the parking garage.

"When you get home, get your shit and get the fuck out!"

"Ma'am, calm down," an officer spoke with his hand on his hip. Musa attempted to get her back in his grasp and into the nearby car, and Jermel tried to save the face of his client.

Mone't cut her eyes at the officer. "And fuck you too, nigga! I do not care about none of that shit!"

"Mone't!" Austin bellowed, trying to get her to stop. "Stop it!"

The final slap to his face was paired with, "You should have fucking stopped!"

The officer grabbed her in the tussle with Musa. All Mone't could see was red. She thought she was pushing Musa off her, but she was proven wrong once her body was slammed to the dirty concrete floor.

"You fuckin' crazy, nigga?" Austin shouted, rushing the officer. "Get your ass off my wife."

Musa and Austin pushed the officer off Mone't, who was face down on the ground, cuffed. The scuffle forced the officer back with his gun drawn. No matter Austin's star quality, he was still a black man in America. Staring down the barrel of the gun quickly reminded him of that.

The commotion was now out of hand. Nearby officers stormed the group. Musa and Austin were slammed to the ground. While being roughly cuffed, Austin peered into Mone't's heartbroken eyes. The tears hadn't stopped falling. With a dirty face, a scraped nose, and an aching body of sorrow, Mone't stared at him.

"Baby, I'm sorry," Austin spoke before being yanked to his feet.

"Do you know who you're arresting? Are you out your mind?" Jermel shouted. "That's Austin Graham!"

The stunned officer looked up at him. "Oh, shit, I didn't recognize you. Let him go."

"Get my wife up and uncuff her."

Jermel chimed. "You're not in a spot to negotiate right now. Just take this one."

Austin glared at Jermel. "Get my wife off the fucking ground!"

"Hey! Hey! What the fuck is going on out here?" Coach Tatum shouted, running off the elevator. "Do you have my player and his team in handcuffs?"

"Sir, she hit me," the officer defended himself. "That's assault to an officer."

"You think I give a damn about that shit? That's my goddamn wife, nigga!"

The coach stood between Austin and the officers. "Let them go. You don't want this out. Look around you—cameras everywhere. This will go from a domestic issue to a Black Lives Matter show. And I can guarantee you they have the means to make your life in particular a fucking nightmare. Get her off the fucking ground."

"I'm taking the security guard." The officer stood arrogantly in his wrongdoing.

Musa chuckled. "I've been to jail before. That ain't shit. I'll see you for touching her though. That's on everything."

"How fuckin' long are you going to take to get her up?" Austin screeched, taking a giant step toward the officer. Handcuffed or not, he wasn't allowing any further assault to her.

"Let them handle it," Jermel grumbled to Austin, blocking his pursuit. "She started it."

An assisting officer uncuffed Austin. He raced to Mone't's side, helping her to her feet. He brushed her face off, although she refused his touch. Tears formed stains down her dirty cheeks while she was being uncuffed.

Musa was yanked off the ground and thrown into the back of the police car with no regard. He would sacrifice himself a million times over for Mone't and Austin. A night in jail wouldn't faze him like it would Mone't.

"Let's go home," Austin whispered. He observed her disheveled state, and his light face grew brighter with anger. The strappy designer heels were scuffed, her shirt was twisted, exposing the top of her black bra, and the front of her body was dusted with dirt and gravel. "Let's go."

Mone't pulled away from him, still not caring about what the camera and reporters were privy to. It was evident everyone surrounding her knew more than she did, and she shared a name and a bed with him. "No. Find your way back on your own. Or to the condo. I don't give a damn."

She walked her sore body to the car and climbed in the back and closed the door. Once she was far from the arena, she pulled her phone out of her pocket and booked the first flight home.

Nothing mattered to Mone't other than getting home to her children and grounding herself. Austin would need to bring everything back on his own.

"Where to, Mrs. Graham?" the driver questioned, being sure to keep his eyes on the road.

"Eastover airport, private entrance."

Chapter Nine

"All right, guys," Jermel chuckled nervously. He clasped his small hands together the minute Mone't climbed in the back of the car. He was flustered, having to think on his feet to save his client's image. That was always at the forefront of Jermel's mind. Protect the client, protect the bag. What he failed to realize was that if the reason behind Austin's success wasn't protected, all the chips would fall where they may.

Jermel peered at the reporters and cameramen. "There's nothing to see here. Emotions are high. But I assure you, all the rumors of my client having an extramarital affair are false. Mrs. Graham was fully aware of the dealings between Austin and Ms. Herrera. Now if you would, please give them privacy to handle their issues."

Due to already embarrassing the hell out of his wife and himself, Austin smoldered his growing anger and planted himself at a safe distance that kept him from charging Jermel and knocking him out. It had been one thing for Austin to put Mone't in a position, but no one else was going to be able to do it, especially not right now.

Jermel turned to saunter over to Coach Tatum and Austin. He cleared his throat as though Tatum was supposed to walk off. He refused. Coach Tatum looked down at Jermel and chuckled to himself.

"Mone't wasn't aware of shit, nigga," Austin said through gritted teeth. "Yo, what the fuck are you thinkin'?"

"I'm thinking that you have endorsements. Contracts are signed and others are coming in. Your wife's inability to control herself is going to ruin everything. Get it in check or lose out on all the shit I worked hard for."

Austin thumbed his nose and closed the space between him and Jermel. He purposely kept his voice low. "I don't give you twenty percent for your marital advice. I don't give a fuck about what you worked for. I'll get it back, but you and me . . . we're done."

Jermel took a step of his own, and instead of looking up into Austin's face, he shoved his fingers into his chest. "Go cool off. Buy the wife something nice, keep her at home, and remember, I know where the bodies are buried."

With a pat on the arm to emphasize his statement, Jermel smiled that cheesy-ass grin and stepped back. "Have a good night, both of you." Jermel pivoted, nodded toward the reporters, and climbed into a nearby car.

Coach Tatum shook his head and nudged Austin slightly. "I'll take you downtown to get your boy."

"Thanks," Austin muttered. His mind was bogged down. The win meant nothing when he was on the verge of losing everything.

Ready to escape this nightmare, Austin trailed Coach Tatum to his car and climbed into the passenger seat. Clamping his eyes shut, Austin internally scolded himself. His mind replayed the last time he climbed into the passenger seat and every step he'd mistakenly made.

"What a fuckin' night," Coach Tatum huffed, climbing behind the steering wheel. "You sure know how to get everyone's attention."

Austin scoffed, slouching in the seat, hoping the cameras wouldn't get any more photos of him behind the dark tints. Pulling his hoodie over his head, he snaked his phone out of his pocket.

Silence filled the space around them until they were successfully out of the thick of the media frenzy. Austin desperately pecked away at the screen of his phone. Every single message was to his wife. After the twentieth text, the bubbles went from blue to green and were eventually undeliverable.

"Fuck!" he said through gritted teeth, slapping his hands against his face and scrubbing it. His cool, calm, and collected demeanor was fading. Anger was seeping through every pore.

Approaching a red light, Coach Tatum reached over and removed the phone from Austin's hands. Disregarding whatever was on his screen, he powered the phone down and dropped it into the cup holder between them. Austin stewed in his self-inflicted anger. His nostrils flared, his lungs being held hostage from air in his chest.

"Let her cool off. There's no need in blowing her up to get a reaction out of her."

"She's fuckin' livid."

"Rightfully so. She just found out with the rest of the world that things aren't what they seem to be. Flip roles and imagine how you'd feel."

"Tuh," Austin scoffed. "Don't even give me that thought."

Brandon Tatum was all too familiar with the weight Austin felt to succeed, provide, and be in a million places at once. He knew what it felt like to be on the giving and receiving ends of adultery. Seasoned enough now to look back on how he and his ex-wife handled their marriage, Tatum regretted it. He regretted not being forthcoming, not trying to fix his mistake, and more than anything, he regretted letting her slip through his fingers and not fighting for her.

"It's a possibility. No one thinks rationally when their heart has been broken. I know we're in the middle of a series, but I would advise you to do whatever you can to work this out."

"I don't have a fuckin' clue on where to start."

"Start at the truth. Don't withhold anything from her. And take your hits like a man. She has a hell of a left hook."

"And right," Austin rumbled, rubbing his chin. Mone't had beat his ass while being restrained. He might've taken her out of the hood, but that grit never left her. There was a beast in her. As long as she was protected and properly tended to, she kept it tucked away. Austin had committed the worst crime to her heart, and he would have to pay for it.

Tatum chuckled and nodded his head. "True. Listen, you two are young, and you have the world in your hands. Remember why you two joined in this covenant. And when you get on the other side of this, don't ever do it again."

The remainder of the ride was silent. Jermel's threat and the possibility of not being able to cut ties with him to protect Mone't's secret weighed on him heavily in tandem with the present issue. He felt himself needing a drink or a blunt despite it not being a regular occurrence.

When they arrived at the jail, they handled the transaction in the sally port. It was against protocol. However, they made an exception for King Austin. Austin was far from a king tonight, and the reality of that showed in the slump of his shoulders.

Musa appeared thirty minutes later, still running his mouth, unscathed. Only, if you looked closely, you could see the scratches on his face from the altercation with the police and his scuffle to restrain Mone't. He wore them proudly.

"Told y'all I wasn't staying," he arrogantly spoke, strolling past the correctional officer. "I'm outta here."

Coach Tatum arranged for his assistant to meet Austin and Musa at the airport with their things. He even called his pilot to make sure they made it home without having to be bothered by people wanting photos or being in his business. Brandon saw himself in Austin: young, vibrant, and full of talent. Like with all his players, he strived to protect that. When he could step in, he would, despite what the front office said.

Musa hopped into the back seat happily. "You think I can sue them for scuffing up my face like this? Can't be a pretty nigga with scratches and shit."

Austin kissed his teeth after signing papers.

"Oh, Coach, he got an attitude?"

Brandon nodded. "Indeed."

"Musa, I don't want to hear shit," Austin grumbled as the car started to move. Austin's head was pressed against the headrest, eyes shut, his mind trying to imagine the fury of what he was walking into when he arrived home.

Whatever he imagined couldn't hold a candle to Mone't's spiking temperature.

Chapter Ten

"Mmm, baby," Pia Spade groaned against Keyston's lips. They were rooted in the foyer. Rarely did Keyston bring women into Mone't's home, but Pia was the exception to the rule. Pia had a viselike grip on his mind and body as well as his pockets.

Sure, Austin paid them all generously, but with Pia as the mastermind behind the operation, Key was seeing bands from millionaires and billionaires. The shit was out of this world. The rich loved gambling and betting on athletes like they were modern-day slaves.

They were.

Black men, immigrants, and disenfranchised players were bought and traded for millions of dollars. They were required to keep their bodies and images in top-tier shape. Mind the businesses that paid them, be a savior to young children idolizing them, while living the dream of every below-average athlete in the world.

Keyston wasn't alleviating the situation for the athletes in Austin's position of being perfect and elite. He was adding to the problem. Keyston knew how Austin was wired. He knew that between Graham, Jones, and Spade, the game would always turn in his favor.

"You got to stop moaning like that, ma. Got me wanting to take you right here."

Pia purred, "Do it."

Keyston winced, knowing how Mone't got down when it came to her kids and her home. But Pia was so tantalizing that he couldn't think straight. This meeting was supposed to be quick. In and out. Transaction of money. But he'd fallen into other things. And now he wanted more of her. He wanted her as his own. Their three-year stint had been confined to hotel rooms, a number of Austin's rental properties, and the guest house after hours.

He attacked her neck, instantly latching on to that sweet spot that made her body hum with desire for him. Caressing her body with his large hands created a melody of moans from Pia. He couldn't help himself. As he yanked her dress over her slim hips, the front door burst open, exposing an angry Mone't and a troubled Aneica.

Mone't's fiery glare landed on Keyston and his lover. Her lip curled, red-rimmed eyes telling him to remove himself from her space. He studied the evidence of trauma to her being as he pulled away from Pia, the mood instantly zapped from the space.

"I . . . I should get going," Pia announced as she pulled her appearance back together. "Key, we'll talk soon."

"I'll call you," Keyston replied as he maneuvered her around Mone't and Aneica.

Pia exited Mone't's home, leaving Keyston to face her wrath alone.

"You good?" Keyston questioned.

"Did you know Austin was fuckin' her?"

Mone't's response was news to Keyston. Being that Austin had been hell-bent about doing everything on his own, Keyston didn't know the ins and outs of his days and nights.

He shrugged, igniting her already-erupted spirit. He knew there was a fight in her that had been lying dormant for years. Mone't was born and bred in the trenches, and she knew how and when to fight. He could see it in her eyes. Now that Austin had brought out the other side of her, it wasn't going to leave without tearing up everything in its wake.

"Did you know?"

"I can't say, Mo. What the fuck is going on?"

Her brow rose. "Aren't you paid to know? Aren't you supposed to know where he is and what he's doing? That's why you're here, right?" She scoffed and whisked past him. "No one ever seems to know anything when it comes to him and what he's doing. That shit is laughable."

Keyston's eyes trailed her right before his feet began to take off behind her.

"Don't," Aneica advised. "Give her a minute."

"What happened?"

Aneica secured the front door and placed her purse on the foyer table. "That's a woman who just found out in a post-game conference that her husband was cheating on her."

"You're lying."

Aneica shook her head. "I wish I were. Did you know?"

Keyston threw his hands up. "I knew nothing."

"Perhaps you should have known. Told him to get his shit together."

"They can come back from this. Playas mess up," Keyston said, defending him. "They got time in this. The kids and—"

Aneica wryly laughed. "How are the kids? Still sleeping, or did all your . . . fun wake them?"

Keyston's hand smoothed the hairs of his beard. He chuckled before removing himself from Aneica's space. This wasn't the space, time, or person to battle with. He was left with two sleeping children to watch, and the only thing he'd been watching was Pia's body move against his.

Choosing not to answer, he averted his eyes from the tiny woman. "Do I need to meet Musa and Austin at the airport?"

"You should find out." Aneica stepped around him to do exactly what he should have been doing: checking in on the children.

Mone't

She'd pulled every paper out of every drawer in Austin's office. Every contract, every deed, every receipt. Somewhere in her search, she was praying that she would wake up. She prayed it was all a nightmare or her mind playing tricks on her again. But the reality burned in the tightness of her chest.

Her mind was telling her that not only was she losing herself, but she was losing her marriage as a result of not being enough for Austin. Not only couldn't she look at herself, but everything Austin told her was a lie. He didn't love her. He wasn't okay with how she was and how she felt. She wasn't enough for him.

Mone't rifled through papers, counted the amount of the things he'd done, the properties in their name and ones that were solo. She wanted to find more than this. She wanted reasons and answers to why he'd do this to them. Why he'd launch war on her already-tattered mental and emotional states.

The door opened, releasing her momentarily from the mania she was engulfed in. Her eyes drifted to Aneica and then back to the legal documents scattered before her.

"Please don't tell me to think or calm down," she muttered.

"I won't." Aneica took a seat on the edge of the desk and picked up a stack of papers. "You have every right to be mad as hell with him. You have every right to want to beat his ass."

Mone't's eyes drifted to Aneica's.

"A man is only going to do what you allow him to do. Don't let him get away with this. My son or not, he's your husband. I'll never ask you to forgive poor, reckless behavior."

"I'm so angry I can't even think straight. I'm teetering somewhere between wanting to fight him until he feels what I feel and tearing up this fuckin' house, Mama. I don't know what to do." Mone't's words were heavy with emotion. Her voice broke, and the tears stung her orbs. They began to fall all over again. She didn't wipe them or try to cover them. All she could do was sit in this heartbreak.

"Be angry. Be heartbroken. Be mad as hell. But do not be stupid for the sake of your family, or him, or yourself. You are a woman with access to all his shit. No prenup. No restrictions. Teach him his lesson, Mone't."

"You want me to leave him?"

"I want you to honor yourself in whatever way that looks like. If that means you fight that nigga all over this house. If you put him out. If you leave. But know this: whatever you decide, you have to stick to your guns. You have to stay true to you, and don't back down until he's proven, repeatedly, that he's changed."

"And what if he hasn't?"

"Then give his ass those papers, take him for everything, and move on with your life. You deserve to be happy. Those babies deserve to see you happy."

Mone't's brows furrowed. Confusion rested in the creases of her face as every word implanted itself. The truth of the matter was that Aneica had never led Mone't astray. She was more of a mother to her than her actual mother.

There was so much riding on the pending decision, but Mone't couldn't think about Austin's deals, his games, or how he felt. She was consumed by everything she was feeling and thinking, everything that Aneica had taught her over the years.

"Remember what I told you. A woman with money is a powerful being. Make him feel it."

Mone't rolled her lips over one another as her eyes wandered around the space. They landed on their wedding portrait. Mone't wore a white maxi dress, her small belly protruding through the fabric. Austin stood behind her proudly in a white linen shirt with the sleeves rolled up to his elbows. His hands were wrapped around her small belly, and the smiles that pierced their faces, despite the pain in Mone't's eyes, were radiant.

Aneica slipped out of the room, leaving her daughter-in-law deep in her thoughts. Mone't stared at the photos on the wall, all portraying a happy little family. All of Austin's accomplishments that she was front and center for, and none of her own.

Nothing for her to truly be proud of.

It felt like Mone't was losing herself. The truth was that she lost herself the moment she pulled the trigger to protect Austin. How could someone who vowed to love, honor, protect, and respect her leave her out here with the weight of the world on her shoulders?

As if she were having an out-of-body experience, she jolted to her feet. Papers, pictures, awards, and anything she could get her hands on were torn up. She should have been tired from the fight with Austin in Eastover. By the standard of a woman scorned, she should have cried herself to sleep after calling him multiple times. She refused to do either. Sleep would have to wait, along with a clear mind.

Austin's office was the pure representation of what she'd felt like for months, years even. To effectively explain: Mone't was a beautiful mess. No matter what size she was, she was breathtaking in everyone's eyes but her own. She was a hurricane of unfiltered emotions, and the world had seen it.

She rested her head on the back of the wall as the last tear slid down her cheek. Musa stood in the door. Behind him stood Keyston and Austin. She wasn't going to speak to any of them. They were all guilty in her eyes.

"Mo." Austin's voice broke through the thick, uncomfortable silence. "Come on. Let's talk about this."

"Get out," she replied.

"Your hand is bleeding," he pointed out, carefully moving across the mess to get to his wife. He removed his shirt to wrap her hand, and she snatched it away from him.

"More than my hand bleeds. Maybe if you pulled out of that bitch for two seconds, you'd really see," she said through gnashed teeth.

"Baby. It was once."

"I don't give a damn about the number of times. You lied. You did it and came home to me. Had me thinking I was losing my fucking mind."

"I'm sorry," Austin muttered. "I'll do whatever I need to do."

Mone't nodded slowly as she stood. "When my lawyer serves you the divorce papers, sign them. That's what you can do for me. Until then, move out of my way."

Austin launched to his feet, grabbing her roughly by the arm. "You're not leaving me, Mo."

"I am. I should've let you do all of this on your own. I should have followed my first mind and set you free. It wouldn't have hurt this bad."

"You can't leave me, baby." He was pleading with her. She refused to listen. She tried to get out of his hold, but there wasn't any escaping this. Austin had her locked into him, forcing her to look up at him.

"I can. I will. I've been beggin' you to just be here. Be with me. Help me. The second I can't be the doting wife, the perfect partner, you step out on me. I've never hurt you. I've always put you and our family before me, and you can't even have the decency to tell me the truth. Maybe if I knew the truth before, it wouldn't feel like I'm dying."

Austin's heart ached. "I'm sorry, Mo. I swear it was once. She doesn't mean shit to me."

"She meant enough to distract you. She meant enough for you to stay with her. Did you even use a condom? Do you know what that is?" She finally broke away from him, laughing to keep from going across his head again. "Probably not. Because we've used them, what, twice? Miss me with the bullshit, Austin. I've played stupid for a long time. But tonight? I'm done."

"Mo."

She wiggled the heavy diamond ring from her swollen finger and dropped it at his feet. "Jermel won. You're free, King Austin. Go win your championship, fuck as many women as you want. But know this: you and I . . . we're done."

"We will never be done, Mo."

"We will."

"You're not taking my kids from me." Like a desperate man, he tried his hand with control. The smirk on Mone't's face challenged him. Without a word, she pushed past Musa and Keyston.

"If either of you follow me, I'll beat your ass too."

Musa and Keyston shared a look before looking at Austin.

"You're going to let her leave like that?"

Arrogantly trying to save face, Austin grumbled, "She ain't going nowhere." He underestimated her. He took for granted what strength she had at her core when he of all people should have known. "She just needs to sleep this off. I'll let her talk her shit."

He bent down to pick up her wedding ring from the floor. The blows to his face deepened in color. His head was pounding, his body hurt, and his mind didn't want to believe that she was capable of leaving. She'd been with him for so long. She fired a bullet for him. He convinced himself that she wouldn't leave and, as long as they had the children, he had a way in.

Pride.

His pride would further kill the vein of life between them.

As Mone't hiked up the stairs, she wiped her face with the back of her hand. She attempted to muffle the sobs and whimpers until she was behind closed doors. Once barricaded in their bedroom, she stripped down to nothing. Her almond skin showed the traces of being slammed to the ground. Her knees were red, wrists were bruised, but still nothing hurt more than her heart.

Cradled in the middle of the shower, she sobbed into her knees. Her body shook with the pain, and reality swaddled her in the bitterness of its taste. Adding insult to injury was Austin's reappearance. He tried to leave her to herself, but that vein that slowly pulsed lured him back to her. His naked body wrapped around hers.

"I'm so sorry, baby. I'm so sorry," he repeated into her wet, curly hair.

Weak with agony, she couldn't fight him off. She could only weep.

"I promise I'm going to make this right. I'm going to fix everything," he muttered against her skin. Austin planted soft kisses on her skin, but Mone't was cold to him. There wasn't a touch in the world that could make her warm up to him. She wouldn't be distracted by a kiss or any other intimate gesture.

When the sobs grew silent and the tears were depleted, she removed herself from his hold. Now too tired to fight or to care, she dried off, oiled her body down, and crawled into bed. Although she saved her exit for another day, she stood firm on leaving.

Nestled into her side of the bed, she let the sniffing and exhaustion from fighting usher her into a restless sleep. She tossed and turned and whimpered. She even kicked him a few times. Austin took it all, knowing he deserved far more than she'd unleashed on him thus far.

Wide awake while the last week of events played on a time loop in his mind, Austin's truth was unleashed into the dark. "You're too good for me, Mo. You always have been."

Her eyes remained shut, but she heard every syllable.

"So pure and innocent, even coming from the same block I came from. You gave me everything. A career and wealth I wouldn't have without you. Two beautiful kids. I know I hurt you, Mo, but you can't leave me. I ain't shit without you."

His thoughts were loud, and his words re-sounded. Mone't would have loved to snap her fingers and their relationship be whole and fun again. They were in a storm, and his words weren't going to change that.

"I love you more than you know," he said. "Even when you're angry, don't forget that. I'm really sorry I fucked up. It was one night. I was drinking. I got caught up. I used a condom the first time."

"But not the second."

"Baby, I—"

"I know you. You're a two-round man. The first one, you're going to put in work. The second, you want it to get you through the day. I know you, Austin, and I know you hate them. I knew you'd been somewhere else. You wouldn't let me touch you. You were running around here like someone was after you. Save all the 'sorrys' and 'I'll do betters.' It's bullshit and it means nothing.

"If you wanted to do better, if you loved me, you wouldn't have done it. You would've brought your ass home. You would've made up with me. Listened to me. But being with me like this is too much for you. Don't deny it. It's the truth. You don't know how to love me at my lowest. Or how to support me. It's the money and the things you provided I should be okay with. This isn't any different.

"I'm supposed to accept this betrayal and stay and fight with you. Here's some truth for you—if it were me who opened my legs to another man and gave away what was yours, my head would've been knocked through a wall. If I weren't pregnant when you got drafted, you wouldn't have married me. If we had a prenup, this would've been over. You would have thrown me a stack to keep quiet and gone on to live your life."

Mone't sat up and swung her legs over the bed. "You can't satisfy me, but you can be everything to everyone else. That's the truth. I don't care about your apologies. It's not even out of your system yet. It'll happen again. I just won't be around to feel like this again." She removed her body from the bed.

He followed suit. "I told you you're not leaving."

"You also told me it was nothing, she was nothing, and I was tripping."

"Goddamn it, Mo. Just—"

"Just what? Just what? Accept the bullshit? Accept that you need to figure your shit out, and until then, I should wait? I've been fucking waiting! I've been waiting for you to win, waiting on you to elevate, waiting on you to see that I am one second away from losing my fucking mind! You can't see shit past you. I'm not waiting."

"I will sit out the rest of the postseason, Mone't," he offered. "I'll forfeit the rest of my salary. I'll take the fines."

She scoffed, then laughed. "All right, Austin."

Mone't exited the bedroom and traveled down the hall to check in on her sleeping children before roaming down the back stairs. She found herself in the kitchen, attempting to keep her day-to-day routine. She hadn't pumped. She had no clue where the bags of milk were and couldn't care.

Her children needed to eat, and she needed to pump her swollen breasts. She also needed Austin, Musa, and Keyston to leave her alone so she could do so.

"What's up, Tyson?" Keyston greeted her.

Mone't yanked the fridge open, paying neither of them any attention.

Musa chuckled softly. "She didn't bite him, nigga."

"I saw every video. She should have. I forgot her ass could fight like that," Keyston said, chomping on a mouthful of Frosted Flakes. "They're going to have to change the picture on this box."

Musa's eyes landed on Austin's pose on the box of cereal.

"They gotta add the bruises and shit. Probably need to put Mo on the box. She's the lightweight champ."

Mone't rolled her eyes in irritation.

"Shorty, laugh. It's funny," Keyston urged.

"Why are y'all even here?" she snapped.

"It's my job to be here," Musa spoke up. "You can cuss me out and all of that. I ain't backin' up off you and these kids."

"I'm not going nowhere. Eman ain't about to beat my ass behind you," Keyston chimed.

"Can y'all give us a minute?" Austin asked, appearing in the doorway with his bruises more prominent on his face.

Keyston studied him, trying not to laugh. There was never a serious bone in his body. He yielded last night, but now the jokes were writing themselves.

"Goddamn, nigga!" Keyston bellowed. "Did you even try to stop her from rocking your ass like that?"

Austin cut his eyes at them. "Give us a minute, damn."

Musa stood up. "Nah, y'all been at it all night. Even a boxer has to take a minute. You got practice in an hour. It's going to be a media storm. We need to beat them."

"I'm not going."

The front door opened and closed. Jermel was walking on thin ice. The tension all around could be felt and sliced with a machete. Mone't busied herself with making oatmeal and bottles as Jermel moved deeper into the kitchen.

"Here goes this nigga," Musa grumbled, standing. "Can't you see we're in the middle of some shit?"

"Considering none of you are in jail, it should be a good day. I've gotten the officer to apologize for throwing your wife to the ground. Unfortunately, she's banned from that arena for the rest of her life, but at least it isn't the moneymaker."

Mone't grunted. "You want to be the next motherfucker in this house with black and blue rings around their eyes?"

"Are you admitting to domestic violence?" Jermel posed.

"Ay, that's enough," Austin spoke up, stepping to Jermel. "I fired your ass."

"And I told you it wasn't happening, not unless you really want that secret out for the world to know," Jermel shared, forming his fingers in a gun.

Tired, embarrassed, and over the bullshit Jermel was stirring up in his life, Austin rushed him. He grabbed him by the collar and slammed him into a nearby wall, his nostrils flaring as they tussled throughout the kitchen.

Mone't nonchalantly removed herself from the mix. All of that was between them. She was going to follow up on the threat and make it a promise. When Austin left, she'd pack up the kids and remove herself from this space.

The tussle turned into a full-fledged fight. Neither Musa nor Keyston bothered to help Jermel in the ass whipping Austin was delivering. He'd gotten himself in this predicament. He'd disrespected Austin's home, his wife, and their marriage one too many times.

None of Jermel's swings landed. As for Austin, he tapped into who he used to be, rearranging Jermel's face in a blinding rage before Musa could pull him away from his agent.

Heaving and still trying to finish what he started, Austin shouted as Musa contained him in a corner.

"Don't talk to my wife, don't look at my wife, don't make a statement on behalf of any of us. If you say shit, I will ruin your fucking life!"

Jermel staggered to his feet, wiping the leaking blood from his face. Like the bitch nigga Jermel was, he pulled his phone out of his pocket. Keyston swooped in to retrieve it, throwing it on the ground and stomping the phone until it shattered into pieces.

"What else you got on you, bitch? Huh?" Keyston further assaulted Jermel, tearing him from his suit jacket, shoes, and pants. "The fuck type of time you on walking in here recording them?"

The question didn't need an answer. Jermel couldn't answer anyway as he was dragged from the kitchen, through the foyer, and out the door he'd entered through minutes ago without invitation.

"Get your bitch ass out of here," Keyston shouted, launching Jermel's key across the street into the thick vegetation. "Happy hunting, nigga."

Mone't had disappeared, and Austin was attempting to calm down. It was useless. The damage was done. He had to feel everything that his actions set into motion.

"We got to get going," Musa announced.

"I told y'all I'm not going," Austin fired back.

Aneica walked into the kitchen with an empty bottle. "You are. No need to be jobless and wifeless, son."

"Ma." Austin stepped toward her.

"What?" Aneica snapped, looking at her son. "What? What do you want to say to me? Hm?"

He backed down. "Don't let her leave."

Aneica winced. "I can't make her do nothing. You better pray she's here when you get back. Good luck." She grabbed another bottle and exited the kitchen.

Musa couldn't help but feel like his unwillingness to assist in Austin's destruction got them to this point. He wouldn't turn his back on Austin or give him the cold shoulder. Austin needed brotherhood to guide him through the series of dark days he was headed to.

"Let's go."

Chapter Eleven

"I'm not practicing."

Musa smacked his lips and scoffed in reply to Austin. "You sound stupid, man. What the fuck you mean you not practicing? You'll be the only nigga on the bench with a long lip. Block out everything else until you get home. You need this shit. Sitting at home fighting with your wife all day ain't good for anyone involved."

"I'm just trying to get her from leaving," he protested.

Austin was younger than Musa and Keyston, who'd experienced life. Austin hadn't been free. He had no idea what freedom tasted like. He and Mone't had been pinned to each other's sides since the day they met.

"That ain't going to keep her. You can lie on top of her. If she doesn't want to be there, she isn't going to be there. Y'all barely twenty-four with two kids and a multimillion-dollar empire, and you've never been apart long enough to feel what it feels like to miss each other," Keyston spoke up. "You got to let her breathe, or she's going to keep going off, keep crying, and before you know it, you two are really divorced with the kids being forever bounced from house to house, you two hating each other, the kids hating both of y'all, and regret."

"What you saying? Just let her leave? Hell nah. I'll be damned if another nigga steps to her on some funny shit." Austin's bruised face balled up as he thought about another man knowing Mone't the way he did.

"But you let a bitch step to you on some funny shit, and you fell into it on some funny shit, and you had this bitch popping up like it was more than just a one-night fuck. You did that. You made that bed, nigga. You're going to have to lie in it. Mo is good, she's true, she loves you, but she's not going to love you more than she loves herself," Musa shared, pulling out through the gate of Austin's estate. "Not anymore."

Austin groaned and slouched into the back seat and looked down at his tattooed finger. "I'll give her some space, but she ain't coming off of me."

Keyston laughed. "Don't fumble the ball again, my nigga. She might be tight, but she's going to be watching your moves. Angie is going to tell her how you handle these bitches stepping to you now that they think they have an in."

"I'm surprised Angie didn't tell her prior to the news breaking," Keyston said.

Musa grunted. "Nah, she probably told his ass and his stubborn ass thought he could handle it."

Austin sank down deeper into his seat and pulled his hoodie over his head in a single motion. He didn't want to think about how he got here. He wanted to figure out how to make this shit go away, how to put a smile back on her face. But he'd missed every mark, every sign, and every opportunity to heal her brokenness.

Austin remained silent until he was fully submerged into the locker room. With his endorsed Beatsville headphones over his ears, he sat at his locker, lacing up his sneakers. He purposely avoided the huddled players whispering about the last twenty-four hours. It would be a miracle if he could make it through practice without incident.

Cypress Jones and Paul Spade shared neighboring lockers and followed Austin's lead. Locker room drama wasn't their thing. Austin tended to stay clear of the bullshit until now.

Cypress nudged him and nodded toward his headphones. "You good, G?"

Austin returned the gesture, taking his eyes off of his sneakers only for a moment. "I'm straight."

"Nah, you ain't, nigga. What's going on for real? You and your lady been all over the news since we left Eastover," Paul added. "Shit at home hell right now, ain't it?"

"She asked for a divorce. Well, didn't ask. She told me she was filing and didn't back down off of it," Austin informed him, rubbing his hands over his face. "I'm not trying to get into all that shit right now though."

Cypress bobbed his head up and down. "I feel you. I do. But we here. You ain't going through this shit alone. We all fuck up. It's how we bounce back that matters."

Being that neither Cypress nor Paul was or had been in a significant relationship, Austin took Cypress's comment with a grain of salt. If he would have taken advice from anyone, it would've been Winston Smith, the OG of the team. They all joked about Winston playing ball with Jesus, but the man was a fountain of wisdom. He didn't care about being the star. He cared about the team as a whole.

"I appreciate y'all," Austin responded with a dap to both men as he pushed his feet into his sneakers.

His mind wasn't in practice. It wasn't in the shooting drills, the sprints, the teams scrimmage. It was at home with Mone't and their children. His mind was where it should have been days, weeks, and months ago.

This was the price he had to pay: the swelling anxiety in his chest, the hypersensitivity along with holding his head in the midst of his peers. It was multilayered.

"You ain't no king, nigga." The low growl came from Kayden Moore, who was facing off with Austin. He was used to this line of taunting from Kayden. It was a mind game preparing him for game one of the finals. Brighton Heights was going to come and fight them game for game for the throne.

"Back the fuck up off me," Austin growled just as menacingly as Kayden assumed he would sound. "You ain't getting close to this rock. Or my throne."

"I'm coming to take your crown, your throne, and your wife. I heard the queen was up for sale. Heard you couldn't do her the way she needs to be done," Kayden taunted, reaching for the ball as he pressed Austin down court.

Usually, Austin's mind in the clutch was strong. Kayden was making a mockery of the pain plaguing him. This was the very pain that was reminding Austin of who he was without the spotlight and money. That hungry dog that rested inside of him was waiting to be awakened, waiting for Austin to remember who and what was the most important thing in his world.

Austin read the screen. Spade broke out the pressure to receive the rock, which shot from Austin's palms to Spade, to Jones, and back to Austin. One bounce, one shot, forced the players back to the top of the court. Kayden didn't yield to his normal routine of rushing to the rock. His sole purpose today was to taunt the great King Austin, shake him up, and throw him off his square. Kayden Moore wanted nothing more than to steal the spotlight from Austin. He thought Austin was unfit to carry the team and the city on his back. The latest stunt had proven that Austin couldn't lead his family or his team.

"I'll have your kids calling me Daddy," Kayden grumbled as he charged his body into Austin's, a rough attempt at keeping him from the ball. Kayden was used to Austin playing smooth, keeping the calm about him.

As much as it was an uphill battle for Austin to keep the air of coolness around him, Kayden Moore's last comment had every exposed inch of Austin's light skin glowing red. Where he was or what he was doing wasn't a distraction from Kayden's pry.

"Nigga, fuck you!" The eruption of words left Austin's mouth as he shoved Kayden backward. Without missing a beat, Kayden swung in an attempt to add another blotch of color to Austin's face.

He was too quick for that. He'd expected Kayden's response. He swerved away from the fist coming toward him. The impact of Austin's fist to Kayden Moore's body alerted the rest of the team. Their scuffle was intensifying by the second. The court flooded with teammates and coaches trying to pry the two men apart.

Austin's dark-ringed eyes danced with fire. "Keep my wife and my kids out your fucking mouth, nigga. I'll show you who the fuck I am."

The venomous words were graced with a smirk.

"That's a threat?"

"A motherfuckin' promise," Austin coolly answered from the other side of Winston Smith's body.

Coach Tatum walked off the court with fury burning in his veins. He blew the whistle, directing the team to the locker room. Spade and Jones lingered until Winston waved them off, signaling that he had it under control.

"Cool out, young buck."

Austin shoved Winston away from him. The shove made little impact to Winston's solid frame. Austin's eyes scanned him, lip curled in annoyance. It was more so with himself than anything else. "I'm cool. Back up off me."

Winston's disposition didn't waver. He saw himself in the young bull. He knew the turmoil he was experiencing, and if only Austin was open, he'd help him through the muck of what was his new life. "Nah, let's take a walk."

"I don't need to walk. I'm good."

Winston placed his hands on his hips and looked Austin in the eye. "Ain't shit about you good, young buck. Look at you. You look like me when I was going through it with my ol' lady."

Austin turned his back to Winston, hoping to collect himself. "Everyone keeps saying that. 'I know what you going through.' Ain't no way. My whole fuckin' world is crumbling. Endorsements are pulling out, my wife wants a divorce, and my agent is . . ." He cut himself off, running his hand over his face. "It's not something I can sweep under the rug. Everywhere I turn there's a reminder of how I fucked this shit up. I can't be angry with nobody but me."

Winston leaned on the wall, listening and watching him pace the floor. He assumed this was the first time he really talked to someone else about it. Austin was experiencing the mania of living in his shit. Winston knew those trenches all too well. Unfortunately, his wife wasn't as strong as Mone't was in the beginning.

"I would tell you it's easy, but it's not. It's a fight. You come to work fighting for respect, and you go home fighting the woman who brings you peace because you waged war on her."

"If I could go back—"

"You ain't got time or space for what-ifs, young'un. You can't go back. This is the bed you made for yourself, and as long as you display that shit on your shoulders, the more Kayden and every other opponent you have is going to poke at it. Don't give them ammunition to get into your head."

Clenching his jaws and taking a deep inhale, Austin calmed himself as much as he could before walking past Winston. Winston scoffed. "That's that shit that got you here. Let's play ball!"

"Practice is over."

"Not for you. Check the ball."

Musa and Keyston sat in the stands of the practice stadium watching Austin and Winston play an intense game of one-on-one.

"You only have one shot. At everything. If you get another, you don't squander it. You keep one eye on the ball and the other on the shot clock," Winston coached him, cutting past Austin and taking the ball to the hoop. "Think about life like this game you cry, bleed, and sweat for. Hours on the court and off the court."

Austin checked the ball, then slowly bounced it down the court as his ears clung to every word Winston spoke.

"You put the work in, you study it, and know without a doubt in your mind you know it through and through. That's how winners stay winners. That's how men are made. It's more than the money and what you can provide." Winston stole the ball and made the final shot. "No matter how many cars, houses, jewels, and whatever else, you vowed your life to that woman. A man keeps his word, he's honest, and he holds himself and everyone he loves at a level no one can touch."

"All that is good, but how do I fix this?"

Winston laughed. "Start with being honest with yourself."

Chapter Twelve

"Mo!" Angie shouted throughout the giant house. There were a number of bags packed up by the side door leading to the garage. Baby bottles, cups, and anything else Mone't would need to get through the beginning stages of her new life without Austin were staged and ready to go.

"Mone't?" Angie shouted as she took the stairs two at a time. She raced down the hall, barreling into Mone't and Austin's bedroom. The heaviness of Mone't's heart met Angie at the door. She shared that pain. Unlike the weight of her best friend's broken heart, Angie was riddled with guilt.

The moment Mone't's flip-flop-covered soles touched the plush light carpet of the bedroom, their eyes connected. Sure, Austin had done damage to Mone't's heart along with intensifying the war she was waging with herself. But Angie . . . Angie was supposed to be the one to protect her from things seen and unseen.

"Why are you here?" Mone't asked, her vocal cords weighted with emotions she was tired of feeling.

"I came to check on you. You won't answer the phone." Angie moved closer, but Mone't held her hands up, stopping her. "Mo—"

"You knew."

"I told Austin to tell you."

"Austin isn't you. I asked you about her, and you shrugged it off. When did we start doing that?" Mone't waited for an answer, and when Angie fumbled over her words, she turned to continue packing her things.

"Mone't, just let me explain. I got the photos—"

"Was it you who leaked them? Or did you sell them to Shady Palms?"

"Why would I do that to you?"

"Because I am trying to make sense of why you didn't tell me and you tell everything else!" Mone't threw her hands in the air. "I can't help but to keep going through this in my head. Over and over and over again. Why would my husband cheat on me? Why does everyone know but me? Why wouldn't my best friend tell me what the fuck was up so I wouldn't be standing at a press conference with egg on my face? Did you think about what that would have done to me?"

Angie's eyes floated closed as her head swayed. "What can I do?"

"Leave. Tell Austin I'm gone, since you're his advisor. Outside of that, nothing."

Angie didn't move. How could she? Just like Austin had made a promise to Mone't, Angie had too. From where Mone't stood, she'd violated her too.

"Mo, I'm sorry. I thought it would be better coming from Austin," Angie admitted.

"You know if it were never leaked, he wouldn't have told me shit. What's really fucking with me is that I've cried to both of you about this postpartum depression, full-on depression, whatever the fuck it is, and I felt crazy this whole time. Am I not good enough for him to care about what's going on with me? Does he even want to be here, or is being married to me some type of protection for him?"

Mone't was on a spiral. As best as she thought she was hiding it, she wasn't. She stood in the middle of the large walk-in closet. She was right at the epicenter of luxury fabrics, exclusive handbags, shoes, and custom jewelry, and yet she was scrubbing her face while hot tears rushed from her eyes.

"I dedicated my life to that nigga, and this is what I get?" Mone't spun around, grabbed a crystal figurine, and launched it into the floor-to-ceiling sliding mirror. The crash resounded throughout the room. "I need to get out of here."

"Can I at least help?"

"Mone't," Aneica shouted as she ran into the room. "Are you okay?"

Sorrow filled her small almond-shaped pools. "I'm ready to go."

***

"I'm home!" Austin announced, carrying his tired body into his mansion.

Ragged.

Emotionally, physically, and mentally ragged was Austin's current state. So he thought. He hadn't even seen the tip of the iceberg of the wounds he single-handedly opened.

"Izzy! AJ!" Austin called, shuffling his slides through the length of the house. It was unusual for the kids not to greet him at the door. There were no toys scattered over the floor. Mone't wasn't huffing and puffing. And there wasn't any food cooking.

"Yo! Where y'all at?"

Between Aneica and Mone't, they were always on top of the kids' schedules. By the time Austin made it home from practice, dinner was on the stove, and AJ and Izzy were dancing to their final video and getting ready to wind down.

"Damn, ain't shit in here to eat?" Keyston asked, rummaging through the kitchen like a dumpster diver. "I told you we should've stopped on the way home. But nah. 'I need to eat with wifey.' Now look. Where is wifey?"

The deeper Austin travelled into the house, the more he was met with still rooms, empty closets, and shattered glass. The tightening in his chest seemed to swallow his lungs and squeeze his heart. All the pressure paused his heart midbeat.

Stupidly, he'd thought Mone't was bluffing. He thought she was putting on a show and would come around. In Austin's mind, he could have wined and dined her, filled her ears and head with words that made her feel good. Shit, he even thought the dick he took out of their home would stroke this ship back on course.

It was foolish of him to assume that Mone't didn't mean the words she spoke or the actions she took. She could show him better than she could tell him. If he wouldn't listen, he was going to feel it all.

Austin spun around as though what he was seeing weren't real. Most of Mone't's side of the closet was empty. The kids' things were gone. His mother was gone.

Snaking his phone from his pocket, he searched the locations of Mone't and his mother. Mone't's location on her phone and truck were undiscoverable. His mother's location was pinged to a nearby grocery store.

If he didn't get an answer, he was going to lose his mind. Wifey was the first name the pad of his finger tapped. The call went to voicemail. He repeated this until his brain grasped the insanity settling in. The next name was his mother's.

Aneica couldn't answer fast enough before Austin was shouting into the receiver, "Where the hell is Mo?"

"Who the hell are you hollerin' at, boy?" Aneica shouted back. "Have you lost your damn mind?"

"Mama." Austin winced.

He ran back through the house again as though something would change. No matter what rooms he walked into, everything was the same. Mone't and the children were gone. Sweat poured from Austin's hairline, and the beats of his heart increased while his hand vigorously rubbed against his chest. He tried to stand steady.

The room was spinning. Mone't had the gun locked and loaded. Her aim was directly at his heart. If he found her now, he could sway her from pulling the trigger and killing that vein. If not, they'd be dead before he could right his wrong.

"Ma . . . I don't have time for that. Where is she?" Austin asked in a panic. His breathing sounded as though he'd run miles. Light on his feet, he jogged down the stairs, circling the living room for any sign of a joke. There wasn't any. "Tell me something, Ma. Where is she?"

"Austin, you need to calm down until I get there."

"I can't calm down! You serious? Yo, you can't be serious. You let my wife just pack up and—"

"I didn't let her do anything," Aneica replied in an even tone. She was prepared for this explosion. She was actually proud he hadn't started punching holes in the walls.

Then again, he was still in shock. He was still processing the fact that Mone't wasn't bluffing at all.

Austin whisked through the kitchen, past Musa and Keyston, who were coolly watching Austin unravel. Aneica had already put them on game. It was precautionary to keep them from rolling through the city with guns blazing.

"Y'all knew about this shit?" Austin quizzed. His wild eyes bounced between the two men he viewed as his brothers.

Neither Musa nor Keyston could lie to him now, or period for that matter. They held integrity at the highest height on their moral compasses. If you didn't ask, they wouldn't have to answer.

Keyston wavered in his planted position. Musa shook his head, followed by his hand running down his face. "We'll help you look for her, but we don't know where she is."

"Nigga," Keyston blew under his breath. "You can't hold shit."

Austin scoffed, his demeanor becoming more bewildered. "Y'all fucking knew! Nah, don't help me. I'll do this shit myself."

Musa shrugged his shoulders and took a seat at the island. "A'ight. You know where we are if you need backup. I saw how she whipped your ass the first time."

"Fuck both y'all," Austin hissed as he snatched a pair of keys from the small cabinet and rushed out the garage door.

"Why is it always fuck us when he gets his ass into bullshit he can't get out of? Huh?" Keyston questioned as the door slammed shut.

Musa waited until the engine revved up to Austin's Ferrari before he commented, "Young niggas. You know how they get down. You know his ass is going to come back here crying, so we might as well get gone."

Keyston took a deep breath. "I'll see you in the morning at Mo's spot?"

"Make sure his ass gets to practice on time."

Musa and Keyston dapped each other before parting ways.

Austin was speeding down the neighborhood streets. Mone't couldn't have gone far. She was either at one of his realty spots he had in the city or at Angie's. He spent hours racing from one building to another, checking every apartment, condo, and loft due to his own paranoia. In Austin's mind, everyone was going to protect Mone't for the sake of being on the right side of the story. His ego told him they weren't going to point him in her direction for the sake of a headline.

He didn't have room for his ego. His ego and pride had done enough damage to his livelihood. He couldn't afford any more disruption from either. Their costs were far too high for him to live comfortably.

Austin pulled up to Angie's building, threw the valet his keys, and hopped on the elevator. With his hands pressed against the railing of the elevator, he huffed while listening to his heart thunder inside of its cage. He couldn't focus on how bad his heart hurt at the possibility of Mone't never coming back. The fight in him wouldn't allow it. He had to fight until he was the champ. He needed that trophy. Fifty years from now, he needed to look back at these days and down into his wife's eyes and know that they fought like hell for them. Who knew this was what it would take for Austin to put his life back into perspective?

Once he reached Angie's floor, he ran down the hallway and banged on the door until she pulled it open. Angie stood before him in a soft pink onesie with hearts all over it. On her face was a shimmery gold mask. He could see the illumination from a ring light in the background.

"Nigga. Could you calm yo' ass down?" Angie snapped. "You're about to scare my damn neighbors."

Austin pushed past her, barging into the apartment to see if there were any signs of Mone't and his children.

"She's not here, Austin," Angie announced. That didn't stop him from going from room to room. He wasn't going to rest until he found her. "You know, if she doesn't want to be found, you won't find her."

"LeAngelique, don't play with me. Where is she?"

She shrugged. "She ain't talking to me either. Apparently, I'm just as guilty as you are."

Austin blew a sharp breath. "But you saw her."

"I did. Saw her pack the rest of her shit, break a mirror, and tell me where I could go and how I could get there."

Austin's shoulder's fell. "Dammit."

"Exactly. You fucked this up for all of us. I'll be able to get my best friend back, though. But will you?"

He cut his eyes at her. "Don't play with me."

"Is there any part of me that looks like I'm playing with you? I told you to tell her. You thought it was easier to make the shit go away instead of just telling her. Now here we are."

"Shit," Austin blew, dropping his back on a nearby wall. "When you find out where she is, call me."

Angie laughed. "I'm not. I've already hurt her once. I won't do it again. You have to fix this one yourself."

"No offense or nothing, but I know that, and I'm tired of hearing that shit. When you see her, drop me the pin."

"All right, I got to go. I have sponsorship content to post. Run along and find your wife."

Defeated, Austin dragged himself out of her apartment and drove home. When he shuffled into the house, the aroma of food hit his nose. He perked up, hoping that Mone't was back and she'd just left to scare him.

"She's not here," Aneica announced as Austin rounded the corner. "Just me."

"I ain't hungry, Ma."

Aneica hated this for Austin and Mone't, but she knew it was necessary. She studied his demeanor and sighed heavily as he hung the keys back in their respective place.

"You don't have to eat. You're grown. You know how to feed yourself." Aneica stirred whatever she was cooking in the pot. There were containers lined up on the counter and stickers with dates on them. "You don't have to eat tonight, but you will eat."

"You leaving me too?"

Aneica nodded. "I am. Mama has to have a life too. Well, more life. There's a man who needs more attention from me, and since you don't—"

"I need you," Austin protested.

"I'll be in to check on you. My time is valuable."

"Who's watching my kids if you're out doing whatever?"

"Their mother and their nannies. I'll be around when y'all need me, but while everyone is taking a break, I might as well too."

Without question Austin was defeated. The pressure resting on his shoulders tripled in weight. His heart was on his sleeve, and his head was spinning. He was sick to his stomach.

"Ma."

"I love you, son. With my whole heart. I love her, too. If I keep coddling you, you wouldn't learn."

"Ma, what kind of—"

Austin raised his voice, causing Aneica to round the counter and meet him. She'd implanted discipline in him. Better than anyone, Aneica knew her son's temper, and she knew the root. Austin hadn't been without her, and when he found Mone't, he wasn't without her either. The women in his life made him. They made it easy for him to get by. They tolerated the mess he had become because they allowed him to. Aneica's hold on Austin was his downfall. She'd done all she could to make a man out of him when the truth of the matter was that Austin needed a man to make a man out of him.

"You have to man up, son. Don't be like your father and fumble this."

Austin's thick brows fused into one. "I wouldn't know how he fumbled. Never met the nigga."

Immediately, she was flooded with guilt, though she was too proud to show it. Austin had grown up living the truth according to Aneica's story, although there was another side for him to explore. There was another side *of* him to explore.

"Take my word for it."

He studied her before nodding. "Yeah, I've been doing that."

Austin trekked away. Emotion defeated him as he hiked the stairs to the bedroom he'd shared with Mone't. Her scent lingered in the sheets, the curtains, and the pillows.

Mone't was activating her power over him. Austin would find her, only to crawl and grovel at her feet in remorse of playing with her trust and love. It wouldn't be enough. Her absence was unfamiliar to him, but he didn't truly miss her yet.

When that hit him, he would feel like he was on the brink of death.

"Mommy, is this our new house?" Izzy asked, looking around the small room painted powder pink.

The house on the other side of Brentwood was considerably smaller than the mansion they all were accustomed to. Mone't bought this house in Aneica's name months after Isabella was born. Up until today, she had no intention of ever using it. In fact, before giving birth to AJ, she was going to sell it. Aneica had advised her against it. She told her that no matter how good things appeared to be, she always needed money in an account that Austin had no clue of and a place to lay her head. If it weren't for Aneica, Mone't would either be stuck in the house resenting Austin or back in the hood shielding two babies from the life she used to live.

"Yeah, for now," Mone't muttered. She hoped that Austin would come to his senses, find her, and make this shit right. She'd been hoping for that for over a year to no avail, so this was her only option.

Leave. Adjust to living without him and thrive on her own. The account Austin set up for her had more than enough in it for her to be okay, but her personal account was what she planned on using. She wasn't going to give him any idea of where she went. Austin needed to sweat it out and learn how to miss her and appreciate her.

"For now?" Izzy shouted. "Is Daddy coming? He owes me a movie. Is Mama going to be here?"

Mone't's brain couldn't process everything Isabella was asking. Her concerns were firing off a mile a minute. On the outside, she showed a cool, put-together front. On the inside, she was a mess. She tried to tell herself this would be over soon, that she could make it through the first night alone. The truth of the matter was, "I can't do this," Mone't muttered to herself.

"Uh-uh, we don't say can't," Izzy chimed as she pulled the covers over her body.

Faintly smiling, Mone't nodded in agreement. "You are right about that, princess. We don't say can't." Leaning over to kiss her feisty daughter on the forehead, Monet lingered. "I love you, Izzy. I know you don't get it now, but remember, everything Mommy does is to show you how strong you can be. Okay?"

Izzy nodded her tiny head. "Can you call Daddy and tell him I love him and I want him to come soon?"

Mone't's heart dropped. Her nerves ran rapidly. She wasn't prepared to be a single mother. Saving face, she exited the room. Once closed behind her room door, she tried to breathe. Letting a shaky breath escape, she took in the coldness and unfamiliarity of the place she found herself in.

Chapter Thirteen

"Y'all," Angie huffed, tension falling from her shoulders, "this moisturizer is amazing. It smells so good. It's silky."

She put on a good show for the hundreds of thousands of people watching her do her night-time routine live. With endorsements from Mone't and Austin, the viewers came, hoping to get some tea on her friends' relationship and not the meaningless tea she was dishing out as she sipped her also-sponsored wine. Angie knew there was a fine line between disrespecting her friends' privacy and entertaining the nosy public.

Love, Angie may have been a gossip blog for the Hills and surrounding areas, but she wasn't going to bite the hands that fed her. Austin was right. He'd invested a lot in her. He single-handedly fueled her dreams. Although she was a high-paid gossip blog operator and owner, she wasn't expecting this to be her path.

In her mind and heart, she knew that she and Eman would be taking over the world. Eman had a hustler's gift of gab, and she knew everything about everything. Between the two of them, they could have been something.

Her life with him was stripped away before its maturity date, but she held on like a soldier. "Don't forget your coupon code LOVEANGIE for twenty percent off your first purchase from Allure Spa. Tell them I sent you, and as always, Angie's Angels, glow with love! See ya!"

Angie ended the Live and took a true sigh of relief. She was happy it was over, happy that the fake smiling was over and that the bombarding questions about Mone't going Donkey Kong on Austin were silent for the night. For the last week, subscribers had been sending to her pictures and "tea" about Austin and his whereabouts. She was confident that his mishap happened once, so she ignored them.

What other blogs were doing weren't any of her concern. Those messy hoes would dime out their mother if there were clickbait in it. Angie was recordable. She had access to exclusive events, sports' media rooms, and private industry events.

Taking her phone off the ring light stand, she moved from her poshly decorated office into the living room full of vibrant pinks, yellows, oranges, deep blues, and greens. Plants outlined the floors and shelves on the wall. Candles were lit, allowing her to bask in the fragrant sandalwood, bergamot, and vanilla notes from their throw.

As she curled her body into the nook of the couch, she scrolled through her phone mindlessly. She called Mone't every day as though everything between them were still normal. Aneica would always send an update. Sadly, nothing on Mone't's end was improving. She wasn't expecting Mone't to get better in seven days or for Austin to repair what he broke. Angie wanted to be a supporting element in the healing. She'd seen Mone't through two childbirths, a wedding, and the day-to-day adjustment of being the wife of a sports superstar.

Sucking in a deep sigh, she pulled the plush canary yellow throw blanket over her feet and looked out the window at the twinkling lights of the city. She wasn't a far cry from Fiftieth, but now she floated above the city that had molded her. Angie's dreams continued from the trenches to the clouds. Nights like these, when she was truly alone, she dreamt of Eman's strong arms wrapped around her body. His nose would be nestled into the crook of her neck. The hint of mint and ganja would be on his breath as he whispered his plans in her ear.

Her mind floated back on all the stolen moments they had. And then the shots would ring out, and she would hear him say, *"I'm no good for you, shorty."*

Never knowing six words would break her heart, she clung to them as a reminder that what she felt, what they shared, was real.

The buzzing of her phone pulled her from her drifting thoughts to an unknown caller badge scrolling over her screen. Typically, she never answered these calls. Whoever on the line was usually a "scam likely" call. But tonight, she needed to hear someone's voice. She needed someone to talk to her even if it was bullshit.

Tapping the icon, Angie hit the speaker button and answered, "Hello."

"You have a collect call from an inmate at the—"

"I'll accept! I'll accept!" She scrambled, unfolding herself from the position she was in. "Yes, all charges, I'll accept."

The line connected, and she was greeted by the soothing sounds of Eman laughing in her ear. "You miss a nigga?"

Embarrassed by her hasty answer to the automated voice, her chestnut brown cheeks flushed like he was standing in front of her, casting that gaze over her. She could see him standing tall and in control while trying not to lose control. He'd bite his lip as his gaze softened as it graced her burning flesh.

"No. I don't even know why you're calling me after about three years and a million letters," she huffed, taking him off speaker and pressing the phone to her ear. Angie needed to hear the cadence of his breathing. She missed him, and it was picking away at the wall she built around her.

"LeAngelique. You missed me?" Eman asked. This time his voice was softer. The amusement was gone. He was serious, and his time was long but precious.

Her voice came out just above a whisper. "Yes."

"I miss you too. I'm sorry I haven't called or written back. I've been trying to pass this time without thinking too much about what you're doing . . . who you're doing."

She looked around her space, full of things she hoped would ease this process for her. Unfortunately, nothing could replace the gaping hole Eman left in her heart. Implying someone was filling his spot was insulting. "You're full of shit. You know no one is here. You know it's always been you."

Eman released a breath it felt like he'd been holding for years. He grunted. "I know. I wouldn't be tripping if you were. I get it. A nigga is gone for a minute. I told you—"

"I don't care what you told me, E. I heard what you said, but it's your heart I listen to. Three, six, twelve, or a lifetime. I can't unglue myself from you." Angie's voice broke. "I've tried. I can't."

Eman grew quiet, his breathing growing shallower. "I'm going to come home and give you everything I said I would."

Now Angie's breathing was shallow. "Your appeal was approved?"

"Don't tell anyone. I heard about the shit going on out there. I want to see it for myself."

Angie moved to the edge of the seat. "I won't. I won't say anything. You can stay here. I have enough room."

"You know I ain't coming in your spot without shit. Trust me, though. When I get my shit right, it's us. Okay?"

"Okay," Angie replied, swallowing her stifling emotions.

"Hold it down. I'm coming home." The confidence in Eman's voice when he spoke invoked a series of chills that took over her being. "I'll be seeing you."

"Time is up," the automated voice spoke, and the call ended.

The phone dropped into her lap as the tears pricked away at her eyes. Tears had been few and far between over the last three years. Angie managed to hold it together. It wasn't just for her. It was for Mone't, too. Eman was the scale balancing everything out. Without him, nothing seemed to be even.

Sucking in a deep breath to fill her lungs, Angie pushed herself back into the nook of the couch. She prayed silently that she'd drift off to sleep to sweet thoughts of Eman, desperately needing her mind to drift off on anything else but what was happening.

Unfortunately, sleep wouldn't be in her cards. The constant dinging from her phone wouldn't allow it. With a long, exaggerated sigh, she picked it up. There were over a dozen submissions of Austin in a club in Brighton Heights. Austin was garbed in the hoochie daddy short special. Silk material that bore exotic designs was paired with fresh white designer sneakers and bright dazzling diamonds around his neck and wrist and hanging from the small hoops in his ears. Austin didn't appear as though he was a man who was losing his family. He looked like the fuck boy of the year. Every photo was attached with some sort of disdain for his behavior.

His wife is at home embarrassed and he's out partying.

Looks like the golden boy ain't really all he said he was.

Angie, is this the family man you've been hyping up? Huh?

She pinched the bridge of her nose, irritation and anxiousness toppling over. If she saw these, she knew Mone't had too. Despite Mone't being upset with her, she pushed herself off the couch and trampled to the front door. Angie's feet were clad in fuzzy slides, her purse swinging from her forearm and her keys in hand. En route to do what she should have done weeks ago, Angie sashayed through the parking garage.

Everyone but Austin knew where Mone't was holed up with his children. And from the look of the constant photos, it seemed like everyone but Austin cared about it.

"Come on, Austin," Angie muttered. "She's been gone for a week. This ain't how you get her to come home."

Hopelessly romantic, Angie wanted her friends to get this together sooner rather than later. The longer apart they were, the more damage would be done. Angie swerved her Mercedes in and out of the lanes, sailing from the city to the suburbs to rush to Mone't's aid.

Mo wasn't going to ask for help anymore. She had already done it once, and her cry fell on deaf ears. If it were up to her, she'd wave a wand and not feel how she felt. She'd bury it under work, the kids, and whatever else she could so she wouldn't have to think or talk about it.

Twenty minutes later, Angie was punching in the code to the front door and making her way in. Having spent most of their lives together, Angie could feel Mone't's heaviness. Some days it was interchangeable, and the text would always read: Is what I'm feeling you or me? Best friends by divine intervention and sisters by choice, regardless of the temperature, they were showing up for one another.

The modest four-bedroom, three-and-a-half-bath home felt cold. As beautiful as it was aesthetically, outside and in, it didn't feel warm and welcoming. Heartbreak, self-doubt, sadness, anxiety, and shame lived here. It greeted her at the door as she eased inside its darkness. Seemingly, the house was quiet.

Taking the short staircase two steps at a time, Angie peeked in on her godchildren before reaching Mone't's bedroom at the end of the hall. Easing into the room, Angie called her name softly. "Mo."

The bed was unmade with covers and pillows in disarray, leading Angie to believe that sleep hadn't come for Mone't in some time. The latest Mahogany channel series flashed scenes on the mounted TV. All the duffle bags and suitcases they'd dragged in over a week ago were still packed as if they were waiting, along with Mone't, to return to their rightful places.

She moved her feet to the ajar bathroom door where she found Mone't in shambles. Handfuls of hair surrounded Mone't. Immediately, Angie dropped her things and crawled to Mone't's side.

"He doesn't even care, Angie. He doesn't care. Look at him. This is what he wanted," Mone't sobbed like a baby into Angie's chest. Her arms tightened around Mone't as her eyes scanned the chunks of hair Mone't had cut and the post on her phone that drove her to this point. "He doesn't want me."

Those four words were so weighted. It wasn't just Austin who had broken Mone't's heart. These were the sobs of having the mother she had, the father who turned her away from knowing him, the brother who was her protector but unable physically to be her rock. These sobs were the sounds of feeling trapped inside her mind without a way out.

Angie let Mone't cry until the sound of pain had tapered off along with the tears. Angie pulled Mone't's face away, holding it firmly in her palms, thumbing her tears from her cheeks. "You have sacrificed so much for him, his career, and your children. You are more than enough. But do you know that, Mo?"

Mone't's reddened eyes dropped to her lap. Then they trailed to the hair she'd chopped. Springing to her feet, she gaped in the mirror at the state of her mane. "Oh, my God."

Angie stood behind her and grabbed the hair shears. "New haircut. New chapter. New journey." Calmly would be the most effective way to get Mone't to come as close to center as possible. "I think you can pull off the Nia Long nineties look, too." Angie cut thick locks of Mone't's hair. The tears were back, slowly streaming down her cheeks.

"I'm sorry, Ang."

"I'm sorry too. We're going to get through this. Until then, we'll just even this out, try to sleep, and go out in the morning for a new 'do."

Mone't's uncertainty pierced a dimple in her cheek. "I haven't slept in what's felt like days. My mind . . . it doesn't turn off. When I sleep, I dream, and it's more like nightmares."

"Depression is a beast, Mo. There is no way you're going to get through this alone. Let us help you. Let us be there. I know how it feels to feel like you're drowning."

Their eyes connected. Mone't's mouth didn't need to move to ask the question. Her eyes were telling.

"Yeah," Angie softly replied.

"Why didn't you tell me?"

Angie continued to cut. "I wasn't even supposed to be with Eman. So what good would it have done for any of us to cry over him? To outwardly show that the last time I saw him messed me up?"

"I can't help but feel like that's all on me, too."

"It isn't on you, Mo. You did exactly what you needed to do. If you hadn't, where would we be? Hm? On Fiftieth and McClendon? Raising a kid or kids? The guys on the block serving? Probably dead or in jail. You didn't pull that trigger only for Austin. You did it for all of us."

Mone't swiped the tip of her tongue over her tearstained lips. "I wonder, if the tables were turned, would he have done the same? That thought consumes me at times."

Angie finished the misshapen cut and brushed Mone't's shoulders off. "You're constantly heavy with your thoughts. It's not this new body you're adjusting to. It's the weight of overthinking that you're carrying. Lay it down for a night."

Mone't allowed herself to rest for a night. Maybe it was the crying for and over Austin and all the other things she kept locked away. Maybe it was the fact that Angie was a few doors down, willing and ready to help her. Whatever it was, she slept enough not to be on eggshells when she woke up the next morning.

Angie and Aneica worked around each other in the kitchen making coffee and feeding two energetic children. When Mone't shuffled in with a long satin scarf wrapped around her head, Aneica's eyes grew wide before Angie could nudge her.

"Don't mention the hair," Angie had coached Aneica this morning when she arrived. Now wasn't the time to shower her with questions and scenarios of what she would've done.

"Morning, everyone," Mone't greeted them.

"Morning, Mommy!" Izzy chimed back. "Mama is taking us to the park and then the bookstore. I can't wait."

AJ, who was sitting on the counter in his chair, clapped his hands at the sight of his mother. "Mmmaaa. Ma. Maaa," AJ babbled as he kicked his chubby feet and opened and closed his hands.

Mone't forced a smile. These two couldn't see how she felt. They were innocent and needed the best part of her. She kissed the top of Izzy's head prior to picking up AJ and kissing his face. "Hey, big boy. You slept through the night!" she cheered.

"It's the food. Keeps him full longer," Aneica announced. "He's about to have some more. Mama isn't stopping to feed you a million times today. No, she isn't."

AJ laughed at Aneica reaching out and cooing at him.

"Thank you for taking them today," Mone't said.

Aneica waved her hand. "I can't stand being away from them. No need to thank me. You need a day."

"Speaking of which, our appointment is in an hour," Angie announced.

Mone't studied her. "You need something to wear?"

"I feel like that was shady," Angie joked. "I would if I weren't a journalist who always travels with a change of clothes. You never know where your investigation will land you."

Aneica laughed. "I'm so happy you used that nosiness for good."

Angie pursed her lips and stole an eye roll.

"Don't roll your eyes. While you're out, tell this one to ramp up her business and get busy. Lamont Wright called me twice this week hoping to get in touch with her. He's willing to pay, so I say make your money."

Angie smirked. "I'll work on her."

After breakfast was over and the kids were dressed and ready for their day, Mone't got herself together and joined Angie in her car. Mone't hadn't said much. Her mind was still full, but Angie had something up her sleeve to get her friend to let some of it go.

Allure Spa would be the resting spot for Mone't today. Angie arranged for only key stylists and estheticians to be present, with signed NDAs of course. Mo needed to be comfortable and protected. She hadn't been spotted out since the fight.

Angie watched from the adjacent chair as Mone't rubbed her hand over her fresh haircut. She chewed her lip with excitement and uncertainty. "I . . . I can't believe how good it looks," she muttered.

"It fits you," the stylist assured her, removing the cape from around her neck. "That's the haircut for a baaadddd woman."

Mone't smiled faintly. "Thank you."

"Girl, please, don't mention it. A new look is due from time to time. Come with me. Let's get these brows and facial started."

Mone't looked back at Angie, who was flipping through a magazine, sitting underneath the dryer with a headful of rollers. "You have a massage after that, too. Enjoy."

Chapter Fourteen

"Izzy, slow down!" Aneica called from the bench. She was hyper-focused as she typically was when she was in public with her grandchildren. However, considering the air around her family, her attention was heightened.

Izzy couldn't run too fast or shout too loudly without Aneica being on pins and needles. As nervous as she was, they needed fresh air. In the pursuit of that, no child deserved to be bombarded by intrusive paparazzi who wanted to make their father's business theirs.

She bounced AJ cautiously up and down in the cradle of her thighs. Every so often, she would glance around the perimeter to ensure the security she was promised was still in place. There was nothing Aneica disliked more than dishonesty. She never accepted it from Austin, which was why she was so disappointed in his recent actions.

Dishonesty was how Austin came to be. Before he could breathe on his own, he was the poster child for it. Aneica practiced it day after day. The secrecy was starting to chip away at the exterior she built. Austin being like his father was on brand. What she hated to admit was that Austin also ran parallel to her.

Conceived and birthed in dishonesty, now he was navigating through the expensive debt the high price tags brought with it.

As Aneica's dark amber eyes scanned the area, they landed on a very familiar being. A man she knew once upon a time all too well. A man who ruled the orbit of her planet in the same fashion Austin was ruling Mone't's.

He walked like his father, smirked like his father, and at times, he even thought and spoke like him. It was insane considering Austin had never formally met him.

In an instant, Aneica's heart thundered against her chest. Although he was responsible for setting up the security and ensured that Austin was protected from his string of outbursts on and off the court, it didn't help the fact that she didn't want to see him. Or talk to him. Or be caught with him. She'd been put on notice over twenty years ago, and she didn't have it in her to revisit that less-than-gentle conversation.

The rumble of his baritone awakened something inside of Aneica she thought had died the day she left his side and returned to her parents' small home. "Aneica Graham."

She shuddered, clinging tighter to a babbling Austin Jr. AJ was consumed with gnawing on his teething necklace, and Izzy was running herself silly. Neither of them could be used as a means to escape the trembling of her internal organs.

"Francesco De Luca," Aneica returned, wincing at the taste of his name coming off her lips. "I agreed to you providing security, not seeing you."

"Seeing how it's all one in the same, I'm here. It's only right since these are my grandchildren too," he arrogantly responded.

She rolled her eyes and peeled them away from him. After all these years and everything they endured separately, he still smelled the same. It was the aftershave he used. Not much had changed outside of his empty ring finger. But she wasn't here to get caught in his allure, and neither was he.

"From a child you wanted nothing to do with," she snapped in a matter-of-fact tone.

Francesco huffed and took a seat next to Aneica. "I'm not here to dig up the past bones with you. I am here to talk about our son. He's spiraling out of control."

"A show I've seen one too many times before," she sarcastically responded in reference to the glimpses of Francesco's behavior when he was a Ganton Hills Monarch.

"Don't you think it's best that he knows where he got this shit from?"

"Mm, no. Being that we've made it this far . . ." Her words lingered, inducing irritation that fluttered across his thick brows.

Francesco swiped his tan hand over his face. "Aneica. Dammit. You're still stubborn."

She shrugged. "And you're still an arrogant asshole. Please get to your point so I don't have to suffer in your presence anymore."

He groaned. "The point is that it's time for me to step in and for you to allow it to happen."

"No, sorry. No can do. We've made it this far," she said again, this time attempting to balance AJ and his baby bag as she shot to her feet. It was easy to walk away. She had practice.

He caught her arm. The electricity ran from his palm into her being. "We aren't done."

"We are. This was a mistake accepting your help. Accepting anything from you always comes with a cost. And I no longer have the patience to pay it back."

He glared up at her, his piercing blue eyes trailing over her. As if she were under a spell, she sat back down, still holding tighter to AJ and scooting down the bench to put space between them.

"I understand I made my mistakes. I understand that your trust was the price for it."

"Just my trust?" she scoffed, mumbling under her breath. "Try my life."

"And I've been trying to fix that. Did he ever go without? He had clothes, food, a roof over his head, AAU basketball, and a full ride. And when he entered the draft, I made sure he stayed here for you."

She chuckled. "He had clothes, food, a roof over his head in the middle of the hood, where he had to fight the temptation every day. AAU basketball because I worked three jobs to cover what you wouldn't. I'm sorry—what your wife said you wouldn't. A full ride because he was talented and put in the work, and he could've gone to any team. You kept him here for you. I would've followed my son to the edge of the earth."

Aneica took a deep breath, held it for a beat, and slowly released it. "I probably should've talked him out of staying. The Hills haven't brought him anything but trauma."

Francesco scoffed. "Trauma? He has an issue with his temper and keeping his dick in his pants. What trauma does he have?"

Her face tightened with frustration. Francesco didn't have a front row seat to Austin's daily battles, and he wouldn't know what trauma looked like if he got slapped in the face with it. "Austin has been through the unimaginable. Sure, you contributed your athletic ability to him. Sure, you assisted in his growth financially, but you didn't wipe tears, asses, or noses while ducking and dodging crack and bullets. You have no idea who he is outside of your genetic makeup. No idea at all who he is or what we all had to face to get him to this point."

"I'm trying!"

"Twenty-three years later, because if the world finds out your ass fathered a son with a cheer-leader, you would be ruined. Not him."

"You know damn well that's not the case," he semi-shouted.

"Then what is the case?" Her tone met his.

Francesco's need to intervene for his son and the crippling effects of breaking Aneica's heart were overtaking his cool demeanor. "I need to be there for my son. I need to. Aneica, I need you to move out of my way for once and let me do that."

Aneica pressed her lips together, stubbornness still present. "I'll consider it. I'll have to talk to him about this before I let you near him."

"He's a grown-ass man, Aneica. Pop your titty out of his mouth and tell him when and where to meet me."

"Considering he has no clue who you really are to him, it's best you let me take the lead on how this is going to go for once. I did it your way. It's your turn to do it mine."

He had no other choice but to yield. There was so much he wanted to tell her. So many years had passed since he was able to bare everything at her feet. The heartache was shared between them. As difficult as it was for Aneica to see him, the same held true for him. She was the love of his life, and being stuck where he was, the admittance of error would have cost him everything.

He stood, orbs lingering on her and then on his grandson, who had his face, before they floated to Izzy. This was his lineage, and he had chosen his career and bank account over them.

A new haircut, an overdue mani and pedi, and a massage to rival all others had Mone't's shoulders relaxed, brows unpinned, and mood lighter than it had been. That was until the additional guest joined Angie and Mone't at the private dining table in her favorite restaurant.

The very last thing Mone't expected after such a calm day was being asked about her main trigger. She gulped down the wine in her glass, internally cursing herself for drinking more than normal. However, since Angie waved a magic wand that got AJ sucking bottles instead of her twenty-four seven, she had freedom to do so.

"Mone't?" Angie asked, reaching out to softly touch Mone't's hand. "You okay?"

She nodded slightly before licking her wine-stained lips. "I can't get that night out of my head. Sure, there's underlying things like my mother. My father turning me away because he can't bear the thought of his baby girl seeing him shackled. But it's that night and the sound of that bullet leaving the chamber and knowing what I did."

Mone't's voice broke and tapered off toward the end of her sentence. "I did that for him and our family. And my brother covered for me. I'm out here living life, and I have the audacity to hate it."

Angie's eyes filled with tears, but she refused to let them drop.

"How ungrateful do I have to be to hate the life my brother sacrificed his for? I hate my mind, my body, myself."

"Because Austin cheated?" Robyn, the therapist, asked.

Mone't gnawed on her lip. "No. As angry as I am about that, and as hurt as I am, I assumed he would. It was a matter of time. But this isn't about my husband's inability to be whole with me. I can't expect that from him when I can't even be whole for me. I don't like me. There's days that I hate me. I hate the way I talk to myself, the way I sacrifice, denying myself, and I really hate the fact that I can't be happy."

Everyone's food was untouched. Who could eat salads and charcuterie boards when the heaviness weighed down their entire beings? Mone't didn't bother to wipe her tears. She allowed them to fall. She allowed herself to be vulnerable without the fear of cameras and media attention.

"I'm not happy. I haven't been in years. I have no sense of myself. I have no idea how to be a woman in this game that's set out to make me crumble. How strong do I have to be? Who is strong for me? Who looks out for me without needing me to feed them, fuck them, smile on cue, and constantly be present? I am tired."

Robyn's eyes softened. She was trained to separate herself from the patients' problems, but everything Mone't released were the thoughts of many women around the world, regardless of socioeconomic status. Mone't's shuddering voice was the voice of every mother, daughter, and wife.

"I'm just tired. I'm not saying I'll end my life or anything. My babies need me, but I need to be happy."

"And you deserve to be happy. That's going to be the goal. We're going to get you happy and healthy. Despite whatever everyone else needs from you, you have to take care of you first and last . . . for you. You cannot pour from an empty cup. You can't take care of everyone if you can't do that for yourself. What's going to get you out of this?"

Mone't shrugged. "Curating something of my own. Without Austin attached to it. Without having to sacrifice me for it."

"What's going to give you that freedom?"

"The slew of emails I have resting in my inbox. A business opportunity to set up and enhance clients' travels."

"Then that's your homework, along with affirming yourself. Loving on you, taking care of you, so that you can climb out of this space you're in."

Completely yielding to the process, Mone't replied, "Okay."

"And you and I will have weekly check-ins to sort through everything. Keep a journal to keep track of any emotions that may arise."

"Thank you."

Robyn shook her head and waved her hand. "Don't thank me. This is what we do for one another. Keep your head up, Mone't. We got you, and you got you. Reply to those emails."

Chapter Fifteen

"King Graham is not playing like a king tonight and hasn't been since the last game."

"Phil, I tell you what, he cannot afford to lose his head this game. If Austin chokes, the Monarchs are going to have to go after this win on their own."

As the announcers exchanged commentary from the sidelines, the team scrambled to find their rhythm. Austin's frustration with himself was easy to pick up on. His teammates sensed it all week through practice, and it had spread like a cancer.

They were emotional and desperate. They handled the ball recklessly, giving Brighton Heights the advantage they needed to outplay, outhustle, and outtalk the Monarchs.

The opposing team was hungry for the win. They were engaged in a full-on mental battle, hungry to break down every Monarch on the uphill pursuit to their victory. Every player blocked out the cheering, booing, and clashing noise of the sports fans.

It wasn't the noise from the crowd tapping against Austin's crown. No. It was his opponent and the public scrutiny of his own transgressions that were firing shots at his crown.

"You can't handle that rock, nigga," Adeem White taunted him, staying close to Austin.

Elbowing him, Austin grumbled, "Get off me, nigga."

"Nah, I'm on your ass all night." Adeem was pressing Austin. Every move he made was a fight to the goal. The refs weren't calling any fouls. It was on Austin to get Adeem off him. It was on Austin to protect his withering mental.

"The only shots happening around these parts are the ones I'm about to take at your sexy-ass wife. She looks like she tastes like caramel."

Of all the insults Adeem had been hurling at Austin all night, that was the one to set him off. The thought of another man tasting the nectar that was vowed to him set him off. It was all on him. He was solely responsible for any action Mone't took against his pride and ego.

Shoving Adeem out of his face, Austin attempted to keep what Winston and Coach Tatum said at the front of his mind. Austin tried like hell to control himself, but the constant thought of another man suckling the part of his woman he loved increased the fury in his veins.

"Before you know it, I'm going to have your pretty bitch in my bed creaming on the sheets, calling me daddy. Swallowing my dick whole."

That was it. That did it. They were already facing off while the game went on without them. The refs paid no attention to it until Austin erupted.

"Fuck you say, bitch?" His mouth guard flew out in a fury. Adeem returned the physical assault with a shove of his own and a coy smirk fused across his lips.

"You heard me," Adeem taunted him. Both teams had now rushed to defend their mates.

Austin landed the first hit, enticing the scuffle to escalate. Refs blew the whistles, teammates pushed and shoved, and the announcers cut to commercial break. The cancer was spreading from the court to the crowd. All the power that Austin possessed was being used for evil.

It took the entire coaching staff from both teams to pull everyone apart and direct them to their respective locker rooms. Austin was furious. Everything in his path was slung, punched, or kicked out of his way. When he finally made it to his corner, he dropped down and put a towel over his head.

His tawny, tattooed skin flushed red. The anger inside of him was growing daily, and he had no idea how to hold it together anymore. Mone't used to be his compass. One glance or touch from her would bring him back.

"Austin, you're ejected from the game. The rest of you, calm the fuck down, go out there, and play ball. We came here to win, not to act a fucking fool! Get this shit together. If one is weak, we are all weak! Come on. Let's go!"

Spade, Jones, Smith, and even Moore patted Austin's shoulder. Paul Spade and Cypress Jones trailed the team out of the locker room and back onto the court. Kayden lingered. "I ain't mean that shit at practice. I was just trying to get your head ready for what's coming. It's not going to stop either."

Austin didn't move until he was sure he was alone. With a tug of his towel, he was face-to-face with Francesco De Luca.

Being that Francesco was over player relations and had a high stake in the team, he was here on business, not to set his world into a frenzy. With or without Aneica's permission, he was going to do his job.

"That's how you handle adversity?" Francesco asked, sitting back in his NBA padded chair. "The league is watching how you handle this, and I can assure you, they aren't too happy about your ability to maneuver through the messes you're making."

Austin scoffed. "They sent you down from the skybox to check me or something?"

"It's my job," Francesco nonchalantly replied, trying not to stare too long at his son or cross the line between yearning father and professional man. "You're making a spectacle of yourself."

Austin scoffed and waved Francesco off. "Yeah, a'ight. I've been hearing that. I'm cool."

Shooting to his feet, Austin prepared himself to walk away. Francesco wasn't allowing it. For Francesco, it was as if he were looking into the past at his younger, uncontrolled self.

Austin in his rawest form was his father's child. Francesco wasn't above his basketball past. His nickname didn't leave him unscathed either. Francesco was the Punisher, an Italian and black kid from Whitestone with hunger in his heart. Nothing was going to stand in the way of coming into his greatness.

Francesco composed himself and stopped himself from reaching out and holding his hurting son. He could feel the weight oozing from his son, and he shared that weight. Had he made better decisions, his seed wouldn't have been this angry.

"Tell the front office to do what they're going to do. You should know better than anyone around this bitch what's up. You got something else to say to me?"

Francesco scoffed and took a step back. "When we call, answer."

The game came and went along with the post-game conference, which Austin refused to attend. Not wanting to be asked questions about anything circulating in his world, he found himself in the club for the second night in a row. The team was due at the airport first thing in the morning.

Though he should have been sleeping, Austin was standing on the couch in the VIP with a bottle in his hand. Liquor coursed through his body, numbing him from his troubles. Temporarily, the attention from random women and partygoers made him feel like he was floating on top of the world.

"Dance with me, *papi*." A seductive slur flowed from the lips of the woman before him. Drunk enough to make impaired decisions, yet sober enough to know the lasting effects of falling into a trap, Austin was reluctant. That was until she tugged at his arm, forcing him to take a step off the couch to steady himself.

"Yo, shorty, chill with that aggressive shit. I'm cool on the dance," he responded with a slight attitude, curling his lips.

She smirked up at him as she pulled a thick envelope from her purse. "Austin Graham, you should have taken the dance. You've been served."

Shoving the envelope into his chest, she pranced off, leaving Austin's head spinning in the middle of the VIP section. His eyes squinted at the black letters typed across the manila envelope: "Mone't Graham vs. Austin Graham, Requisition for Dissolution of Marriage."

Austin's heart dropped down to his custom-sneaker-covered feet. His heart beat slower and heavier as if he were in the worst shape of his life. She pulled the trigger. Foolish of him to believe that she was bluffing in this game of love. Mone't had a full deck of cards, and Austin was out of chips. Aimlessly, he walked toward the back exit, his eyes still trained on the words. Musa and Keyston stood outside the car, passing a blunt and blowing the smoke into the air.

"Fuck wrong with you?" Keyston quizzed.

"Let's go," Austin replied under his breath. If Musa didn't have keen hearing, he wouldn't have heard him clearly.

Without asking any questions, Musa rounded the front and climbed behind the steering wheel. Austin sank his body into the seat, refusing to speak until he was alone in his team-issued hotel room.

"Baby, come on. You know this ain't how we get down," Austin spoke to Mone't's voicemail, a result of her blocking him. "I'm sorry. I didn't mean none of that shit. She didn't mean shit to me."

He hung up, paced the floor, and rounded the room back to his phone. He hit her name in his favorites and immediately got the voicemail again.

Though Mone't had blocked him, he was going to leave message upon message until he got the result he wanted.

"Mo, just pick up. We got to talk about this. Dissolution of marriage? You mean to tell me there ain't shit I can do? I said I was sorry. I ain't gon' do it no more! Unblock me now and call me back!

"Mone't, pick up this fucking phone!" he shouted into the phone, as if that would make her do what he wanted her to. "You had me served at a club? At a fucking club in front of cameras? You don't want this shit to go away, do you? You want to keep doing this bullshit. Baby . . . I let you go off. But this!"

Like a maniac, he hung up, threw the phone across the room, and continued to pace. If he were a smoker, he'd be chain-smoking out the window, two in his mouth and one behind his ear. He was stressed, alone, and feeling unhinged. His mind drifted back to the game with Adeem taunting him, telling him how his woman tasted.

Austin launched across the room to the phone, repeating his mania once more. "You out with a nigga, Mo? This is how you do me? Just serve me and go out with another nigga? I swear to God, if you fuckin' that nigga, I'm stealing off on him. You know I got niggas in low places! And you! You just going to give away what's mine? You got my kids! You better be at fucking home when I get there.

You ain't divorcing me. I said 'til death. I ain't gon' kill you or nothing 'cause I love your stubborn ass. But dammit, Mo, I'll kidnap you!"

The voicemail cut off, giving him a minute to think about what he'd said. "Shit," he huffed, sliding his hand down his face. He hit her name again as he plopped down on the edge of the bed. "I didn't mean that shit, baby. I didn't mean none of it. Come pick up the phone and let's talk this out."

For his sake, the phone died, and the noise of his racing thoughts took over the silence of the room. As he held his head, Austin's breathing was labored, forcing him to fall back on the mattress and do what he should have done hours prior—sleep.

When the morning met him, it was just as unpleasant as his mania-filled night. He staggered to his feet, holding his head, and with squinted eyes, he surveyed the room for his phone. Figuring at some point during the night he kicked it across the room, he abandoned his search for a moment to pull the papers he was served the night before out of the envelope. He flipped through the pages one by one. She didn't ask for the house, the cars, or a percentage of his earnings. Austin knew the heart of the woman he'd spent his life with. The only thing she ever truly required from him was to be a father.

"Mone't Graham requests to retain her name and a schedule adequate to the children, Isabella

Mone't Graham and Austin Graham Jr., wherein custody will be shared between parties and all decisions would be in the best interest of the minors." Austin muttered the words, ignoring the knocking at the door.

As real as the words were printed in black and white, losing his family wasn't a dream or threat. It was real. Standing and dragging his tired bones to the door, he pulled it open without looking through the peephole. The weight of the details of the pending divorce was distracting.

The moment he opened the door, chaos ensued again. The same woman from the club who'd served him the night before was back with a box in her hand. Tempted to slam the door in her face, he swayed.

"Just give it here," he grumbled, figuring it was something from Mone't to further push the dagger into his chest.

"You've been served." She smirked, running her eyes up and down his tattooed frame.

Austin's attention completely shifted once the box was in his hand and opened. It was a positive pregnancy test and a card.

Congratulations, Daddy.
XO, Pandora.

The flash from the camera caught his reaction.

"Are you fuckin' serious!" Slamming the door shut and tossing the box in the trash, he found his phone, plugged it in, and waited impatiently for it to light up with power. Vigorously tapping the screen of his phone, he called his lawyer, who had called him multiple times prior.

"Austin, where have you been, man? I've been calling you. Mone't's lawyer had me served," Clark Roberts rushed out in a frenzy.

It had been a long time since Austin felt like he was spiraling out of control. Everything was mounting on him. "I know. I got served last night in the club. And again this morning."

"She served you again?"

He scrubbed his face in fury. "No, Pandora did. With a pregnancy test and some other shit."

"Are you serious?" Clark asked, exasperated. "Is there a hearing or—"

"I don't fuckin' know, man. You're my lawyer. This shit needs to go the fuck away."

"They've overturned Roe v. Wade, Austin, and we can't kill her . . . can we?"

"Shh. Shut up and calm down. Is it me or you with the issues right now?"

Clark took a beat to compose himself. "You're right. My bad. I'll order a court-appointed test, and if it's positive, I'll order a paternity test."

"Ay, man, listen and hear me good. I cannot put Mone't through any more shit attached to this. Tell her to shut up until it's a fact that the baby is mine."

"I'll handle it. I'll correspond with Mone't's lawyers. She isn't asking for much, so maybe you have a chance."

"I don't have shit until Pandora is out of the picture."

Austin sucked in a deep breath and clamped his eyes shut. Like a freight train, the weight of his actions buckled him. While his name and reputation were being run through the mud, he would return to the empty home without the people who made everything he worked for worth it.

Chapter Sixteen

"You're up late." Aneica's voice floated into Mone't's range.

Slightly looking up from her iPad, Mone't muttered, "I can't really sleep. Figured I'd get up early, cook breakfast, take the kids on a walk, and try to explain to them what's about to happen."

"You filed?" Aneica asked, taking a shot in the dark.

With a slight nod, Mone't returned her attention to the iPad. "Yeah, and he left me like twenty messages. Not to mention my dad called me last night."

Mone't's energy was heavy. She chewed at the corner of her full lips as she tried to keep up her mindless activities on the screen, overpowering all the emotions she was feeling.

Aneica started the coffee and pushed her daughter-in-law to talk more. The more time Mone't spent outside her head, the more she could help herself heal. "How'd that go?"

Mone't shrugged. "I have daddy issues, I guess. I didn't ask Austin for anything but my name and for him to be a father. Not that I doubt that he would, but I don't want Izzy to feel what I've felt for a very long time."

"You had Eman."

"Eman isn't my father, though. It wasn't Eman's job to be my father. It was my father's." Mone't shrugged. "I imagined talking to him would have made me feel better."

"How do you feel?"

"Like my parents fucking failed, and I can't do that to my kids. My relationship with Austin has to be cordial enough to raise them in a healthy environment so they don't feel this. He took the rap for her only for her to turn around and fail at being a mother. Do you know how many times I went up there to see him and he refused to see me? I just want better for them."

"Bouncing them from house to house is better?" Aneica asked as though she hadn't been the one to suggest this course of action to Mone't.

Mone't's brows dipped in response. "It'll be better than me being in a dark space and having them constantly present to fighting. Right now, this is what's best for all of us. Austin needs to get his shit together, and I need to get my shit together. It's simple."

Aneica threw her hands up and yielded to Mone't's words.

"But I have a question for you," Mone't posed, giving her full attention to Aneica. "Who was this man you had in the park around my babies?"

Aneica squinted her eyes.

"Don't do that, Mama. You got something you want to share?"

She shook her head.

"You sure?"

Her response was almost a squeal from a child who'd gotten caught with their hand in the cookie jar. "Mm-hmm. I'm sure. It was just someone I knew once upon a time."

"With six big men?"

"How about you mind someone else's business but mine?" she quipped.

"Lady. Anytime you and the kids go out, you are my business. If Izzy gave me all the tea, she's going to tell her daddy all the tea too, so get ready for that line of questioning."

"I don't have to take this," Aneica replied, pouring herself a cup of coffee and prancing toward the kitchen's exit. "I'm leaving."

"Uh-huh. Don't get caught up with strange men and their security," Mone't called behind her as she stood and prepared AJ's breakfast before a quick meditation on the screened-in porch.

She had found a routine for herself that worked. If she woke up feeling heavy, she found something to occupy her mind. Lots of screen time on her iPad but off of social media seemed to do the trick. Matter of fact, she'd deleted all social media apps from her devices after her breakdown.

Seeing Austin's face, hearing about their issues, were in fact triggers. She was living in the hell created for her so there was no need to have outside opinions haze her thoughts any further. Turning off the noise was imperative. Sometimes when it came to matters of the heart and mental health, the less time you spent with noise, the better. How could Mone't really find herself if she was trapped under the layers of someone else's projections of who she should be?

She was a great mother because she knew what it was to have a horrible one. In the same fashion, Austin was a great father and provider, being that one was never present in his home coming up. They succeeded in those realms so far, but for themselves, there was a lot of room for growth.

As she sat with her legs crossed and her arms open, she inhaled all the things that she could change and exhaled all the things she couldn't control. Austin's manic voice messages were out of her control. He was entitled to feel how he felt. As was she.

His cheating. She couldn't control it nor go back in time and change it. The woman popping up and teasing her with falsehoods, the media calling her everything but a child of God.

She exhaled it all.

She inhaled clarity, spiritual growth, good mental health, self-love, and the ability to be present for herself and her children while they all navigated through this new chapter of their lives.

Unequivocally, Mone't was intentional about being on this path to healing for herself. She desperately needed it. The ever-so-slight buzzing from her phone caused her to crack her eye open. She wasn't expecting a call back so soon in response to her email to Lamont.

Another task added to her list was to fulfill her own dreams and her own destiny. Relying on Austin's money wasn't going to be the soundtrack to her life anymore.

Pulling one last deep inhale in, she released it slowly. She opened her eyes, slowly grounded herself, and answered the phone just in the nick of time. "Hello."

"Mone't Graham." Lamont's voice came through like rich chocolate. He sounded wonderful, and had this been Angie instead of Mone't, she would have been putty, ready for whatever demand he could make.

"I'm assuming you got my email," Mone't replied, standing.

"I did. I figured calling you would get things set in motion faster. Do you have time today to meet up and discuss what I'm looking for?" Lamont asked, making Mone't wince.

"Today? I promised the kids a day with me—"

"All day? Can you break away tonight? We can have a business dinner."

She winced again. Wanting to say no, she heard Robyn's voice in her head urging her to step out of her comfort zone to get what she wanted for herself. Saying yes would be the first step to her professional growth.

"Can you do seven?"

Lamont laughed, a little surprised that she didn't put up much of a fight. "Seven and uptown. Do I need to send a car your way?"

Mone't shook her head as though he could see her.

"Mone't? You there?"

"Y . . . yeah. I'm sorry. A car won't be necessary. I'll drive myself."

"Whoa, Austin isn't sending you with security?" Lamont probed.

Being that he should have known the answer to that question, she laughed it off. "I am a big girl. I am more than capable of moving around this city without security trailing me wherever I go."

Mone't hadn't talked to Musa or Keyston since she moved. Finding the mental space to know more than she did already was anxiety inducing. Her mind would run on tangents about them keeping secrets for him.

"I hear you, big girl," Lamont replied. "I'll let you get to those babies. I'll see you tonight."

"See you then."

"Stop tugging at your dress," Angie hissed over Mone't's shoulder. "You look fine. When is the last time you handled a business meeting solo?"

Angie was bouncing AJ up and down in her arms while Isabella lay across Mone't's lavender bedspread watching cartoons. Although Izzy seemed wrapped up in her TV watching, she heard and saw everything. If Mone't knew how in tune her daughter was, she would have faked her happiness better, concealing her pain with smiles that pained every frown line of her face.

"I haven't." Mone't and Austin's worlds had been so embedded in one another's that leading separate lives was foreign. Mone't putting on a dress and makeup and rubbing her hands over the finger waves of her new 'do felt like an irreversible sin. "This is the first time. Whenever there was something to handle for Austin or one of the businesses, he was there with me, and when he wasn't, Musa or Keyston were always close by." Mone't muttered, "I feel naked."

Angie hummed slightly, cutting her eyes from Izzy to Mone't. "That feeling is mutual, I'm sure. It's necessary, though. This is your first step into the grown-woman you."

"You've made all of this sound so easy, Ang." Mone't's shoulders slumped slightly. The last twenty-four hours had been a roller-coaster ride for her.

"I've had no other option but to adjust all my life. I practically raised myself. Every step is intentional, and everything has to be set with some sort of intention. If you don't do that, you could be walking in circles, picking up the same ol' thing. No growth, no milestones, just the same misery."

"A hamster wheel."

"Precisely. I know this, all of this, is the very last thing you wanted to do, but trust yourself, Mo. You got this."

Angie could've given her unsolicited advice that would further damage her healing. She didn't. Her growth was dependent on Mo's. As long as Mone't was used to the rut and comfortable with it, Angie would be comfortable with hers. Angie and Mone't sharpened each other. They were each only as strong as the other.

For a while, Angie was the one Mone't leaned on. The time would come when Mone't would need to plant herself in the soil, allowing her roots to run deep and be the one Angie leaned on.

Oftentimes women saw each other as competition, not partners through life. What the duo had was sacred. Their love, faithfulness, and respect for one another would outlive most marriages and relationships.

Mone't smiled faintly at her reflection in the mirror. The sight looking back at her was new. Every day she grew into another version of herself she hadn't dreamt of, from her reflection to the small Rolex Presidential on her wrist. Mone't pivoted on the balls of her designer-heeled feet.

"I'll see you when I get back."

"Mommy, don't be long," Izzy spoke up after listening for the duration of the conversation. Izzy's expression mirrored Aneica's all-knowing brow raise with the pointed glare.

Chuckling softly to herself, Mone't kissed the top of Isabella's head and trampled over toys on her way to the door. "I won't. I promise. Please be good for Auntie Ang."

Isabella smiled wide, which told Mone't all she needed to know. Angie was going to have her niece hyped up on candy as they rummaged through her closet and put on a mini fashion show. It was inevitable. Before Mone't could fully make her exit, she blew a kiss to AJ.

The drive from the quaint suburban house to the restaurant felt long and agonizing. Mone't's heart thundered out of her chest with every mile closer. But the walk up the mural-painted sidewalk to the large oak doors of the restaurant was sure to do her in.

Although this was a business meeting, her mind couldn't stop reminiscing about Austin walking on her left-hand side. Musa and Keyston would be flanked in front and behind while he interlocked his fingers in hers. It had been so long since they had those stolen moments.

The warm breeze of the summer night caused her to shudder. Her memories would need to lie dormant for a night until Mone't had time to entertain them. She didn't have time right now.

The host pushed the door open upon Mone't's foot hitting the first concrete step. "Good evening, Mrs. Graham. Mr. Wright is anticipating your arrival. If you'll follow me."

Briefly, Mone't looked to her left as if Austin were there to put his large hand on the small of her back and walk step in step with her. Snapping out of it, she tilted her chin upward and let a small smile ripple over her lips.

The cadence of her red bottoms alerted Lamont, who was tucked in a corner booth that overlooked the restaurant. He slid out and stood to his feet. Easily, he towered over Mone't. Being used to looking up, she plastered the most genuine smile she could on her face.

Mone't's lonely senses tried to ignore the scent of his cologne and the way his tailored suit draped perfectly over his long limbs. Lamont opened his arms to greet her. Mone't held her hand out, which led to an awkward standoff, making each of them switch greetings, fumbling with arms and hands.

"I'm sorry," she quickly apologized.

Lamont laughed, waving it off. "Don't worry about it. I'm happy you could join me."

Mone't slid into the booth, placing her clutch in the empty spot next to her. "If I haven't learned anything else about money, you answer when it calls."

"I like that." Lamont's eyes lingered on Mone't's upper body a second longer than they should've. Most basketball wives were beautiful. No one was Mone't. There was a soft beauty about her that was striking and even paralyzing at times.

"So." Mone't cleared her throat to break his ogling. "Who are these clients you're trying to woo, and what do you need from me?"

"For starters?" Lamont quizzed.

Mone't nodded. "For starters."

"Dinner. I've selected some things off the menu for you to try. I've had a long day, and I can't focus until my tank is at least halfway full," Lamont stated. "I also want to host them here the first night they arrive, so I'd like you to be familiar with the restaurant."

Unbeknownst to Lamont, this restaurant was one of her favorites. Perhaps that was the reason why she was plagued with the memories of her husband at every turn. She was out of her element without him, but faking it for the duration of this meeting was bound to carry her through it without incident.

Mone't nodded. "All right. Then I should let you know that I know the menu like the back of my hand. The hosts know me by name. I suggest either renting it completely out for your guests or hosting them in the private room."

Lamont relaxed slightly, letting his back sink into the plushness of the high-back velvet seating. A satisfied smirk caused a dimple to pierce his chocolate cheek. "I underestimated you."

"Most do." *Husband included.*

Lamont threw his hands up. "I apologize."

Mone't laughed. It wasn't hearty, and it didn't make her small eyes shut while she fought tears. But nevertheless, it was a smile she didn't have to force. "It's no problem really. People see my name or me and instantly think 'NBA wife' along with all that entails. I'm just a girl from Fiftieth and McClendon."

"I understand that. I got drafted here from Glendale, and everyone thought I wasn't a name to remember."

"It happens."

Small talk turned into a full-blown conversation over seared duck, couscous, broccolini, sweet potato soufflé, and various wines. Mone't effortlessly curated a menu while listening to Lamont talk about how each jeweler had a taste for rich, decadent dishes.

The plates were cleared, and the conversation hadn't dropped a beat. Mone't wrote off her gift of gab in this instance as work, but there was something about Lamont Wright that made it easy for her to forget her troubles and focus on the task at hand.

The chiming of her phone broke her stride of confidence. Foolishly, in the height of her mania, she set alerts. Anytime Austin's name was in the media, she'd get an alert. Outside of him turning up in the club and getting ejected from the game, she wasn't cringing at the tone of the chime.

It was apparent that Lamont had gotten the same alert. As Austin's wife and the general manager, they were invested in his every move. Lamont had a financial stake in him, while Mone't had an emotional, spiritual, mental, and physical stake. That was far more expensive than any amount of money.

Hesitantly, Lamont pulled his phone from the inside of his jacket pocket. The screen illuminated his face. Mone't found herself holding her breath as he read the post. By the dip of his brow, she knew it wasn't good.

Having to see it for herself, she opened her clutch and retrieved the device that would be the source of her agony for tonight.

"Mone't, don't look at it."

"Please," she huffed. "You aren't married to him. I have to."

Shady Palms was the first to report the heart-wrenching news, and then a flood of other non-credible blog posts reported their tea as well. Mone't frantically scrolled through the mentioned blogs to see if she saw *Love, Angie.*

Fallen King Austin Has Fathered a Child with IG Model Pandora Herrera

Unwelcome tears sprang to Mone't's eyes. She gasped before remembering where she was. Her eyes snapped up to Lamont, who was looking at her with concern. The rest of the restaurant seemed to be avoiding eye contact with her while they whispered to one another.

Mone't swiped her tongue over her painted lips and quickly fluttered any remnants of heartbreak from her eyes. The forced smile was back. "I'm going to email you everything we discussed and get the flight chartered and the hotel rooms booked. Gift bags will be in each room upon arrival."

As she rushed the words out of her mouth, she stuffed her phone in her clutch and disregarded the complimentary mints she loved while she fumbled for her keys. Lamont reached his long arm over the white-linen-capped table to stop her.

"Slow down."

"I'm okay. Really. I'm just going to get home to my babies."

"At least let me walk you—"

"Lamont, really, I'm fine." She faked being okay so well it was second nature. She expected him to leave her to her troubles. Against what she thought he would do, Lamont slid out of the booth, stepped to her side, and held his hand out.

"Let me walk you to your car. No matter how much of a big girl you are, even big girls deserve protection."

The spiking emotions threatened to spill over and make a mess of her in this establishment. Mone't didn't give his gesture any further thought. She put her hand in his and allowed his large frame to block looks and camera phones inside and outside of the restaurant.

His car was waiting curbside, ready to take her to the nearby parking garage. She climbed in, refusing to look at the people who were gathered outside, gossiping about her crumbled marriage while waiting to get into the restaurant.

Mone't was determined to hold it together until she was alone. That was unrealistic. She rubbed her hands over one another. The parking garage was just around the corner, but it seemed like it took forever.

Lamont reached over to settle the wringing of her hands. For a moment, they looked at one another. When eye contact broke, Mone't was a second from breaking away herself. She didn't wait for Lamont's driver to open the door. She pushed the door open and hopped out. Without uttering another word, she quickened to her SUV, climbed inside, sparked the engine, and sped to her reprieve.

Chapter Seventeen

"You've reached the voicemail of 640-555-9898. Please leave a message after the beep." The beep resounded around the SUV Mone't was gifted for her twenty-third birthday.

She'd been parked in the driveway for over thirty minutes, and the news of her husband had her calling him back-to-back. She hoped he would answer so she could tell him this. She wished she had the strength to return to their home and tell him this face-to-face. Austin needed to see the damage his actions continued to cause to her mental and emotional well-being.

This was a continuous spiral, and despite having people huddled around who were invested in her healing and her growth, she felt trapped and alone. In the darkest room, she was an angry beast desperately searching for a reprieve of some sort.

"You dirty-dick motherfucker! Are you serious? Not only do you cheat on me and come home to me, you didn't even bother to be safe. I was nice in the request for dissolution, Austin! If you brought me anything from that nasty-ass whore of yours, I swear I'll take everything from you and set it on fire!"

Every syllable was said through gnashed teeth into the stiff air with strings of spit accompanying them. Her eyes were rimmed with red. Her nostrils were the same. Mone't was on an emotional roller coaster that had her bound and wouldn't stop slinging her round and round.

"I gave you everything, Austin. And without question you throw my life away like this?"

Her voice broke. Tears escaped, and the pain she tried to push down every day was bubbling to the surface like reflux.

"What do I have now, Austin? Hm. Tell me. I can't believe you'd do this to us. While I'm like this. I tried to be everything you needed, and everything I am—was—wasn't enough for you. You were probably better off killing me. Because this is bound to. This has to stop."

Mone't's anger went from loud and raging to just above a whisper as the automated voice told her the space in the voicemail was now full. Vigorously wiping her face, she groaned in agony. There was a soul-piercing, heart-wrenching pain that no one could erase from her chest. It hurt.

She hurt.

She could cut her hair, put on makeup, dress herself in the most expensive linens, but with every step she took, she was constantly reminded of the pain she was having to endure, not solely from Austin, but the pain she inflicted on herself.

"Make it stop," she cried. "Please just make this stop. I can't take this shit. It's one thing after another after another after another. What's it going to take, huh? What's it going to take?"

No one was in the car to hear her, but her cries didn't fall on deaf ears, and as long as she kept pushing, she wouldn't be alone. Resting her forehead on the steering wheel, she sobbed until the handle of the door was being pulled on. A stream of brown and black makeup liquified by tears and snot ran down her face.

At the door was Angie. Being the empath she was, tears were cradled in her eyes too. She could make Mone't's life away from Austin a vacation, but it wouldn't take her pain from her. It would only distract her for a moment. What Mone't was experiencing was all-consuming.

"Unlock the door, Mo," Angie calmly coaxed Mone't.

"Angie, leave me alone."

"I'm not doing that. I saw the posts."

Mone't scoffed, her anger and sorrow being misdirected to Angie. "You probably knew about that shit too, didn't you?"

"You know me better than that. I called Robyn. She's on the way. We can do this in the house or in the car. It doesn't matter."

"Why would you call her? Angie, I'm—"

"Fine? This is fine? You screaming in the car for thirty minutes isn't fine. This is heartbreaking. Don't push me away, Mo. Open the door."

Mone't refused. Her stubbornness was front and center. The many facets of her personality and grief were interchanging, taking their spot center stage to effectively convey Mone't's sorrow.

"Mone't."

"Go away, Angie."

Angie had a stubbornness that could rival Mone't's. She refused to leave Mone't until this mess of their marriage was cleaned up. Not Aneica, Angie, Musa, nor Keyston were going to step off until Mone't and Austin were healed and back in their rightful positions.

"All right, fine. We can play this game all night," Angie grumbled, walking away from the car as Robyn's sports car pulled into the driveway behind Mone't's. She was blocked in between Angie's car and Robyn's. In a few seconds, she'd be in for a rude awakening when Angie returned with the spare key fob.

Mone't swiped the back of her hand over her makeup-smeared face. Angie returned with the key fob, unlocking the car for Robyn to climb into the front seat. Angie took the spot in the middle seat of the second row and settled into the silence.

"I'm fine."

"Maybe not right now, but you will be. So let's talk through it," Robyn coached. "What are you feeling?"

After a pause, Mone't finally said, "It won't stop." Her voice was so weighted with discomfort. Her entire being was uncomfortable. Her chest ached, her throat burned, and her soul hurt. "The constant pain. The reminders. I can't even tell myself how to get from point A to B. One step. 'Just take one step, Mone't.' And when I take a step, I feel him. I see him. At the nucleus of who I am, there is him. Consuming how I feel. I want off this ride. I want him to sign the papers and get on."

"And then what?" Robyn asked in response to Mone't's reflection. "He moves on, goes and lives his life, and what do you have? I'm not referring to work or your children, but you. Can you live with yourself like this if Austin does what you tell him to?"

Mone't opened her mouth to answer, but no sound came out. Her mind began its trickery, quickly flashing the memories. The gunshots, the rapid thrust into stardom, the children, the adjustments they never adjusted to, the hope, and the thing that broke the safest place they knew.

Comfort and safety were found in the rut and stagnated growth of a couple who was projected to take over the world together. Money didn't contribute to their growth. It hindered it.

Mone't's phone began to ring out, startling their pause. Mone't clamped her mouth closed. She unblocked Austin to cuss him out only for him to be blowing up her line again. His signature ringtone called out over and over again before Mone't fumbled with the device to silence the call and block him. She answered instead.

"Mone't, baby." Austin's pained grunt froze her. "Mo."

The tears puddled in her eyes.

"You got to talk to me at some point. We have—"

"Kids?" she whispered. "You seem to have a new addition."

"I only have two. With you. That's it. It's just us, Mo."

"But it's not. It's you and her."

Austin groaned, muffling his sorrow the same way Mone't tried to. "It's me and you. That's forever. It's tattooed."

"I can cover that up, Austin."

Her words made him unable to speak for a moment, and then he said, "You could, but you won't."

"Sign the papers."

"No."

"Austin—"

"No. It's been me and you, and it'll be me and you. I'm going to fix this, baby. Just come home so I can."

"I'm not coming back. This is done. Sign the papers, please."

"I love you, Mo. Not enough to let you go, but enough to stay and go through all of this."

Finding the strength to hang up, she pushed the driver's door open and slid out. When her heeled feet hit the concrete, she slowly dragged herself into the house. Everything she was carrying weighed a ton. In pursuit of a break, she found an open bottle of wine and hiked up the stairs.

She shut herself away from the world and drank until she fell asleep. Hopefully, in the morning, she wouldn't remember the dreams that plagued her through the night.

Chapter Eighteen

"I don't know if it's a pleasure having you tonight, Jermel. A lot of controversy has been attached to your name. You lose your biggest client because you doubled down?" the host of *SportsTalk* sounded off throughout the lobby of the front office.

It was a massive building that housed trophies, rings, and retired jerseys to include Lamont Wright and Francesco De Luca. Austin attempted to study the grind of the past players. They had grit and tenacity, and although he didn't want to see himself in any of the old heads, he saw in Francesco his form, footwork, and hands in the post. If Austin didn't know better, he would assume he was a carbon copy of the legend.

However, his nerves had the best of him. Between his pending meeting and his ex-agent talking shit on every available TV throughout the lobby, there wasn't much focus left in him.

Jermel's arrogant laugh made his teeth grit with anger.

"Should've thrown his bitch ass in a lake," Keyston muttered to himself as he hoisted his body off the plush leather armchair.

He's a fuckin' bitch, Austin thought. It was important for him, more so now than ever, to present himself as put together and controlled.

"Double down? I didn't double down. My ex-client was controlled by his wife. You saw her beastly behavior weeks ago. I only spoke the truth. She wanted Pandora in their bed, and she played the broken-hearted wife well."

Jermel's words seeped into Austin's head. He regretted not protecting Mone't the way he should've when Jermel was around. There wasn't a night without her that he didn't see in his mind the angst and irritation on her face when he spoke.

"You ready for this meeting?" Musa asked, studying Austin's ragged appearance. It was evident he needed a distraction from the bullshit being spewed on the TV.

"I'm good," he said, shrugging Musa's hand off his shoulder.

"Bullshit," Keyston grumbled, standing in front of the coffee station and pressing random buttons on the machines. "Mone't called him last night. Nigga been in his feelings all night behind it. Surprised I haven't caught his ass sliding down a wall with a glass of red wine in his hand."

"Shut up, nigga," Austin spat.

"Damn," Musa grumbled, his eyes focused on the screen of his phone. "You about to be in your feelings a lot more."

Keyston scoffed. "I doubt it. Look at him. Looking like ass, and he's about to walk in to meet with Lamont."

Musa winced. "Say, man, can we reschedule this emergency meeting?"

Keyston kissed his teeth and pointed his fingers at Musa. "You straight, man? You're sounding like me right about now. How is he going to reschedule an emergency meeting?"

Musa grimaced and handed his phone to Keyston while Austin was nervously pacing and running his hands down his tie. In the opinion of his boys, he was too big to be so nervous, to be fidgeting, to look like anything other than the king he was meant to be.

Keyston's expression tried to stay the same, but he failed. "This is some shit here."

Austin stopped for a moment to peer over at the men he revered as brothers. They peered back, both swallowing the lumps in their throats.

"What?"

"Nothing," they both responded.

Keyston slid Musa's phone into his pocket discreetly. They were careful not to alarm him with the recent spotting of his wife. Her being hand in hand with another man was bound to send him into a frenzy.

"Yo, stop playing with me. What's going on? Mama good?"

They nodded.

Austin took a step closer. "My kids?"

Keyston took the lead. "Your kids are good."

"They're healthy, too," Musa added.

"What's wrong with Mone't? She text you? I know she didn't sound good last night, but is she okay?"

Neither Keyston nor Musa had time to answer before Austin was fully closing in the space between them. "Is she okay?"

"She's—"

He didn't want to hear that she was fine. He heard her voicemails last night. Played them over and over when she hung up. He heard the tremble in her voice when she spoke, even through the anger. He knew her cadence, and as much as he bypassed her well-being, he knew the disparity in her voice. Regardless of how many times she served him or shouted she wanted to be without him or read him for filth, he knew her. And he knew they were better together than apart. They always had been.

Austin's phone was constantly going off in the jacket pocket of his sage green tailored suit. Musa and Keyston stiffened their spines as Austin reached for it.

"Bro, stay off your phone until after this meeting," Musa spoke up.

"Nah, it could be Mo," Austin said, rejecting him.

"It's Mo all right," Keyston muttered, making Musa nudge him.

"Shut up, nigga," Musa hissed.

Austin peeked at his phone until he landed on the images everyone else had seen: Mone't hand in hand with the man he was set to meet with in mere minutes. His face glowed red.

"This what y'all keeping from me?" His words came out in a growl. "That nigga fuckin' her?"

Musa and Keyston stood silent while Austin's worst nightmare played out in his mind, unhinging him by the second.

"Is that nigga in there fuckin' my wife?" His nostrils flared and his orbs bounced wildly.

"Mr. Graham, Mr. Wright will see you now in the main conference room." The shrill voice of an older woman brought Austin back just for a second.

He pivoted, adjusted his jacket and tie, and started marching toward the conference room. Musa and Keyston quickened on his heels. Keyston reached him and attempted to halt his stride.

Austin roared, "Get the fuck off of me!"

Musa had planted himself in front of Austin to block him from barging into the conference room and making a fool of himself, his woman, and his family. His behavior on and off the court had gotten him attention he didn't want, need, or like, and he'd fed the fire with gasoline every step of the way.

"You don't show not one motherfucker that they got one up on you. Keep your fucking head," Musa said just above a whisper. "Heavy is the head who wears the crown. Kings go to war every day, nigga. You gon' win, or you gon' let these snakes take you out?"

Austin's emotions were as all over the place as Mone't's had been. He wasn't in a position to react emotionally. Not now anyway. "I'm good," he replied, rubbing his hand down his navy tie. "I'm good."

"You sure?" Keyston asked.

Austin stepped around them and made his way into the conference room. Around the table were Lamont, Francesco, and now-minority owner Gerald Bennington. As much as it infuriated him to make eye contact with every man at the table, he did. Swallowing the lump in his throat, he greeted them as a whole. "Gentlemen."

"Austin Graham," Lamont spoke up, a knowing grin shimmying across his lips. "Please take a seat."

He did, graciously playing the game for the powers that be. Austin had one chess move that would shut this entire operation down, but he chose to hold it close to his chest until it was time for checkmate.

"I'm sure you know why we called this meeting today," Gerald spoke right before Lamont began to talk.

"Your behavior on and off the court is not one that aligns with our core values. When we drafted you—"

"When we drafted you"—Gerald cut Lamont off with both his words and a sharp glance of the eyes—"we drafted a family man. A Cinderella story. From the hood to the Hills. You and your wife had your shit together. Your personal life was personal. Whatever proclivities you and your wife shared weren't on our screens, in the gossip column, or in our press conference every day. This is unacceptable."

"What my long-winded friend is saying," Lamont said, taking his power back, "is if you don't pull your shit together, you'll be traded to Whitestone, where careers go to die. I am expecting you to pull this championship out of your ass and get your home in order."

Lamont's closing remarks made Austin chuckle. His orbs lifted to Lamont's smug expression. Lamont thought that the night before with Mone't was something to hold over his head.

"Get my home in order?" Austin quizzed as he nodded coolly. "I'll do that. You stay away from her. I'll do exactly what you suggest. Gerald, Francesco, good day."

He rose from the table, towering over everyone who remained sitting. Francesco was the only one who stood to shake his hand. As annoying as Austin deemed his recurring presence to be, he accepted. Francesco had welcomed him into the league. Against Jermel's advice, Austin had followed Francesco's business suggestions and secured his future for his children's children.

Although Austin showed a cool demeanor, he was reeling on the inside. He wasn't going to stand toe-to-toe with Lamont. It wasn't worth it. However, he was going to go get his wife, regardless of what she said. Mone't had never let another man touch her in an intimate way, and in his quick study of the photos, he could see her distress.

The hard-bottom soles of his Italian designer dress shoes beat against the shiny ceramic floors. His phone was pressed to his ear as he breezed past Musa and Keyston. They joined him in stride until they got to the parking lot.

"Angie, I'm not asking you. Send me her location."

"A . . . Austin. Come on. You think something is going to change?"

"Angie, I'm calling you and not a private investigator," Austin stated firmly. "Send me the location."

"Are you coming over here to harass her or to get her back?"

"What you think?"

Angie released a sigh of relief. "Are you sure? Austin, she's fragile and—"

"Angie." Austin's tone was firm and direct. She had no other choice but to give him what he wanted, or he would use his power and means to find Mone't himself.

"I sent it."

"All right, good looking," he replied before hanging up and stepping into the elevator. "We're headed to Mone't's. I'm sure y'all know the location."

Shortly after leaving the front office, they arrived across town at Mone't's modest Brentwood home. Upon parking the car, Keyston stayed still, waiting for Austin to make his move. Austin's mind was going a million miles a minute, but the agonizing visual of another man having access to her thrust him over the edge.

Jumping out of the car, Austin took long, quick strides to the door. He knocked heavily on the door. "Open up, Mo!"

He waited five seconds before repeating the request. He spotted the Ring doorbell. The ring itself illuminated from gray to blue. He leaned over, face-to-face with the camera. "Open this door, Mo! You hand in hand with niggas now? Got me being dragged into closed-door meetings where that fuck-ass nigga thinks he can tell me how to handle shit with my wife? But you hand in hand with him, laughing and cheesing in the restaurant? Bring your ass to this door, Mo. If you thought I was signing them papers, baby, you out your goddamn mind!"

Austin walked away from the door and pivoted. He hit the button again, although the live recording prevented it from chiming. "You got me fucked up, baby. Fucked up! I know I messed up. Bad. I know I did. But I'm telling you, the bitch is lying!" With every word, his voice got higher. "This ain't how you get me back. You don't take your sexy little ass out with my GM! With the Nia Long shit you got going on. Where is your hair, Mo? Where is it? I don't know where you left it at, but you better go get it!"

Austin pointed down the street. Musa and Keyston were now outside of the car, leaning on the hood, getting a hearty laugh at his expense. Austin twirled in a circle and tapped the camera with his finger.

"Okay, I'm tripping, baby," he laughed. "I'm buggin'. You got me out here tripping, baby. I ain't shit without you, Mo. I ain't shit, baby. This how you wanted me? Broken down? A'ight, you win. I'm coming back here every day now until you let me in."

Austin used all his willpower to turn around and walk back to the car in lieu of kicking Mone't's door in. With his mouth balled up, he stomped to the car and climbed into the back seat. He pulled his tie from around his neck and glared out the window. Mone't was upstairs in the window. He could see her through the sheer curtain. His heart fell and shattered. Feeling his lip quiver, Austin dropped his head and let a few tears fall from his eyes. He was no longer alone.

"You ain't gotta hold it together for us, nigga. That hurt to watch. Fucking funny, but hard. Let that shit out, nigga," Musa spoke up.

What was waiting for Austin when he got home was going to be the turning point he needed. He and Mone't were on a continuum of insanity, and someone had to swoop in and reset the natural balance of things.

In his unbuttoned shirt, overgrown Caesar cut, and facial hair, Austin looked like exactly what he felt like: shit. He dragged his body through the house into the kitchen in search of a drink. He had no business drinking. In two short days, he would be back on the court, playing the final stretch of the championship.

"Why you hanging yo' head, little nigga?"

A baritone voice hit Austin's ears like a freight train. He snapped his attention to the breakfast table his children once occupied.

Austin squinted at the sight of Eman bigger than he remembered. Three years had flown by, and he didn't even know he was up for early release. How could he, when Mone't spearheaded the entire thing?

"Eman. I ain't tripping, right?" Austin asked, stepping in his direction. "You really home?"

"Yeah, nigga. You'd know that if you came to check on a nigga every once in a while," Eman responded.

Austin's shoulders slumped in response.

"Cut that shit out. Change your fucking clothes. Ain't no drinking. Your game is sloppy, and your life is a mess. This ain't what I meant when I said take care of her. I didn't go back in for this to be the result, young'un."

Musa and Keyston smirked. Musa had effortlessly overseen Eman's appeal and release while Austin fought, lost, tried again, and won. While Mone't was going through the motions, Musa made sure that what was meant to be together was going to return itself to wholeness. They were a family, and no one would win if the family feuded.

"Wait, y'all knew he was coming out?" Austin asked, still in disbelief.

"Damn, if you can't believe it, Mone't is going to lose her fuckin' mind when she sees me," Eman said with a chuckle. "This is a nice place you built for her. Seems like the only thing you missing is her."

Austin licked his dry lips and nodded. "Yeah, I fucked up."

"Nigga, that goes without saying. I know you got a basketball court in this castle. We headed there.

I've eaten, slept, and eaten again. It's time to get this shit back on track."

Like Austin was a young boy back in the hood, he clung to Eman's words. He didn't know his father, but Eman was a close replacement for what he needed. Even if he was still trying to figure life out on his own, Eman was a guiding light.

Austin trekked out of the kitchen after releasing Eman from a long-overdue embrace. Everything in him wanted to call Mone't and tell her the news, but he couldn't. He knew without a doubt he was blocked, and after his psychotic behavior on her porch, she more than likely deleted his number.

Clad in a team-issued tank and basketball shorts, Austin found himself mid-court in a game of one-on-one with Eman.

"You got some celebrity in your belt and forgot how to hoop like it's street ball," Eman spoke low, controlling the ball and keeping Austin from it. "Offense and defense. That's what I taught you. Too fucking big to be a bitch nigga on the floor."

Eman drove past Austin, knocking him down in the process.

"Get up!" Eman shouted. "This game is going to knock you down. Life is going to knock you down. You keep getting up!" Eman returned to center court. "You the king, right? Take the rock."

Austin focused in and dug deep to take what belonged to him to the hoop, but Eman outhustled him again.

"This life is going to hustle you. You got to keep up. You got to keep your eyes open. You should have seen that hustle from a mile away. When you take your eyes off the rock for a second, they always slip through."

Eman stepped back and made a three-pointer. "Go get my ball. This is my court now. I'm your daddy. Every time you take your eyes off it, something slips through. Your wife. Your kids. Your business."

Austin jogged behind the ball and checked it back in. He didn't utter a word, his soul thirsty, his ears grasping the knowledge.

"You fall down, you get back up. You're down in one quarter, you play better in the next. This is your life. Play like you own it. Niggas like Jermel and Pandora are out to take you for your check. Keep your eyes on the rock."

Eman stole the ball from Austin and took it back to the hoop. "Every time you get distracted, it'll cost you. Tonight, it's sleep. I'm going to play you until you can't move no more."

Eman and Austin played until Austin outscored and outhustled Eman. The final shot was made, and Eman pounded his palms together. "That's what I'm talking about. Now tomorrow the real work begins."

"We doing this again?"

"Nah, we're cleaning up your image and shutting down these capping-ass bitches. Then you're going to get my sister back home. She shouldn't be living on her own with two small kids because you can't tuck your dick away."

Chapter Nineteen

"Izzy, let's put the puzzles away and get ready for lunch," Mone't announced as she walked into the extra bedroom she'd converted into the playroom.

Today was tough. Outside of her day-to-day challenges with herself, Izzy only wanted her father, only wanted to listen if the directive came from her father, and Mone't was at her wits' end with it. The gentle parenting approach had been something she succeeded at until today.

Isabella huffed and stomped her tiny feet around the spaced painted in primary colors. AJ rested on Mone't's hip, gnawing on his chunky fist. He babbled through the bubbles of his saliva and clung tightly to Mone't with his free hand.

"Don't act up, little girl," Mone't warned, squatting down to put AJ on his blanket. It instantly induced a set of agitated whines from AJ. He hadn't let her go since the night before.

"Mommy, why can't we go home? When is Daddy coming?" Izzy whined in sync with her brother.

Mone't wrestled with both of her children, her own agitation setting in. She refused to dwell on it. Voice notes from Robyn reminded her to not dwell in the turmoil and instead look outward. She had no idea what that meant, but she was going to try like hell today to see where that got her. So far, living outside of her head was just as chaotic as being inside of it.

"Daddy is working, Izzy. Baby, you know this. Please put the puzzles away." Mone't attempted again to get her husband's look-alike to do what she needed to do.

"Mama would let me play," Izzy sassed, pushing Mone't further to the edge.

"Isabella Mone't Graham, pick these puzzles up now, put them away, and then bring your little behind downstairs for lunch."

"No!"

Mone't's head snapped back, and her tiny nostrils flared open with shock at the audacity of her daughter's defiance. She quickly recalled the times when she pushed against her mother and was met with some form of punishment. Spankings were hard and long, always resulting in raw welts on Mone't's legs and butt. When she got older, it was a backhand across the face and a challenge to fight. She never had the option of turning down the fight. She had to fight her mother. Isabella saved Mone't from that cycle of abuse she rarely spoke of.

She governed herself. It was easy to snatch Isabella up, spank her, and make her do what she wanted. But Mone't knew the lingering effects that her mother's discipline had on her. She still suffered from her mothering.

"Isabella." Aneica's stern voice shattered the thick glass of tension between mother and daughter. "I believe your mother told you to clean up these puzzles and go downstairs for lunch."

Isabella froze in place, orbs bouncing from grandmother to mother.

"And if I ever hear you tell your mother no again, you can cancel puzzles, books, and playdates. Apologize."

"I'm sorry, Mommy," Isabella muttered as she cleaned her mess.

Mone't closed her eyes and took a deep breath before slowly releasing it. "Thank you."

"Don't mention it," Aneica responded, reaching for AJ. "I'm going to take them out for a playdate after lunch. Your phone has been blowing up."

Aneica and Mone't traded the baby for her phone. "You might need to handle that."

"Are they going to see . . ."

Aneica shook her head. "We all need each other, regardless of the circumstances. Sometimes it's twirling on the porch and shouting in the Ring camera or outside in the car cussing them out on the voicemail. Whatever the communication, hearts are fighting to get back to one another."

"Is there anything you don't know?" Mone't asked with a squint.

Aneica smirked and waved her off. "If I were to tell you all that I know, you'd miss another work call and possibly a contract. Go."

Mone't lingered momentarily before pulling herself away from her children and mother-in-law. Once she was inside her room, she tapped Lamont's name on the screen and placed the phone on the countertop of the bathroom.

"You are one hard woman to get in contact with," he responded with a tinge of frustration in his voice.

"Two children are a handful. Are you calling about the confirmations I sent over?"

"No, those are perfect. I have a last-minute meeting in Oakridge. There's a luncheon I need your skills for."

"Okay, I can make some phone calls and have that done. I'll invoice the—"

"In person. It's just a day trip. We'll be there and back. I'm headed to the airport now. Can you meet me?"

"It doesn't sound like I have much of an option, Mr. Wright."

"Lamont," he corrected her. "I'd prefer your presence. It seems to make the passing time worth it."

Mone't's eyes dropped to the screen, and her brow rose. She wasn't one to let someone run game on her, but it felt good to be appreciated, even if it was just for business. "I can swing a day trip, but I need to be back to tuck them in."

"I promise you we will. I'll send a car to come get you. See you soon."

He ended the call before she could object. An audible huff pushed from her lips as she pulled the silk scarf from her hair. She'd be trading in her comfortable matching leggings set for a dress, a pair of heels, and a soft beat that would be able to combat the summer heat.

Almost thirty minutes later, she was clad in a beautiful formfitting canary yellow dress and metallic gold Tom Ford lock heels. She was stunning. If only she could see how breathtaking she was, everyone in her path would be subjected to bowing at her feet.

Packing her Christian Dior tote with her backup sandals, iPad, cosmetics bag, and phone accessories, she headed down to the kitchen, where her tiny family was gathered around the countertop, eating sandwiches and listening to a children's audiobook.

Aneica's attention landed on Mone't and skated up and down her attire. Aneica would rather Mone't be a little more covered up, but Mone't's body was that of a giving grown woman, and hiding womanly curves wasn't the easiest feat. Her expression was unreadable as a soft smile crossed her lips. "You look good. Meeting?"

"Yeah. I'll be back by the time they have to go to bed, or sooner."

Aneica hummed and nodded her head. Her lips were pursed together in her signature disapproving glint.

"Smell yummy, too," Izzy chimed in, enjoying the softness of Mone't's signature scent. "You going to see Daddy?"

Mone't ignored Aneica's look and let a gentle smile cross her lips before placing a kiss in the nest of Isabella's curls. "No, not today. I have to go to work. Auntie Angie will be back this afternoon with pizza."

"Pepperoni?" Izzy asked excitedly.

Mone't rounded the table to kiss AJ's cheeks. "You know it. Are you going to behave while I'm away?"

"Yes, Mommy," Izzy responded. "When you get back, can we please see Daddy?"

Mone't's eyes met Aneica's. "We can arrange it, okay?"

The doorbell chimed, signaling Mone't's ride to the airport.

"Mommy, you promise? I saw him yesterday at the door. He looked mad. And you're sad. Can't we go home?" Her jawline tightened, prompting her to suck in a sharp breath.

"I promise. I love y'all. Please act right. I'll be back in time to read you a book and tuck you in."

Mone't's tone was dipped in sadness. Whether she liked it or not, she would have to sit down and have a conversation with Austin about their children bouncing back and forth. The effect of this pending divorce was starting to take shape in Isabella's behavior. That was the last thing Mone't wanted for her children.

"Okay, Mommy. Be good too."

"Yeah," Aneica chimed along with the doorbell again. "Be good."

Mone't gave Aneica a smirk before blowing the kids another kiss and scurrying to the door. A suited driver was on the other side with a smile on his face. "Ms. Graham."

"Mrs." Correcting her title was second nature. The moment she realized she did it, she snapped her mouth shut. "I'm sorry."

"Don't be. This way. Mr. Wright is on the private jet awaiting your arrival."

Mone't coached herself to take one step and then another and another until she was safely strapped into the back seat on her way to the airport.

Mone't: Headed to Oakridge for a day meeting. Can you grab pepperoni pizza for the kids?

Angie: What about you? Super Supreme and wine?

Mone't: You know it!

Angie: Bring me back some tea.

Mone't chuckled to herself and tilted her head back and closed her eyes. Sleep came like a thief in the night. She didn't realize she'd drifted off until the driver announced their arrival. Quickly checking her appearance in her compact she retrieved from her bag, she reapplied a fresh layer of nude lipstick and waited for her door to be opened.

Lamont met her at the foot of the stairs. He tugged at the knot of his tie, his temperature instantly rising when he spotted her. Clearing his throat, he waited until she got closer to greet her. "Thank you for joining me."

Mone't smiled kindly, her eyes barely visible behind the mascara and her cheeks. "You didn't give me much of a choice."

Lamont smirked evenly. "I did. You chose what I would have."

"And that's, what, working?"

"No, spending time together, because whether or not you want to admit it, I make you smile."

She tucked her lip between her teeth, feeling warmth flutter throughout her. It felt wrong to enjoy being in another man's presence. She recalled how Austin shouted and cursed the day before because of the photos. Her taking action to feel anything was bound to kill him.

She couldn't focus on what he wanted or how he would feel. She was looking outward, and Lamont was right. She hated to admit that someone else made her feel good. Even if it was for a tiny wrinkle in time.

Instead of answering, Mone't took it upon herself to board the sizeable private jet and find a comfortable window seat. She texted Angie and Aneica to let them know she would soon be wheels up. Placing her phone on airplane mode and stowing her bag, she looked out the window.

The two didn't exchange words until the plane had successfully taken off and was at cruising altitude. The flight attendant made her rounds with a flute of chilled champagne for her and neat glasses of whiskey for him.

"Who is the client?" she inquired, post the thankful nod to the flight attendant.

"There's a new vineyard and distillery trying to make its stamp in the Oakridge wine and whiskey sector. They want investors, and I need to see what exactly I'm really investing in."

"I'm assuming your whiskey is a gift."

"It is. How'd you know?"

"My dad and my brother. They were brown drinkers. Judging by the darkness of it, it's a good barrel. Aged well. Smells fragrant. It might be a good investment."

"Your dad and brother were brown drinkers?"

"They're both in prison."

"Can I ask what for?"

Mone't rubbed her hands over one another. "Not really something I like getting into."

He nodded. "I can respect that. I see it's a heavy place for you."

"Yeah, one of many. So what's my role today?"

"You tell me whether the investment is worth taking. If it is, I'll sign the paper and wire them the money. If not, we go home."

Silence fell again until they landed on the hillside of Oakridge. After Isabella was born, Austin took her here for a mini work vacation. The vineyard that was her namesake was a few hills over. A place that held laughter and joy would be all Austin's when the divorce was final.

Choosing to continue to walk in the guidance from Robyn, Mone't shut her mind off and followed Lamont. She stood by his side, took in the numbers, and tasted more wine and whiskey than she had in a long time. She ate from decadent charcuterie boards and had grapes straight off the vines.

Mone't was a good look. No matter the man's side she stood by, she made him look good. Unbeknownst to Mone't, Lamont was using it to his advantage. He knew that no matter where she was to step foot, there was always a camera ready to catch her.

He made sure to lean into her path and whisper jokes in her ear. He was sure to put his hand on the small of her back when she laughed. Lamont was a snake, and he was growing to size. Soon he'd have her where he wanted her. Mone't was the piece on the board that would kill Austin's chances of winning. She didn't even know it.

Subsequently, due to Mone't's advice, Lamont signed the papers to become an investor. They embraced, and she blushed, feeling a sweet kiss to her cheek. She felt a sensation in her body that was only meant for Austin. She blamed it on her alcohol consumption and the excitement, and she quickly pulled away.

"We'd love to host you both for dinner to celebrate this partnership," the host of the tour, Michala, spoke excitedly.

Mone't smiled her smile. "Unfortunately, I have to get back."

Those were the words Lamont wanted to hear. Mone't's inhibitions were slipping, and to have her alone on a plane with the "do not disturb" light only opened up a world of possibilities.

"We would love to, but responsibilities call. Expect my wire shortly. I look forward to doing business with you."

Michala smiled. Mone't noticed there was something else behind that smile but didn't dwell on it. "We are looking forward to this ourselves."

The groups parted ways, leaving Lamont to escort his prey back to the jet.

"I've never gotten to close a deal like that before," she gushed as she slipped her flat sandals off her feet. She was buzzing and chose to be barefoot.

"We definitely should do that more often." His voice was a low rumble. There was no pace left in his actions. The flight staff had been alerted to distance themselves from the two upon arrival.

Mone't, unknowingly, was in the belly of the beast.

She threw him a look over her shoulder. "We?"

Lamont reached out for her and pulled her soft body into his. His erection alerted her to his motives. And then the kiss made her body tense more. This was wrong. Yes, Austin had broken their vows. Yes, he'd hurt her, but she was too good of a woman to do it back to him. She only knew Austin, and from the way Lamont sloppily kissed her, squeezing her in place while groping her body, that was all she wanted. She was Austin's girl.

"Lamont. Please stop." She struggled to get loose from his hold, but he continued forcefully kissing her neck and roughly tugging her dress up her body. "We can't do this."

"Mone't, you want this. I want this."

"I can't hurt him," she announced in tandem with Lamont refusing to listen and swiping his long fingers against the seat of her panties.

She hated that sensation didn't come from Austin. She hated how good it felt to be touched and desired. He'd latched on to the spot on her neck that could drive her crazy.

"I can't do what he d—" Her words were cut short from the pressure of Lamont's fingers fully slipping into her aroused center. The liquor amplified the sensation. For a few moments, she halted her protest. Her mind refused to give her mouth the courage to stop this and not fall victim to bad choices.

"Your pussy, Mone't," Lamont growled into her skin, "is tighter than a motherfucker. I want it."

All she could do was moan as the plane raced down the runway. Caution was thrown to the wind while Lamont's fingers worked her in and out. The skilled pilot got them into the sky without them tumbling.

She moaned a sinful pleasure she regretted with every sensation. Her sense was in a battle, and it was about to lose when Lamont dropped to his knees and buried his face between her thighs. He latched on to her bud, and all euphoria halted. Sense was back, and Mone't was disgusted with herself and him.

Lamont was too big, too fine, and too old to not be doing this right. "Stop." It took all her might to push him away from her. She looked at him with a frown and brows pinned together. "Don't come closer. Just stay there."

Mone't fought to pull her dress down and fix herself.

"Don't let him stand in the way of what you want."

She groaned. "I'm married, Lamont. Regardless of what he did. I'm still his wife, his girl, and this is wrong."

"It's right, Mo."

She held her finger up. "Don't call me that for starters. Secondly, it is. You are too old not to know how to eat pussy. My clit isn't a piece of bubblegum."

Barefoot, ashamed, and disgusted, she whisked off to the lavatory to clean herself up. "Chewing on my clit like that. Who taught him how to do that? All I know is Austin, but he would never . . ." she angrily muttered to herself, snatching paper towels from the holder to wipe her juices from between her thighs. She caught a glimpse of herself and stared at the woman looking back at her. "You don't have to do what Austin did to you to feel better. You feel better because you deserve to feel better. That's not attached to any man. Especially not Bad Eating Eddie out there."

Mone't stayed in the space until she had enough control to walk back out, grab her things, and find a place to sit away from him.

"Mone't, I'm—"

"Please don't make this any worse than it is. I'm owning this one. I know better."

"Your husband doesn't deserve you. That girl is pregnant."

"What my husband does or does not deserve is solely for me to determine. I am tied to his soul as long as there is breath in my being. Understand that. Respect that."

She sat down and turned to the window for the rest of the flight. She made her own arrangements to get home that wouldn't include Lamont's charity. She'd also gone so far as to send him her final invoice and the contact's name for the venue coordinators. They no longer needed to be within each other's orbits.

"Are you telling me a man that fine and that big can't do something as simple as eating pussy?" Angie asked in disbelief. Aneica was inside watching movies, the children were sound asleep, and after Mone't had washed her body until it was sore, she was in shorts and a T-shirt outside, eating pizza with her girl.

"I'm telling you! He was gnawing on my shit like AJ does to his fists. Sure, it would have felt good to feel good. Only for a minute or two, you know. A good get back. But it didn't feel good, regardless of the moans and my body doing what it does. As angry as I am with Austin, he's all I wanted in that moment. He's all I want, period."

"Then why not go home?"

"And fall back into the same rut, being over-looked and underappreciated? Not to mention, he did cheat on me. I'm not ready, and he hasn't learned his lesson."

Angie took a sip of her wine and hummed. "And you telling him that his GM got a taste of his cookie is bound to kill him."

"The same way some woman was bouncing up and down on my dick made me feel? Probably, but this is where we are, and I want out. My kids want out."

"You know I'm supporting you every step. If this break is what y'all need, stick to it. Just remember why you're doing it. Is it to be chewed on like a piece of Bubblicious, or is it to heal your marriage?" Angie asked in a fit of laughter.

Mone't couldn't help but join in. "It was really terrible. I was locked in that small bathroom, fussing, 'Austin would never. Austin would never.' At least he would've done the shit right and had me considering listening and yielding."

Their giggles were cut short when Aneica's voice penetrated the air. "Mone't, your mother is here."

All laughing ended. "My what?"

Aneica threw a nod over her shoulder and stepped out of the way, making room for Mone't's

One Final Shot

mother to come barging into her space. "So this is where you've chosen to hide out instead of that big-ass house? What's this about you not taking a dime of his money?"

There was no "Hi, how are you? Sorry for missing the last three years of your life and failing to show up when you called me." She wasn't here to see about her daughter. She was here to come up off her daughter.

Mone't jolted from her seat to meet her mother halfway. It was clear she'd been living the life. Her brown-hued face showed signs of Botox and a few surgeries. Her eye color was different now, and the BBL could be seen fully through her skintight clothing.

"Austin is the highest-paid player in the league with property and businesses, and you are choosing to let him off the hook."

Mone't scoffed. "Well, thank you for asking about me."

"If it were about you, Mone't, you would have turned an eye to his wayward dick or broken it and him. You didn't. You ran. So this isn't about you. It's about him. Always has been. But don't fret. Mama is here, and I'll show you how to make a nigga pay." She placed her hand on her daughter's cheek and smirked.

Mone't stepped out of her touch and scoffed. "Like you made my daddy pay?"

"It was his operation. He made all his choices to lie, cheat, and steal. But you're one to talk. Isn't your brother serving time for you?"

Mone't glared at her.

"That's what I thought. Now, my little naive daughter, show me where I'm sleeping."

"Hopefully in hell," Angie muttered.

"Agatha, no one is talking to you."

"Arayna, cut it out."

"Absolutely not," she snapped. "I sacrificed my life to have you, and you're going to repay me."

Aneica chose to insert herself, feeling more like Mone't's mother than the vessel who had granted her life. "That's enough. I'm sure there's a whorehouse or a motel you can stay in."

"That would make it easy for you and your secrets to continue to hide behind the greatness of your son. If you want me to keep what I know to myself, I suggest you stay out of my way."

Aneica snarled and looked at Mone't, Angie, and then back at the monster of a woman. "One thing about my secrets. I'm not as afraid of them as you are of the truth."

Chapter Twenty

On the balls of his feet, Austin danced around the ring, avoiding the heavy blows from Eman. This dance had started off as a workout before Austin was scheduled to board a flight later that night. It was his last solo workout to fight with his teammates for another title. It was supposed to be uplifting, and now the egos of two men were feuding for a place to be.

Eman was all brawn. Muscles ripped out of his melanated skin, his eyes cut in an angry glare, and Austin knew he deserved it. The bruises Mone't left behind as a parting gift were beginning to fade. He didn't want more. But Eman had left the well-being of his sister in Austin's hands.

"Whoa, this shit getting a little hot, huh?" Musa asked, taking a break from punching the fifty-pound sandbag Keyston was holding. He peeled the gloves off his hands and turned fully to face the ring set up in the middle of the home gym as the focal point.

"They 'bout to scrap. Can't say I didn't see it coming," Keyston replied, taking a seat on the nearby bench. "I'm surprised it took this long for E to let loose."

Musa grunted, joining Keyston on the far end of the bench. "You know how that nigga likes to get down. He assesses, then attacks. My money is on him."

"Hell yeah it is. That's where Mone't learned that shit from. Nigga had to start the series black and blue, and he's going to finish it black and blue," Keyston joked, making himself laugh. "Fuckin' piston."

Musa chuckled prior to taking a gulp of his water. "He's going to play the rest of the series pissed off, too."

Keyston's shoulder bounced. "Makes for good TV."

Musa threw his head to the ring after Eman landed a harder-than-normal punch and Austin landed a series. "So would this, if we were into letting the world into our shit."

"Calm the fuck down," Austin grunted, bouncing around Eman. "You wildin'."

"You wildin', young buck. I've been cool, but I can't help thinking about how it's going to feel to see her."

"Probably better than the last time I saw her," Austin replied to Eman. Honestly, he was tired of revisiting the same thing in the forms of different people. Although he knew they all were right, no one was feeding into his ego.

When the ego wasn't being fueled, the soul started to take over, snatching every ounce of nurturing it could to repair itself. Austin was being forced to look long, hard, and deep at himself. Sure, he could say some sweet, slick words to Mone't to get her back home, but if his ego took up more room than he did, they'd be back in this same predicament.

"Maybe you can talk some sense into her, get her ass back home, and cut this shit out," he grumbled, making everyone in the room scoff in tandem.

"Ain't shit I can say to make her come back here. She ain't hearing shit from you unless it's the truth. When you start lying?"

"We boxing or talking?" Austin asked annoyingly.

"What part of 'take care of her' did you forget?" Eman quizzed, making Austin change the rhythm of his dance. As long as Austin allowed someone else to be in control, he'd never win a fight. There were no victories to be claimed when playing the game was all you knew. Eman wanted Austin to step out of that mindset and go for broke in pursuit of everything he wanted.

Eman swung, but Austin bobbed and weaved, seemingly making Eman change course. "Pandora ain't going away, and Jermel got his short, cheesy ass on every little gossip channel that will give that nigga the time of day."

Reliving the night that ruined his life and threatened his livelihood, he said, "I didn't forget. I'm watching this bullshit every day just like you are."

"Why haven't you made it stop then? Huh, King?"

"Yo, cut that shit out." Austin was prideful, a trait he'd unknowingly gotten from both parents. Telling Eman everything that transpired between him, his wife, and another woman would make him feel like more of a failure than he already looked at himself as.

Eman hit him. "What you doing about it, King? Can you answer that shit?"

The press was evoking anger in Austin. Anger these days was an ever-present emotion Austin couldn't shake. It was showing up everywhere. It controlled how he conducted himself. Right now, it had him. He swung a triple punch: two to the body and one blocked attempt to Eman's helmet-covered head.

Eman returned the favor. The force behind the hits had Austin's fit core tightening to absorb the shock. They were in a scuffle. "I did what I said I was going to do. I took care of her. Still taking care of her. I fucked up once! And no one can look at all the shit I sacrifice?"

"Protecting her. Taking care of her. Honoring her ain't about no one in the world but you. What you missing?" Eman's words were gritty as they locked into one another. "You are the product of how you treat her. What you missing?"

They heaved and grunted, and neither was willing to surrender to the other. Austin and Eman were toe-to-toe over a woman they both cherished. Eman wasn't going to let Austin out of the hold until he started speaking some truths.

Aneica entered the gym with her mind spinning with texts from Francesco about the closed-door meeting Austin attended a couple days ago. She was hoping Austin was alone and calm to tell him the secret Francesco was pushing to expose. She was greeted with cursing and grunts from the grown men who were trying to settle their differences in the middle of the boxing ring. The sight captured her pained expression.

"Y'all are going to sit there and watch?" she asked, dropping her phone and rushing toward the pair. "Stop it! Stop it now, hear?"

"They grown. What I got to do with that?" Keyston asked nonchalantly as he grabbed her phone off the rubber mat on the floor. The texts from Francesco were still popping up in their thread, and Keyston's curiosity wouldn't allow him to look away.

When Austin finally broke away from Eman, he snatched his head gear off and tossed his mouth guard across the ring. He heaved like a raging bull. In and out, his chest swelled and deflated.

"You think I thought that shit through? I didn't, and now it's all I can think about! You know how it feels to look at her in these pictures and through windows and see that I did that? I hurt her like that?" His voice broke, and his hands scrubbed over his face. "I broke up my home for one night with a crazy-ass bitch who won't fucking go away. I allowed her to be uncomfortable around Jermel. I didn't stop to really check on her. You know how heavy this shit is? I am out of my fuckin' mind behind this, E.

"Nah, I didn't want to hurt her. No, I don't want no one but her. Mone't is the safest place I know. I don't have that shit. I'm out here naked. Niggas think they can talk about my woman, and I did that. Jermel pushing fuckin' lies. It's all on me."

The silence was so thick you could hear a pin drop. Austin's body was weak with emotion. He leaned on the ropes, letting the sweat and tears stream into one. "It's all on me. I can't keep doing this shit too much longer alone. I ain't shit without her or my kids."

Aneica stood on the stairs with tears in her eyes. She wanted to hug her son, but this was the moment Francesco had been talking about. Austin needed another man to show him how to stand up in the face of adversity. He didn't need to be coddled.

Against her better judgment, she took a step closer, and Keyston stopped her. "Let him go through that. E is here. 'Sides, it looks like you got your own shit to sort out."

"Wha—"

Keyston placed her phone in her palm and nodded toward the door she walked through moments before.

"Key, please don't say—"

"I ain't finna blow up your spot, Mama. He can't handle this shit right now."

Aneica hesitated before pulling herself away from the group of men who found themselves standing up to support their brother. Blood couldn't have made them any closer.

Eman took a seat in the corner of the ring after Aneica reluctantly left the gym. He didn't need to talk anymore.

"My mind don't stop fucking going. This is probably how she felt," Austin huffed and dropped his tired body on the mat. He sat upright with his back against the post. Removing the gloves from his hands, Austin sniffled. "I'm losing my fucking mind."

Musa took the lead. "You need to talk to someone."

"Who am I going to talk to? Y'all think this shit is funny. None of you niggas gotta get up and choose to hold your head up every day. I can't lock myself in this house or chase her ass down. There's payroll. There's people who depend on me. I gotta win a championship and smile knowing she ain't there and really might not be comin' back."

"We black men in America. Don't nobody love us," Keyston chimed. "Ain't shit about watching the breakdown of a black family, man, woman, and children funny. We keep passing on the same curses our parents passed on to us."

"All the more reason for you to get yourself some help, man. We from the hood that don't teach us about mental health," Musa spoke up. "We're not even comfortable showing affection or talking about this shit because of the taboo around it."

"The shit is taboo. You ain't a man if you cry. You ain't a real nigga if you love your woman out loud. But you that nigga for how much time you did. You that nigga for all the bitches you got. At the end of the day, we left with a bunch of fucking trauma," Eman added. "I got in the streets because my mother let the only father I knew take a charge. Mone't had to eat, she needed clothes and the basic shit, and I would be damned if I let her trick for it. She was safe with you. She smiled with you. She didn't smile much at home and definitely didn't do much of it when I left the first time. My only focus has always been to make sure her happiness and everyone attached to her was safe so she could thrive. I would have happily taken that last charge for her because I knew, finally, she'd be free to be happy.

"I didn't hear shit from you. Not a visit, a letter. Yeah, money on the books was cool. Thank you for that. I'm forever grateful. But if Mone't hurts, I feel that shit. I need you to get you right so she can get right. Mo is all I got."

"We need you to get right," Musa corrected him. The energy in the room was heavy. A tear slipped from his eyes, but he didn't wipe it. "You so busy trying to carry us when you should've let us step in and carry you."

"But we can't turn back. What's done is done. We've been dancing around this long enough. We've been watching it long enough. It's time to fix this shit."

"So y'all gon' let that nigga come for my top then give me a nigga therapy session?" Austin questioned, lightening the mood in the room.

Eman chuckled slightly. "Listen, you hurt my sister. I had to. I wanted to tussle with your billion-dollar ass last night, but I was too full."

Austin kissed his teeth and waved him off. "Get out of here, nigga."

Laughter erupted.

"For real, young blood. We got you," Eman said as he stood up. "If you focus on getting your family back, I'll take care of everything else."

"Finally!" Keyston said, throwing his hands up. "I thought I was going to have to step in."

"I'm happy your ass didn't," Austin spoke up.

"I ain't that damn bad." Keyston defended himself.

In unison, they said, "You are."

Once the smoke settled and the group had split into their separate corners of the house, Austin found himself in the cabana with his eyes closed, wanting nothing more than to lay his head in Mone't's lap and listen to her talk about her day with the kids.

The faint footsteps were getting louder until they reached his side. "You need to eat."

Austin grunted. Not really having an appetite, he sat up anyway. "I could've sworn you were out of here with Mone't."

Aneica sighed, setting a tray of food between them. She sat on the edge and pressed her lips together. "Mone't's mother popped up at the house. I needed to get away from her before I end up in jail."

Knowing the turmoil Mone't's mother brought along with her, Austin frowned, his chest tightened, and his anxiety spiked more. "What she back for?"

"What you think? The world knows Mone't filed for divorce. Everyone saw you get served. She wants a piece of your worth. Like Pandora."

Austin groaned, scratching his growing hair. "This is too fucking much."

"Indeed. So fix it. Please." Aneica's tone was desperate as she stood. She was on borrowed time. At least if Mone't and Austin started working things out, the coming blow would knock him down to a soft spot.

The chime from the doorbell made Eman's chest swell with angst. He hadn't seen his sister, other than in photos, since that fatal night. She was so much more than the little girl he left behind who was holding a secret. From the photos he'd seen of her, Mone't was grown. No matter how grown she was, she was still his baby sister.

He stood at her stained-glass door combatting the heat until he was greeted by a familiar face. Somewhere under all the plastic surgery, his mother was there. He wasn't surprised she'd mutated herself. He wasn't surprised that she was here. His mother was an opportunist. Surely, she wasn't here for his sister's well-being. She was here for the money that would be awarded to Mone't if Austin signed the papers.

"I see you're out of the pen." She said it with so much disgust that Eman almost assumed she was talking to herself.

"I ain't here to see you," he stated, refusing to feed into her nonsense.

"Only way to her is through me. You know how this goes," his mother stated. She evoked trauma in him that he should have taken the last three years to heal.

Eman had the same double dose Mone't suffered with when it came to parenting: mommy and daddy issues. Although Mone't's father wasn't his father, he was enough of an influence to teach Eman how to hold himself as a man. He was a man because of Mone't's father. But Mone't lacked that development from him, and in a sense, he felt guilty about it.

"Ma, listen, I don't have it in me to fight with whoever you are this month. Let me in."

Just as their mother refused to step out of the way, Mone't was coming down the stairs, eyes puffy, face devoid of joy, holding a cranky boy on her hip. Right behind her was Angie, who froze in her tracks the moment she heard his raspy baritone.

Eman's body locked up as he saw Angie in the mirror. Sure, he missed Mone't, wanted to catch up on the years he missed being there for her, but more than anything he wanted Angie's body on his. Even if it was just for a hug. He'd spent every night of the past three years trying to forget her only for her, and her alone, to consume his thoughts.

The family wasn't the family without him. He'd certainly felt the void. "Ma, let me in."

"Eman?" Mone't asked over AJ screaming at the top of his lungs for a snack. She pushed her mother out of the way to see if she was dreaming. Musa hadn't given her an update on the status of his appeal. She thought she'd have to wait months or years to see him again. Here he was, standing on her doorstep with a mirrored expression. They shared the same set of narrow eyes that disappeared the moment emotion showed across their faces.

Mone't's eyes flooded, distorting her vision. It was Eman. It smelled like him, looked like him, and felt like him as she wrapped her arm around his bulky body. "I can't believe you're home."

Eman's wide arms encircled her, holding both her and his nephew tightly in his embrace. "I'm sorry it took me so long to get here."

Before Mone't could become fully consumed with emotion, she broke away to tend to AJ. "Come in. I cooked."

Eman stepped into the house, now face-to-face with Angie. Her full eyes held tears she fought to keep at the brim. His eyes swept over her, and he was pleased by how she'd formed out without him. Eman's mind quickly ran on how his body was desperate to connect with hers again.

"LeAngelique," he commented proudly, happily. "You look good."

"You look real," she replied. Her lips quivered into a painful smile. "Are you real? I'm not dreaming this, am I?"

"Nah." Eman's voice rattled with emotion.

Mone't and her mother had left them to their reunion.

"I'm here. Can a nigga get a hug?"

Angie denied herself logic and trampled down the rest of the stairs. She ran into his arms, and they clashed, and she took a deep inhale of his white tee. The pads of her fingers sank into his muscular flesh. "I never thought this was coming."

Eman held her without words. He'd played this moment with her in his mind too many times to ruin it with a stupid comment. They held their embrace for minutes. It was necessary.

"You need to spend time with her," Angie said once she pulled away slightly to look into his handsome face.

"You're not leaving, are you?"

"No, I'm not."

He kissed her forehead tenderly before pulling completely away. "Wait for me."

"I've waited three years. I can wait a few more hours."

Eman smiled before roaming into the kitchen to see Mone't multitasking. She was assisting Izzy with a book and feeding AJ all while monitoring a pot of brown stew chicken. Aneica taught her how to cook it, being that it was Austin's favorite, along with peas and rice, cabbage, plantains, and macaroni and cheese.

This was their staple Sunday dinner, and now that the kids were used to having it, Mone't couldn't deny them.

"You're really a mom," Eman said with amusement, still ignoring their mother.

"I'm really a mom. How are you?"

"I'll be better when you're better," Eman stated, instantly making tears prick Mone't's eyes.

She waved her hands, hoping to wave off the emotion as well. "I'm okay."

"You aren't okay, Mo."

"I'm okay as I'm going to be, though."

Eman hummed. "You deserve to be better, and that's why I'm here."

"Is he outside?"

Eman shook his head. "No, I wouldn't do that to you."

Mone't sighed in relief. She wasn't ready to come face-to-face with Austin yet. If she saw him now, she'd crumble, fall into his arms, and attempt to forget his sins against her. Without a doubt, she missed him, their home, and the good times they had. But she still needed to know and feel a change within him.

"Thank you," Mone't said before grabbing Izzy's attention. She was a millisecond late, because Isabella was out of her seat, walking toward Eman.

"I saw pictures of you."

Eman squatted down to her level. "I've seen pictures of you too."

"How?" Isabella questioned.

"Your uncle Musa sent them while I was at school."

"Big-boy school. Mommy told Daddy she wanted to go to big-girl school. I always hear them . . . but not anymore."

"You miss your daddy, huh?"

"So much. I miss him hugging Mommy. Mommy needs a hug."

Eman cut a look at Mone't, who pretended not to listen. "I know she does. She and Daddy are going to be okay."

"I hope so. She's sad."

Eman was pleasantly surprised by how much Isabella looked like Austin, but her heart was that of her mother's. The little girl before him was so much like his sister that his sense of protection was heightened.

Before the two could dive into any more, Angie chose this as the perfect time to take over the handling of the kids for Mone't. Since her mother had shown up, Aneica had made herself busy with Austin's affairs to keep herself out of jail. If it weren't for Angie staying with Mone't day in and day out, she would be handling this solo, which would have caused the emotions to boil out of control.

Mone't slowly turned around with a plate in each hand. Eman remained silent as he trailed her outside to the screened-in patio. "I've been trying to keep all this from them."

"You can't uproot kids and think they don't notice what's going on with their parents, Mo. You know that when Mom did, it threw our world into chaos," Eman stated as he pulled Mone't's seat out. He took his, thanked her for the food, and studied her. Mone't was proud of her tresses. They were nonexistent now. It was the loudest cry for help he'd ever seen.

"How long have you been home?"

"Long enough to see what's going on. I don't like this shit, Mo. You and Austin apart don't feel right."

"Having him cheat on me at my lowest didn't feel right either," she countered.

"Mo."

"Eman, don't do that. Don't tell me it's not the lowest or it was a rough patch. It wasn't that. It was me feeling, and sometimes still feeling, like it's just me. I have to be pretty and take care of him, the kids, and the house all while feeling like I'm fucking alone. There's nothing no one can say to me. It's me, all me, and it's dark in here, every day telling myself to just get through this minute to make it to the next. And then just when I feel like it's getting better, he cheats on me . . . with her. Now there's supposed to be a baby on the way? No. I can't handle all this."

"When did this start?" Eman was concerned. Depression was a real thing, and they were birthed into a community that swept it under the rug. They'd tell you shit like, "Shake it off. It's a bad day. You're being dramatic. Black people don't suffer from mental health issues. We're too strong." All of that was misleading and always counterproductive to the mission of undoing generational trauma and healing the wounds of the soul.

"Honestly?"

"I ain't fight this hard to get out for some bullshit, li'l bit."

"When Dad left. I'm sorry, let me correct that. When he got dragged away from me at a traffic stop. I've always been going through these patches of darkness. I don't know. After I pulled that trigger, and knowing what I did and why I did it . . . it haunts me. It fucks with me. I did it to save him, but really, E, it was for me, and then it turned into a lot more than I thought."

"You know I'd do that shit a million times over for you. At some point you have to forgive yourself and reevaluate what you want for you. You ain't doing this for nothing, Mo. You aren't here for nothing. The same way Austin can't come back to you broken, y'all can't fix this family broken. You can't teach your children how to push forward if you're broken."

Mone't quickly wiped the tears from her cheeks. "I'm tired."

Eman scoffed. "You ain't got time to be tired. Tired means you'll sit down on the job. Sitting down on the job means you'll quit. You two built a life together despite how you started. You can say you pulled that trigger for you. But you pulled that trigger for all four of you.

"Shit, me going away saved my damn life. I know it's dark inside because you live in there, but I promise you, if you come out, you'll see you how we see you. There's life after heartbreak. There's light after darkness if it's something you desire. Fix you so you can be ready to receive what's yours."

Eman stood up and rounded the table. Pulling her to her feet by lifting her hands, Eman held her close. Mone't had broken down several times, but this particular time was the one she needed. This was the comfort outside of Austin's that was going to comfort her into healing.

"I love you. You're supposed to be here. Nothing you've done has been in vain. You are not alone, and such a precious flower doesn't grow in the dark. Say it," Eman coached.

Mone't sobbed into her brother's chest. "I . . . I love you. You're supposed to be here. Nothing you've done has been in vain. You are not alone, and such a precious flower doesn't grow in the dark."

"Say it again, baby girl."

"I love you. You're supposed to be here. Nothing you've done has been in vain. You are not alone, and such a precious flower doesn't grow in the dark."

"Now breathe."

While her hands were clasped around his waist, she inhaled deeply and slowly released it. He broke their embrace and placed his massive hands on her shoulders. "I ain't letting y'all quit. I ain't letting you fail."

Chapter Twenty-one

"Zone, zone, zone!" Austin shouted through the cluster of bodies. He was calling a new play, not the one the coach called moments ago. Brighton Heights saw the AAU play coming from a mile away.

Winston, Cypress, Paul, and Kayden got into position for the ball to be thrown to any of them. Austin glanced around the court as the ball left his fingers and went past his opponent and to Cypress, who pulled back and shot the ball across the court to Kayden. He took it to the hoop, and the crowd erupted. They didn't have time to celebrate. They were down by twelve and had to make the last two minutes of the game be the last minutes of the championship.

Ten players followed the lead to the other end of the court. For the first time all season, all five starters and closers were on the same wavelength. They flawlessly reclaimed the ball with assistance from Winston. A three.

The Monarchs were never the team to try to outscore. They were going to let their opponent run themselves down in the paint and put it in the hands of their king. Austin shot a three and got in position to steal the ball. Another three.

The energy in the building was unmatched. It was contagious, jumping from the crowd to the players. Brighton Heights was going to be shut down in their own house, and Austin was going to take great joy in it. The third championship was on the way, and he felt like this was the road to vindication. One more win, and his life would be whole again.

The noise of the arena was off the scale. They couldn't shout over their opponents and hear themselves anymore. They needed to fully buy into the trust they'd built throughout the years.

Winston glanced at Kayden and threw Austin a nod. While Cypress chased down the ball to steal it, Austin and Kayden set up down court to receive it. Steal, pass, shot. Three. Foul.

Austin fell to his back, sliding across the glossy pine, groaning in agony at the sting of the burn. One point away from tying them again. Another point away from winning. They were down to the wire, and despite the crowd chanting his name, he was deaf to it all.

With the assistance of Kayden and Winston, Austin hopped to his feet, shook off the fall, and stood at the line. Two shots. The coaching, the cheers, the boos, and his teammates' encouragement fell on deaf ears. The ball hitting the pine and bouncing back into his hands was all he heard over the thundering of his heart.

He made the first shot, took custody of the ball, and did it again. Jogging backward, Austin got into position. He wouldn't celebrate until their lead was more than a point.

Brighton Heights tried to take a play out of Ganton Hills' book and fire off a three-pointer that bricked. Cypress rebounded it, traveled down court, and threw it behind his back to Austin. The final shot, the final second of the game. Swoosh. Three points sealed the series and delivered.

"Game!" Austin shouted, sweat pouring down his face, proudly pointing at his fourth finger on his right hand. "Give me my ring."

"Three-peat, young buck!" Winston shouted, wrapping his arms around Austin.

Consumed with emotion, Austin looked into the crowd for that face. The face with the small eyes hidden behind high, smiling cheeks, the perfect white teeth glistening behind bright red rouge. His chest was pained, his eyes watered, and he dropped to his knees. To the spectators it looked as though Austin was overcome with emotion due to his third consecutive win. In reality, the one he started this with wasn't there excitedly rushing to the floor to hug him and kiss his face.

Aneica excitedly cheered between Eman and Musa. Keyston pointed at him, grinning from ear to ear. Unbeknownst to Austin, he'd made Keyston a millionaire with one shot. "You the one!"

Aneica fought through the crowd to get to Austin. Throwing her arms around his neck, she kneeled on the floor with him. "I am so proud of you. You did it, Austin. You did it!"

Pulling himself together, he stood and pulled his shoulder back. Everything was in perspective. At the height of his career, Austin was the GOAT. At the height of his career, Austin was alone.

The moment he stepped foot off the jet, he was going to start the process of putting himself back together for the sake of himself and knowing that if Mone't was going to take him back, he was going to be a whole man deserving of her love.

"So, Austin," Robyn spoke up from her seated position next to the window, "why'd you call?"

Austin rubbed his hands on the material of his pants. His hands were clammy, and nervousness swirled in the pit of his gut. His mind danced around the answer. He had flashes of the fights, the events that led to him falling into Pandora, and the guilt that plagued him thereafter.

"I didn't call," he stated just above a mumble. "My mother did because sleeping the days away isn't acceptable, I guess."

"Is it sadness or—"

Austin sucked in a deep breath and slowly exhaled. "I cheated on my wife."

Robyn nodded. She knew Mone't's side. She couldn't and wouldn't discuss it, but she observed the way Austin's tall body slumped in the chair. There were no chains, no diamonds glistening, and no aura of a great season and postseason. He was sad, truly sad, and although Mone't was a big part of it, there was something in Austin that motivated his steps.

It had been days since Austin had been outside of the house. Days since he really ate, and it showed in his face. The overgrown facial hair and the thick silk coils were untamed. He didn't care what he looked like. What he knew was there were things he had to sort through.

"I've learned in these instances there's always something underlying to make us do something irrational. What was happening with you that made you feel like stepping out would make you feel better?"

"Let me stop you there," Austin said, lifting his glance slightly. "I didn't think it would make me feel good. Honestly, cheating on my wife was never something I thought I would do. I dodged groupies and crazed women for three years just to slip up when she needed me. It made me feel like shit, and I still didn't lay it all at her feet. I hid. I tried to, anyway. All it did was feed into the insecurities she was having with herself. I still feel like shit."

"What was the root for you? Your wife is just a branch on the tree. What's happening at the root of this?"

He grew silent again. His eyes traced the pattern of the carpet. From the carpet, his eyes landed on her wall of awards. Without invitation, his feet led him there. He stood at the awards and read each of them. "Did these make you feel good?"

Robyn chuckled nervously, feeling as though Austin was on the cusp of hijacking her session. "They did."

"Proud, right?"

She nodded. "Yes."

"I didn't feel proud when I got the third title. Yeah, sure, I was happy my teammates and I pulled it off, especially with all the shit surrounding me. I looked up in the section reserved for my family, and only my mother, my new agent, and my boys were there. Not my father, not my wife. Not my kids. The extension of who I am precedes and succeeds me.

"I don't know who I am, where I came from, why my temper is so bad, why I'm arrogant. How am I supposed to raise a son, show my daughter how a man is supposed to care for her and love her, if I have no idea who I am and I don't know how to be a man for their mother? I don't know who I am. I know damn well I don't deserve her."

"Let's dive into that. Why do you feel undeserving?"

Austin's head dropped, and he slid his hands into his pockets to keep from fidgeting. "We have a privacy clause, right?"

"Doctor-patient privacy and the NDA, yes."

He fell quiet again. "It was the night before I was supposed to be drafted. My final hoorah in the old neighborhood. We were at the courts, balling, clowning, having fun. My homeboy ran bets on the games. We were hustlers. I was the talent. I knew who I could take and how I could outplay them. I really balled out when I knew Mone't was there watching. Her smile always gave me that extra push. Anyway, that night felt different. She looked different. Shit, it was different.

"There was this guy—G, they called him. He was pushing me for another game. They wanted to win their money back. Long story short, it got heated. A fight broke out, and a bullet was fired. That bullet saved my life. I probably would have wasted away if I didn't have basketball.

"She saved my life, our life. She carried all that weight, that guilt of taking a life and being able to bring one into the world. How does someone do that? How do they stay strong like that? I don't deserve that. Never did. I fought since meeting her to protect her, to be there for her, and somewhere along the way, I thought money and success were enough. For a woman who is so strong to have a man so fuckin' weak . . ."

Austin's skin reddened with every passing moment. He fought the tears, but as of late, the tears didn't know any respective person or place. They formed into giant droplets and rushed out of his eyes. "I hate to tell you this, Doc. You're wrong. She is the root. She's the only thing that matters, and when you don't deserve something that fucking good, you try to kill it. Unintentionally. I love the ground she walks on because she walked on it. It's more than just her being my wife. Mone't is my best friend, my safe place. I tried to kill that because I wasn't right. It hurts. Shit, I don't know what I need to do for me. All I know is what I need to do for her, and that's to never make her feel this type of pain again."

"Why?"

Through the tears and snot, Austin answered, "Because she doesn't deserve to ever feel like this again."

"Is she deserving of someone else?"

It burned his throat to reply, "I'm sure."

"Are you willing to let her go to get what she deserves?"

Austin spun around in a whirlwind. "Hell nah! I ain't here to accept that shit. I'm here to fix me and get her back. Help me. I ain't never letting her go."

"Austin, what if she has?"

"She ain't with that nigga. Is she?"

Robyn placed her iPad down on the table near her emerald armchair. Sliding her glasses down on the bridge of her nose, she watched Austin pace. It was becoming clearer to her that everything Austin said was indeed fact. Mone't was his compass, the rhythm to his rhyme. The one thing that made him tick. She controlled his vibration, his movements, and his energy. They'd done this to each other. When one part of the duo was off, everything was thrown off-kilter.

Austin's erratic behavior was a prime example.

"Austin, let's stay focused on the task. We're talking about you, not Mone't."

"Nah, we're talkin' about her. She's a part of me. If you talk about me, you got to talk about her. There ain't no other way around it. I've been trying to find me. I've found me in her. I ain't got that. Don't you get that, Doc? That's why I need her back. Since fourteen, she imprinted on me. My first kiss. My first lover. My first love. To unravel the nucleus of who I am, you have to pass her."

That was the truth.

Austin plopped down in another chair and stared into space, tears still falling freely from his face. He refused to wipe them. Ego didn't live here, and he rejected the idea that men didn't cry. All he'd been doing was crying.

"I knew her from around the neighborhood. She was always too good for me. Always quiet, always in her books. That's how I made her talk to me, you know? I was heavy into sports. My mama said I wasn't getting stuck in the hood like she did. She was walking home one day, nose in a book, and her friend was talking her ear off. This was after her brother told me to leave her alone. I purposely stopped in her way so she could run into me. I had a baby crush on her, but the second her eyes looked up at me, I was stuck. Nothing has ever held me hostage like that.

"She was sad, and I promised her she'd never know what that was again. In the same season when I was a rookie, we had our first kid, and she was sad again. Postpartum depression. I was scared as fuck 'cause I couldn't take that away. That one was easy. The second time, though, the pregnancy was rough. I was barely there for it, and all she wanted was me. I couldn't fly her out. AJ wasn't having it." Austin paused to laugh through his tears. "He still ain't. He for sure made his mama stop and feel everything. It was hard watching her go through that and not have the tools to really care for her. Thank God for my mother, who was there, is still there, every step of the way. But I wasn't.

"Work, appearances, endorsements, and whatever else my janky-ass agent occupied my time with . . . All I saw was the fact that no one in my camp would ever go back to the hood again. I didn't see or hear that she was in distress and needed me to put on my cape."

He lifted his eyes to Robyn, who was all in, not daring to interrupt.

"I failed her. I broke her heart far before I cheated. That's probably why she's angry with me. Why she hates me. I get it. I deserve her rage and her cuss-outs. But I'll fight for her love."

"How are you going to do that?"

"Do what I did when I made her talk to me. I'll put myself in her way until she talks."

Robyn nodded. "May I offer a suggestion?"

"That's why I'm paying you all this money."

"Convince her to do a joint session. I don't want y'all in jail."

"Even then, we'll be together."

Mone't's feet pounded the pavement. She'd been whisking around the city all day. Aneica had sent her on a hunt to gather things for her brother's welcome home party, and her mother insisted on having a cup of coffee from Triple B's. If it were up to her, her mother would fly off on whatever broom of delusion she flew in on.

Since her mother's abrupt arrival, Mone't had done her best tucking away her feelings, avoiding

Aubreé Pynn

her, and trying her best not to explode. There were points in her life when she thought that she would have been better off if she had never known her. If she could have traded in her mother for her father, she would have done it in a second. Life with Eman and her father would have been different but better. Arayna's only concern was how much money Mone't was going to get from Austin when he signed the papers and how much she figured she was entitled to.

It would kill her to know that no matter how much she snooped, pried, or lingered around, Arayna Swift was never seeing a dime of the money Mone't was entitled to. Hell, if she knew how much her daughter really had in the bank because of Austin's acknowledgment of his wife's worth to his wealth, she'd stroke out in the middle of the floor. Perhaps Mone't should have told her so she could. Unfortunately, her mother was a leech. She'd seen her mother hook on to man after man for a come-up. Hustler after hustler, dealers, and scammers alike. Wherever she had been holed up had her content for years.

With her mother, anything was bound to happen. Though Aneica didn't want to be in the same house with Arayna, Mone't refused to leave her children with Arayna. They didn't even take to her the way they did to Aneica. Getting Aneica back in the house came with a long list of things to get.

This dash around the city was worth the security she felt keeping Arayna away from her kids. Arayna was liable to have some man she was sexing stupid kidnap them for ransom.

The thought made Mone't scoff as she walked into Triple B's, happy that she was finally in an air-conditioned building. She wasn't dressed to the nines today. A pair of Graham 11's, biker shorts, an oversized graphic tee, and a fitted cap was her steel. Her frame could be spotted a mile away.

It made it easy for Lamont to enter the restaurant and stand in line beside her without being seen. "Catching up with you has been a task."

His voice damn near made her jump out of her skin. Irritation instantly struck her face when her eyes landed on him. "I sent you a replacement concierge and figured there wasn't anything else we needed to discuss."

"You know there is so much we need to discuss. What happened—"

Mone't held her hands up, still trying to forget that she had been seconds away from allowing him to enter her body. "We don't need to rehash this. You and I aren't compatible."

"How can you use that one time as a deal sealer?"

Her lips curled. She didn't even want to answer him. There was another pressing question. "Did you follow me here?"

"You told me to meet you here. I've been waiting outside for you."

"Lamont, are you out of your mind? I didn't ask you—"

He held his phone up and showed her the thread of text messages between the two. The only issue was that Mone't never sent him a text or answered a call following the terrible display of fellatio on the flight from Oakridge.

Her already-narrowed eyes squinted tighter. "I didn't text you any of that."

"You're not going to have me out here lookin' like a sucker for you, Mone't. I ain't Austin." Lamont mumbled the comment, but Mone't was a mother who listened to her children's calm breathing in the dead of the night. She could hear anything.

She dug into the designer fanny pack strapped around her waist and pulled her phone out. Scrolling to Lamont's name, she saw the slew of texts and immediately put two and two together. Arayna was up to her bullshit.

As she sucked in a deep, unsettled breath, she put the phone back and spun around on her heels. She refused to share another word with such a pressed man. Lamont didn't get the hint. He was desperate to get Mone't to fall into his trap.

At this point, if she didn't give him what he wanted freely, he was heavily considering taking it. Lamont was banking on Mone't being completely naive. Unfortunately, he was being met by opposition at every turn.

He chased her up the sidewalk to the parking garage until he finally got her to stop. "Mone't!"

"What? What aren't you getting?" she bellowed, heaving in and out. She felt her anger growing more and more, and this was a dangerous space for her to be in. "I don't want to be with you. I don't want you in my space. I don't need the issues atta—"

Lamont roughly grabbed her face, cutting her off midsentence. She smacked him across the face and pivoted her escape once more. Her quick, short steps were nothing for Lamont, who took one step and had her in his possession again, this time to keep her in place.

He needed her to be in place, in a position that would matter for his benefit later. Mone't fought. She tried to wriggle away from him. No one had ever handled her like this, and she was afraid and unprotected.

To no avail. He had her in a hold she wasn't strong enough to break away from. Every available phone from every bystander snapped the photos of Mone't Graham being tongued down by Lamont Wright. It was a mess, a circus all orchestrated by her gold-digging, meddling mother. Mustering up all the strength in her body, Mone't pushed him off her and wiped his sloppy kiss from her lips.

The swipe of his saliva from her face was followed by another slap across his. He ate it and smirked. "I like that shit, Mone't. When I'm done with you, you'll jump to every command."

Her eyes darted around, seeing the people—some paparazzi, some nosy-ass people who'd done nothing to assist her. Everyone wanted a story. They wanted to be the first to post. The world they lived in was more concerned with how many clicks, likes, and shares they could generate. There was no humanity left.

"You are out of your fuckin' mind. You are seconds away from me making sure you don't manage another team. Stay away from me!"

Mone't cut through the maze of cars with rage leading her way. Making it to the spot on the second level where she parked her SUV, she climbed in and dropped her head onto the steering wheel. A plethora of emotions moved through her body, making her nauseated. She wanted to blame Austin for all of this. She couldn't. She couldn't even bring herself to go home and curse her mother out for this setup.

Instead, she dug through her bag for her phone she'd tucked away before fleeing Triple B's. She unlocked the screen, which still displayed the most recent family photo of Austin smiling brightly as he tossed Isabella in the air and her with AJ cradled in her arms. They were in the backyard, the plush green of the landscape and hills providing the backdrop.

As she tapped the screen, she landed on the number she desperately needed right now. She needed to be grounded, needed a calm voice, and needed some reason. If left to her own devices, she would back out of this parking spot and run Lamont over for daring to handle her the way he had.

Mone't placed the call and gritted her teeth while the line trilled throughout the Bluetooth of the car.

"Mone't, are you okay?" Robyn's voice came through the speakers with concern.

Mone't hadn't solicited Robyn's help for herself. Both interactions had been because Angie had sense enough to stand in the gap for her friend. Mone't had to do it for herself.

"I, uh . . . I need an appointment or something. I need something," she stammered.

Robyn chuckled lightly. "Have you had lunch?"

"I don't even think I can eat right now."

"How about we try? I'm on Fiftieth, headed to Prophet Park for a give back. Come out," Robyn urged.

Mone't tensed up. She hadn't been to Prophet Park in years. It was different now, or so she'd heard. Ever since Austin moved her into the mansion on the hill, she tried to consume herself with what was happening only in their bubble.

She hesitated before answering, "Okay."

"I'll see you when you get here."

Mone't sent Aneica and Angie a text letting them know she was headed to a therapy appointment. The rest of the details didn't need to be discussed until later.

When Mone't reached her old stomping grounds, she barely recognized anything. The old house she lived in was renovated. Big Dawg Construction in partnership with The Black Hero Project had flipped so many homes. She smiled seeing the children run down the street without fear of a bullet flying.

Mone't and Austin were born and raised in Prophet territory. Gang wars were a norm for them, and without protection, anyone could get touched. Parallel parking across the street from the park, she got out and looked up at the mural painted on the side of the corner store.

All the greats who had come from Fiftieth were painted on the wall. In the center was Austin, smiling the way he did, holding the basketball proudly. She smirked, remembering the times his smile illuminated a room and hers matched.

The music coming from the park grasped her attention. Securing her car, she trotted across the street where the throngs of people were dancing to the music, eating from food trucks, and enjoying face paint.

Duke and Tanya happily served the neighborhood, side by side, from their food truck. Lehana painted faces. Shilo was giving free noninvasive checkups, Dania was offering her doula services, and Robyn was on the opposite side, by the courts, speaking about black mental health.

The energy from everyone was good. As she walked through, she felt the anger slowly fall from her shoulders. She blended in with the crowd, trying to stay as undetectable as she could.

Robyn spotted her, smiled, and continued to wrap up her presentation. "Everyone who came over here to sit through my rambling will receive an hour with me. Regardless of whether you have insurance, you can book a session. Remember, self-care starts with your mental health. Thank you all for coming. Enjoy the event."

Mone't counted thirty people out of the hundred who were there stand up and thank her for hosting the Black Mental Health Circle. As gracious as she was, Robyn smiled, hugged them, and shook their hands. She treated everyone with the same respect. She loved people and believed that her love would rub off on everyone she encountered.

"Mone't Graham. How does it feel being back here?" she asked as she replenished her pamphlets.

Mone't winced and looked around, trying to avoid the courts. "Surreal. It doesn't even look the same anymore."

"When was the last time you were here?" Robyn asked, studying Mone't's inability to look at the things she'd trapped away: the courts and the other side of the park, where her father was ripped from her, thrown to the ground, and had a knee on his neck until she screamed so much that they had to stop.

"Three years. I never thought about coming back or giving back. I just pushed this to the side."

"Hm," Robyn hummed. "Like everything else?"

Mone't nodded. "Just like that."

"Let's walk. I need water and some of that good Caribbean food Sir Duke has. Do you like Caribbean cuisine?"

"I can't live without it. Mama is Jamaican American. Every Sunday is either curry goat or brown stew chicken."

Robyn laughed. "That explains the hips. That's Austin's mother?"

"Yeah. She's been more of a mother to me than my own," Mone't said, feeling that lump in her throat. "Speaking of which, my mother has popped up out of nowhere with a new body. Like, head to toe. She's been meddling, talking to my lawyer about changing the demands of my divorce, and setting me up to meet with people I don't want to."

"It sounds like there's no boundaries set in place."

Mone't laughed, walking shoulder to shoulder with Robyn through the crowd. "She doesn't even know what that is, if we're being honest."

"How do you feel about it?"

"I hate it. She's the reason why I allow people to go so far until I can't take anymore. You know, she had my father set up. He's serving life in prison because of her. And my father also has blocked me from contacting him in any form for the rest of his days.

"When Dad went away, she pushed my brother into the life. Then she put him out when he wanted to do things his way because he knew what kind of woman she was. She never wanted to be a mother. She was a hustler who, as she loved to say, thought that having us was going to keep around whatever man's pockets she had her hands in. It kept my dad until it didn't."

"Did she ever make you hustle?" Robyn asked.

Mone't shook her head. "Eman wouldn't allow it, and then Aneica took me under her wing. My mother is a representation of what I never want to be. I don't want to be with any man I have to accept the bare minimum from to survive."

"Did Austin represent that?"

"Austin holds such a huge part of my life that no one can compare to what building that feels like. No, it hasn't always been great, and this is the worst it's been, but no one else is him."

The pair stood in line and Robyn sighed, swiping sweat from her brow. "At some point, you do have to admit that although he hurt you, you allowed it because you felt like you owed him. From what it sounds like, Austin and his mother saved you from falling into the ways of life your mother taught you. You two created a codependency, so when trouble knocked on your door, what you thought you had shattered."

Mone't sucked in air, filled her lungs, and slowly released it. "We did. Being without him has been the hardest, most uncomfortable thing. Yeah, I am mad as hell at what he did, but everything good in my life leads back to him."

"Mone't, love is beautiful. But love without growth shrivels up and dies. We outgrow spaces and situations. If we stay trapped in our minds, we can't look outside of that. We can't grow while we're trapped in the darkness of what's happening up here." Robyn lightly pressed her finger into her temple. "Don't look at your separation at his infidelity as the end. Look at it as the end of this chapter. You and Austin have been wrapped around each other since you met. You two need space to grow. You're growing. You're placing boundaries around yourself.

"If your mother causes you so much stress and anxiety, tell her she can't be in your space. As black people, we have this toxic habit of thinking that because it's our mother, father, sister, brother, cousin, aunt, uncle, or grandparents, we have to tolerate their behaviors. We don't. That doesn't mean we don't love them or respect or honor them.

"However, to break the cycle for you and your daughter and her daughter, you do it differently. Honor you, respect you, and love you. We repeat learned habits instead of doing something new. This is your chance to do it differently and change it for every generation after you. It's not all about you. Look outside of yourself and set your boundaries. Watch how things turn around."

They stepped to the window, and Duke shouted, "Mrs. Three-peat. What you want? All of it's on the house. Queen Graham can get whatever she wants."

Tanya giggled and smiled brightly at Mone't. "He's a fan. Congratulations on the win."

Mone't nodded. The win wasn't hers, but she would gladly accept the praise on behalf of Austin. "Thank you. He worked really hard for it."

"I hope he's working even harder for you," Tanya responded.

"You're a real one, that's for sure. Tanya was looking at me all kinds of crazy when the news broke, like it was me."

Mone't laughed it off. "I appreciate y'all."

"We appreciate you. Tell your brother to link up with me when he gets home."

Mone't's smile grew. "He's home. I'll tell him to see you."

"Bet!"

Duke and Tanya loaded Mone't down with food and took a picture with her in front of the truck.

Duke held her hostage at a table with Tanya and Robyn. Mone't thought returning to her old hood would spike her anxiety. It was refreshing to be back around the people she came up with.

Duke went from serving corners to serving cuisine all around the world. Greatness and perseverance were embedded in the blood of the inhabitants of Ganton Hills. Failing was never an option, and when you fell, there was a neighborhood of people who wanted better for you.

Although Mone't was trying to blend in, Duke had outed her, causing swarms of people to come shake her hand, talk to her, and tell her how things would turn around for her and Austin.

Unsure if Robyn had orchestrated all of this, Mone't was grateful either way. She was unaware that so many strangers would pour back into her empty cup. If she could stay all day, she would, but there was a daunting task waiting for her at home. Not to mention, it was a matter of time before Arayna brought the gangster out of Angie or Aneica.

Mone't said her goodbyes and left the festival with hands and arms full of food, teddy bears for the kids, and other knickknacks she'd bought from the vendors. She even graciously signed up to be a sponsor next year. She needed to be a part of this every year moving forward.

After maneuvering her way out of the parallel parking job, she crept home. The euphoria of the festival could only last so long. As she drove home, she remembered the reasons she ended up over here in the first place: her mother, Lamont's inability to accept no as an answer, and the constant fight to get her head and spirit right.

Arayna was outside on the patio sipping Mone't's special wine, sunbathing in a bikini that barely covered her overgrown parts. Mone't's lip curled at the sight.

"Oh, you're home. Since you've been gone for hours, I suspect it went well."

Mone't's lips twitched in irritation. "I would have rather been home enjoying my children."

Her mother scoffed. "They have nannies and Aneica. You only need them to get half of Austin's wealth. Be smarter than me, please."

"How about I just be better than you? I need you to get up, pack your shit, and get gone."

"You are certainly not speaking to me that way."

"Oh, I most certainly am. You show up after three years. Uninvited at that. You don't help out with anything. You meddle, you snoop, and you pry. What's the worst is that you're hijacking my phone to text a man I don't want to be with. And my lawyer telling him I want more. You are unhinged, and I can't have you around me or my kids."

"Oh, so Austin has you that far gone?" Arayna sat up and looked at her daughter like she had three heads.

Mone't scoffed, throwing her hands in the air. "He doesn't have me any kind of way. I am grown, and what I choose to do and who I choose to do it with doesn't concern you, Arayna!"

"It does. Because if it were up to me, you wouldn't be in this tiny house divorcing a man who has the world falling at his feet."

"If it were up to you, I wouldn't have anything. You would have made me hold his children hostage from him and demand thousands of dollars a month while turning tricks for you and your madam. Something is wrong with you. You've never been a mother but want to show up because you see dollar signs."

"I have been a great mother to you. Are you still crying because I spanked you and sold your little clothes your daddy bought you with drug money?"

"Are you on crack? It's crack. You set my father up, took that from me. Beat the shit out of me repeatedly for not doing whatever with whomever. If it weren't for Austin and Mama, I would still be in the hood or dead."

"Oh, King Austin the savior. How quickly you forget what your little light-skinned savior did to you."

"Oh, I remember. There's not a minute of the day I don't think about it. He cheated on me. He also might have a baby on the way that didn't come from me. That's such a small piece of what we really fought, cried, and bled for. And because you know that, you have never once asked me how it felt."

"Oh, please, Mone't. Your little feelings don't matter to the bigger picture. Suck it up." Arayna stood and studied her daughter. "Tell me, what do you have besides your name? Hm? Sure, you're pretty, but you've gained weight, and you have two kids. You didn't finish school. You have nothing for yourself but what Austin gave you. What man is going to really take you seriously outside of the ones who want to use you and then leave you?"

Every word spoken made Mone't feel like she was that little helpless girl all over again. Tears piled up, blurring her vision. "Men like Lamont?"

"If they want your pussy, you might as well make them pay for it."

Tears spilled over now. "I'm sorry that's the life you had to live. I'm sorry no one ever protected you, so you have no clue how to protect me. I am so sorry that that's your reality. But it's not mine, and I won't carry that cross for you. I have a lot going for myself whether I finished school or not. None of that gaslighting distracts me from the issue. You gotta go. I didn't need you as a mother then, and I sure as hell don't need you for one now."

Her mother scoffed. "You don't know what you need."

"I do. I don't need you, Lamont, your advice, or the trauma associated with any of that. The real issue is that you never healed, so you bounce from dick to dick, trying to feel something other than shame. Because you sent to prison the only man who loved your used ass. You can change your face and your body, but you're still the rotten soul of a shell of a woman inside. You've done enough damage to me. You aren't allowed to do any more. Get your things and get going. The Ganton Hills MARTA runs on the half hour."

Mone't didn't notice that Aneica was standing in the doorway with her arms folded across her chest, kissing her teeth and humming the entire time. "You heard her. Get going before I make you go."

"Ain't no need for that, Mama. She's going to be leaving," Mone't stated, stepping back and watching her mother wade in her worn flip-flops. "The trash always takes itself out."

"You'll regret talking to me like this one day." After unnecessary silence, Arayna chose to follow Mone't's advice and leave.

The house was completely silent. Angie slipped out to see Eman after she put the kids down for a nap, and Aneica gladly waited by the door with a machete. It took Arayna all of twenty minutes to gather her things and drag them to the door. She stopped and glared at Mone't, jealousy seeping through her pores. Mone't would have something she would never feel. Love. Pure love. Not just from her kids, but from Aneica and Austin.

"You are a fool for that man."

Mone't held her face and smirked. "I'd rather be foolish for one than thirty."

"You'll see you're just like me."

"I'll go blind before I do. Get the hell on."

Knowing that this would be the last time she saw her daughter in person, Arayna took her in. She adored how she looked like the only man who loved her without regard of her past. She would never admit that she was proud of her for loving and standing up for herself the way she did.

Mone't stood with pride, and not an ounce of shame wiggled over her face. She was grown. She was growing. She was evolving and healing, and everyone noticed, including the woman who failed her.

"I wish you the best."

Aneica couldn't wait for both of her feet to cross the threshold before slamming the door behind her. "Your mother is a piece—"

"I need a minute," Mone't whispered. "Just a minute, please."

Aneica gently placed her hand on Mone't's shoulder before walking away. Once alone, Mone't took a series of deep breaths and muttered the affirmations she'd been chanting most of the week. "I'm okay. I'm worthy of love without trauma. I'm honoring my boundaries. Love starts with honoring myself."

Robyn's approaches with Austin and Mone't were different. Austin needed to talk through his issues, but Mone't needed to talk herself through her moments instead of living inside the darkness her mind created for her to dwell in.

"I'm okay. I'm worthy of love without trauma. I'm honoring my boundaries. Love starts with honoring myself."

She repeated it a few more times until the heaviness in her chest subsided. Despite being angry with Austin and wanting nothing more than for him to give in to her request, her mind couldn't stay off him. Lamont mentioned he wasn't like him. It was a definite fact, because, since she was a girl, no one was like Austin.

"Don't," she groaned to herself. "Don't start this tonight."

Her brain and her heart were in accord, regardless of what her broken spirit muttered. Healing and destruction were all attached to one person. She couldn't look at herself or her children without seeing him. Whether this was closure or another chance to get this right, Mone't knew that right now she just needed a nap.

She climbed the steps to her bedroom and found herself curling up in the middle of the bed, reminiscing about the times when he was only centimeters away. He was the first man to show her pure love outside of her father and Eman, and the second to cause her pain. Nevertheless, all the roads to her healing started and ended with Austin Graham.

It was almost three hours later when Mone't reemerged. She strolled into the playroom, a smile instantly displaying on her face when her children called for her.

"Mommy, where you was?" Izzy asked, disregarding all the lessons she'd gotten from school, Mone't, and Aneica.

"Where were you?" Mone't gently corrected her, leaning down to kiss her face before plopping down and tickling AJ's chunky feet.

"Yeah, that. Where were you?" Izzy corrected herself, probing again.

"I was praying and affirming," Mone't stated, feeling Aneica's presence enter the room.

"Why? Because you're sad?" Izzy quizzed.

Choosing to tell the truth to a child who already knew the answer was the right thing to do. There were things that Mone't fought so hard not to expose them to. If she wanted to be a better mother than the one she was assigned to, she had to keep it real. In appropriate doses, of course.

"Yes. I'm sad sometimes, but it's okay to be sad."

"Are you sad 'cause Daddy isn't here?"

Mone't pressed her lips together. "Yes."

Izzy hadn't taken her eyes off her dolls. They were in a house happily coexisting. The black male and female dolls with their black plastic children were a gift from Angie for Christmas.

"Do you pray for Daddy?"

The truth was that when Mone't stopped being able to look outside her own darkness, she couldn't pray over herself, her family, or her partner. She forgot for a brief moment in time who God was and the healing she could tap into by simply tapping back into the divine.

The beauty of this healing was that it was the process that would teach her daughter and son how to heal. She wasn't going through these emotions in vain. There was something greater happening here.

"I do."

"You miss him?"

"I do."

"Can he come see us?" Now Izzy looked up at her mother, who was holding AJ in the seat of her lap, bouncing him up and down to keep him from crying.

Mone't nodded. "I'll talk to him."

"No yelling. Remember? We talk nice." Izzy was sure to add the ending for extra sprinkles so her mother knew the rules. "AJ, don't eat that!"

And just like that, Isabella was back to being the dominating sister. She removed her brother from her mother's lap and put him back on his mat. "These are your toys. Gee! Give me a sister next time."

Mone't swiveled her head to look at Aneica, who was just as amused as she was. "You should hear the things she says when you're not here."

"I don't think I want to know what comes out of her smart mouth. What's that look on your face?" Mone't asked, reading Aneica's posture and expression. "My mom's gone, so it's not that."

Aneica winced. "Uh, I'd tell you my business, but it's my business."

Mone't laughed and smiled as she threw Aneica a nod. "I hear you, Mama. You up to something. Don't worry, I'll find out."

"Mm-hmm. Until then, we all have been summoned to the front office for a meeting tomorrow. I've called Angie. She'll be here first thing in the morning."

Mone't's brows dipped in confusion. "What they want with us? We don't work for them."

Aneica shrugged her shoulders and kept her poker face. Francesco played a part in Austin's longevity. Not because of the physical ability he passed to his son, but because of the advice he gave Austin his first season. Whether Aneica was prepared or not, everything was about to come full circle.

"I don't know. I got the call from Francesco De Luca. We need to be there at nine. Make sure when you pray again tonight, pray your husband doesn't blow a fuse."

Chapter Twenty-two

"How was therapy?" Musa asked from the driver's seat.

Keyston was to his right, and Eman sat in the back seat with Austin. They were all clad in designer suits, tailored to fit their builds. Musa and Keyston were in the dark about why they were attending a meeting. Austin had put Eman up on game days ago.

Eman knew more about the ins and outs of Austin's businesses and dealings than the other two. Austin may have not shown up for visits, but Eman received quarterly reports for every business he held a stake in. Austin's job was to recognize the players on his team. Keyston wasn't as responsible as Musa. Musa wasn't ready to step into his full potential, which was why he stayed so close to the family. He'd used protecting Eman's sister as a crutch. Austin knew Musa was destined to be great. He just needed the push.

Eman was willing and ready, and he proved to be the one Austin could trust the most. After all, he'd taken a bid for his sister for the greater good of their legacy. For that reason alone, Eman was Austin's right hand.

Austin scrolled through the text from Francesco, who'd been texting him frequently since his ejection. He'd laid out the purpose of the meeting in detail and listed all of its attendees so Austin wouldn't be blindsided.

"Therapy was . . . dismantling." Austin had been deep within himself since he walked out of Robyn's office. The first day was the hardest. He'd been in a daze during the season, but without any distractions, he had no other option than to look at himself.

"Don't lose your head when you see her today," Keyston spoke up. "You can't be going all topsy-turvy in here with these owners."

A chuckle was shared between Musa and Keyston.

Ignoring the clowns in the front of the Cullinan, Eman glanced over at Austin. "Pandora refused the pregnancy test and the paternity test."

"That's 'cause her ass ain't pregnant," Musa said with a scoff. "She been quiet as hell since she got hit with those papers."

Austin shook his head. He'd made a mess of things and could only pray that everything would reveal itself and he could bounce back from this. He refused to speak about Pandora until he was sure that his gut was right. If only he'd listened to his gut months ago.

Today, he chose the calmer resolve. He adhered to the notes Robyn gave him after his series of breakdowns. "Stay clearheaded, know you aren't always entitled to control, and the only person you're responsible for is yourself."

Austin didn't dive into the conversation surrounding whether Pandora was really carrying his child. Either way, he'd have to accept it. When they pulled up to the headquarters of the Ganton Hills Monarchs, Austin inhaled deeply and centered himself before opening the door and stepping out into the media frenzy.

Eman, Musa, and Keyston surrounded and ushered him inside. Once inside of the building, he saw Mone't's car pull up. Without regard for the media, he darted back out of the building to retrieve her. He opened her door, his heart and lungs seizing when he laid his eyes on her. Her scent was enough to make him pass out. Mone't's makeup was her signature look: natural beat, full red lips, small eyes outlined with mascara. Her body filled out the off-white wrap dress she wore.

"Please don't cause a scene in front of these cameras," Mone't muttered, hesitant to take his hand. The group of men took it upon themselves to divide and conquer. Keyston and Musa escorted Aneica into the building to ride up to the conference room with Francesco, and Eman maneuvered the estranged couple through the swarm of intrusive media.

Mone't latched her hand tightly around Austin's, keeping her head down, trying to keep her anxiety down. Once inside, she let it go and walked away to the elevator.

Austin and Eman stepped on and silently rode with her. Austin couldn't take his eyes off her. Everything in him wanted to stop the elevator and hash all this out. This wasn't the time or the place. And the last time they were in the elevator, she'd put bruises on him that seemed to take weeks to fade off his body.

She was beautiful. Not the beauty he'd been used to seeing, but something was radiant and attractive about it, so magnetizing that he wanted to stay in that light. It was healing.

Her own healing had done something to him.

"Are you going to stare a hole in my face or tell me why I've been summoned?"

Mone't's words were soft. She stood with her back pressed to the back wall of the elevator, and her eyes were closed. Austin wondered if she was feeling the same flood of emotions he was.

She had to be. They were imprinted on one another.

Austin wasn't going to let the big news go before it was time to show his hand. "You'll see soon."

"Austin, it's in your best interest to tell me what I'm walking into." Mone't's piercing eyes finally opened and floated over toward him. They trailed over him, taking in every inch of him that she could see: tailored periwinkle suit, paisley tie, tightened jaw, focused, fiery eyes, and thick, curly coils pulled into a tight man bun. His beard and mustache were trimmed and full.

Just the sight of him had her mind playing back the times she would straddle his face, before she was insecure about the weight she gained from AJ. Mone't could've gained 150 pounds and he would still want her on his face.

Before her mind could dig into all the nasty, freaky things they'd done to each other, she cut her eyes away.

"You're not walking into anything that's going to embarrass you or cause you to cuss me out."

She scoffed. "I thought that the last time I attended something with you. What's it today? Another woman? Or she's really having a baby that's yours? What is it, Austin?"

The door of the elevator glided open, and Austin motioned for her to step off. His attention was solely on her and not the intense conversation his mother and Francesco were having in the corner. Mone't saw it, though. She quickly picked up on the history between them.

Austin stood behind Mone't, feeling the shiver from the slightest touch of their bodies. He placed his hand on the small of her back, and it fit perfectly in the dip. "Trust me."

Mone't scoffed under her breath, and she stepped out of his hold. "Trust?"

"Baby, this ain't the time or the place. You'll see, and when you do, you owe me a conversation without rolling your eyes or sucking your teeth."

Regaining his possession of her, he led her to a waiting area. Aneica had removed herself from Francesco's space and waited impatiently by the coffee maker. There was no time to talk. The doors to the conference room opened, promptly drawing everyone's attention. They were waved into the space, and Austin took the lead. They all took their seats and waited for Lamont to say something.

He peered at Mone't for moments before he shifted his attention to Austin. "I'm sure you're wondering why you all are here. Quite frankly, I am too, being that Mr. Graham is set to be traded to Whitestone in a few weeks."

Mone't cut her eyes at Austin, who sat coolly, hands clasped in his lap as he pretended to be interested in what Lamont had to say. "Traded. I'm here for a trade?"

Austin held his hand up, gently silencing her.

"Austin, we think it best to send you somewhere where the spotlight isn't on you at all times. Somewhere you and your family can thrive," Gerald added.

The room was silent. A smile crept across Austin's face. "That sounds like y'all thought long and hard about it. It's going to be a no from me. I'm not going anywhere."

"You are," Lamont commented. "We don't need a meeting to negotiate the details. We honored your request because of your status."

"That only means you didn't do a good job of really finding out what my status is. If you did, you would know that Gerald only owns five percent of the team. The only reason he's still in his role is because the other ninety-five percent of the owners have been silent for, what, three years now?" Austin looked to Francesco to confirm.

"Three years, six months, and two weeks," Francesco stated.

"Gerald, you remember when you damn near gambled the company away with Spade Enterprises and needed that bailout? Did you ever read the contingency?"

"I remained acting owner. What are you getting at, Austin?"

"You remained acting owner because a member of the team couldn't own and operate the team while playing." Austin sat up, making sure not to miss the color drain from Gerald Bennington's face. "You're looking at the ninety-five percent.

MoGraham Consultants owns thirty-nine percent. That's my wife, sole owner of the umbrella company that provides this arena lively nightlife experiences during the games. Eman owns thirty percent, and between my mother and my boys here, they take up the remainder. You can't trade me without the majority vote. Baby, am I leaving the Hills?"

Austin turned to Mone't, who was still processing the fact that he'd given her majority of a team and never uttered a word. "N . . . no."

"Eman, am I leaving?" Austin asked.

"Not at all," Eman returned.

"Ma, Key, Musa, where am I going?"

"Nowhere," they responded, sealing the vote in Austin's favor.

"Do we vote to remove Gerald Bennington as acting owner? All in favor, say aye." Austin sat proudly as the ayes resounded without hesitation.

"Do we vote to remove Lamont Wright as general manager?" Austin asked.

"Aye."

Gerald shot up from his seat. "You're not taking my team from me!"

"You took it from yourself," Austin replied calmly.

Gerald's secretary stopped recording the minutes and bounced her eyes from Austin to Gerald.

"Keep taking notes, sweetheart," Eman spoke up. "He's about to hit a fade-away."

Austin nodded. "I vote to elect Francesco De Luca into the seat of acting owner, transferring five percent ownership from Gerald Bennington to Francesco De Luca. All in favor, say aye."

Once again, the decision was unanimous.

Lamont stood up from his seat, steam shooting out of his nose. "I will sue your ass."

"Not before I sue yours. Have a seat. We're not done," Eman spoke up with authority in his voice.

Since Eman's return home, he'd been working overtime to figure out the connection between Jermel, Pandora, and Lamont's sudden interest with his sister. With Angie's top-tier journalist skills and his ability to strong-arm people, he unearthed information worse than the video of Austin slamming Pandora into a wall.

Eman swiveled in his seat. "Sweetheart, tell my guests they can enter."

"This is some bullshit. I'm not standing for this," Lamont huffed, marching to the door behind the secretary who'd made her way there and pulled the door open. On the other side stood Jermel and Pandora with Detective Blake. Days ago, he'd been given all the findings of Angie and Eman's investigation. With much persuasion, she talked him into not only pressing charges, along with a kickback, but giving the victims the satisfaction of watching them being dragged out in handcuffs. Dramatic, sure, but she was a fan of theatrics. Though she wasn't keen on getting the police involved in their business, this was necessary to protect her friends' business and ultimately hers.

Lamont froze. Mone't cut her eyes back at Austin. "What is this about, Austin?"

"I told you to trust me. Just watch," Austin whispered in her ear.

Eman took the lead of the meeting. "It has been brought to my attention that you three knew about the shell company that held majority ownership of the team. To my understanding, if the majority owner was in violation of the character clause, he or she would forfeit their rights and the team and its holdings would be transferred."

"That's right," the secretary spoke out of turn. "I've read the bylaws front to back for the last year for Mr. Wright."

"And what else?" Eman asked. A sly smirk crossed over his face as he awaited the reveal of how he and Angie uncovered the fraud happening under Austin's nose.

She gulped before continuing. "And I've reviewed all the closed-door meeting minutes. The system is set to record anytime someone enters this room. I gave them to Angie and Eman, and they handed it over to the detective. In my contract it states that in the event a takeover is set into motion, I have to share it with the majority owners."

"Thank you for confirming that," Eman said. His smirk formed into a full grin. "Your star athlete has been a prime family man, until he wasn't. Dissension brewed between him and his wife, caused by an agent underqualified to do his job. You know, for that body I caught. But I thank you, my guy, because without you, I'd still be sitting in a cell with no motivation to sign my appeal papers. But you and your shady-ass business dealings prompted me to come out and ensure your entire plan crumbled. Pandora was strategically placed into position, low-hanging fruit that was easy to bite, especially after half an ecstasy pill was dropped into my boy's drink. And before you deny it, we have the video from the club of Pandora doing it. You may have been the agent, but I've received every report and contract for the last three years. I gave Austin advice about what deals to take and what to pass on. I know you thought that was you, didn't you?"

While Eman shared the private details of his and Austin's business relationship from over the years, Mone't's and Aneica's eyes were burning holes into a not-even-a-little-bit pregnant Pandora. She was full of shame, though. Her eyes were low, her skin was clammy, and if she could make herself disappear, she would. Eman had been hustling since the time he came home to track her down and get the truth. He wasn't dismissing Austin from fucking up his family. Austin was responsible for that without a doubt.

"And even after maneuvering your way into the back end of deals, you still weren't satisfied, Jermel. You then teamed up with Lamont and his sister Pandora to ruin the character of Mone't and Austin. It was simple, right, Lamont? Record Austin sleeping with your sister, shop the photos and videos around, and then weasel your way in with Mone't and snatch the team from under their noses. You gave it your best effort, but unfortunately for you, it was in vain. Detective Blake, now that we've strung all the details together for you, you can move forward with the arrest of Lamont Wright, Pandora Herrera, and Jermel Green."

"I gave you everything you wanted!" Pandora shouted. It was foolish of her to believe that ratting her brother and Jermel out would make her immune to the cold shackles relaxing over the jewelry she scammed men out of. The reality that this lick was over caused tears and a confession to spill from her being. "I was never pregnant. I can't even have kids. Jermel sold Angie the tape of me pressing Austin for money. He told me to keep him in the city. It was all for money and a small percentage of the team. I was wrong, but I helped them. I can't go to jail!"

Mone't felt like she was having an out-of-body experience. This was so much information in such a short window of time.

"I have nothing to do with this," Lamont spoke up arrogantly. "She came on to me."

Mone't's head snapped in his direction. Austin knew that look. Reaching under the table to grab her knee, his touch warned her against responding.

"And I'm assuming you dug up her mother to press her for a divorce because she told you to?" Eman asked. "Meeting adjourned."

"Angie and Eman, thank you for the information. Unfortunately, Austin and Mone't weren't the first entity they tried to take over. But this is the first time they've gotten caught. Efficiently, I might add." Detective Blake opened the door, waving to the officers he had on standby.

Austin walked around the table, unbuttoning his suit jacket. "One thing before you take Lamont, Officer." Austin pulled his hand back and slapped Lamont like he was the pimp and Lamont was the ho who owed him money. "I figured I owed you for putting your hands on my wife. Y'all can take him now."

The cops read the Miranda rights to the three conspirators. Eman was confident that, in a few minutes, Angie was going to blast the news of Lamont, Pandora, and Jermel being charged with conspiracy to defraud a franchise, and Gerald was going to be an accessory to the crime committed. Mone't anxiously watched as all four were cuffed and escorted out of the conference room.

"Did everyone know about all of this?" Mone't asked.

Keyston and Musa were the first to speak up.

"News to us, shorty."

"Nah, he don't tell us shit."

Aneica chimed in. "I didn't know about anything. And I feel like I just sat through *The Twilight Zone*."

"Yeah, me too. I need some air," Mone't muttered, standing and walking out of the conference room into the hallway. Austin was hot on her trail, calling her name until she stopped.

"Mo. Baby, stop."

She finally stopped once she found a corner in a vacant hallway to pause and exhale. "All of this . . . for money?"

Staying at a safe distance, Austin placed his hands in his pockets. "Anything could happen to me at any time. I needed to make sure you and the kids were good."

"What else have you kept from me?" she asked. "How long did you know she wasn't pregnant?"

"I always had a feeling, but today confirmed it. Mo, we need to talk, and not here."

"Austin, I don't want to talk. This has already been a lot for one day."

"At least let me see the kids. I can't go another day without seeing them. Or you for that matter."

"You're looking at me now. I'll bring the kids tomorrow to the party."

"That's not enough, Mo."

She nodded. "Neither is this, Austin. So what? It was a setup? You still did it. None of this changes that. Sign the papers, and let's just be done with this."

Austin didn't block her exit. He swiveled to watch her walk away.

"We'll never be done with this. You and I made a pact, in blood. I ain't never backing off of that."

Chapter Twenty-three

"Take this dish to the table on the patio," Aneica directed Mone't. They'd been setting up and cooking since the wee hours of the morning. Aneica insisted that everything had to be perfect for Eman's welcome home party.

What was a simple family gathering at Aneica's house turned into a big to-do at the home Austin and Mone't once shared. Being back in this place was nerve-racking for Mone't. She was constantly feeling its pull on her and looking for any signs of another woman. She doubted Austin was that stupid, but she wouldn't put it past him. Rather, she couldn't put it past him. She didn't want to. She wanted a reason to fight him and fully remove her love from his possession.

"Mone't," Aneica huffed as she threw the kitchen towel over her shoulder and placed her free hand on her hip. "If you keep looking for something, you're going to drive yourself insane."

"We could have done this at your house," Mone't muttered, picking up the dish.

Aneica scoffed in amusement before turning back to the pot of chicken she was overlooking. "Put that on the table."

Mone't inched closer to the back door, and the sounds of joy from her children made her heart thunder. Austin had a glow about him, and a laugh she hadn't heard from either child in a long time consumed the vast backyard. Austin spun them in a circle in the middle of the pool.

Since it was warm enough for Isabella to jump in, they were out here whooping, hollering, and laughing. Mone't sucked in a deep breath and took a step out on the patio. Her eyes skated around the area at the decorators putting the final touches on the decor.

White linens covered the several tables placed around the yard. Balloons, a photo booth, DJ booth, and dance floor were all ready for today's celebration. They had a lot to celebrate, and that was what Mone't tried to focus on, not her husband and children happily splashing away and turning her into putty.

"Mommy, get in!" Izzy shouted.

Mone't had no intention of even being here, so she wasn't prepared to be in a pool or needing a plan to escape from Austin. Polishing her face with a fake smile and the voice to match, Mone't replied, "Mommy is okay. Enjoy Daddy."

"Are we staying?" Izzy fired off another question. This time Austin stopped splashing with AJ to look in Mone't's direction for confirmation. "Say yes."

"We're going home after the party," she stated, standing her ground.

She could feel the switch in Austin's attitude from where she stood. "This is their home, Mo. It's our home."

"We'll talk about it later. Not now," Mone't said as she placed the dish down and scurried back into the house.

"You know, you can keep running away, but eventually you two will have to talk. You have kids," Aneica chimed the moment Mone't appeared in the kitchen.

She rolled her eyes. "I was just hoping you could be a liaison between that. Talking to him means I feel things again."

Aneica could relate heavily to that. After all these years, her stomach still danced and released butterflies when she saw Francesco. She'd spent plenty of years hating him for something she willfully participated in. Austin was a direct payment for their actions and her hurt. She was determined to make him into the man he was without the help of his father. Before, she didn't think she'd made a mistake, but as of late, she was seeing the error of her ways more and more.

"Mone't, I've been right a lot, and I've been wrong. God knows I have been wrong. I have to pay for that in the way my child reacts to issues. Do not repeat the mistakes I made and have your children pay for it."

Mone't leaned on the counter and folded her arms across her chest. "I don't want to feel like I did before."

"Then don't. Talk to him. Find some kind of common ground. It's not about what you two feel. It's about those kids. At this point, you two are either going to work this thing out or go your separate ways. But regardless of the decision, those kids are top priority. You've spent enough time feeling. Now do something."

The advice allowed Mone't to straighten up, but it was really Aneica speaking to herself. She hated being wrong, but the time was coming when she would have to tell her truth and lie in the bed she'd made. Without a doubt, she knew that when the blow came, Austin and Mone't needed to be in close proximity to one another. He was going to need his wife. They'd done a lot of healing on their own, but he was going to need her for this next phase of closing the circle.

"I hear you," Mone't said.

"Then do something about it. In two hours, this house is going to be full of Monarch players, Beatsville rappers, and family. You need to tighten up. Matter of fact, drink some of that and go change." Aneica slid Mone't a cup of rum punch she'd made the night before.

Immediately, Mone't wanted to use breastfeeding as an excuse not to drink, but Angie the Baby Whisperer had made AJ forget about the titty and whine and babble for real food or a bottle.

There wasn't an excuse. She took the cup and roamed to a guest bathroom to change. As she walked down the hall, Austin trekked inside with a towel wrapped around his waist. Mone't froze momentarily, her mind reminding her of the young boy with the bird chest she'd fallen for. He was a full-grown man now, glaring back at her with a pensive expression chiseled into the fine lines of his sun-kissed skin.

"Why you changing down here? Our room hasn't moved," he grumbled.

"It hasn't, but I have. I don't live here anymore, Austin."

He scoffed and rolled his eyes. "You're going to get on my nerves with that. You just pack up, take my kids, and think I was cool with that?"

"You didn't come after us."

"I had to work, Mo. You didn't even give me a chance to fix this shit." With every word he spoke, he stepped closer to her. "The kids are staying here. They need to be in their house, not bouncing back and forth because we can't work this shit out."

"I'm not leaving my kids."

"Then take your ass to our room."

She chuckled in annoyance. "Could you move?"

He didn't budge.

"Austin."

"What, Mo? What you want me to do? Sign the papers and let someone do what I'm supposed to be doing for you? Get that shit out your head. I'm not signing them papers, and the kids ain't leaving tonight. And if it's up to me, you ain't either."

Mone't gently pushed Austin out of her way, quickly snatching her hands back when she felt the shock of their skin touching. "I need to change."

She scurried away to the bathroom, leaving Austin standing in his irritation. He pivoted and stomped into the kitchen like a child. "I'm going to put that woman's head through a goddamn wall. Has she always been that stubborn?"

"She's gotten worse over the last two months. She gets on my damn nerves too," Aneica spoke up, placing the stew chicken into a dish.

Austin huffed and picked in the pot of curry goat. "Damn, Eman gotta come home from jail for me to get curry goat?"

"Yeah, and a championship ring." She smiled up at her son, who smirked.

"It didn't feel right without her there," Austin admitted. "I didn't leave the house after we won."

"You gonna tell her that?"

"She won't listen."

Aneica put the tongs down, wiped her hands on the towel, and handed Austin a cup of rum punch. "That's because you keep rolling up on her with your chest out. She doesn't want to see that shit. She doesn't want that side of you either. She wants to see the raw parts of you. She wants to know that you've changed and she won't have to feel pain at your hands again. That's what she needs from you. All the crying you've been doing, she hasn't seen a tear."

Austin took the cup and took it to the head. "Pour me some more."

She smirked and followed his instructions. "Be vulnerable, son. Be honest. Get your wife back."

"Daddy! Come on!" Izzy shouted loudly. Austin had briefly left them in the baby pool, but Isabella had the patience of her mother.

He took the second cup to the head and rushed back outside. "A'ight, a'ight, don't be so bossy."

If Aneica had her way, the two would either be tearing up the house and the party or off somewhere tearing up sheets. "If I'm lucky, I'll get the latter," she muttered to herself.

A few drinks later, Mone't was made-up and sitting at the decorated table with Davina LeRoux—the music manager of the Hills and surrounding area, stellar mom, and businesswoman—Emya, Angie, Braxton Rivers, and Sienna Lawrence.

There was so much greatness at this table, and they all seemed to have their lives together, while Mone't felt like she was still sitting in the middle of a mess.

The business opportunity she thought she found with Lamont had only turned out to add more of a mess to her plate. She sat quietly, sipping from her cup, listening to the women talk, and watching how Austin was so attentive to their children while entertaining all the guests.

"Mone't," Davina called with a slight giggle. She turned to look over her shoulder to see what had Mone't's attention so captured that she couldn't answer her for the last thirty seconds. "Ah, I see."

"Mm-hmm," Sienna chimed. "The effect of that man."

"Girl, I know that look," Emya added. "You want to hate his ass, but you can't."

"You know, Zaim and I separated when I was carrying our first baby. We're three in now." Davina observed Mone't's expression. "You are still in love with that man."

"I wish I weren't," Mone't muttered. "I really wish I weren't."

"Why? Because you think it'll be easier to pull away from him? I'm telling you, that's not the case," Sienna spoke up.

"It's never to pull away from these men. Once they imprint on you, that's it. It could be a year, three, or five. They're going to get you back. The question is, are you going to be ready when it happens?" Braxton asked Mone't.

"Girl, who you telling?" Emya scoffed, sipping her rum punch. "Tony wouldn't let me breathe until I talked to him. Mind you, we'd been friends since college."

"I got to give it to them. When they know what they want, they don't stop until they have it. You and Austin aren't done, Mo," Davina spoke up. "I'd like to see you get out this house tonight."

"She won't," Angie added.

"I thought you were on my side," Mone't protested, watching Angie stand from the table and trot toward Eman, who was nice and liquored up.

"I am, but my man is calling. So I have to go," Angie threw over her shoulder.

"Ayo, wassup, niggas! Big Daddy Zaim on the ones and twos!" Zaim shouted into the mic as he hijacked the DJ's booth. He was more than honored to be snubbed by the star. "How y'all feeling tonight? I just wanna thank Austin for inviting me to this dope-ass party and wearing my dope-ass headphones!"

"Ah, shit," Davina groaned. "Let me go get his big drunk ass down."

"Baby number four, Davina!" Sienna shouted behind Davina, who was whisking away to get Zaim away from the DJ booth.

"It's the damn punch," Emya said in a fit of giggles. Sienna, Braxton, and Emya laughed among themselves.

"Shit, it's about to have me pulling Prynce out of here," Braxton muttered into the cup. "Let me get him another cup."

Mone't was in a daze again. Austin's orbs were holding hers captive. When she could break away, she excused herself from the table and walked inside the house. She hadn't been in their room, but she knew that was the only place no one would interrupt her.

Outside, Austin had handed the children to Aneica and followed her inside.

"Girl, she ain't leaving this house," Sienna muttered to Emya now that Braxton had excused herself and went to refresh her and her husband's cups.

"Nope," Emya said, high-fiving her. "Baby number three compliments of this rum punch."

"I'm going to tell her to name the next one Rumi. She's getting knocked up tonight. Did you see the way he passed those kids off like an assist?" Sienna asked in a fit of giggles. "Shit, I'm drunk."

While they laughed among themselves, Austin was climbing the steps two at a time. Like a bloodhound, he had Mone't's scent and was going to follow it until he latched on to her flesh, making her whimper until she succumbed.

Walking into the bedroom he hadn't slept in since she left, he found her at her vanity, taking deep breaths. Austin locked the door behind him and pursued his wife. Before Mone't could protest, she was already locked in the bathroom with him, trapped in a stare-off.

The rum punch, tension, and unspoken words had them in a chokehold, the silence speaking the words their mouths stubbornly refused to say. Austin's impairment didn't obscure the view of the woman before him. In all the rawness of their relationship, he was drawn to her like a moth to a flame.

"You enjoy your time with that nigga?" Austin questioned. It was no secret that Mone't had been seen with Lamont more than once on what looked like more than business. Though Austin knew Mone't was well within her rights, he didn't have to like how another man touched her and attempted to leave his scent on her.

Mone't didn't answer, slightly ashamed that she almost slipped into Lamont's demands to have her as a ploy.

"Nah," Austin's baritone rumbled. "So much to say. Serving me papers, blocking me. Keeping me from my kids, from you. You're going to answer me. Look me in the eyes so I can tell if you lying."

Mone't scoffed, rolled her eyes, and looked up at him. "What if I did?"

"Then you would have defended him yesterday. You didn't. Didn't even look at him."

"What's the point, Austin? Is this a dick-measuring contest?"

Austin pressed his body against hers, bending his neck so he wouldn't miss the flutter in her eyes when she felt his nature rise against her flesh. "It ain't a contest if I already won."

"And gave it away. Tell me, if I had slept with him, what would you have to say?"

"We even, and I'll fuck that nigga up the way I did Jermel. But that shit is trivial, Mo." His large hands went from her hips up the side of her body. They found their resting place at the base of her neck, squeezing just enough for him to hear the low groan she was trying to suppress.

"It's not."

"It is. 'Cause he ain't me. Never could be. He'll never know you like I know you. He'll never know that right now you're ovulating. He'll never know the smell you emit when you're on your cycle or when you're craving me. He'll never know how that one tear slides down your cheek when it's good for you. He'll never know that you whimper in your sleep on rainy nights. He'll never know that you like when I take my time with you."

Austin flicked his tongue out to taste her pouty lips. He latched on to them, slowly kissing her, applying enough pressure to her throat to make her head spin.

"He'll never know that I'm your first, last, and only. Ain't no one after me. What he had was a sample. I got the whole damn buffet. He'll never know I'm responsible for those titties. For that ass. For that pussy jumping and throbbing." He bit down on her lips while his hands groped and smacked her ass. "He'll never know that I know where the stretch marks start and stop and when they developed. You're my girl, Mo. Mine. I fucked up, but I'm still yours."

"Please, stop," Mone't whined so sexily. If he considered letting her walk out the same way she walked in, he would've disregarded it after hearing that.

"No. I'm clean. Wasn't no baby, and I want you."

"You don't deserrrvv . . ." Her breathing hitched when Austin's mouth found her neck and his long fingers slipped up her sundress, easily finding the treasure nestled between her thick thighs. "Austin."

"I want you, baby. Just you. All of you."

He sucked her neck, pressed his fingers into her hot apex, and slipped the straps of her dress off her shoulders, exposing her perfect breasts. Mone't whimpered, unable to speak or protest. The rum punch was doing what it needed to. They were locked beneath its spell.

Austin greedily suckled at her breast, not wanting to pull himself away from her. How could he? Months without her felt like an eternity, and it was something he never wanted to experience again.

Her moans were so sweet, and if he grew any harder, he'd bust through the constraints of his boxer briefs. "He'll never know how fucking beautiful you sound when you moan for me like that. That moan is mine, Mo."

Lifting her body up, he placed her bare ass on the countertop. The sundress was bunched around her waist, giving Austin access to whatever he wanted. Mone't was on fire, lost in the entrancement of how beautiful they were without the forces working to pull them apart. She tugged at the waistband of his pants. Forcefully pushing them down his hips along with his boxers, Mone't groaned when Austin's length bobbed out.

It was darker than the rest of his skin, and veins wrapped their way up and down the shaft. It was the perfect length and girth, with a slight hook at the tip. It jumped at her, slowly leaking precum she wanted to taste.

Mone't couldn't bring herself to drop to her knees before Austin pushed her thighs open, and she was spread-eagle. The next motion was lining up with her opening, and the third was falling into her depths with loud groans of pleasure escaping from their lips.

In a frenzy of nerves shooting off, she threw her arms and legs around him, pushing him fully into the depths of her.

"I fucking missed you, baby," Austin grunted roughly in her ear. He ground inside of her heat, kissing her, smacking her ass, loving every pulse and grip of her pussy. "I'm sorry, Mo."

Mone't matched his rhythm. This romp in their bathroom wasn't in their plans. She planned to gather herself, sober up, and go home. That would give him a night with his kids before Aneica returned them.

Sexing her husband like they were two horny teenagers wasn't even on the list of things to do. But she was loving every minute of it. Loving the way he chanted her name.

"Mone't, Mone't, Mone't."

She relished the way he kissed every inch of her flesh while keeping his rhythm. In this sacred space, with just them, there was no room for doubt or thought of mistakes. It was just them letting their bodies do the talking while a party went on in their backyard.

Sprawled in the middle of their bed, Austin drank from her river, burying his face as far as it could go. She gripped the sheets, cumming again and not committing the count to thought. She returned the favor, sucking him, riding him, telling him how good he felt inside of her.

Austin looked up at his wife, adoring her sex faces while she rode him into their personal dimension of ecstasy. His hands gripped her waist tightly as if she would run away from him the minute he came.

Mone't's walls tightened around him as their bodies quaked in tandem. Synchronized moans, squeals, and incoherent words swirled throughout the room until she fell to his side, sighing in relief at the feel of the pillows and sheets against her skin.

Normally, it would have taken her hours to fall asleep. She would have tossed and turned, trying to turn her mind off, but with Austin's heavy arm draped over her and his breathing in her ear, she faded quickly, her body still throbbing with desire.

Chapter Twenty-four

Austin woke up to an empty bed. Mone't's scent lingered, but she was far gone. With no true sense of time, he sat up and peered into the darkness of the room. Like every night before this, he couldn't sleep without her unless he'd taken several drinks to the head. Even then, it only lasted a couple of hours. He refused to be in this bed without her. Sleeping in the guest bedroom on the firmer mattress and shivering from the draft or running himself into exhaustion was better than this.

Staggering to his feet, he found something to clothe himself with before traveling down the stairs. There was minimal light coming from the first floor, but the loud whispers told him not everyone was gone or passed out in various corners of the house.

Glancing at a clock on the way to the intense whispering, he groaned to himself. It was only three in the morning. He wasn't going to be able to go back to sleep without Mone't's body on his, and he was far too tired to run, hit sandbags, or shoot the night away.

Finally reaching the noise, his ears burned at the conversation Francesco was having with his mother.

"How long do you think I'm going to keep this up with you without telling him the truth?" Francesco asked as he put his shirt back on. The sight alone spiked the irritation in Austin's body.

The first strike was that they were putting the articles of clothing back on in his kitchen, and the second was that he was talking to his mother as if he didn't have any sense. How Francesco moved next would determine the third strike.

"Fuck y'all got going on in here?" he asked harshly, watching his mother jump out of her skin, and Francesco's shoulders squared. "That's why you been on my line all this time. Y'all fuckin'?"

"Austin, watch your mouth," Aneica hissed.

Francesco turned to him, blocking the view of Aneica pulling her dress back together. "I told her it was time to tell you."

"Austin, just hear me out," Aneica softly pleaded. "I wanted to tell you."

"Ma, you could have told me y'all had something going on. You didn't have to do that shit in my kitchen, though." Disgust immediately hit him in the gut. "My kids eat off the counter."

"We weren't on the counter. It was the floor," Aneica corrected him, causing Austin's dramatic behavior to turn up a notch.

"I'ma be sick. Please stop."

"Aneica, you need to stop deflecting, dammit."

"Ay ay ay, playa," Austin warned. "I don't give a damn if that's your lady. That's my mother. You don't talk to her like that."

"Austin," Aneica called his name again. "Go to sleep. We'll talk about this later."

"When, Aneica, huh? In another twenty-three years?" Francesco asked, making Austin freeze and count back like a flood of film going through his mind. He squinted his eyes, looking closely at Francesco and seeing himself: his height, build, and that terrible-ass attitude on the court from time to time. "Son, I wanted to tell you."

"You got to be fuckin' kidding me," Austin replied in disbelief. "Ma, you fucking serious?"

"Watch how you talk to your mother," Francesco spoke up.

Austin held his hand up, silencing him and peering at his mother. Aneica wished she could disappear. There was no running or vanishing from this moment. It was the inevitable, and her time to tell on herself was up.

"I'm not talking to you. Ma, you serious? This whole time you had me around this motherfucker and didn't say shit?"

"Austin, let me just explain," Aneica said, trying to calm her son. There wasn't any calming him. There was only one person who could, and she'd run off like a thief in the night.

"You ain't got shit to explain to me when you had twenty-three years to! I'm out here thinking my daddy didn't give two fucks about me, and he was around the whole time? You didn't say shit, Ma. Nothing."

Aneica's eyes pricked with tears. "I didn't know how."

"You didn't know how? Yo, you trippin'. How long were you gonna keep this? When we start this, Ma?" Austin looked to his mother with tears pricking in his eyes. "And you were in my face for three years and didn't say nothing. Posing as a friend when the whole time you were the nigga who busted and ran off."

"Austin, let me explain. It was complicated," Francesco spoke up, stepping toward him.

"Ain't shit complicated about sending your kid and his mom off to live in the hood, dodging gangs and bullets, hating-ass niggas, and scheming-ass bitches. Ain't nothing complicated about it. It's fucked up." Austin shook his head and palmed his face. "Get out."

"Austin!" Aneica shouted in disbelief.

He wasn't budging. "I got you a house. Do this shit there. I don't want to see neither of y'all."

"If you let me tell you what happened—"

Austin cut Francesco off. "Ain't no need. I don't want to hear that shit. Take your woman and get out my house before I put your ass out."

Austin moved out of the way so they could walk past him. Sure, he was angry at the news. But the hurt coursing through him was overwhelming. Austin recalled every night he wished he had his father to talk to then stared at the ceiling of the small house he grew up in. He recalled the nights he would have rather had a real meal instead of a pack of noodles.

They trekked to the door, and Aneica stopped to look at her son.

"Don't even give me the eyes, Ma. Get out."

When they left, Austin hit the wall, not realizing that Isabella was at the top of the stairs watching his breakdown. Hot tears and anger made his surroundings the last thing he was aware of. That soft, "Daddy?" snatched him out of his feelings.

He quickly wiped his face with the back of his hand and sniffled. "What you doing up, baby girl?" He avoided her eyes.

"Where is Mommy?"

It was a valid question, and whether Mone't was sound asleep in the bed she didn't belong in or wide awake, he and their children were going to find out. "You want her?"

"You two together," Izzy answered honestly. "Can I have both?"

Austin nodded. "You can." He climbed the stairs and scooped her up. "You have to help me with your brother. Can you get your blanket while I get him?"

Isabella nodded and rested her head on his shoulder until they arrived at her room, and he placed her back on her feet. Isabella wasted no time going to get her blanket and her favorite teddy bear for the car ride while Austin put AJ in his carrier. His son was heavy and healthy. Although Mone't was going through her own emotions, he could tell she didn't neglect taking care of them.

There was so much about his woman that deserved to be praised, and he was going to do it every chance he got. For this early morning, all he needed was to lay his head in her lap while she massaged his scalp.

Once the kids were secured in the seats of the spare family vehicle he rarely drove, they quietly made their way to Mone't. Isabella had fallen asleep next to her brother, clutching her teddy bear and blanket.

He arrived at the house and noticed the light on in the bedroom where she watched him weeks ago. She was up, and he needed her. Balancing both sleeping children, he walked up the sidewalk and rang the doorbell. It took Mone't a matter of seconds to get from wherever she was to the door.

"It's late," she whispered, reaching out to take Isabella.

"It's early," he muttered. "Point me in the right direction for him."

"Up the stairs to the left, first door." Mone't secured the door and climbed the stairs with Isabella slumped over her shoulder. Fixing the tiny bonnet on her head and kissing her forehead, she fixed the blanket and stepped out of Izzy's room, leaving the door slightly ajar.

Austin stepped out of AJ's room at the same time and looked at her. By the way his eyes cast over her, she knew his appearance was driven by something deeper than her leaving him in the middle of the night.

"Downstairs," she directed him.

Austin followed her down the narrow stairway into the small kitchen. This house didn't have the high ceilings or tall doorways their home had. Every time he entered a new room, he had to duck to avoid hitting the frame.

"You could have called and told me you were on the way," she spoke up with her back to him.

"I wouldn't need to if you were still in the bed."

The baritone of her husband made her chest swell.

"I need you to be there."

Mone't could've easily fired off all the times she needed Austin and he wasn't there for her, but she chose to look forward and not at where they came from. "You going to tell me about it?"

"I will." Austin's voice was soft and undetectable of his hesitation of what was next for him with the information he received almost an hour ago. He envisioned the moment he came to Mone't, laid his head in her lap, and broke down to be so much different than this.

He was torn. It would have been easy to give into the temptation of distracting them both with sex. At least that way he could have been lulled back to sleep by her soft breathing while her body was pressed against his.

His tall body slumped. He didn't feel like the king or the crusader who'd put his entire family on. Owning the Ganton Hills Monarchs and a successful clothing line and collaborating with the biggest names in hip-hop weren't shit and didn't mean shit to him. The amount of humbling happening in this moment was unreal. He had to look at the woman he loved, the woman he'd hurt, and cry.

Mone't turned on the tea kettle and slowly turned around to face the gentle giant she fell in love with. Vulnerability dripped off him. She stood torn between wanting to watch his breakdown, enjoy it, and say something that would dig into his heart deeper, or open her arms and hold him.

Seeing him fighting back tears while trying to gather his thoughts was the sexiest thing she'd seen from him. Sexier than claiming her body while their minds spun. Sexier than taking control of the situation that had gotten too far out of control.

Her back stiffened, and her thighs clenched. Austin still had a hold on her. She watched as he planted his hands on the countertop and groaned as though his heart hurt.

"Is this how you felt? When I lied to you? Like someone reached into your chest, took your heart out, and crushed the fuck out of it? Because this feels like heartbreak. I ain't never had nobody break my heart, Mo. Nobody."

Mone't's nostrils flared. She felt his pain. Now that their bodies had connected again, she could feel him, and it was heavy.

"It felt like death. Like the safest place on earth I knew was stolen from me. Like it had been invaded and I was left in the rubble, trying to find anything that reminded me of what I once had. Just like someone took the heart I left in their hands and threw it into flames."

Austin groaned, dropped his body into a seat, and slightly looked over at his wife. She was dressed in a King Graham T-shirt with a silk scarf tied around the short cut he'd fucked into a mess hours prior. "I made you feel like this. This shit is no joke. I can see why you beat my ass like that."

"Who did it?" Mone't held her breath after asking the question. She didn't know what he was going to tell her. She didn't know where this was going, so she stopped breathing until she knew it was safe to do so.

"Would you ever keep something from me?" Austin questioned, not ready to share the information. "Something that would fuck me up?"

Like the woman she was, Mone't stepped to him, cautiously hoping that Austin wasn't going to hit her with another blow to her mending heart. Just above a whisper, she said, "No."

"That's because you're pure, and I tainted you," he scoffed, hazel eyes trailing over his wife. "I'm really sorry I did this to you, Mo."

The rumble of his velvety voice froze her. He'd said it over a hundred times, but this was the only one she believed. This was the one that changed their course. Mone't stood between his gaped legs and placed her hands softly on both sides of his face. "Talk to me. Tell me what's happening with you."

"I thought about it. I stared at his photos, the posters, emulated him only for him to be the man who implanted me." Austin started off in a mumble. "He didn't have any other involvement after that, though. Not a letter, a smoke signal. Nothing. Just let us live like shit. I should really be thanking him for being a piece of shit. It would have never taught me how to get out of the trenches. I wouldn't have you or our family. But that doesn't negate that fact that he threw me and my mom to the wolves."

Mone't released the breath she was holding. She listened to every word he spoke.

"She would have never told me if I didn't hear her. I've been searching my whole life for some type of inkling of who am I besides what I was told to be, and he was here the whole time?" Austin scoffed, eyes lifting to hers that intently focused on him. "The star. The player relations. The man who's found some way to been in my space since I got drafted, and not a word from her. Why would she hide that from me?"

She inaudibly gasped at the revelation. Francesco De Luca was her husband's father. She studied his face and saw the similarities. But still she saw Aneica's son. Her pride and joy. Although Austin was devastated by the news, Mone't wasn't going to dismiss all the hard work Aneica did to raise him and then turn around and take her as her own. "Shame."

His face screwed up. "Shame? She fucked him then and again now. That's not shame. That's some wild form of control. Avoidance or something."

"Which could be true, Austin. She's human. She's made her mistakes. We all have."

"You ain't never done nothing like this, Mo," Austin said, defending his feelings, and he removed her hands from his face.

The kettle began to whistle, drawing her attention away from him as he stood. Austin roamed into the living room, sitting on the couch, staring down at his hands. Mone't allowed Austin his space while she made his tea: one bag of green tea, one bag of lemon ginger, three squeezes of honey, and a cinnamon stick.

It was best if she allowed him to talk, knowing that when he got like this, his mind was liable to jump from topic to topic until he was all talked out. She placed their mugs down on the coffee table and sat on the other end of the sofa.

"You don't want to be close to me?" he asked. "I need you close to me, Mo. You keep me calm."

She moved closer and sat in his silence. Austin stared at the steam dancing off his tea.

"I'm not pure, Austin. Not anymore," she announced.

"All of that is a direct reflection of me. I pushed you to do whatever you did with that nigga." Austin shrugged his shoulders. "I don't care about that, Mo. For real. I did that. This shit here I didn't ask for. But I get it. When you hurt something God gave you, He has to teach you a lesson."

Austin laid his head in Mone't's lap. His next set of words made the tears spill from their eyes. "You're my Garden of Eden. Everything I needed was always right here. I'm safe here. I'm protected here. I'm allowed to be raw here."

The wetness of his tears seeped into her lap. Naturally, she allowed her fingers to sink in his curls.

"Everything starts and ends with you, baby. I don't want to be without it. I can't be without it. I'm not signing those papers. I need you to understand that."

She sniffled. The lump in her throat was holding her voice hostage. "What do we do then?"

"Fight for this shit. 'Cause if I lose you, you might as well kill me."

She closed her eyes, letting the tears fall. "Is it worth it?"

"As worth it as taking my next breath. Because if losing you means I have to relive this feeling over and over again, I won't make it."

She licked her dry lips and inhaled. "Okay."

"All I'm asking you is for a chance to make this right. All I need is that final shot, baby."

"Don't miss."

Austin softly kissed the exposed part of her thigh. "I won't."

He settled back into her lap and lived in their silence until the sun came up. Mone't slept with her head propped up on her hand. Austin slept in the cradle of her lap. His tall body hung off the couch, but he'd sacrifice comfort to be able to rest here with her.

Before she could wake up from AJ's whining, he sat up and cracked his neck. He watched her sleep, mouth slightly open, her breathing heavy but relaxing.

Mone't was bad, and they both knew it. The five-foot five-inch, almond-toned flesh glistened with specks of gold underneath the low light of the sun peeking in through the curtains. Although he threw a fit about her trading in the thick, long tresses for a short pixie cut, he loved how beautifully she was coming into herself, not just as his woman but as a woman tapping into her divinity. Her healing was his, and he needed to submerge himself in it.

He was in awe of her. Kissing her face softly, he reached behind himself and spread the throw blanket over her. AJ was beginning to crank up his cry. Austin whisked up the stairs to change his diaper and clothes, then brought him down to the kitchen to find something to feed him.

Luckily, Isabella had followed him downstairs. "Mommy has bottles. Microwave for ten seconds."

"You know a lot, don't you?" he asked his growing daughter.

"I do. I'm Mommy's right hand."

"What am I then?"

"Her boyfriend," Izzy replied, laughing.

Austin shook his head as he followed her instructions to feed his son. "You want to get Mommy some pancakes and eggs from FlapJacks?"

"What's in this for me?"

"Mickey Mouse pancakes with extra whipped cream."

"Add chocolate chips and we have a deal."

"Then it's a deal, little mama. But we can't wake up Mommy."

"Did you make her cry?"

Austin shook his head. "No. I'll never make Mommy cry again."

"You promise? I don't like sad Mommy. Happy Mommy is funner."

"I love happy Mommy, and I promise to keep a smile on her face. And your face and this chunky man's face."

"You better. I do not have time to go alllllll the way to your house, then alllllll the way to this house, then allllll the way back. I want to be in the big house, and I want happy. Happy for everyone. You, Mommy, Mama, and even AJ."

"Even AJ?" Austin asked, laughing at his daughter's backhanded compliment. Sometimes he had to stop and evaluate whether she was 3 going on 4 or 3 going on 40. Isabella's mouth and sassiness definitely came from Mone't. But he wasn't without fault. He and his mother molded her into the monster she was.

"Even AJ. He's my brother. I love him. He just needs his own toys."

Austin chuckled and nodded his head. "You got it, little mama."

Chapter Twenty-five

"Daddy, Mommy is going to love these flowers and pancakes," Izzy shouted excitedly as Austin maneuvered his way into Mone't's house. He didn't have a key, so he was forced into breaking and entering and didn't mind. She had no business being away from him anyway.

"Remember her favorites in case one day Daddy forgets," he said with a grunt as he popped the lock and pushed the door open. On the other side was Mone't. Her tiny hands were propped on her hips, her eyes were damn near nonexistent behind her squint, and her mouth was tooted up.

Austin smirked, licking his lips and instantly turned on by her little attitude.

"You could've just called for the code," she huffed, taking AJ out of his arms.

"I did. I'm still blocked. You need to do something about that," he commented. "I'll fix the knob before we put this on the market."

Mone't was sashaying away from him and removing AJ's saturated bib from around his neck. "Hold up. You speaking French. What is this 'we'?"

Austin and Isabella followed her into the kitchen, where she'd been enjoying her morning tea before Austin broke in with his kids in tow.

"You and I. This is a great rental property."

"Like the other ones you have stashed around the city?" she questioned, wiping AJ's face and kissing his chubby cheeks. "Did Daddy make you an accessory to his crime? Hm? Is he turning my sweet boy into a criminal? I expected this from your uncles."

"None of my uncles are cri-animals," Izzy interjected. "They all went to college. Uncle E is the smartest. He was there the most."

Mone't cut her eyes from Isabella to Austin. He threw his full hands up in defense. "I didn't tell her that."

"Mama told me that. But you went for a little bit, Mommy. Are you going back? You don't want to be smart?"

Mone't's mouth fell open as she prepared herself to answer her, but she decided to fire off more questions.

"She said Daddy only went for a little bit too. So my Mommy and Daddy are dumb."

"Whoa! Ain't nothing dumb about your daddy, girl." Austin defended himself. "I'm smart, handsome—"

"Arrogant," Mone't added. "Furthermore, your mom is the smartest of everyone."

"Even Mama?" Izzy asked, kneeling in her chair.

Mone't smirked, her lip quivering with laughter and a smart comment daring to escape her mouth. "Sometimes I am."

Isabella scoffed. "Hm, that ain't what I heard."

"See, she needs friends." Austin used this conversation to argue his case to get Mone't to come home. "Her friends are back in the neighborhood."

"Austin, don't do that," Mone't warned with a slight smile on her face.

"Don't do what? Point out the fact that my mother has our daughter hanging out with Blanche and Dorothy and Rose every other afternoon? Why is she gossiping about us to us like she eighty?"

Mone't couldn't help but laugh. It made Austin's heart thunder with pride. This was what he expected to feel when he won his third championship. The laugh of his wife was better than any MVP, any championship trophy, and any max contract he could sign.

"All right. You have a point. We can do biweekly visits," Mone't countered. She balanced AJ on one hip while she undid the bags Austin placed down on the counter seconds prior.

His brows dipped in confusion. "If I recall, last night we agreed to work on this."

"Yeah, with you at your place and me at mine."

He waited until she gave Isabella her food and returned to the island before he leaned in to hiss at her. "Girl, are you on that stuff?"

"What stuff, Graham?"

"Percs, zannies, coke, crack, molly, X? You on something if you think that after last night I'm letting up off you."

Mone't smacked her teeth and rolled her eyes. "You're being dramatic."

"Oh, well. Whether you come home or not, I'm going to be wherever you are."

Mone't's lip curled up. "I knew I should've left you on the doorstep last night."

"I would have broken in."

"So you're really going to be a criminal?" Mone't sassed.

Austin smirked and looked her up and down. Mone't knew better than to be prancing around him in those shorts and that tank top. "Don't forget I went to college, girl. I know how to do a lot of things."

"And I'm assuming that 'doing a lot of things' somehow translates to you're not going to leave."

"Nah, we attached again. You fucked around and found out." He took their trays to the table and motioned for her to sit down. "You didn't mention your flowers."

Mone't was so caught up in trying to argue against his proposition and clean AJ up that she missed the bouquet of assorted flowers: sunflowers, white and yellow roses, and pink daisies. "Well, I do apologize. Izzy, they're beautiful."

Izzy shot Austin a sassy look and pranced over to the table, just to spite his effort. Mone't's inherited attitude was on full display.

"You're welcome. I used Daddy's money. The lady at the store told him he better be taking them to you. Daddy said she was in our bidness." Isabella stuffed her mouth with chocolate chip pancakes oozing with whipped cream. "They're always in our bidness."

Mone't closed her eyes and shook her head.

"She really was in our business, then asked me for a photo after calling me all types of dogs," he huffed. "I thought they loved me. They really love you. I saw someone at a game with a sign that said, 'Make the shot for Mone't.'"

Mone't was never one to be caught up in how the public felt about her. She was just his wife. To her, it was that simple. Her husband was the superstar, and she was along for the ride. However, their status had made their issues bigger than life. She flashed him a look, begging him to table it until Isabella and AJ were both out of earshot.

They sat in a comfortable silence, enjoying the first meal together in a long while. AJ smacked on Mone't's fingers as she fed him pieces of her sweet potato pancakes. Austin tended to Isabella's messy face as she knocked down a stack of pancakes, bacon, and eggs.

"Where are you putting this food, girl?" he muttered, watching her eat like him.

"She's having a growth spurt. She'll eat crazy like this and then won't want anything. I've just paid attention to the phases."

"I can't believe I missed all of this," Austin said, feeling defeated. "This ain't going to ever happen again."

Mone't hummed as though she didn't believe him. It wasn't that she didn't. She did. She didn't want to, though. The raw and hurt part of her didn't want to. But Austin had finally come back for her and their family, and he was dead set on mending the things he'd broken.

Breakfast was over, and Isabella and AJ were in their playroom, wreaking havoc on the room and each other. Mone't was close by, cleaning and making herself busy. Avoidance. She'd felt things last night into the early morning that she scolded herself for. She was a sucker, falling back into him off some rum punch and tears. That was what weak women did.

Austin sat on the bench at the end of the bed and watched her between texting Angie. He had to credit her on his recent turnaround. From putting him in contact with Robyn to arranging a fake girls' night so he could surprise Mone't, every gesture had to be grand and consistent. The woman occupying his mind and heart was deserving of that. She'd more than proved that.

"Why are you watching me like a hawk? Like I'm going to escape or something?"

"Because you did once. I came home to an empty house, and that shit fucked me up."

"You also found yourself in the club grinding up on random women and having the time of your life."

"I wasn't having the time of my life. I was drinking heavy to feel nothing and then drinking some more to sleep throughout the night and not see you."

She rolled her eyes.

"Roll them as much as you want. I'm not lying."

"But you have."

He chuckled in annoyance. "Mo, there isn't anything you can say that I'm going to dispute. It's all true. I slept with her. I hid it. I put my hands on her to keep her ass silent. I pushed you away before because I was guilty as hell. I clubbed and drank heavy. I fought people for talking about you because I was wrong. I allowed Jermel to form a wedge between us. I left you alone for a minute because I couldn't get my head right. I cried a lot. I fought some more, and then I went to therapy. Still going to therapy."

Mone't stopped occupying herself. "You're in therapy?"

He nodded. "I hate it, honestly. All I talk about is you. She tries to redirect me to how my actions affect me and childhood trauma and all that shit. To be honest, all that shit is what it is. Well, was."

Mone't leaned against her dresser, studying him as he rubbed his temples. "You know you're going to have to talk to him and your mom at some point."

"The point ain't today."

She sighed and went back to her mindless cleaning. "Well, bring it up in therapy."

"You know, the crazy part is I look like him. I play like him. I talk and walk like him and didn't meet him until I'd already developed."

"Genetics don't lie. Look at Izzy and AJ." Mone't pointed across the room, gesturing like the children were there.

Austin leaned back and spread his arms over the end of the bed. "You know what else doesn't lie?"

"I'm sure you're going to tell me."

"The heart. Like I was saying earlier: either here or there, this separation shit is over. I don't care if we here tussling all night until there's a resolve. It's over, Mo."

"What brought this on? I can't help but feel like this new development of your father is causing you to be here."

"Baby, I was going to be here if that nigga showed his hand or not. But I can't go through that without you. I need you. And that's it. I need you. Ain't shit without you."

She hummed, stepped between his legs, and replied, "Well, I have a hair appointment at one, and I need you to father your children. Let's start there."

"I don't know why you're getting it done when I'm going to fuck it up again."

She curled her lip. "You won't. Last night was a moment of weakness."

"There's strength in weakness, and the way your pussy welcomed me home was strong as hell. No mistakes, baby. Just purpose."

"We're not fucking through this, Austin."

"Touché. But we will make love through it. Period. No discussion. Now back up off me before I drop your ass down on me with my kids down the hall."

Mone't quickly pulled herself away from him only for Austin to pull her down and kiss her. He saw that glint of desire in her eyes. He was chipping at the wall around her heart. When he reclaimed it, he would never fumble it again.

Mone't pulled herself away from him to get ready for her appointment, and Austin went to gather the kids for snacks, a movie, and a nap while Mone't was gone. When he had them comfortably tucked around him, Isabella lay on his thigh, watching the colorful animation of the new Mahogany Kids streaming channel.

"Daddy," she spoke through a yawn.

"Hmm?" he grunted, eyes barely open. AJ's dead weight on his chest was putting him to sleep too.

"Mommy didn't call your name in her sleep last night or call the lady, crying. That's good. Don't leave, okay?"

"Okay, baby."

Isabella nuzzled in closer, knocked out before they could get ten minutes into the movie. Mone't crept down the stairs and into the living room. She draped the blanket over them, snapped a photo, and left for her hair appointment.

Chapter Twenty-six

"I didn't find the curry, but she had a whole bowl of oxtail she stashed," Austin spoke as he walked into Mone't's house. This time he used the code to get in. "You're going to have to make some rice and peas and cabbage."

"Austin." Mone't rushed to the door to warn him before he cut the corner. But it was too late. He was already face-to-face with Francesco.

"Fuck is he doing here? Y'all fucking in this kitchen, too?"

"Whoa, what?" Mone't asked, missing that bit of information before. "I've only been upstairs ten minutes. I hope not."

"So you knew they were coming?" he asked Mone't, who chose this moment to be smart instead of direct.

"When you say 'coming' . . ."

"Mo, right now ain't the time to play with me, baby. Did they show up, or did you invite them?" he questioned. "It don't even matter. Y'all can go. We don't have nothing to discuss. I want to eat with my family."

Francesco's presence had instantly provoked the need to drink. Austin was trying to stay away from the bottle, but it quickly gave him an escape from all the nonsense.

"They are your family, Austin, whether you like it or not. Just hear them out and understand why. We all make mistakes," Mone't urged. She couldn't stand seeing the hurt on Aneica's face or the sadness in their eyes. Austin had opened her up to feeling more than herself, and she couldn't stop feeling. Especially him.

Austin was on the trail to the liquor cabinet he knew she had. He stepped heavy, deliberate footsteps on the way to the fully stocked wine rack in the cabinet. That was all there was. No brown liquor, no rum punch, just bottles of red, white, and blush wine with Mone't's silhouette on them. "This all you got, baby?"

He questioned her as though he didn't know that his woman wasn't big on drinking. This was the most she'd drunk since turning 21, and she'd tapered off since ushering herself out of her haze.

"That's all, and you don't need to drink. Just listen."

He erupted. Thankfully, Angie and Eman had picked up the kids almost an hour before Austin came back from grabbing clothes and food from his house. "Goddamn it, Mo! I don't want to listen. What part of that are you missing? I don't want to

look at the nigga, talk to the nigga, hear that nigga.
He said fuck me twenty-three years ago. What I got
to talk to him about now?"

Although she jumped slightly at his bellowing,
she stepped to him. Austin had tried his damned-
est to cover up how he felt by using Mone't as a
Band-Aid. She was his Band-Aid, his balm, his
healer, but she couldn't heal him from this. She
couldn't make this go away. This was one thing he
had to look in the face.

"Austin," she softly spoke, touching his frigid demeanor. Austin's frame was so tense she worried
the slightest touch would shatter him into pieces.

Tears danced on the brims of his eyes. His nostrils flared, and his mouth was balled up. "Don't,
Mo. Don't."

"Listen, please."

"I needed him," Austin admitted. "I needed him.
I needed more than just the block to raise me.
More than just my mama. I needed him, and he
didn't give a damn. Why should I?"

She reached up, placing her soft, tiny hands on
his swollen chest. "Because you still need him. You
don't have to look at him, but listen."

"Son, just—" Aneica started, and Francesco
placed his hand on her back.

"Let me. Please," he muttered in her ear. She
yielded. "You have every right to hate me. To want
me gone. I didn't do half of what I could've done

for you. Don't blame your mom for this. Blame me. I knew I would never be able to have a life with her then, and I wanted to. I was already in a situation, and my livelihood was attached to it."

"So you left us in gangland for some fuckin' bands? That's crazy. I bet you've never seen no one get popped or had to do it. You never took a life, did you? Had to watch someone you love take a life to protect you? My girl and her brother did more for me than you did."

Francesco moved closer to him. Austin was a direct reflection of him. For Austin to understand his inherited anger, he needed to know that Francesco was a reflection of his father, a lineage of fatherless boys who turned into angry men. The cycle had to be broken. The generational curses attached to their Blackness had to stop, and it would have to stop tonight. Francesco had a grandson who needed to live a life free of trauma. In order to see that through, he had to be the one to take ownership.

"I was married to a woman I hated so I could sit at a table full of men who didn't respect me otherwise. I am the product of a broken-hearted black woman and an Italian man who was looking for excitement, not partnership. My mother, your grandmother, Frances, gave me my father's name because she wanted to ensure that I always felt like I belonged somewhere."

"I don't give a damn about none of that."

Francesco moved closer, urging Mone't out of the way. "I know, but listen. It'll make sense."

Austin huffed. The anger that coursed through his veins was manageable. But Mone't stayed close just in case he lost it again.

"My mother worked her fingers to the bone and killed herself doing it so I could have a future. Basketball saved my life the same way it did yours."

"Nah, my wife did that," he muttered. "With or without a rock, she did that."

Knowing the depth of their relationship, Francesco nodded. "Thank God you have her. All I had was a drive to make it by any means necessary until I met your mother. By then, falling in love with her was out of the question, but I did. Jeopardizing everything."

"And his wife found out," Aneica spoke up. "I didn't have many options. It was get rid of you and keep my spot or leave the team. I chose you. I know I should have told you. We should have said something, but I let my own hurt cloud what was best for you. I can't let him take all the blame because it's on me, too. I'm sorry, Austin, for keeping it secret. I thought I was doing my best until I wasn't."

"I know you're angry. I missed years, but I'm here."

"And what you want me to do? Ask you to play catch or some shit? Nah. I've been searching for myself for years, taking bad advice, hurting the one who, without question, stepped to the plate to protect her family. She didn't ask me for shit. She didn't require shit. I got two kids I have to be my best for. I'm not abandoning them, and I sure as hell ain't leaving them in the hood to figure this shit out. Yeah, you fucked up. Both of you did. Being selfish. I see I get it from both sides. But y'all were too ashamed to do right by me. I'm never going to be that man. I'm never going to let my shame keep me from owning up and fixing what I messed up. So maybe you served a purpose. You taught me how not to be. How to not leave my son with my blessings and curses to maneuver alone. I don't need to break bread with you tonight. This is too much."

"Can we try?" Mone't pleaded. "Can we just try? I know you are heartbroken. I can feel it. But tonight, just try. Not for you, but for AJ."

Austin cut his eyes at Mone't and studied her. That woman was powerful, because against Austin's reluctance, he would do anything she said. He found himself at the table with his wife to his right, his mother to his left, and the man responsible for his being at the opposite end.

"I came to all of your AAU games," Francesco shared, breaking the silence.

Austin ate as though he didn't hear him.

"Austin." Mone't's tone was so soft, and that was the only reason he listened.

The mere sound of his name flowing from her lips made the tiny hairs all over his body stand at attention. "Yeah?"

Taking her time pouring her bold red wine in the teal glass, her eyes lifted to his. She took him in with his freshly groomed beard. It was as thick and full as his sorrowful eyes. As she placed the bottle down, she shifted her weight. The glass was held between her fingers. "Talk to him. Don't be so stubborn."

He couldn't combat that. She was 100 percent right, although he prayed she would be as unhinged as he felt so he could kick them out, curl his body around hers, and try to sleep this away. Mone't was too good for that. Not in the stuck-up sense of the phrase. She was good. Good to him and the children they'd created. Good to his parents, regardless of what they'd done to him. Mone't had popped out of character once for the world to see, and she wouldn't do it again. Especially not tonight while he was so fragile.

"You came as a scout. Not as my father. When I lost games and got angry, I needed you to tell me how to conduct myself. You could've attended a million games and it still wouldn't change the truth. Now if you want to talk about how we move forward, then okay. Talk about that. Trying to take me down memory lane doesn't work."

"Aneica, let's grab the dessert," Mone't suggested, clearly seeing that these men needed space to sort out their issues.

Aneica obliged without pushback. As the women cleared the table, Austin and Francesco stared at one another. They each accessed their ego and temper and the nucleus of who they were as men.

Austin waited until Mone't and his mother were gone to ask, "How long you and my mama been messing around and debating when and how to tell me?"

"Just the last couple of months. Ever since the scandal."

Austin nodded in response. "Since I publicly embarrassed my wife. Got it."

"At least you got it on track faster than I did."

"I'm not patient. I'm not comfortable being away from her or building a life that she's not a part of. I see we don't have that in common."

"I'm sure the more time we spend together, you will."

"I doubt it."

"I'm proud you're doing this consistently," Robyn spoke up as Austin made himself comfortable on the parallel couch. "How's everything? Have you talked to Mone't?"

Austin smirked a devilish smirk that told Robyn all that she needed to know. She scribbled down a note to herself and softly chuckled. "I assume it's going well."

"I don't know about well, but better than before. I can look at her and tell that when she sees me, that's all she sees, even if she's trying to move past it."

"Heartbreak is like grieving. It comes in phases. Some days are better than others, but if every day you make an effort to make it better than the last, eventually the days are good again."

"You know, you're like some Baby Yoda with the jewels you be dropping," Austin pointed out.

"Uh, thanks. However, I get a feeling that today isn't about Mone't."

Austin fidgeted with his hands before hopping to his feet. Instead of distracting himself with her awards, degrees, and certificates, he stared at the abstract painting. He felt as chaotic as it looked. "It's always about Mo. Karma hit my ass in the chest. I don't know if it's a good or bad thing that I've never been heartbroken. I mean, it ain't no secret I did it to my wife. Probably disappointed my mother a time or two, but the way she had me walking around . . ." Austin paused, took a deep breath, and further studied the painting. "I feel like this painting. Spinning and shit. Trying to make sense of it, and nothing is making sense to me. Honestly the only thing that's kept me grounded is Mo."

While Austin sorted through his thoughts, Robyn got comfortable in her chair and listened. She realized Austin needed to talk without interruption. He typically found his solution within his own thoughts.

"I never expected my mother to be the person to deliver the blow to my heart like that. Part of me hoped my heartbreak would come from Mo. It was only right she holds it in her hand even when she didn't want to. But I didn't even care that she let another man touch her. I deserved it. I settled with that. But my mom . . . You know, she and my father have been doing this on-again, off-again shit, and none of them ever said, 'Hey, little nigga, this is your pops. You look like him, talk like him, walk like him. You got his temper and all.' She had me in this man's face for years and didn't say shit. My favorite player. The reason I picked up a ball and took it serious for real. I've been searching for who I am for a long-ass time. Now I know, and I don't know how I feel about it."

"Austin," Robyn finally spoke up, "there's another way to look at this."

"Is there? Because right now it's looking like Aneica Graham is a liar who tried to keep her nose clean for years."

Robyn sat up and pushed her glasses up. "There's always another way. Have a seat."

Reluctantly, Austin sat down and groaned. "What's the other way?"

"Grace."

"Grace?"

"Grace. Having some grace. The same grace Mone't has extended to you. Have some grace."

He scoffed. "That man let me struggle."

"And if you had had a silver spoon, where would you be now? Would you have worked this hard? Would you have your wife, your kids, your accomplishments? Sometimes we put our parents on a pedestal, forgetting that they were just figuring it out too. I'm not saying that they weren't wrong and you're not entitled to those feelings, but remember, your parents were young. You and Mone't were young. What if something happened where you weren't in your daughter's life—"

"I wouldn't do that."

"Because of who you are now. But if you weren't? You can't say what you would've done. Lead with the same grace you want."

Austin scoffed. "I don't want to do that."

"Okay, don't. Rob your children of having active grandparents."

Austin cut his eyes at her, and Robyn shrugged. He could adhere to her advice or not. His payment for five sessions had already cleared.

"I hate when you're right."

"I get that a lot."

He smirked. "I'm sure. You think you can do this with Mone't and me? I know there's a lot she's holding back from me."

"I can facilitate the space, but are you ready for that? There might be some things you don't want to know."

"I gotta go through it one way or another. I want her to look at me with that fire again."

Robyn bobbed her head. "You bring her, and we'll work through it. Keep in mind it might be a hard conversation."

"It needs to be had, and I don't want her walking away from me."

Austin returned to a quiet house. Mone't wasn't in any of the rooms. He still hadn't familiarized himself with her space. He gladly slept on the couch in the playroom because at least that meant they were all under the same roof.

Ending his hunt, he found his beautiful wife on the far side of the yard. There was a nook dressed in thick green plants, cobblestone, a pair of reclined lawn chairs, and a small table that sat between them. He spotted the bottle of wine and the drinking glass before he spotted her sorrowful face.

He quickened his steps toward her, his brows dipped in, and his chest tightened. He was unsure of what had her so distraught. "What's wrong?"

Mone't sniffled. "Nothing. I'm okay."

She didn't trust him with her emotions, and he knew it. He'd ruined that part of them, and he was desperate to have it back. Austin wanted so badly not only to be her best friend but to be her man, the man she laid her burdens on, and he'd carry them with pride.

"If you were fine, you wouldn't be crying," he commented, sitting in the chair on the opposite side of her. "Tell me."

Her eyes were fixated on the paper tightly clutched between her fingers and palm. She couldn't peel them away. Every time she traced her eyes over the last line, tears flowed again. Thankfully, today was bookstore day with Aneica. The children were gone, and Mone't could cry in peace.

Unfortunately, diving into these emotions surrounding her father wasn't quite what she expected her quiet time to be consumed with. Crying over her and Austin, praying for their marriage to be mended, was easy. As for the relationship with her father, there would never be a chance to mend that.

There would never be a chance for him to hold his daughter.

Mone't bit her lip as hard as she could, trying to turn her pain elsewhere. She couldn't. She swung her legs over the chair and stood up. The two-page letter fell into Austin's hands, and she walked away.

Austin watched Mone't walk away, sobbing quietly to herself. Giving her space, he looked down at the final paragraph:

Know that as a man I prayed for you to have someone with my heart. I prayed that the one you've tied yourself to can heal the parts of you I broke and didn't know. Mone't, you were my pride and joy. I was a hood nigga with a daughter who clung to his every word. Most men hope for boys. But you were a treasure. Please forgive me for being the one to break your heart first. Forgive me for not being there to wipe your tears, to give you the game. Forgive me for not walking you down the aisle. Forgive me for allowing you to be ripped from me. Even after my life is over, understand that you never deserved to see me at my lowest. You are a queen, Mone't. That's probably why you married the king. I love you. Know that. When you tell your kids about me, tell them your father stood on principle and he gave you his heart. I pray I make it to heaven so I can hold you again.

Austin took in a deeper breath and shut his eyes. He allowed one tear to slide down his cheek. There was a stack of letters wrapped in a rubber band and resting behind the wine bottle, and she'd read every last one. Collecting them, the wine bottle, and the glass, Austin walked into the house. Mone't was in the kitchen, attempting to prep dinner.

He'd seen this before. She occupied herself when she was trying to distract her mind. He couldn't stop replaying those words in his head, so he knew she was wrapped in them.

"What happened to him, Mo?"

"He's dead," she responded, chopping the potatoes vigorously and slicing her finger. "Shit!"

Austin rushed to her side and assisted her. She snatched away from him, but he gently regained possession. Her hand rested in his. He moved closer to her, completely closing the space between them. The pain exuding from her body was undeniable. Space and time didn't sever the connection they had. Despite Mone't's temperament and stubbornness, the universe needed them together to cling to one another.

Austin took the sliced finger and placed it in his mouth. As if Mone't were his baby, he sucked the blood from the cut, removed it from his mouth, and ran it under water. Mone't was a mess. Tears slowly fell down her face.

"He had congestive heart failure. Apparently, he found out weeks before he was arrested. That's why he never fought the case. He gave all the letters to Eman. Imagine that. Eman got closure with him, and I had to get it from letters. Twenty-four letters and one phone call weeks ago explaining why he couldn't see me. How much he loved me. I don't know why the people who say they love me disregard me so effortlessly."

Austin swiped the tears from her cheeks.

"I married a man just like him. So good for everyone but for me, the very last on the list."

"That's not true, Mo."

"It is, Austin. I clung to you because you reminded me of him. You felt like him. I was safe with him until I wasn't and safe with you until I wasn't. I can't help but think of how my life would have turned out if this weren't it."

Austin wrapped his arms around her, holding her tightly, surrounding her in warmth and security. He kissed the top of her head and muttered, "I'm sorry."

She didn't reply. She could only sob in his chest. Heartbreak at this point was ever-present. The very thing that pulled them apart was pulling them together. Neither could deny it. Space fought to erase the foundation their young love was built on. If anything, they missed each other more.

Mone't tried to suck it up and push him away from her. Little did she know, this newfound confidence, attitude, and willingness to be vulnerable with him was drawing him in more. That, and he was tired of the space between them. Tired of them not keeping it real. This love ran deep. It was a soul tie.

While Austin held her, he thought about all the things that came full circle for them. Sure, Mone't had let him off his leash to run wild, and he'd hated every second of being available for the streets. Women were different out there. They were treacherous. They came with motives, implants, constant risks, and headaches that weren't worth it. That one taste was so detrimental to them. He only wanted her—her pain, her pleasure, and all of her broken pieces.

"What do you need, baby?"

"Just hold me," she whispered. "I just need you to hold me."

He lifted her off her feet. She wrapped her legs around his waist, and he carried her up the stairs to her bedroom. Laying her down on the bed, he removed the slides she wore on her pedicured feet and the cardigan from her arms. Austin pulled his shirt off and climbed in bed behind her. He pulled her body into his. His thumb glided over her bare skin.

She shuddered. Her fight was fleeting with the gracious touch of her love. "I read all of them three times. Every letter was about love and the deepness of sacrifice and forgiveness. He said he forgave my mother for what she did. He talked about how much he loved her for giving him a family. Even though Eman wasn't his, he still loved him the same. I can't help but find peace in it, but it's unnerving."

"Which part of it?"

"Forgiveness. Loving when it hurts." Mone't turned over so she could be face-to-face with Austin. "I miss us."

"I've missed us like crazy."

"I don't want to blink and have you be gone. I don't want to waste another moment, Austin. I'm tired of hating you. I'm tired of crying. I'm tired of trying to figure life out without you."

"If we were supposed to do life alone, we would've never crossed paths. I want to be your man again, Mo. I know I fumbled that ball. I know I got distracted."

"You did."

"I'm going to be better. I promise. Therapy is helping with that. She's teaching me shit like giving grace."

"Grace?"

"Yeah. She said I have to lead with the same grace you've extended to me."

"I couldn't let you stand out there like that. You looked like a lost puppy." She sniffled and snuggled deeper into his embrace.

"I came home. Doesn't matter what house it is. You're home. Let's fix this. Let's learn from this loss."

"Tomorrow isn't ours. Only right now."

He kissed her sweetly and tenderly, hoping to take away a fraction of her pain. "Let's go to therapy to work through this shit so we can get better and do better."

She nodded.

"You with it?"

"Yeah. I'm with it." Mone't threw her legs over his and settled in his arms. She needed rest, and there was no better place to do that than in his arms.

Chapter Twenty-seven

Avoidance.

That had been Mone't's emotional state since learning of her father's passing. She didn't talk to Austin much, avoided him touching her, avoided being alone with him. She was experiencing the heartache again, and anything that represented that for her, she stayed clear of. She hadn't even answered the calls from her brother. Part of her felt like she would have been better off living in a delusion of her father's existence. She could have made peace with that at some point. Death and loss and heartache seemed to be on a soundtrack that looped over and over again.

The door of the locked bedroom was opened by Mone't. Isabella ran in first, and Austin sauntered behind her, holding a babbling AJ. "Mommy, love you. We're going to Grandma's to have some fun!"

Mone't's eyes skirted to Austin, AJ, and then to Isabella. "Oh, yeah? What kind of fun?"

"Uh, library, ice cream, movies, pool, and then we're baking cookies," Izzy said, running down the list of things she was looking forward to.

Although Austin wasn't too hot on his mother and Francesco, he recognized that Mone't needed a change of scenery, and he had to lean on his resources to make it happen. Over his needs were Mone't's. Regardless of whether she wanted to talk or be touched or accept comfort when it wasn't convenient, she needed him.

"Oh, that sounds like fun. I have to spend the night without you?"

"Mm-hmm. Daddy said he's taking you somewhere special," Izzy announced, jumping on the bed to get to Mone't's level.

Mone't sat in the middle of the bed, legs crossed, folding piles of laundry she'd neglected over the last week. "Is he?"

"Mm-hmm. So smile and have fun!" Isabella cheered, hopping over to Mone't to kiss her face. "I'll see you tomorrow with a million cookies."

"All right, big boy, give your mama a wet one." Austin leaned over the bed and handed his junior to Mone't. She held him tight, kissed his chubby face, and inhaled his scent. "All right, that's enough of taking my lovin', boy."

Mone't chuckled and released him back to Austin. "Izzy, be good for Mama, and be nice to your brother."

Isabella bounced out of the room, her comment floating behind her. "Only if he's nice to me."

Austin cut Mone't a look with a smirk resting on his lips. "That's your daughter. That mouth."

"That's Aneica. Don't put that on me."

"Maybe. Wrap this up and pack an overnight bag. There's an outfit hanging up in the closet."

He exited the room before she could combat the statement. While Austin was gone, Mone't returned to folding and her silent talk to herself to overcome another hurdle.

While she moved around the room in one of Austin's T-shirts and a pair of short shorts, she put the clothes away and took deep breaths.

"The Ian Sanders designer called Eman this morning," Austin announced, walking back into the room and interrupting her stilling moment.

Before, she ignored Austin's half-dressed state. Tailored pants hung off his waist, his chiseled core on full display. She was tempted to touch him, but in the back of her mind, her pain was reminding her that some time ago, another woman was having her way with him. She felt irrational for feeling that way and especially displaying it. They agreed to move forward, but how could they do so if she kept bringing up the past?

Shaking off her feelings and sweeping them under the rug, she pretended to be fine. "So after parting ways, they want you to come back on board?"

"Yeah, we're meeting at the vineyard."

"We?" Mone't asked like Austin was speaking a foreign language. "You sure you want me there?"

Austin's eyes cast over her. "I wouldn't be asking you if I didn't want you to come with me, Mo." He knew that if she stayed in this house and locked herself in rooms, she was going to slip back into the same habits as before. Depression was a constant fight. He watched her fight it for so long without support and refused to do it any longer.

She shrugged. "I don't want to be in your way."

Austin took a deep breath, walked over to her, pulled the clothes from her hands, and wrapped his arms around her waist. Kissing the base of her neck, he groaned into the curve. She smelled like vanilla and bergamot. It was the most arousing and relaxing scent.

"Trust me, you ain't in my way," he growled, kissing the base of her neck again.

Mone't wriggled away, and Austin pulled her back, pressing his hardness against her butt. "See? I'm in your way and a distraction."

"Who told you to smell this damn good? Shit." Austin attacked her neck, and Mone't was growing into putty in his hands.

"Austin," she groaned, pulling fully away from him, "I don't want to go. I don't want to be touched right now. Just go."

He swiped his face with his hand. "Nah. I did that before. We've done that before. You can have an attitude the whole time, and that's cool. I know how to handle that shit. You're coming."

"We've also fucked through it, and then you went and fucked someone else."

Austin dropped his head, pressed his hands into the dips of his waist, and groaned inwardly. His face twisted, and he bit his tongue. All the comments he wanted to fire off in response were counterproductive. "Baby, get dressed. The jet leaves in an hour."

Mone't huffed and looked him up and down. Her mood was jumping from her to him, and if Austin weren't in a metamorphosis, he would've fed it, and neither of them would take steps forward.

He left her presence to finish getting dressed. Eman, Angie, and Keyston were on their way to the airport. Austin made plans for him and his wife and her and Angie. He wanted her to enjoy herself outside of her head. He wanted to celebrate the wins with her. They were on a road to healing, and together they were going to feel and be present in every step of life.

Mone't sighed, trying her best to not feed into the gaping darkness of her mind. She didn't allow herself any more time to wallow in the gravity of it.

Thirty minutes later, she was dressed in a custom maxi dress and designer heels Austin provided, and she met him at the door, overnight bag in tow.

"You look good," he complimented her. Austin wore black tailored slacks and a crisp white oxford with the sleeves rolled up, the top three buttons open and exposing his tattooed chest and diamond necklace bearing the initials of his wife and his children. He was a hoop star who could pass as a rapper.

"Thanks. So do you."

Graciously assisting her to the Cullinan waiting for them, Austin and Mone't's new driver nodded his head. Since announcing the ownership to Musa and Keyston, Austin had hired more security to be with his mother and wife. Now that he'd given Musa and Keyston the keys to unlock their destinies, he set them free to fly.

Two hours later, the entire crew landed on an exclusive tarmac and proceeded to their meeting. Everyone was dressed in some variation of black-and-white, proudly representing the family and the strength of moving as a unit. Austin was the proudest. His failure had humbled him, and his mistakes in business and his personal life had provided clarity. He was nothing without the people who only had the best in mind for him and his growth. His hand clasped Mone't's while the Sprinter van took the group to the top of the hill to meet with Ian.

"You know that spot on the other side of the hill we didn't buy?" Austin asked softly enough so only Mone't could hear him.

"Mm-hmm." She nodded, her eyes catching details of nature's beauty.

"I bought it. Put it in the kids' names," he informed her.

Mone't turned to look at him, searching to see if he knew that she was the one who helped close the deal on it before he made that move.

He didn't.

It was only a matter of time before he did, and she was unsure of how he would respond to it.

"The pending owner needed to liquidate their assets, so Michele called, and I swooped in. We're staying there tonight. Everyone else will be on the other side."

Mone't feigned excitement, letting a tiny smile cross her lips. "You're full of surprises."

Her hand was brought to his full lips for him to kiss, and then he tenderly repeated the motion. "Love you, baby."

"Love you."

Exiting the van, the group walked into the private dining area where Ian and his business partner were receiving their drinks from the bartender. It was the same bartender who had served Mone't and Lamont previously.

"Ian Sanders," Austin greeted him, closing the space between them and extending his free hand.

"Austin, it's good to see you," Ian greeted him, gripping his hand for a firm shake. "This is the beautiful wife?"

Austin released his hand and pulled Mone't in closer. She always played her part well, smiling brightly and making Austin look good. What she didn't know was that the deal being made wasn't through Austin's corporation. It was through hers. After Eman and Austin had their initial phone call with Ian and understood that Jermel brokered the first deal and was entitled to a piece of the pie, they headed in a different direction.

"Mone't Graham," she oozed sweetly, extending her hand.

"It's nice to meet you in person. Austin hasn't stopped talking about you."

Mone't was sure that Ian, along with his team, had done their share of research when it came to the two of them. It wasn't hard, either. Their relationship and rumors of their relationship had been plastered everywhere.

"I'm sure," Mone't responded.

"He actually wouldn't entertain the idea of meeting unless there was something in the plans that included you."

Mone't looked up at Austin in slight confusion. "Oh, really?"

"Really," Ian replied, taking a sip of his drink. "You two ready to talk shop? I heard dinner is on the way, and I want to get all the boring shit out of the way so we can celebrate."

"Uh, yeah, sure," Mone't commented, taking a step and expecting Austin to do the same. "Babe . . ."

Austin smiled, knowing the capability Mone't possessed. She didn't need a degree to close a deal. She had what she needed, and he would gladly sit this one out. "It's all you, baby."

Austin stepped back and nodded Mone't over to the small table in the corner dedicated to this meeting. She sat and seemingly held her breath until Ian began to talk.

"When Austin's former management reached out about this video game, it was just like the others. He's on the cover of the packaging for a percentage. Typical, right? We expect that. When his new management answered my call, they presented something different. Something empowering." Ian reached for a binder from his associate and handed it to Mone't. "*Izzy's Full Court*. A gender-fluid interactive game. It has beginner, intermediate, and advanced settings. It'll feature matching, colors, shapes, math, science, and the history of basketball. As the children advance, they'll have problems to solve that support learning and development.

"We highlight the players a lot, but Austin brought up a good point this morning. The player is only one piece of the bigger picture. They have a home team: the wife, kids, parents, and extended family who prop them up. This is a game for the family."

Mone't flipped through the pages of the binder while Ian presented the genius idea to her. The numbers had been negotiated prior to them arriving. For Isabella, 30 percent was designated into a trust. Sanders Tech would hold 40 percent, and Mone't and Austin would hold the remainder.

"What do you say, Mone't?"

"It's a great deal. I'm only going to ask for one thing."

"Sure, lay it on me," Ian said, thinking Mone't was going to ask for content control or something along those lines.

"A contingency clause. If this game does double the number projected in the first quarter of the launch, we will launch interactive toys for infants and toddlers. Austin will handle teenagers to adults, and Angie will have interactive fashion apps and video games."

Ian sat back in his seat and marveled over the way Mone't expanded her brand and his with one clause. "Mone't"—he stood—"you have yourself a deal. I look forward to working with you and your beautiful family."

They shook hands and signed the papers. While everyone popped bottles and cheered as the dinner rolled out, Austin held a conversation with the passing bartender. He was always welcoming and personable with people who stopped to talk to him. Austin was a guy from the neighborhood, and he understood what he represented.

"Bro, hell of a season. I knew you could pull that off," the bartender cheered, giving Austin some dap.

Austin laughed, accepted the gesture, and said, "I had to pull it out and take it home."

"And you got your woman back. And bought the last spot she was up here looking at."

Austin's brows dipped in instant confusion. "What?"

The messy bartender reached in his pocket, pulled out his phone, and pulled up the photos with Lamont and Mone't too close for comfort. It was one thing to see glimpses of her hand in hand with him leaving her favorite restaurant and another to see her in a parking garage visibly upset, but this . . . Austin felt every inch of his skin burn with anger. Austin knew there was time they spent together. He had an idea of what happened, but seeing it in 4K was liable to kill him.

"He was all up on your woman, man. I hope you Will Smith slapped him for disrespecting you like that. I'm happy y'all working it out. The king ain't nothing without his queen." The bartender spotted Mone't sauntering back over to Austin and stuffed the phone in his pocket. She reached the pair and accepted the flute of champagne in thanks.

The bearer of unsolicited news retreated from the couple, leaving Austin in a vortex of swirling thoughts.

"I can't believe you put all this together," Mone't gushed. "I'm so happy for the kids. I negotiated another deal for AJ, you, and Angie if the first quarter numbers are doubled."

Austin fought through a clenched jaw and flared nostrils. He refused to swipe this victory from her. This was her moment. In every moment of victory, she somehow, in some way, supported him. It was only right to do the same.

Dinner went on without a hitch. They drank, laughed, and enjoyed the company of Ian and his team. Parting to their separate locations for the night couldn't come soon enough. Mone't's attitude had done a 180-degree turn from earlier. The golf cart ride to the luxury home was included with the price of the property.

Upon Austin's request, the staff had filled the home with five types of roses in an array of shades, and candles, champagne, and chocolate-covered strawberries were waiting at the entrance for them.

Mone't was already buzzing. Another glass was going to activate a side of her that neither she nor Austin had seen since finding out she was pregnant a second time.

"You didn't have to do all this."

Austin scoffed, clenching his jaw. He was swirling and thinking of sexing his wife so good that her mind would never remember what it was like without him, fucking through it. It wasn't productive, but it was something to do other than fussing, cussing, and taking three steps backward.

He reached out and pulled her into his body, wrapped his hand gently around the base of her neck and kissed her roughly. He pulled the lingering champagne off her tongue. Mone't's body was in submission, and the alcohol was to thank for that. It helped her throw her inhibitions to the wind.

Hoisted around his body, she kissed his face and his neck, panted, and moaned as he thumbed her bud. "Put me down."

Listening to his wife, he watched between inebriated lenses. Mone't undid his belt and his pants and yanked them down his thighs. Freeing him from his briefs, she took his length into her mouth and sucked him like a porn star. She had come out of her bag. Austin needed physical touch constantly. He needed to have her upon request, and she was going to try her best to accommodate his needs.

Austin pushed his fingers over the minimal amount of hair on her head and groaned. That cut was sexy, but there was something about gripping her by the roots of her hair that he needed. Still in her dress and heels, she wrapped her hands around the back of his legs, digging into his skin to steady herself.

He winced, enjoying the pleasure and pain she was creating. He wanted her, needed to be buried inside the softest, warmest, safest place on earth. She groaned when he removed himself from her mouth. Red lipstick had smeared across her face and the length of him.

"Turn around," he ordered. "Dress over your ass and hold on to the railing."

With a devious grin, Mone't did exactly as she was told. Austin let a carnal groan go as he smacked her ass and watched it ripple. He did it again and again, coaxing a yelp from her. Then he leaned down, kissed both cheeks, and ripped the thong from her body. "Spread 'em."

Mone't spread her legs wide, anticipating the sweet invasion of Austin and his stroke. He rocked two fingers in and out of her and added another, pressing his thumb against her back door.

She moaned, groaned, and whimpered. Just as he pulled her to her brink, he pulled them out, reached around, and shoved them in her mouth. It was in tandem with his entry into her super grip.

Mone't was made for him. Her grip was perfect. Her arch was perfect. She was perfect for him. The thought of someone trying to feel his treasure was driving him crazy.

Austin drilled inside of her, and she threw it back, rotating her hips, calling his name, and taking every inch without protest. They climbed the mountain to ecstasy and exploded together. He leaned into her, sure not to waste a drop of his seed. His lips found the base of her neck and kissed it.

"I'll meet you in the shower," he growled and pulled out.

Mone't tried to steady her wobbly legs. It was no use. She held on to the railing and followed the rose petals to the bedroom. It was full of flowers and candles. She smiled, still in the haze of the euphoria. Removing her heels and dress, she got into the shower and washed the day off her.

Austin joined, ready for round two, and she gave it to him. There was a change, though. She felt it. When the round was over and the shower was done, Austin exited and went to sit in the dark.

Concerned about her husband, she wrapped her body in a plush robe and padded over the hardwood floor until she was toe-to-toe with him. "What's wrong?"

"Why didn't you tell me you came up here with him?" Austin asked in a low tone.

She sighed and pulled at the lapels of the robe. "I didn't think it was important to say after the party. I thought you knew."

"Nah," he scoffed. "I had an idea, but seeing pictures of you with him smiling and laughing and holding hands and shit . . . Did you fuck him?"

"Austin."

"Did you?"

Mone't inhaled deeply and released it. She moved his arms and straddled him. "Can you look at me?"

Hurt filled his eyes as he considered the idea and readied himself to hear the truth. Mone't held his face in her hands. "I am your girl, Austin. Yours. You were my first, you're my last, and you've been the only. I was here thinking I was coming to set up accommodations, not to close a deal. I—"

"I don't want to hear no more, Mo." His ego was taking the lead. He gently pushed her off and stood up. "I'm going to get some air."

Mone't scrubbed her face, then drew her legs into her chest and groaned into her knees. She was tired, and the feeling of bliss she'd gotten from the past several hours was gone. The thoughts running through her head were wild and threatening her peace. Ultimately, there was nothing she could say or do tonight to make Austin feel better.

The truth was the truth, and once she woke up in the morning, she planned on tackling it. Now she would rest her mind and body and protect the handful of peace she'd fought to maintain.

Austin rode the golf cart down the hill with no particular destination in mind. He reached the other side of the property and parked at the house he and Mone't stayed at years ago.

The music and splashes from the pool could be heard from the front of the house. He refused to knock, arrogantly figuring that if he paid the property taxes, he could walk in at will.

His heavy feet followed the noise into the lavish backyard. Angie was holding the foam basketball hostage while Musa waited on the other side of the mesh fence that ran across the pool. Eman was on her side, talking junk until she released the ball, and Musa smacked it back over the net.

Austin helped himself to a drink and plopped down in a nearby seat. Keyston noticed the long expression on his face and ended his cheering to poke fun at his homeboy. "This man got a dime in his bed and got the nerve to be over here with that look on his face."

"What you do, bust prematurely? It happens. We all been there," Musa added. All he did was activate Keyston's foolishness.

"I busted while putting the condom on once. It was embarrassing."

Eman frowned at the comment and shook his head.

Angie gagged and covered her ears. "Why would you tell someone that?"

"For real," Eman blew. "I would have taken that shit to my grave. Wouldn't no one ever know that."

"Man, we got to keep it honest with the kid. You know what psychological damage that does to someone?" Keyston defended himself.

Musa cut his eyes at him. "Is that what turned you into a psycho?"

"Nah. My mama cut my hair too early. That's why I'm a psycho," Keyston returned, making Eman holler on his way out of the pool. "What? I'm serious. You know what kinda brain damage you do when you hit the soft spot repeatedly."

Musa blankly stared at him, getting ready to fire off a barrage of jokes, but he remembered his mother was a sensitive topic. "You need help, nigga."

Angie swam over to the edge of the pool and looked up at Austin. He looked pitiful. Not as bad as he did the previous months, but he was without a doubt in his feelings.

"What's wrong with you, Austin, and where is my friend?" Angie quizzed.

"Back at the house," he muttered.

Angie nodded. "So what you do this time?"

Austin frowned, and his voice became pitchy. "Why I always gotta be the one doing something?"

"Because you're always the one doing something. Duh."

Austin rolled his eyes and took his drink to the head. "Well, this time it was your friend. Got the nerve to come up here with that nigga, hugging and kissing on him and all that. Got the staff coming up to me, showing me pictures, talking about, 'Oh, you got your girl back, that's what's up.'"

Angie's head tilted to the side, and her eyes squinted. "But did she sleep with him?"

"Whoa, wait a minute. Mo fucked that nigga?" Keyston asked, walking through the water to hoist his body out of the pool.

"You might need to pay that nigga a visit," Musa chimed in.

Eman scoffed. "I would have made that nigga go night-night."

Angie looked around at the guys as if they had two heads. "Are y'all missing this part where he cheated on her? Hid it only for it to come out? Not to mention the crazy-ass girl was showing up everywhere and lying about a baby? Or is it me?"

"That ain't how you get a nigga back, LeAngelique," Eman spoke up, shooting her a telling look.

She shot him one back. "Y'all bugging. He cheated on her. So what if she took Lamont's snake ass for a ride?"

"That's my wife," Austin said, defending himself.

"Then you should have acted like a husband. Y'all got to stop this double standard shit. You can fuck around, cause us all this emotional and mental damage, and come back like, 'Oh, I'm sorry, baby. I didn't mean it.' Get out of here with that! The minute we let a nigga sniff the pussy, y'all ready to slide down walls, pull up, and spin the block. That's crazy to me."

"Because you're a woman. When we cheat, it's not about y'all," Keyston said. "It's about our dicks and what we want right then. When y'all cheat, there is emotional attachment to it."

"Oh, shut up," Angie squealed. "The lack of self-control is repulsive, and the arrogance after is worse. Austin, you made this bed, and you got to lie in it. Whether or not she slept with him shouldn't matter to you because you started this."

"So you saying she did and she's lying to me?" Austin questioned.

Angie was inclined to let him believe it, but that would reverse his progress. "I really thought you were growing up. This is some little-boy shit. You should know her better than any of us. If you believe she gave away something so sacred, you need to reevaluate your relationship. And maybe you really should sign the papers and let her be."

She scoffed in disgust and swam to the far end of the pool and got out. It was silent among the men as she wrapped her body in a towel and stomped inside. When Eman was sure she was out of earshot, he popped Austin across the head.

"You big dummy. Why are you that big and that stupid?" he hissed. "Considering your track record, you can't even be mad at Mo. Hurt? Yeah, it's a pride killer. But Angie ain't wrong."

"You did all that cappin' in front of her for what?" Musa asked, snickering.

"I can't let her little ass know she's right all the time. But we can all agree that this sun-kissed nigga is slow," Eman said.

Austin kissed his teeth. "I should have taken my ass home."

"You ain't going nowhere until you resolve this. You aren't supposed to be adding to her plate. Some shit you got to take with your chest. We out here fighting every day, and you're going to add this, too?" Eman asked. "You crazy, bro."

Musa shrugged his shoulders as he sparked a blunt he had laid on a table. "The wise one has a point. You got to eat that one. Mo wasn't even looking in his direction until you gave her a reason." Musa toked the blunt and handed it over to Austin. "Take some puffs, and take your big ass back to her. We over here having drunk fun, and you bringing me down."

"Facts." Keyston nodded in agreement.

"Big facts," Eman said. "If anything, I know my sister, and she's faithful, loyal, and honest to a fault. If she took it there, I'm sure she would have told you she did."

Austin rubbed his temples and lay back. Eman, Keyston, and Musa stayed outside with him until the blunts in rotation were gone and the bottle of 1942 was gone. They staggered off one by one. Soon after Keyston was gone, Austin slowly stood and made his way back to the other side.

The candles had burnt out. He felt like shit for storming out the way he did. They were right. Again. Arrogance was a beast, and continuing to feed it would ruin his family for good. He climbed the stairs to the room and found Mone't curled in the middle of the bed on top of the covers.

He hummed to himself and grabbed the throw at the end of the bed and draped it over her. Moving to the closet where the staff had unpacked their things, he opened the drawers until he found a bonnet. Mone't's hair coiled, and considering she didn't put any products on it after she got out of the shower, he didn't want her to wake up with a dry scalp.

Austin bypassed lying in the bed next to her and sat on the couch across the room. He watched her sleep until his eyes floated closed.

Morning came, and Austin woke up to Mone't in the bathroom, molding her hair. Stretching and yawning, he watched her from his spot. He was the luckiest man in the world to have someone as beautifully complex as Mone't. His eyes didn't peel away from her as she wrapped her hair in a designer silk scarf, washed her face, moisturized it, and brushed her teeth.

As she walked out of the bathroom, she went to the dresser to moisturize her hands. "You might want to shower and get dressed. I called my therapist. She'll be pulling up in a half hour."

"I already made an appointment for when we get back."

"Yeah, I don't feel like leaving here with this between us, and I really don't want to talk to you about this without a mediator."

"Mo," Austin said with a sigh and sat up.

"You don't have to say anything right now. Take the next thirty minutes telling your arrogance there's no room for it between us."

Mone't slipped her tiny feet into some slippers and trekked out of the room. Austin sat with himself for twenty minutes. Being sure not to piss his wife off, he did as he was told and met them outside. When he saw Robyn, he paused.

"We have the same therapist?" he questioned.

Robyn smiled. "You both came recommended by Angie, so here we are."

He took a seat next to Mone't, who hadn't acknowledged him. She sipped her tea, preparing herself to tell Austin the truth and hear his.

"Yeah, here we are," Austin mumbled.

"Mone't told me after a night of connection you two had a hiccup," Robyn jumped right in, snatching the Band-Aid off. "I've heard how she feels—"

"I'd like to hear it too." Austin cut her off. "I need to hear it."

Mone't nibbled at the corner of her mouth before she slightly turned to him. "I didn't sleep with him. But I'd be lying if I said that if the opportunity had presented itself, I wouldn't have. I would have. We were close."

Austin cringed. Through gritted teeth, he asked, "How close?"

Mone't licked her dry lips and fidgeted with her sleeves. "Fingers and really bad head."

"Did you cum?"

"No. I stopped him."

"Why?"

"He wasn't you."

Austin peered at his wife, tears dancing in his eyes.

"Austin." Robyn called his name. "How are you feeling?"

"Like shit," he answered. "Like a piece of shit, honestly."

"Why?" she asked.

"Because me feeding my arrogance and my ego, sleeping with Pandora, hiding it, lying about it, and trying to pacify Mone't led to this. I did that to her," he answered. "I can't lie. That shit hurts my pride. No man wants to know another man was tasting what was his, but what can I do? I did that."

"Austin, I'm sorry," Mone't spoke up. "It's not all on you. I made that decision to step into that realm knowing it wasn't what it seemed like. I did it. I regret doing it. I don't feel vindicated. I don't like knowing that it hurt you even though you did what you did. It doesn't make it or me right. I feel like shit for keeping it, for not being forthcoming. For being so stubborn."

Austin turned Mone't's seat completely around to face him. "I know what I said. And I meant that. I'm still a work in progress, Mo. I'm a prideful man because I'm insecure. I know that, at any moment, you can pack up everything and be gone. I put you in the position to. Since reconnecting, I've gone to sleep every night in fear. You can wake up at any point of the day and say you want out. And what am I going to do about it? You are the one thing in my life that's right. That pushes me. I'm sorry for even placing this on your shoulders and making you carry it on top of everything you're already carrying."

She sniffled and nodded.

"Austin, is there anything you need from her?" Robyn asked.

"There's one thing I need you to let go of."

Mone't small eyes pierced his as she asked, "What's that?"

"Let go of that night. Wash the blood off your hands and let it go. You carry that. It weighs you down. I hear you in your sleep some nights. We can't live if the dead are holding us hostage."

Mone't dropped her head, and the tears fell into her lap. Austin lifted her chin. "We don't do that, baby. You hold your head high."

"Mone't, let Austin know what you need from him." Robyn's voice was so peaceful it helped smooth the conversation that otherwise would've taken a turn for the worse.

"I need you to listen to me even when I don't have the words to tell you I need you. I know I make it look easy, like I have everything I need, and I'm okay. Sometimes there's a war going on in my head, and I just need you to hold me, tell me it's going to be all right."

"I can do that."

"I also want a vacation and family time during the season."

"I can do that, too. What else? Tell me what to do so we never have to experience this again. I can't take this shit."

"Be good to me, Austin, and I'll be great to you."

Robyn didn't see any need for her to be present. She quietly excused herself from the table while the couple reconciled their issues. It was beautiful to watch the love they had for one another fight like hell to grow and mold them into the new versions of themselves.

As Robyn collected her things to head to the room Mone't booked for her, she spun and bumped into Keyston. The impact was hard enough to knock the blunt from between his lips.

"Damn, shorty, you in a rush?" he gruffly asked, steadying her, then retrieving his blunt from the ground. "Shit, I just rolled it."

Robyn yelped during the impact and found herself entranced by Keyston. She couldn't figure it out and was embarrassed by the way she was ogling this stranger.

Keyston smirked. "You good, little mama? Mouth all gaped like you lookin' at a fly nigga or something."

"Leave her alone," Angie huffed, giving Robyn enough time to scurry away.

Keyston watched her rush away until Musa blocked his sight. "You drooling, creep."

Keyston quickly checked his face and nudged Musa. "Shorty bad."

"She's a therapist. Therapists always got a lot of shit with them. You don't like baggage. You like easy."

"I could like baggage."

"Anything for some damn pussy," Musa scoffed, nudging him forward.

"Ain't that the goal?"

"Nah, building to have that generation shit is the goal. Look around you. Austin's great-great-grand-children are set. That's my goal."

"That might be yours. Mine is pussy until I'm in the ground."

Angie strolled in, proceeding Eman, and scoffed. "You're disgusting, Keyston."

"But I'm honest."

"They straight?" Eman asked.

Angie peeked down the hall to the patio and giggled at Mone't straddling Austin's lap and tonguing him down. "Looks like it to me."

Eman grimaced. "A'ight, I don't want to see that shit. Y'all had all night. We got wheels up in two hours, so let's get this show moving."

Austin groaned. "Our family is cock blockers."

Mone't wiped the residual saliva from his lips prior to removing herself from his lap. "We can resume."

"Please do," Eman said as he walked out. "We have numbers to go over and deals to decide on. Summer Fest is in a week, and we got to talk about y'all hosting the family day. Zaim already printed your names on the flyers, so there's that."

Chapter Twenty-eight

"Ay," Angie cheered, encouraging Mone't to twerk along with the beat of the music. Beatsville was hosting this year's Summer Fest and had introduced two new artists. Trio G was closing the show tonight.

Between the music, the liquor, and the weed, Mone't was vibing with Austin and enjoying being out and free to be herself. She didn't care about the cameras or what the trolls on the internet had to say about her dancing on her man.

Austin was definitely benefiting from the rewards of Mone't's newfound freedom. All that mattered in their world was them and their family. No one was allowed to penetrate that bubble, and it was up to them and their circle to protect that.

Eman and Angie rocked to the beat. He was trying his best to distract Angie from the work she was here to do. Angie had all-access passes along with a few other bloggers to highlight the week-long event on her site. After a day of Mone't and Austin hosting the family day, it was time to turn up.

They didn't have to worry about the kids until the day after tomorrow. Austin was slowly accepting the fact that Francesco wanted to be there for his kids. He wouldn't make his children suffer the way he had because of ego. Plus, Aneica wanted them all to be a happy family, and this was the first step. Austin figured if Francesco won Isabella over, he'd win him over eventually.

Placing his hand on Mone't's waist as she whined, he bit his lip and grunted.

"They trying to make another baby." Keyston laughed, loving the way they had tuned everyone out and enjoyed being in marital bliss.

"If they haven't already made one." Musa chuckled as Zaim got their attention. Tapping Austin's shoulder, he nodded him to the stage. It took Austin a minute to move away from Mone't. He had to calm himself before breaking away from her and standing in front of thousands of people, showing the handiwork of his wife.

"Come with me," he whispered in her ear.

Mone't looked around at what seemed like millions of people in her mind. "I am not going up there."

Austin chuckled, kissed her cheek, and laced his fingers in hers. "Bring your fine ass up on stage with me."

She flashed him a wary look, but he returned one of hers, dropping the anxiousness from the fine lines of her beautiful face. She softly replied, but despite the music blaring, he could hear her. "Okay, baby."

Mone't and Austin were flanked by security as he led her to the side of the stage where Zaim and Davina were standing side by side. Davina threw her arms around Mone't's neck.

"I'm so happy you're here! Y'all look like y'all have been enjoying yourselves. Thank you for hosting the family day," Davina gushed as she let Mone't go. "Izzy is a superstar."

"Thank you for having us. I'm loving this. It's definitely a vibe," Mone't responded as Trio G thanked Ganton Hills for coming out and sharing the night with him. Zaim walked on stage happily, in his element.

"Ganton Hills, what the fuck is up! Y'all enjoyed that? Y'all thought I was done, huh? Nahhhh." Zaim's voice was so hypnotic, captivating the entire field of the attendees.

"Damn, that nigga is sexy," Davina said with lust.

Mone't chuckled. "And you get to take him home."

"Doesn't that feel good to know people love your man but you get to have him completely? They really won," Davina said. "Two larger-than-life men with two bad-ass women holding them down. I love it here."

Mone't's smile grew by the passing second. For the first time in a while, she felt true happiness. There weren't any thoughts about the what-ifs or past transgressions. She was happy and free and needed this bliss to have a lasting effect on her and Austin, who was now on stage.

"I would be remiss to end a hell of a weekend and a festival without shouting out my guy, Austin Graham. When he said he put the city on his back, he meant that shit. Brought us home another championship after a hell of a year. I'm going to let you take it from here, brother."

Davina anxiously awaited Austin's moment to shine. Hell, everyone backstage was grinning from ear to ear, and Mone't had no clue what was going to happen.

"Thanks, brotha," Austin said as he and Zaim dapped and pulled one another into a brotherly hug. "Thank you."

"Do your thing, nigga," Zaim praised him, patting his shoulder before walking off stage.

Austin looked out at the crowd and started talking. "Before y'all go home and back to your lives, I want to thank you for riding with me and all my teammates here. But above all of that, I want to thank my wife. This year was hell for us. Y'all saw who really ran shit, and I'm telling you, I ain't shit without her. Mo, come here."

Mone't tensed up before Davina nudged her. "Go to your man, girl."

Putting one heeled foot in front of the other, Mone't made her way to center stage. Austin pulled the designer frames from his face so she could see his eyes. "You are the real MVP. You sacrificed so much for me to be who I am and to be on the stage. You've given me a beautiful family. You've held my strengths as well as my fears. Nothing I have in this life would have been possible without you. I wanted to first apologize for putting you through the hell I did. I fucked up in public, and it's only right I apologize just as loudly, if not louder."

Mone't quickly tried the wipe the lone tear that ran down her cheek.

Austin dug in his pocket and pulled out a small velvet box. "I also want to ask you this the right way." He lowered himself to one knee. "Mone't Graham, will you marry me again?"

The crowd erupted in cheers and proceeded to chant, "Say yes, say yes, say yes."

Mone't and Austin had tunnel vision. Neither of them could hear nor see anything other than each other.

"Yes," Mone't cried. "I will."

Austin adorned her empty finger with a new diamond ring that was almost as heavy as his newest championship ring. He stood, abruptly captured her face, and tongued her down, not giving a damn about the thousands of people watching, screaming, and aahing.

"I love you."
"I love you too," Mone't sniffled.

> *When I say I'm sorry*
> *I meant that*
> *When I say you're my world*
> *I meant that*
> *When I laid myself at your feet, girl*
> *I meant that*

Every speaker on stage was filled with the silky sounds of Jamarcus Hill, the R&B king. He was the first man Mone't loved if Austin told it. She had every album and poster that had come out since he hit the scene her junior year of high school.

Austin draped his arms around her shoulders while Jamarcus sang Mone't's favorite song. She stood, body pressing against Austin, squealing like his biggest fan.

> *I'd do whatever I gotta do to bring you home*
> *Baby, say you love me, say you love me*
> *Even if you don't love me, say you love me*

Jamarcus handed Mone't a massive bouquet of flowers and continued to sing to her before turning to the crowd, who was in the zone along with Mone't and Austin.

When the song ended, Jamarcus shook Austin's hand and hugged Mone't. "I want to be at the wedding."

"You know it. Thank you."

"Anything for the lady," Jamarcus joked.

The DJ finished the set and wished the crowd a good night. Mone't pulled Austin to their Sprinter, not caring whether their friends were waiting. When they were alone behind the privacy window, she wasted no time getting to what she wanted.

With assistance, Austin and Mone't stripped each other down, assuring that the only thing she wore was her ring. She pushed Austin down into the seat and mounted him. Their eyes connected as she inched her body down on his and clenched her walls.

Austin's mouth fell open, releasing a carnal moan of ecstasy. "Ride your dick, baby."

Mone't did, happily being his personal freak. He sucked, bit, and smacked her flesh while she rode him through the city.

"Baby," Austin tiredly hummed.

Mone't was sprawled out in the sheets. The evidence of their night of lovemaking was all over the room. Clothes hung from various places, their phones were dead, and the slow-jam playlist that had played had turned into relaxing sounds of rain.

"Hmm?" Mone't hummed into the pillow. "I'm not cooking, baby. Just order food."

"I already got you food. I need you to wake up and eat," Austin replied with a tired laugh. He kissed her face. "Wake up, baby."

Mone't groaned and rolled over to her back. She looked up at him and then to the tray between them. "You did this?"

"I'm not even going to lie. I tried. I had egg and batter all over the kitchen. Mom did. She brought the kids back early, and I had to run down there and clean up."

Mone't giggled, remembering all the nasty things they did to each other from last night leading into the early morning. "Whoops."

"You wild," Austin grumbled, biting his lip. His mind recalled the way she bounced, sucked, and ground her body over his. "Eat. I'm going to get these rugrats ready to go."

"Where y'all going?" Mone't asked, throwing a piece of pineapple into her mouth.

"We're going on vacation. Don't freak out. We don't need to pack. Everything is already there. I just need to get their bags for the plane ready."

"Vacation? Austin, I have to get my hair done." Mone't grabbed her short nest of curls and frowned. "I can't go anywhere like this."

"Baby, you can get it done when you get there. I mean, I'm going to mess it up again, but you can."

She squinted at him.

"Don't close your eyes at me, girl."

She kissed her teeth and threw a pillow at him. "You got jokes. You know they only open a quarter of the way."

"And I love it. All of you."

She blushed. "Don't distract me from this vacation you sprang on me."

"Listen, you want a vacation, you got it. Eat up and get your panties off the fan before your nosy daughter comes in here."

Mone't giggled and stretched her sore body. "That's your daughter."

"That mouth ain't mine, I'll tell you that," Austin said over his shoulder while walking out of the room.

Mone't looked around the room. She grabbed a handful of fruit and shimmied out of the bed to pick up their mess. In the process, she turned on the TV to listen to the news while she cleaned quickly.

"Former General Manager Lamont Wright, owner Gerald Bennington, agent Jermel Green, and social media influencer Pandora Herrera have all pleaded guilty to the charges of defrauding a franchise. The plea comes after three-time NBA Championship MVP Austin Graham announced the new ownership of the Ganton Hills Monarchs. While Austin finishes out his six-year contract

with the Monarchs, Prynce Rivers, head coach of
Eastover University, will come on board as the new
acting owner.

"The team's front office has also announced
that Francesco De Luca will be the new general
manager, and they've partnered with Beatsville
Entertainment for new innovative halftime shows.
It looks like redemption for the Graham franchise
is on the way. Back to you in the studio, Emya."

Mone't leaned on the post of the bed and looked
around the room that was becoming far too small
for her and Austin. The house and the break had
served its purpose. She knew life wasn't always
going to be crystal stairs and rainbows for her and
Austin. They would have good days and bad days,
but they would have each other. That was what
was important.

"Mommmyyyyy," Izzy called, walking into the
room. "Did you hear? We're going on vacation!"
Excitement coursed through her body as she
jumped up and down. "And this time, you and
Daddy can't leave us!"

Mone't chuckled and picked her up. "Do you
know where we're going?"

"Nope. Daddy said it's a secret, but it's okay. I
like your ring. Is it going to stay?"

"It is, and guess what?"

"What?" Izzy and Austin asked in unison.

"We're going back to the big house," Mone't
announced.

Isabella cheered, jumping out of Mone't's arms to do the same dance she'd seen her daddy do time and time again when he won games.

Austin's brow peaked. "You selling this one or . . ."

"I'm thinking about partnering with the Black Heroes Project and selecting a deserving family to give it to. I'm sure someone would love it, but it's time we came home."

"You damn right it is." Austin pumped his fist. "I'll have all of this packed up."

"Just our things. Whoever we select can use the furniture."

Austin stared at her in amazement. "Whatever you want, I got it."

"Ditto."

Epilogue

"You look so beautiful." Aneica's voice broke as she looked over at Mone't dressed in a custom Kendya Couture gown.

She had to be stitched into the off-white beaded dress. Mone't's makeup was flawless. The makeup artist traded her signature red lipstick for nude.

"Thank you," Mone't said, pulling in a deep breath.

"There is something to be said about the strength and sacredness you hold as a young woman. So many women don't unlock what you have so soon. They don't leave, they don't stick to their guns, they don't require fullness. But you, baby, you have shown me something." Aneica praised her, holding Mone't's hands in hers.

"I don't want to ruin my makeup," Mone't whispered. "I learned it from you. I didn't have much of a mother, but you loved me and taught me and took care of me. You raised me. I wouldn't be me without you, Mama. You're my mom, and I thank you for taking me in and on. You didn't have to. Lord knows you didn't have the time for another kid, but you loved me. Thank you for that. For protecting me, always. I couldn't have gotten through any of this without you."

Aneica sniffled and softly dapped Mone't's face. "It has been my pleasure. God knew what we needed, and He gave me you. I love you, Mone't. Now let's stop this crying and get you renewed."

"Yeah, let's do that." Mone't laughed through her tears and turned toward the door.

The intimate group of family and friends was gathered on the terrace, awaiting Mone't's entry. Jamarcus Hill sang a song he wrote especially for this occasion. Austin stood proudly at the altar. Everyone watching would have thought that this was their actual wedding with the way Austin fidgeted and licked his lips, anticipating seeing his bride.

He was overcome with emotion. What a journey they'd embarked on together. What was time if he didn't spend it with her? He grew his legacy with her, created spaces for improvement with her.

Eman walked arm in arm with his sister down the tabby aisleway. Mone't's eyes were fixed on Austin. Austin was trying to contain himself and not run down the aisle and sweep her off her feet.

She wasn't the quiet girl who refused to talk to him anymore. She was his woman, and he was her man. That was his greatest accomplishment. Being a whole, emotionally intelligent, healed man for Mone't Graham. For their children. For himself.

"Who gives this woman to this man?" Robyn asked.

"I do," Eman proudly spoke.

Austin took a step forward, embraced Eman in a brotherly hug, then reached for Mone't's hand. Hand in hand, they stood in front of Robyn and the people who poured into them.

"What a journey it has been," Robyn started. "To watch these two actively heal themselves and reconnect has been the most beautiful thing I've seen in a long time. What you two have is sacred, and I want you to always remember you have a love that not only heals each other but everyone you come in contact with. Austin and Mone't have prepared their own vows."

Mone't took a deep, settling breath. Her eyes roamed from Austin to his groomsmen—Eman, Musa, Keyston, and Winston—then to the portrait of her father just how she remembered him, to their children, and finally, to his parents. "When I met you, I was young and overcome with that puppy love. That's what your mom called it. God, it was so easy loving you, being there for you, caring for you because you encompassed me in the rays of a sun I never thought I would feel.

"Loving you has been the most complex, difficult, soul-stirring thing I've ever done. And I don't ever want to know what life would be like without you. You are my person. My hairdresser in the middle of the night when I forget to put my bonnet on. The one who carries me up and down the stairs when I'm being a brat. The one who protects, provides, and loves me. You're the one who will lose himself just to be in my presence. I love you with every fiber of me, Austin Luca Graham. Thank you for imprinting on me. Who knows where I would be or who I would be without you?"

Austin nodded. "You're trying to break me down like a pound. I see you, Mone't Graham. Not only are you fine, but your soul is gold. Not gold-plated. Pure gold. You are so full of strength I have no other choice but to rise to the occasion. Loving you and growing with you has been my greatest honor. Time, sunlight, life means nothing if I'm not spending time with you, standing in the sun with you, or living with you.

"Thank you for taking a chance on the scrawny kid with big hoop dreams. You've been my personal chef, my nurse, my secret keeper, the loudest one cheering my name. But most of all, you've been the safest place I can lay my head and rest after fighting wars I don't talk about. I love you, and I will spend every day of the rest of my life showing you how much I do."

"Whew," Robyn blew. "Well, there is nothing to say after that. Austin, kiss your wife."

Austin pulled Mone't into him and tongued her down. Their attendees cheered, clapped, and shouted their excitement for them. The love was the reason, but the fight and effort to win was the star of the show.

That Fall

Austin dribbled the ball down court, pointing to Winston. His teammates scrambled into their spots, preparing for the ball to come. Mone't and the gang stood in the family section, cheering for Austin. They were down by twenty in the first game of the season opener.

Austin and the rest of the team were fighting to come back, but time was trickling. The final shot would close the gap some, but it wouldn't bring a win tonight. The buzzer sounded, and fans looked defeated, but the team walked off the court with hunger in their eyes, and she knew that this would be the last time they played like this.

While Austin did his post-game conference, his family waited at the restaurant for his arrival. Austin would have a reason to celebrate tonight. Although, every night he lay down with his family, he won.

When he and the starters of the team arrived at Lydia's, cheers erupted. Mone't stood in the middle of the crowd, holding a secret that would surely turn his night around.

"I lost. Why are you smiling so big?" he asked after kissing her face.

Everyone grew quiet so they could hear the announcement. The staff rolled out a cake with an ultrasound printed on it. Austin studied it, brows dipped, then studied Mone't, then the cake again.

"You're pregnant?" he asked as if he didn't think it could happen. "You're having my baby?"

"Yes, the third one," Mone't said between giggles.

He reached out and swooped her off her feet.

"Remember, every shot you take always goes in," Mone't mumbled against his lips. "You might have lost the season opener, but you won me."

"I know that's right," Angie shouted. "He won him a trophy! Owee!"

Laughter ensued. This was what it meant to be family. They celebrated together, cried together, fought together. As long as they took every shot together, they would never lose.

Francesco hugged his son tightly. "That's my boy! Love you, son."

"Love you, Pops." He let him go. "All right y'all, drink, eat up! We got another championship to bring home. I got to afford all these kids!"

The End

Also by APXCB

Ganton Hills Series

Olive and Oak
Red
Gangsta Lovin'
Purple
Green
Come to The Ghetto
Gas Station Drug Money
Pressure
Keeper of My Soul
Yellow
Orange
Leather and Wood
The Trenches: Loyalty Over Everything
A Christmas Creed

Beatsville

Make Me Feel It

Ganton Hills Romance Stand-Alone Series

The Remnants Love Left Behind
Because of You
A Lonely Christmas

Spinnin' the Block
Give Good Love
Lavendale
Savage
Gunner
Judah
Menace

The Way You Lie
The Way you Lie: The Aftershock
All to Myself 1
All to Myself 2

Love the Series

Love Over All
The Game of Love
Love Knockout
Fight for Love

Indigo Haze: The Collection

Indigo Haze 1
Indigo Haze 2
Indigo Haze 3
Indigo Haze 4

Forbidden Lust Series

As We Lay
As We Lust
As We Lie
As We Wade

One Last Chance Series

Now or Never
Break Down Your Wall
Break My Fall by Skye Moon

Poetry Collections

Coldest Summer Ever
Sumwhereovarainbows
Queendom
The Essence of You
Stranger Things